THE END OF SNOW

MURDER IN SQUAW VALLEY

A LAURA BAILEY SNOW SCIENCE MYSTERY

Prudy Grimes

Prudy Grimes

ISBN: 1503177629
ISBN 13: 9781503177628

This is a work of fiction. Though Squaw Valley Ski Resort is real, and many of the places in this novel are real, or were real in the big winter of 2010/2011, I have changed places to make them fit my needs. Any resemblance to people living or dead is coincidental.

For Rich, thank you for living this Tahoe dream with me.

My deep thanks to Darla Sharp for spurring me on. Thank you to Michael T. Colee for his patience, and his expert snow science advice. Thank you also to Thomas Painter for last minute expert insight into snow behavior. Any mistakes in the science are mine, not theirs. Thanks are also due to Alan Rinzler, Developmental Editor. For the stories of the early days of Squaw, I'd like to thank Leroy Hills. Finally, thank you to Beth Dickey and Marilyn Annucci for somehow shoehorning into their busy lives time to help with copyediting.

The first fall of snow is not only an event, it is a magical event. You go to bed in one kind of world and wake up in another quite different, and if this is not enchantment then where is it to be found?

Priestley, J. B. *Apes and Angels: A Book of Essays.* London: 1928 Methuen & Co., Ltd

THE END OF SNOW

MURDER IN SQUAW VALLEY

ACT I

Chapter 1

THURSDAY, MARCH 31, 9 PM

I put the rented Nissan Murano in drive and pulled out of Reno Tahoe Airport. The gear shifted effortlessly, a nice change from my ten-year old Subaru at home. The Murano was dark maroon, a perfect color to fade to invisible in the gloomy weather, but at least the car came equipped with four-wheel drive and snow tires. If it didn't, I wouldn't be going anywhere because giant signs over the highway told me that chain restrictions were up on I-80.

As I started the drive up into the mountains of the Sierra Nevada Range that rings Lake Tahoe, nobody was going anywhere fast. A dozen Nevada Highway Patrol troopers stood out in the snow wearing bright yellow rain slickers, checking vehicles over with flashlights as they wended their way through a bottleneck of semis lining both sides of the highway, leaving a single narrow lane in each direction for traffic to pass. A mile past the exit for Boomtown, the traffic stopped. It was 34 degrees at 9:37 p.m., and a sloppy snow pounded down from a black sky.

A highway patrolman made his way from car to car. After he spoke to the drivers, I noticed they all turned their cars around and headed back into Reno. There was no way I was going to do that, so I had my window rolled down ready to make my case by the time it was my turn. The trooper leaned down and, beneath his hat, his cheeks had flushed red. He was soaked and looked miserable. But he dog-shook the weariness and cold and struggled to keep an open expression on his face. Having felt that way so many times myself, my heart went out to the guy.

"Ma'am," he said, "you're going to have to turn around. There's a wreck around Floriston, and nobody's getting through but emergency vehicles."

Before I could reply, his sat phone blared, and he spoke into it for a moment. Over the static, I could hear a man say the accident had been cleared, but they were still shutting I-80 down due to the road conditions. He turned back to me.

"So, ma'am, due to the snow, you're going to need to turn around and head back into Reno."

I pulled out my driver's license and my university ID.

"Actually, I'm here because of the snow. I'm a snow hydrologist."

His face went blank. He had no idea what I was talking about. Why couldn't I just come out and say, Back off, Trooper, I'm Laura Bailey, snow scientist?" I fought back a laugh and smiled up at him.

"The head of the Squaw Valley Ski Patrol expects me to be on mountain early tomorrow. I've got to get up there tonight." I held that bright smile.

He looked my license over in the beam of his flashlight.

"Laura Bailey," he said to himself. His face brightened up all of a sudden. "Was there an article about you in *The Tahoe Times* a while back?"

I nodded and tried not to grin—almost famous.

"I didn't remember your name, but the photo made a big impression," he said, smiling. "That head of hair is hard to forget."

"So I've heard." I leaned forward and said confidentially, "It's a pain in the ass." People have called my hair "honey-colored"—I call it blondie-brown—but whatever it's called, it's always been a riotous big head of hair. Many is the time I've wanted to cut it off down to three inches of poodle fuzz. But being a woman in science, I needed something that marked me as feminine when my professional life did the opposite.

"You can call Dave Geisner, the head of the ski patrol at Squaw," I told him. "He'll verify I'm coming in to work with him."

He took my license and school ID and turned away. I lost sight of him in the wall of white just a few steps from the car. A moment later he came back with a fellow trooper. The new patrolman was older and obviously in charge.

"Miss Bailey?"

I nodded, "Yes?"

"Or is it Dr. Bailey?"

"Either one."

"You really need to get up to Squaw tonight?"

"Just to Truckee."

He looked at me sideways as if he wasn't sure whether or not to trust me. He glanced at my license picture and then at me.

"Fort Collins, Colorado, huh?"

I nodded.

He turned his attention to my Colorado State University ID. "Associate Professor of Hydrology. What brings you up here?"

Just then a squadron of emergency vehicles pulled up behind me, so the lead Patrolman, whose nametag said he was "Trooper Bates of the Nevada Highway Patrol," pointed me over to a gap between semis on the side of the highway in what would ordinarily be the slow lane of I-80. I parked the Murano. The heater worked great, but maybe because I was sitting still, the windshield started fogging up, and I couldn't see much.

What was bringing me up here? The question resonated. Three years ago my team and I constructed a large platform back in the mountains and lugged in all kinds of equipment to measure snowfall, snow density, relative humidity, wind speed, relative temperature, and all kinds of other stuff having to do with my specialty, the effects of dirt and carbon on snow melt. Last summer, I used a big chunk of grant money for remote microwave sensors that would have made it so we didn't have to hike back there in the middle of winter and take readings. Something had happened, though, and the sensors weren't working.

I needed to get the readings from the massive snowfall that winter—more snow than the area had seen in twenty or thirty years—and to install replacement remote sensors.

A moment later, Trooper Bates came back, looming up suddenly through the veil of snow.

"We've got a convoy of cars headed up in ten, fifteen minutes. I'm going to talk to Dave Geisner. If he confirms your story, I'm going to let you go up in the middle of the convoy."

I nodded. "Thanks." I was starving and impatient to get going, still hoping to hit the Safeway in Truckee before it closed.

By this time, the last few vehicles coming up the highway had been routed back to Reno, and the night hung around me, black and hushed by snow. The reflections on the wet pavement made the highway look like polished onyx. Even the rumbling of diesel engines from the semis lining both sides of the highway dampened and sounded far away.

I'd bumped my trip up by a day in order to get out to Squaw and ski around with Dave. I felt curious as to what could have a curmudgeon like him asking for my opinion. He'd called a few days earlier and, in his usual way, skipped the pleasantries.

"Laura, time for some kickback."

"Meaning what?"

"Squaw's helped you out and given you access to the resources to help with your station. We've taken snow sleds up and hauled your gear. Helped you install everything. We give you lift access to reach your site by skiing in rather than coming around backcountry. We've been scratching your back, so scratch ours just a little bit. I'm curious about what's going on here. I'm seeing stuff I've never seen over my thirty odd years. I'd like you to ski around and check out some shit with me."

"Jeez, Dave," I told him. "You don't need to guilt trip me to get me to fly out a day early, ski around, make some turns, and talk snow management. That's hardly odious work. I'd be happy to."

In fact, this was the second reason I felt anxious to get up there. I couldn't stop thinking about what Dave told me. It had been an epic winter, but the melt was coming in earlier than usual. It was still dumping snow, and temperatures were low, yet snow packs were being undercut with flow that seemed bizarre to him. He also said that twice in the past month, soot or dirt had come down with a big dump of snow. Since that's my area of expertise, I guessed that was what he wanted to show me.

Historically the snow around Squaw contained non-trivial traces of dust from Asia, even the Sahara, and, in dry years, dust from the Sacramento Valley. But, as wet as this season had been, that hardly seemed likely. The nearly constant rain in the valley and snow in the mountains had surely kept the dust and carbon washed out of the atmosphere, yet Dave's claims had me curious and a little worried.

I've had experience with what happens with dirty snowfall in Colorado. Dirty snow absorbs the sun, whereas white snow reflects it, meaning the dirty snow melts faster than white snow. In Colorado, this leaves longer and longer periods without water. The dirt in Colorado's snow seems to be coming from poorly done agriculture from certain areas in Utah and even from western Colorado. There's a practice large farmers do of plowing the land after harvest that makes it easier and faster to get a spring crop in, but it leaves the topsoil vulnerable to erosion by rain and wind during the winter. Huge dust plumes from these plowed fields come up and get incorporated into the snow. And in the melt process the snow melts down out from underneath the dust particles, and the particles tend to accumulate on the top. Meaning they don't just melt away with the snow. The dust, and I think the carbon, too–that's actually one of the questions I'm doing research on—remains to continue the fast melt. Dust events in Colorado are localized, but soot from pollution sources happens all over the world. I'm hoping, if we can find a way to get the dirt out of the snow, we can slow down or even reverse the climate change we see going on all over the world.

That may seem like a stretch, but the name of my field is "The Desertification of the Rockies." Losing the trees and the grassy fields of the Rockies is going to have a huge effect on weather patterns in all the land east of the Rockies. If it can happen, *is* happening, in Colorado, it's likely happening all over the world.

That was my three-minute, chatting-at-a-party explanation of my field. I also have the elevator-ride version, and of course, the long, detailed scientific version.

I looked up just in time to see Trooper Bates materialize through the snow. I rolled down my window, and he bent forward to talk to me.

"I spoke to Dave Geisner, and you're good to go. The convoy is just coming up to Boomtown. So after the second vehicle, there'll be a break, and that's where you pull in behind. Take it easy driving up."

"Thanks for letting me through."

He nodded. "You're welcome. Be careful, Dr. Bailey." He banged his hand on the side of the car and stepped aside as the first highway patrol car passed. An ambulance with chains on the tires followed the patrol car. They paused a second, and I pulled the Murano out into the open lane behind the ambulance. More vehicles followed, but through the snow, all I could see were the two pickup trucks immediately behind me. I occasionally caught a glimpse of several more sets of headlights following behind. We started up 80 towards Truckee, and it was 10:32 p.m. and 31 degrees, according to the car thermometer.

=

As we moved further up into the mountains at twenty-five or thirty-miles an hour, a fog sifted down through the pass. It settled along the highway and spilled down lower to the banks of the Truckee River. It was tedious driving, hard not to get hypnotized by the fog, so I turned on the XM radio and tried to find the NPR station, I couldn't, so I ended up listening to a '90's grunge channel. Before leaving the airport, I latched my iPhone into the Bluetooth in the car, so when my phone rang I just had to push a button on the steering wheel to talk. I loved it; my shabby ride at home had nothing in the tech department.

I recognized the voice immediately. "Laura, it's Tim Schneider." He's a postdoc who works for me. "I want to touch base with you about who's bringing up what."

"Hey Tim. Glad to hear from you. I'm just driving up to Truckee now through the fog. Anyway, I brought my pit kit: snow stakes, a shovel, a precipitation gauge, a scale and measuring stick—that kind of stuff. You know, mountain money, flares. Nothing technical." Mountain money, otherwise known as toilet paper.

8

"I'm wondering about the sensors. Should I bring those?"

"You need to work with Manfred. He's in charge of packing that stuff up." My friend Manfred Heimler was in Fort Collins on sabbatical. He'd be heading into Reno with Tim and Sara Wilkins, a hardworking graduate student, and together we'd all head out into the backcountry behind Squaw.

"I talked to Sara, and she said you're thinking about building a wind shield for the snow gauge."

"I'm worried we're still catching some wind up there. Sara suggested bringing up the stuff we need to build baffles for a shield. Then if we want it, we've got the materials, and, if we don't think it's necessary, no harm done."

"I wasn't along when you put up the platform. How far in exactly is it?"

"If we have to ski in on skins, it's going to be fourteen or fifteen miles. If we can ski out the back of Squaw, down the back of Granite Chief, it'll just be a short hike—couple miles. So I'll be checking that out in the next few days." Historically, skins were strips of goat or seal fur you'd strap onto the bottom of your skis. Going uphill, the fur digs into the snow and stops you from sliding backwards. Going downhill, the fur lays flat, and you can ski normally, or you can easily slip them off. Nowadays in the States, most people use technical material in place of fur. Manfred, being European, still uses mohair goat fur. But whatever you used, we still called them skins.

"Tell me again why we can't take snowmobiles?" Schneider was always looking to do things the easy way.

"The snow's too deep. They don't work well in such deep snow."

"And you like to do it old school," he said with a groan.

"That, too, Tim. If you don't love being out in snow, you've got no business in this field."

He laughed. "Yeah, you've mentioned that before." And we rang off.

I was working with three snow research sites: one behind Squaw Valley, one behind Colorado's Aspen Highlands, and one with Manfred at a research site he managed in the Italian Alps near the border with

France. I used these sites to collect data to start computer models that I used to extrapolate the snowmelt for given areas. I'd come back and use these field sites to compare with my models and assess the accuracy of my computer modeling. I also work with satellite imagery and a whole plethora of other stuff to study snow covered area (SCA) patterns and how they're changing with the new and different storm patterns we're seeing. Snow science wasn't just measuring snowfall and how much water the snow holds any more

It can sound more complicated than it is. Sometimes my students' eyes glazed over at the beginning of the semester, but I've been pretty good at making it clear.

When soot falls on bright white snow, the energy balance changes because more sunlight is absorbed meaning the snow melts faster. The reason this becomes a problem is that seventy-five or eighty percent of water in the west comes from snowmelt: water for things like hydropower, electrical dams and turbines, and agriculture. If farmers can feel certain about how much water they'll have from a snowmelt, they can plant more lucrative crops.

I forget the exact statistics, but something like every one percent we're off in our prediction of how much water comes from a snowmelt costs about a billion dollars. When we see evidence that soot or dirt in snow is causing melts to go off a whole month earlier, that's a huge problem. One month earlier for the melt means one month longer without water. Already winter in the Sierra Nevada is two and a half weeks shorter than it used to be.

So while a bit of dirt or carbon mixed into the snow in the Lake Tahoe area may not seem like a big deal, I worry it may be the beginning of the end of snow in the lower forty-eight states. Snow scientists have long predicted that the last area in the United States with regular, yearly snowfall will be the West Coast mountain ranges, including the Sierra Nevada mountain range. Faster snowmelt is going to speed up climate change. It's all tied together. There's no pulling one single thread out of the weave of factors that go into making up the climate: less snow, less water; less water, fewer crops and higher costs for electricity. Not to mention an increase in fire danger. Climate patterns are changing, and none of us know for sure where it's going to end up. But it seems clear from historical patterns kept over the past eighty years that there is less snow at lower altitudes in the Sierra, and in mountain ranges all over the world, than there used to be.

A few minutes later, the convoy stopped at the Agricultural Check Point a few miles over the California state line. We were almost there. The Nevada highway patrolman who led the convoy pulled to the side and waved me through behind the ambulance. The Agricultural Check Point was closed and dark as I drove through the gates. I took the next exit off I-80 into the little mountain town of Truckee with a surge of nostalgia. I've always loved this town with its old-fashioned wooden sidewalks and the trains running through it.

I was staying at a shack in Truckee owned by my friend Rita Chambers. Rita, at forty-seven, was seventeen years older than me, and had worked for twenty-five years on the Aspen Mountain Ski Patrol. Eight years ago, with some money I inherited from my grandmother and my great aunts, I bought a small dacha in Aspen's west end next door to Rita, and we'd been friends ever since. Rita got the Truckee house in a nasty divorce, and always let me stay there when I visited nearby Squaw Valley. Tough and stringy as a coyote, and just like a coyote, I am certain Rita could survive the harshest winter on not much more than sunflower seeds left behind in a bird feeder. Rita's wicked sense of humor saved her from being just plain dour, dour and mean. Instead, she was mean and hilarious. The kind of personality you wanted to make sure you stayed on the good side of. I wouldn't want to hear what she'd have to say about me if we ever fell out.

I pulled into the driveway of the faded pink bungalow on West River Street. Thank the gods it was shoveled. I had expected to be doing that myself before bed. Rita must have been paying for a snow service, which was funny because she swore she'd never spend a penny on the dilapidated old house, as evidenced by the torn lace curtains in the dirty windows. I guess $200 for a season's worth of snow removal wasn't exactly upkeep, more a necessity. I breathed a sigh of relief–it was one less thing standing between me and getting something to eat and going to bed.

The house was an eighty year old Victorian with a tilting porch, hardwood floors, and lots of small rooms. When I opened the front door and walked in, it was about 20 degrees inside. I headed back outside, fought my way through snow drifts around to the back of the house, and found the ancient furnace in a dirt-floored storage room sitting cold and dead. I fiddled around with it, lit the pilot light, and got it breathing out a weak plume of lukewarm air. Back inside, the kitchen had a big farm sink and a creaky refrigerator. I opened some cupboards hoping for the rental house staples of dry pasta and a bottle of marina sauce, and instead found a few sticky bottles of spices, some olive oil long since gone rancid, an unopened box of Frosted Flakes, and a box of long-shelf-life milk with a couple months yet before its expiration date.

I lugged my suitcase into the small master bedroom and spotted a gray knit cap with a brim hanging from a coat rack. It took me a few seconds to realize whose hat it was, and then a wave of sadness nearly shattered me.

So this is where Peter left it. We had searched everywhere for that hat, Peter's favorite. Three years ago, the last time I borrowed Rita's house, he was here with me. It was a few months before his death in an avalanche in the backcountry behind Aspen Highlands. I could see his green eyes beneath the brim of that cap, his dark hair in curls around his face, and his year-round goggle suntan. It was hard to wrap my head around the idea that his cap was still here, and he wasn't. It felt like it happened in another lifetime, but so raw it was like it happened yesterday.

His friends had been able to reach him and dig him out quickly. Then one had skied out for help while another stayed with him. They told me later that he couldn't move, but he was lucid and in no pain. They talked for almost an hour as he lay staring up at the blue Colorado sky. At least a friend who loved him was with him until the end. At least he was out in the mountains on the snow and not lying in some hospital bed eaten away with cancer.

I didn't let myself think about it very often. He had an infectious spirit, and such a love of the mountains. He was my mountain man, my one true love. It had been three years, and I still couldn't talk about him. Three years after his death, our time together had become a slide show in my memory. I remembered the pictures, but the essence of the man had begun to slip away and become almost impossible to grasp.

As I walked back out of the bedroom, still stunned by the flood of memories, my phone rang, again, and it was Dave Geisner.

"So you made it up?" he said. "Good. Be here at 5:00 tomorrow morning for the early sweep on Red Dog."

I looked at my watch, and it was after midnight. "Uh, sure Dave," I told him. "Where should I meet you?"

"You know where the Avalanche Command Center is?"

"Meet you there at 5:00?"

"Yeah. Be sure and bring water and plenty of food. It's going to be a long day."

I stiffened my resolve for what I suspected would become an argument.

"Dave, I'm happy to ski around with you tomorrow, but I can only give you the one day."

"I know, I know," he said. "Haven't we been through this already?"

"I just want to make certain we're clear on this. My team comes in Sunday, and by then I have to decide what the state of the backcountry is, how we're going to trek in, buy provisions for snow camping, and talk to a couple people here and at UC Davis."

From past experiences with Dave, I knew that he'd happily turn one day into every minute between then and the arrival of my team on Sunday afternoon. No knock on him.. He was responsible for the safety of every single person skiing at Squaw Valley USA. And on a busy Saturday, that could be upwards of fifteen-thousand people. I had a lot of respect for him and his job

"See you at 5:00," he replied, and cut off the call.

I was relieved I had some dried apricots and a couple battered Cliff Bars buried in my ski pack. And, of course, I had my baby-blue Snow Angel CamelBak. I figured I'd have to get up at 3:30 in order to get there by 5:00, since with the bad weather, it could easily be up to a forty-minute drive to Squaw. I unpacked my gear and laid everything out ready for the morning, then climbed into the same bed where Peter and I slept the last time we were here. I fell asleep holding his cap and pretending I could still smell him in the sheets, ignoring the gnawing hunger in my belly.

Chapter 2

FRIDAY, APRIL 1, 4:45 AM

It was still dark when I pulled into the Far East parking lot at Squaw and parked as close as I could to the concrete building that housed the Squaw Valley Ski Patrol, so I wouldn't have to lug my gear any farther than necessary. I could see a snowcat's bright headlights scrape across a meadow to a special fortified bunker fourteen-hundred feet from the patrol building to collect the explosives needed for the day. Two patrollers drove snowmobiles following the snowcat to help the driver gather and load up the explosives.

By 5:20 I had geared up and said hello to a few acquaintances. The avalanche control room was packed with people and dogs. It was a cold, dank room lined with wooden lockers and benches, with gear scattered everywhere. Smelled to me like life in the mountains, and I loved it. Patrollers buckled boots and loaded their packs with crimpers to cut fuses, and igniters to light the hand charges that would be used to clear loose snow from the mountain. Avalanche dogs chased each other through the crowd. Most of their lives were spent in training, so that was their form of play. They only worked during the frantic minutes when someone lay buried beneath an avalanche.

I made eye contact with Dave, and he gave an easy nod in my direction, pointing a finger at me. He was dressed in a red flannel shirt with black stretched-out suspenders hanging loose over his shoulders, and worn black ski pants. His graying dark hair hung longer than I'd ever seen it even though Squaw Valley USA liked their employees' clean cut. Sixty years of sun damage had burned his face a hard brick red.

I hadn't been here during the winter for three years, so a few people looked surprised to see me and said a quick hello. But they all had jobs to do and no time to fool around.

Dave stood up and prepared to make the morning announcements. He had a grumbly, authoritative voice that cut through the chatter of the group. Immediately, the room fell quiet. Dave said that today it would take twenty patrollers to toss almost two-hundred-fifty hand-charge explosives. These weigh approximately four-hundred-forty pounds and were made up of ammonium nitrate emulsion, the same explosive used in the Oklahoma City bombing. Teams of two full-time ski patrollers would head out onto the five mountains of Squaw to make the mountains safe for skiers by blasting away snow that might avalanche, and then cleaning up afterwards by ski cutting, which is skiing across precarious aspects to loosen snow and cause it to avalanche harmlessly.

Eight years before this, Rita tried to talk me into being a ski patroller. I went out on Ajax Mountain early one day in February with her and one of the head guys on the Aspen Ski Patrol. Rita told me to throw a hand-charge way over to my right and down a steep headwall. I threw like a girl, and it ended up about six feet in front of us. Rita calmly said, "That's ok. Just hit the ground. NOW!" We all three threw ourselves down onto the snow, and the blast from that explosion still echoes in my ears today.

At Squaw, each blast team was composed of two patrollers: one rated "K," for known–a licensed blaster and intimately familiar with the terrain he or she patrols–and a partner rated, "F" for familiar on the terrain. They can both ski and blast the terrain they're responsible for blindfolded in a blizzard, and they probably have, many times.

As the teams assembled caps and fuses, Dave gave the rundown on the day's patrol activities. By 9:30, when lifts were projected to open, there would be twenty-four paid patrollers on the mountain and upwards of sixty volunteers. It wasn't going to be an especially crowded day, since it was a Friday, and the new snow was heavy and wet. By 10:00 a.m., the snow should end and be followed by rapidly dropping temperatures as a cold front blew in. Winds were expected to top out at seventy miles per hour at High Camp. On the tail end of the cold front, another storm was forecast to arrive from the Pacific, and this one was expected to drop significant precipitation and lead to a spectacular powder day to start off the weekend.

It took another fifteen minutes after his announcements for Dave to extricate himself. Around 5:45, we headed outside together into the dark and the cold, and clicked into our bindings as patrollers finished loading cases of hand-charges onto a waiting snowcat, we each grabbed a long rope, and the snowcat towed us to the base of Red Dog chairlift where we dropped the ropes. The snowcat moved off into the darkness towing another four patrollers to the next drop-off point.

There was no one around but the two of us and the lift operator who had the lift running. He stood sweeping off the metal frame as each chair came past.

We all said good morning then Dave told the liftie, "Be sure to stay awake. And no smoking pot," he added. Which seemed to me a weird and sort of random comment—especially seeing how hard the guy was working—until I remembered Dave's personal crusade against people employed by Squaw Valley smoking dope.

"OK," the liftie said, and moved forward to knock the snow off our chair then flip down the seat in time for us to board. I rolled my eyes at Dave.

"What?" he asked. "I don't want a lawsuit because some idiot kid decides he's bored and wants to get high. Is that so bad? I'm responsible for this whole freaking place, don't forget."

"I know," I said. "It's not bad. Just sort of a losing battle."

"Yeah, if I catch some liftie letting guests pileup on the off-loading ramp because he's asleep again, we'll see who ends up the loser."

The sky lightened to gray as we rode up through a forest of pine trees. The patrol shack at the top of Snow King Mountain sat to the left of the main thoroughfare. It had been buried so deeply by the twenty feet of snow on the ground that we had to clamber down a set of stairs dug into the snow to reach the shack. Inside, it was just a wood-lined cabin with a wooden table and benches built around the sides.

The first thing that hit me was the warmth. I gravitated close to a wood-burning stove chugging out the BTUs in a corner. It was going to be hours before I felt warm again. I was still starving, and I took a stretch, feeling the glorious ache in my muscles from a two hour Pilates session the day before.

Matt McCoughlin, a big Irishman I've known for years, looked up from where he was assembling caps and fuses for the hand charges.

"Laura Bailey!" he said and moved across the crowded space to sweep me up in a hug. Why do people always use my entire name? "How are you? It's been too long since I've seen your pretty face."

"Pretty" may be a stretch. I have even features and an Octoberfest serving wench body, with a big chest, small waist and way too much hips for my taste. I'd rather be skinny and straight up and down. But I'm not really that pretty. He set me down and fluffed my hair, then turned to a petite blonde who stood behind him packing bright yellow hand charges into a ski patrol backpack used only for explosives. Two dogs bounded up from the floor and hurried over to say hi, one of them, a little black and white mutt, already wore his ski patrol harness, which like the patrol parkas was red with a white cross.

"Hey Dave," Matt said to his boss. "Laura, you haven't met Janis Murphy. She's a new member of the patrol this year and already an 'F.' She comes to us from the Whistler/Blackcomb area where she worked as a heli guide." Whistler/Blackcomb is a huge resort in Canada outside of Vancouver.

Janis stepped forward and smiled. She looked me straight in the eye, and shook my hand. "Nice to meet you, Laura. I've heard nothing but good things about you from these two."

"Really? Matt I can believe. But I've never heard Geisner say a nice thing about anybody." I winked at Dave, but he scowled. "Just kidding, Dave. You say nice things all the time." He gave me a grudging sideways smile. Matt and Janis both burst out laughing. Dave never had a nice thing to say about anybody; it was part of his charm.

Janis wore green dangly earrings and half a dozen silver bracelets. Her turtleneck was pale blue with a rhinestone snowflake on the front. Ski Patrols are usually a last bastion of alpha males, type-A personalities, and reluctant to embrace women. So to find a woman hired on in a paid position, and part of a blasting crew, in her first year on the patrol, and, on top of that, she still dressed like a woman—told me she must really have it going on. I wanted to know her better. I needed all the friends like her I could get since snow science is just as alpha male heavy as any ski patrol.

Matt and Janis turned back to packing up the hand charges and all the gear that went along with them. The dogs quieted down and fell asleep in front of the fire.

"Ready for a hike?" Dave asked.

"Sure," I told him. "Absolutely."

We climbed up out of the patrol shack and clicked into our bindings, then skated on our skis across the open expanse of snow where two different chairlifts dropped their riders. Fifty yards above us, up through what looked like virgin snow, lay the first snow station Dave said he wanted me to take a look at. We took off our skis and started climbing up the mountain in our ski boots. There was no trail and there was a reason. Every time a new trail was made in the snow in a big resort like Squaw, a hundred people would follow it on the hunch that someone knew something they didn't: an unexpected powder stash, or a steep line no one else knew about. So each time the snow station got checked, it had to be reached by a different route, a pain for sure, but it had to be done, so that all it took was a new snow fall to cover up the boot tracks. And the way it was dumping snow, our tracks would disappear long before the lifts opened.

Dave was huffing and out of breath by the time we waded straight up a steep slope through hip-high snow to reach the station. I guess at sixty-five, age was finally starting to catch up with him. We took some measurements of the snow depth. Just by kicking the snow I could tell it had a high density of water. Dave jammed a cube-shaped snow cutter into the snowpack, and removed it. Together we weighed it with a hanging scale from my pit kit to get a more exact read of the amount of water in the snow. That gave us the snow water equivalent, or the SWE.

"Looks like twenty-four percent SWE, Dave," I told him.

He filled in the data in a notebook. "Officially, Sierra Cement, then."

We worked quickly. We both knew what we were doing. On the downhill side of the slope I dug a quick snow pit, not digging really, just sort of encouraging the snow to move on down the mountainside. That left us with a flat wall of snow on the uphill side. We didn't need to dig deeper than four feet since other mountains at Squaw had deep burly pits that were used all winter to a get a historical reading of the snowpack.

I immediately saw all the layers of snow, and that gave me a history of what had been going on at Snow King Mountain. I could see the whole integrity of the snowpack, which told us how well it would hold up under varying stresses. There were textural differences: rotten pockets of snow with depth hoar, which are large cohesionless snow crystals caused by the presence of strong temperature gradients within the snowpack; ice lenses where small puddles of water refroze into ice, and all kinds of stuff. A thick layer of pine needles about six inches down told me there had been a wind event that stripped the pine trees down below and blew the needles up mountain. This meant there was an inversion that night, meaning the temperature down below was colder than it was up high on the mountain.

We ran a few pressure tests on the snow. That way we could see how well the different layers of snow held together. I put a slight pressure on the new, wet snow with a shovel, and it slid forward away from the old snow easily. I looked over at Dave, and he frowned. That wasn't a good sign. The facets between the old snow and the new, wet snow were weak and fractured, meaning this new snow would avalanche easily. Hopefully, this facet would firm up between now and Monday so it would be safe to venture out into the backcountry.

Down in the snow pit, it was still too dark to see subtle traces of dirt, if there were any. I found it hard to understand how dust or soot could have been blowing around during the constant storm cycle that had been going on at Squaw for the past month. But then sometimes the Sierra got dust transport from Asia, or locally derived dust, in pre-frontal blowing. The big winds that came in prior to storms. Dust in the snow layer would have a big effect on anomalous melt. Also, early season dust or early season warm temps could cause early melt.

"Dave," I shouted up at him. "You're not selling me a line about this dirt you saw in the snow just to get me out here to help you?"

I was joking, but then I was also serious. It seemed hard to believe there could be dirt in the snow during a winter as wet as this one.

His dark red face glared down at me from the top of the cut.

"For God's sake, Bailey! What do you take me for? I can't believe you'd even think that let alone say it. Try censoring the big ideas in your head before spouting off like that!"

Methinks he protests too much, but I placated him with a smile as I gathered some snow from three different layers of snow pack, scraped the snow into a separate plastic bag for each layer and carefully labeled the bags. I was standing there, four feet down into the snowpack on the side of a steep mountain thinking I should have my crew pull up the satellite imagery for this area from last December, January, and February, so I could see for sure if there had been dirt or carbon mixed into those early snows when Dave shouted at me in his usual manner.

"Laura!" He was leaning down to one side offering me his hand to help me out of the pit. I noticed he'd already packed his gear up. He seemed anxious to get going.

"Ready? Ready?" he asked me. "We've got a lot of ground to cover and since you're only giving me the day—there's no time for stargazing, girl."

"Hardly stargazing," I told him as I picked up my shovel, dried the blade, and folded it carefully. His rushing was not going to make me leave part of my pit kit behind. I took my time packing everything into my backpack.

"Any idea where the winds were coming from when this dirt you thought you saw came down?"

"I don't know. Where they always come from–the West? Who cares? It doesn't have anything to do with getting the resort open."

I stared at him for a few seconds amazed at his shortsightedness. He just didn't get it—how fragile, how fleeting, this snow was. I felt surprised again at how long his hair was because he'd always been such a by-the-rules guy.

"The new owners don't mind you having long hair? That's a switch, huh?"

After several years of negotiations, Squaw Valley had recently been sold by one of the original families that started the resort to a corporate entity that owned and managed several other big resorts. Rumor had it the same company would soon buy neighboring Alpine Meadows as well. The company had a plan to sink a lot of money into the resort over the course of a five-year plan, and then sell it. So naturally, people around Squaw were nervous.

He laughed. "Oh the new owners mind. I've been reminded several times that I need a haircut. With all the snow we've had this winter, I haven't had time to do shit. It's just been relentless."

I looked around at the abundant snow. There was more this season than in the last twenty, and all the burden of keeping skiers safe fell on his shoulders. I nodded sympathetically.

"I can imagine." We helped each other hoist on our backpacks and turned around just in time to see the sun rise up over the mountains and flood Lake Tahoe with pink light.

"Wow," I said.

Dave stood still next to me and, uncharacteristically, put his arm around my shoulders and gave me a quick squeeze.

"Yeah," he said. "This is my payola. Not exactly jobs our parents will ever be proud of, but moments like these are when we get our pay-off."

He turned to face me.

"What do your parents think of you being a ski bum?"

"First off, they died when I was seven," I said, "and secondly I'm not a ski bum. I'm working hard every day to make sure we keep the snow we have now, or even to reverse trends and get back more snow. The kind of snow that was around when my grandma and my great aunts—and that's who raised me—were girls."

Behind us echoing up the mountain we heard the big BOOM of a howitzer over at Alpine Meadows. Their blasting had begun.

Squaw's situation was geographically unique. Since Squaw Valley's five mountains were linked by a series of ridgelines, all potential avalanche sites in the resort can be reached by hand charges. That made it possible for Squaw to be one of the few resorts in the country that did avalanche clearance work with only hand charges and ski cutting, and without the use of big guns. Because of the immense amount of snow Squaw received, and the vastness of their terrain, they were one of the largest users of hand charges in the country. Behind us on the expert terrain of KT-22—some of the steepest in-bounds terrain in the country—-we heard the WHOMP of patrol blast teams setting off hand charges.

Once we reached the open area where the Red Dog lift emptied out, Dave clicked back into his skis.

"Let's head down and get some coffee, Doctor."

"That sounds great. I'm starving. By the way, I don't consider you a ski bum, either. But if that's how you want to think of yourself, feel free."

Dave grunted, meaning *what* I had no idea, and shook his head, "Not a ski bum," he said to himself.

We spun around, turning our backs on the view of Lake Tahoe, and started down Red Dog, the local racing mountain. We took it easy, carving smooth turns into the corduroy snow. Though the conditions weren't ideal, it was lovely to be out early on the freshly groomed run. The lifts had yet to open for the guests, so we had it all to ourselves, and instead of racing we took our time enjoying the morning, carving long, sweet turns.

Back down in the village, Dave got caught up talking to a blast team that had just finished its sweep, so I headed into a shop advertising breakfast burritos. I ordered a soy latte for myself, extra hot, and a plain black coffee for Dave and two breakfast burritos with eggs, salsa, and cheese. By the time I came back out, Dave was shouting into his squawking satellite phone, which was the size of a brick and strapped to his chest, and that's right where he needed it since he yelled into it all daylong. We walked together over to the Funitel with our takeout and loaded up with two other ski patrollers. The four of us plopped down onto the metal bench that rings the car. Most resorts in the

States have Gondolas, but Squaw went the European way and had both a large cable car lift–everyone at Squaw called it a tram, but I could never get used to calling it anything but a cable car–and a Funitel that unlike most gondolas that hold six or eight people tops, holds up to twenty-eight—though not comfortably. Both of these upload skiers about halfway up. From there you can head up higher onto Granite Chief, Emigrant, or Squaw Peak.

The Funitel lurched out of the building and by then Dave had finished talking on the sat phone, and the patrollers, a husband and wife team of volunteers, started quizzing Dave about what kind of crowds he expected for the weekend.

"It depends on when the snow starts," Dave told them. "If it comes in early and dumps all night then clears out for a bluebird powder day tomorrow—I'll need all bodies available on skis. It'll be a zoo. Especially if they get 80 open. But if the snow comes in later in the night, and it's still dumping in the morning, it won't be so bad. Mostly locals."

The two nod.

"How many bodies are available for you?" I asked.

"This winter we've got forty full-time paid patrollers, four out with injuries. And around ninety volunteers."

As Dave and I drank coffee and finished our burritos, the talk turned to the new owners of Squaw. Nobody trusted them, seeing as they were a large corporation looking to make money, but the fifty-million they'd promised to spend on Squaw over the next five years was sorely needed in infrastructure repair to lifts and village updating. So everyone seemed to be waiting to see how long it took this corporation out of Colorado to show their hand.

"Jesus," the husband said. His nametag read "Glenn from Chico, CA," "What's with people from Colorado buying up all our resorts?" He was an older man, a retired physician, compact and fit.

His wife, "Janelle from Chico" looked older, and her bulk strained the seams of her pants and parka as if she had recently gained twenty pounds.

"Laura here is a snow scientist from Colorado," Dave told them by way of introduction. "Ask her."

"Well, thanks Dave. It's complicated and hard for me to boil down to half a Funitel ride, but I think this area looks good because Colorado is really being hurt by the red snows. Tourists get put off by the way it looks. It's not that pristine vision of an alpine setting. It doesn't look the way a ski resort is supposed to look. And then, of course, Colorado gets less snow, and their season is shorter. In the long run, the Sierra will probably be the last area in the continental US that has snow. I think all these things tie in with the idea that California resorts aren't as commercialized as ours, leaving room for development. So Tahoe resorts look pretty attractive. You've certainly got the terrain."

Glenn said leaning forward, "Even though we're at lower altitude, we're supposed to have snow longer than Colorado?"

I didn't have time to do more than nod since the Funitel was rumbling into the entrance to the Gold Coast Building where we unloaded. Hardly enough time to begin explaining that California storms source their moisture over the Pacific as the jet stream comes out of Alaska, hits the uplift of the Sierra. This orographic lift is what wrings out so much snow for Tahoe area resorts. Colorado storms generally come from the same place and are caused by fluctuations in the jet stream that bring this moisture up through Canada and then back down into the Rockies. So being farther from the ocean, they've got less juice.

Dave and I hefted our skis and marched off to the main exit–I felt ready to get some of that juicy Sierra snow underfoot—while Glenn and Janelle ducked out a side door to cut down to a different area of the resort.

Dave and I headed over to the Siberia chair to check the snow station on top of Squaw Peak, which at nearly nine-thousand feet is the second highest of the five mountains that comprise Squaw Valley, USA. The Siberia snow platform was a fifteen minute hike up from the top of the lift. This time we packed along our skis, so once we finished we could just ski out. The Siberia snow station was more of a research station than the stripped-down platforms on the other mountains at Squaw. A winter-long burly pit was maintained at the top of Siberia, so there was no digging involved. I climbed down and started reading the snow history of the epic season Squaw had had up to that point in the winter.

It was full daylight by then, so I could see much better than when we were on Snow King. We once again checked the depth of new snow, and did tests to see how easily the new snow slid off the layer beneath it. Dave rammed the ten x ten x ten centimeter cube into the snow, and we weighed it, subtracting the weight of the cube, to measure the exact amount of water in the snow, while I gathered samples of snow in plastic bags to check for soot or dirt once I got back to Fort Collins. We also ran a test to check the heat capacity of the ice, how much mass of snow cold content there was in the snow pack in Joules per square meter.

An hour later, around 10:15 a.m., we were once again in the Patrol Shack at the top of Snow King Mountain. Matt and Janis had long since finished their avie clearance work, snow slang for avalanche work, and were hanging out in the shack waiting for somebody to come by or call and say they were needed. Once in a while a guest dropped in to purchase a T-shirt to support the Squaw avalanche rescue dogs—-featuring a silkscreen of the dogs on a chairlift with Lake Tahoe in the background. Obviously, neither Matt nor Janis were fans of Dave's old school approach to ski patrol where the senior team on any terrain had to sit in the patrol shack and wait for a casualty call. They'd much rather be out skiing and being a presence on the mountain. Nobody had to say a word for me to read the undercurrent. We sat in the shack warming up for five minutes or so in the tense environment, then Dave stood up suddenly.

"Come on, Laura. Let's ski down." I said good-bye to Matt and Janis, grabbed my gloves and helmet, and started out the door.

We pulled our skis out of the snowdrift where we stuck them. "To hell with them if they don't like the way I run it. When they're in charge they can run it any way they want," Dave complained to me.

I tried to get my helmet down over my hair. I should have braided it, but it had been a rush of a day. I suddenly remembered I had a hair tie in my pocket, so I quickly weaved it into a single braid and tied the end off while Dave watched smirking.

"What?" I asked, as I snugged my helmet down onto my head.

"It's just a wonder you can get all that hair into a helmet."

"For anything on my head, I have to size up. Or I wouldn't."

We laughed about that for a second, and the tension from inside the shack fell away.

"There's something I'd like to show you over here under the Squaw Creek Chair," he said. "Let's head over this way."

We stood on top of the headwall of a long, groomed run leading down to The Resort At Squaw Creek, a high-end resort of condos rented out like a hotel. Before us, Lake Tahoe stretched out ringed round with snow-covered mountains. The snow had mostly stopped, but the skies were still overcast, and the lake reflected the pewter color of the sky. Tahoe looked like a big, long cave of the gods. The day had turned cold, and the wind swirled snow around us. Dave dove down off the headwall, and I pushed off, swooping down behind him. His shaggy hair flew loose in the wind: no helmet or hat for him. I felt a familiar rush of joy as I flew down the mountain and let my skis rip, no longer fighting the speed but relaxing into it so that I moved up alongside Dave.

He motioned off to the left. I followed him over a lip of snow and down off the main run into a field of pristine snow that lay heavy and knee deep. We were going fast and sliced right through it. The mountain fell away steeply beneath our skis. Hundred foot Jeffrey Pines looked like bonsais buried as they were twenty feet up in snow. The clean rush of air stung my face, and trees whipped past as Dave moved ahead and dove off further to the left, weaving into a stand of pine trees. Dave brushed up against a pine limb and knocked loose a flutter of snow that sparkled before my eyes for an instant before pinging into my face. I breathed in the sudden scent of pine and carved silently through the snow behind him. Everything seemed to flow in slow motion. All around, the forest settled in silence except for the whoosh of snow. Though we flew through the trees, it felt like everything moved slowly—the trees gliding past, the rhythmic movement of one foot up, one foot down, like riding a bike along the bottom of the ocean, no need for air, no need for eyesight.

A shout from Dave roused me from the quiet snow world.

"To your right," he shouted again, pointing with his pole into a glade of pines in front of us and slightly uphill. I spotted a person standing and waving a ski pole, yelling.

"Hey! Help!"

As we moved closer through the trees, I could see another person, a dark-haired woman sprawled out buried in the deep snow. I steered over into the trees and smeared my tails to a fast stop next to Dave who stands at least six-foot-two, and I noticed that even on him the snow came up well above his knees.

I'm five-six, and the snow was up to my crotch and eased higher every second. I quickly began stamping out a platform on the snow. It took me a good thirty seconds to get solid snow to stand on without sinking, but I was still a foot or so beneath the top of the snow.

The woman stuck in the snow looked like a snow child from a Russian fairy tale with her dark hair covered in snowflakes, and her fair complexion flushed rosy from either cold or the effort of trying to get out, or both. It can take forever, an hour or more, to dig out of a fall in deep snow, and the process leaves a person exhausted. Without someone to help, an inexperienced person can suffocate. The other woman, a tall blonde in a cobalt blue parka, wore an inordinate amount of makeup for skiing on a wet, messy day–heavy foundation, lots of black eye shadow, dark lipstick, and it looked like even fake eyelashes.

"We've been here over an hour digging her out," the blonde said, accusingly.

It was about 10:30, and the lifts had opened at almost 10:00, so they'd hardly been there over an hour, but she didn't look in the mood to quibble. Her chopped-off, chin-length bob moved emphatically as she spoke. She seemed angry and spin class fit.

Dave smiled. "Yeah. Falling in deep snow's hard. Are you hurt?" he asked the dark-haired one.

"I don't think so," she said.

What a sweet face she had. She looked like a much nicer person than her friend. They were both a little older than me, maybe mid-to-late-thirties.

"Let's get you up," Dave told her, and moved to help her up. Just then, an angry squawk came from his chest. He ripped the phone free from its harness, and we all listened for a minute, before he put it back into the harness on his chest.

"I've got to go. Serious pileup casualty. You heard it. Laura, you stay and help her get sorted out."

"Dave! Wait!" I shouted to him as he hopped his skis around and poled himself downhill to get some speed, then cut uphill to get back onto the main, groomed run, which was a hundred yards above us. He quickly disappeared among the pines.

What in the hell was he doing? The brunette could likely be hurt. I'd skied a lot of mountains all over the world, and I knew damn well that he should deal with the possible casualty at his feet before taking off to check out another one.

"What the fuck?" the blonde said.

I was thinking the same thing.

I moved around awkwardly in the deep snow to get below the fallen skier. I had to crouch down low, then pull backwards to get her up. It's like what I'd imagine pulling someone out of quicksand would feel like. As she came free from the snow, she screamed sharply, then continued to groan.

"Are you okay? What hurts?"

She didn't say anything, just gritted her teeth and grimaced as I pulled her loose. By the time I finally got her on her feet, she had tears in her eyes.

"Where do you hurt?" I asked her again.

She put her hands around her ribs. "Here."

"Can you cough?" I asked.

She tried, but blanched pale with the pain.

I moved beside her and braced her for a second, so she didn't end up back in the snow.

"Looks like you've got a cracked rib or two."

She nodded. She was tiny, barely five feet tall, and dressed all in black except for her red gloves–black parka, black pants, black hair. I looked around and saw no sign of a helmet or a hat. As I dug out my cell phone, I asked her if anything else hurt.

She looked uncertain. "I don't know. I'm just so cold and shaky. I can't move my hands very well."

"I don't mean to be rude," the blonde said. "But what do you know about this? What are your qualifications? Are you even on the ski patrol?"

"I'm not on the ski patrol, but I spend a lot of time in the back-country, and I'm a certified Wilderness First Responder."

That shut her up.

The little brunette was shivering uncontrollably. It was obvious that there was no way she could ski down from this field of heavy deep snow they'd gotten themselves into. By the way the blonde was standing, I didn't think she was an experienced skier either. I certainly didn't think either of them had any business being on an unmarked and unpatrolled off-piste slope in this mashed-potato snow.

I tried dialing the ski patrol number, but got no reception. I looked around and realized we were in a deep glade with rock cliffs behind us, and a wall of huge pine trees around us.

I unzipped my parka, took it off, and unfastened the harness for my CamelBak, handing it to the dark-haired woman who looped it over her shoulder as I zipped back up.

"Here," I told her. "I'm going to have to ski down and get some help." I stepped up closer. "Let me have a look at your hands." She pulled her red gloves off, and her fingers were cold and pale but still slightly pink, so I knew she didn't have frostbite yet.

Her dark eyes looked up at me with a twinkle. Obviously, she had a zest for life.

"What are you looking for?" she asked.

"If your fingers were white, it might mean you had frostbite, but yours still have a little pink. So you just need to warm up."

I pulled out some green and gold hand-warmers from the CSU ski team, I'm an Assistant Coach, and helped her slip them inside her gloves. "Crush those up," I told her. "Move them around, and they'll get hot faster." From the depths of my backpack, I pulled out an old

Cliff Bar and some dried apricots and handed these over to her as well. "I'm sure you're exhausted and in the midst of a blood sugar crash. If you eat something and drink some water, you're going to feel better. I'll be back as soon as I can. It won't be much more than a half hour."

As an afterthought, I pulled out a credit-card sized wafer containing a silver foil blanket.

"If you get really cold and shaky wrap up in this."

During all this time, the blonde stood five feet uphill from us, huffing and sighing. It was obvious she thought her day had taken a dreadful turn.

"I saw a client of mine skiing through here earlier," she finally blurted out. "I'll ski down for help. Then I want to see if I can find him. You stay here with her," she told me.

She put her hands back into the wrist straps for her poles, and started trying to turn her skis around.

Uphill, way above where the blonde stood, I could see people skiing past through the trees.

"For Christ's sake, Alexis!" the brunette snapped. "She's the pro. Let her ski down. You can wait here with your best friend a little longer."

I couldn't help but laugh. "You've got spunk. I like that," I told the brunette.

"I've been told that before," she said, and groaned in discomfort. "This is exactly what my husband warned me was going to happen." She turned up to look at her friend, "No offense, Alexis. You know I love you, but you're not a patient person. You wanted to take this shortcut that wasn't safe, and now look what's happened." She shook her head, a rueful look on her face. "It's a fine mess you've gotten us into now, Alexis!"

"Sorry," Alexis said, and for an instant she looked it.

"How long do you think it'll take?" the injured woman asked.

"As fast as I can make it down and back. Promise you won't try to ski out on your own?"

"Yes," Alexis said. "Please do hurry. My friend can barely ski. I should never have brought her down here. It's going to be harder than hell to get her out."

"How did you end up down here?" I asked.

"I wanted her to get a chance to ski in powder."

"Be honest, Alexis, you followed some guy down here," the brunette added.

"This isn't powder," I told Alexis. "Powder snow is light with a low water content. This is more like cement. Now promise me you two will stay right here till I get back."

"Are you crazy?" the brunette said, shaking her head. "I can't go anywhere except on a toboggan."

"OK," I said, as I kicked out of the snow and followed Dave's tracks out.

Chapter 3

FRIDAY, APRIL 1, 10:45 AM

I flew off the mountain as fast as I could. At the bottom of the mountain, back within cell phone range, I called the ski patrol office. Apparently, the casualty Dave left us for involved a bunch of guys from Google sneaking onto an out-of-bounds racing hill, getting in way over their heads, and four of them colliding. All four of them had fairly serious injuries. I'd laugh if it wasn't so pathetic. So there was currently no sled—snow slang for the Ski Patrol's toboggan they use to haul injuries off the mountain—available on Snow King Mountain. It'd be about forty-five minutes before they could get a team over from neighboring KT-22 to bring the dark-haired woman down off the mountain.

This was bad news. I headed back up in the chairlift; figuring that I had a couple more aluminum blankets in my back-pack I could wrap her up in to keep her from getting colder. I could build a platform with skis and poles she could recline on. Though moving around that much might cause her more pain than it was worth, and in the deep snow I'm not sure how well that would work. But hopefully, I'd be able to make her waiting a little less painful.

I arrived back to the stand of trees where I left them a half hour ago to find more bad news. I could see the divot in the snow where the brunette fell, and our tracks stomping around all over the place, but the two women were gone. The temperature was dropping fast, and a stiff wind had come up, even back in the big pines. My tracks were beginning to freeze beneath my skis.

Gone! Or at least out of sight.

I looked around. They had to be here somewhere. Skiing out didn't seem like a possibility for the little brunette. I stood there confused for a few minutes yelling, "Alexis! Hey!" But the only sound was the wind soughing through the trees up high. I skied down around the tracks we made in the snow and found tracks skiing out and down. I'm certainly not "F" rated at Squaw, but I know enough to feel certain there was no real way out going straight down. Dave skied down and to the right prior to cutting up, and I followed in his tracks when I'd left them earlier. So it couldn't have been either of us who made those tracks straight down. It had to have been the women. I felt confused not to mention shocked as hell.

As I stood looking straight down the mountain toward the old riding stables down below, there was a double fall line, meaning the ground fell away straight downhill in front of me, and it also fell away to my right. So I could have skied downhill either straight down, or to the right. To the right, they could have skied another couple hundred yards and met up with a major groomed run. Straight down, I didn't think there was anything but a forest of huge pine and fir trees. Maybe I should wait for the ski patrol, I thought. But they said it would be at least another half hour before anyone got there. I hated leaving the ski patrollers to just wonder where we went, but I figured ski patrollers were better able to fend for themselves than Alexis and her buddy, so I headed straight down mountain in their tracks.

It was tough going. The trees had grown up so thick there was no going fast as I weaved between them avoiding the huge tree wells the previous few days' warm weather had caused to expand around the big trees. Many a skier and snowboarder dies every year taking a header into a tree well. You slip in sideways, or fall in backwards, then fall straight down, and end up hanging upside down by your skis, or board, which are caught way up above on the snow. This is an absolute death trap unless someone finds you fast, or you're able to catch onto the trunk of the tree on your way down, or somehow you're enough of a contortionist to twist around and get your feet loose from your bindings, in which case you can kind of shimmy up the tree. Snowboarders lack that safety hatch. There's no way they can get out of their bindings hanging upside down. With twenty feet of snow on the ground, I didn't see a bottom to any of the tree wells.

Twenty or thirty foot rock cliffs littered the area. The tracks I followed wound through them gracefully. The temperature had taken a nosedive from the mid-twenties when I left the women to what I bet was the low-teens judging by the way the snow squeaked beneath my skis. Most of the time I saw one or two sets of tracks, which made sense because the brunette could have followed behind in her friend's tracks. But every once in a while I saw what looked like three sets of tracks. Some powder hound must have come along and found the women's tracks and followed them, hoping to find a personal ski nirvana. Hardcore skiers always have an eye peeled for a set of tracks wandering off into the unknown.

A sudden howling gust of wind came up and the trees around me shook loose their snow loads on my head. I had to wait for it to subside and wipe my goggles in order to see where I was going. The day had gone from messy to miserable.

Five minutes later, I reached a huge Ponderosa pine that stood backed up to a rock cliff that was maybe thirty or forty feet high. The face was steep enough that it was bare rock. The women's tracks led underneath the snow load the big pine had dropped. I skied around the tree and spotted something red, and half covered in fresh snow, back under a fallen tree. I moved over and picked it up. It looked exactly like one of the brunette's gloves. I reached inside and pulled out a CSU hand warmer. It was hers. They had gotten this far. I moved around beneath the big tree and realized that tracks skied out on the downhill side. So the tree probably had just dropped its snow load in the big wind. It looked like a cornice had also broken off the top of the cliff the big tree backed up to. The snow was so deep and littered with globs of wet fallen snow from the big pine that I wasn't sure whether I was seeing one, two or three sets of tracks skiing out on the downhill side. I stood there baffled. How in the hell had her glove ended up here. It was freezing out. It all felt crazy making.

I skied around the big tree once again, then followed the tracks on down into the thick, steep pine forest. What in the hell were those women doing? Another fifteen yards or so and the tracks emptied out onto a snowcat track. Breathing a sigh of relief to be out of that hellish forest, I stopped and once again dried my goggles. Maybe the brunette wasn't hurt as badly as I thought? Just some pulled oblique muscles, not a cracked rib? Maybe once she got some food and water in her she started feeling better? The thought forced its way into my mind that maybe she left her glove as a sign. Maybe that was the only bread crumb she had. But a sign of what? God knows her friend was eager to get going. I pushed off and headed down the cat trail fast.

At the bottom, I stopped at the Squaw Creek chairlift, which started up just outside the big resort.

"Did you see a couple women ski out down that cat track?" I asked the lift operator. He was in his mid-twenties, with a goggle-suntan and a big cheery smile.

"No, ma'am," he said "I don't think so. Just you."

"Did you by chance notice a little brunette dressed all in black, skiing with a tall blonde in a bright blue parka?"

He shook his head. "I don't think so."

"Any calls for a casualty in the woods up there?" I pointed up mountain.

"No, ma'am," he said. "There's no place to ski up there in the trees. Too thick."

"OK. Thanks." When did I become a "ma'am" to a good-looking guy like that? It kind of stung.

I kicked my skis off and left them lying on the snow off to the side of the main path up to The Resort at Squaw Creek: The Crystal Palace as the locals call it, since the whole front façade of the sprawling resort is covered in black glass. I walked into the vast lobby, all stone floors and intimate seating areas with an impressive view of the valley. I asked after the two women at the front desk, no luck. I clomped downstairs in my ski boots and asked the bartender—"Justin from Okemo, NH"—-at Sandy's Pub if he'd seen them. No joy there either.

My phone rang as I headed back up the stairs. By the time I'd dug it out of my parka, it stopped. On my way back outside, I heard the ding for voicemail. As expected, it was Dave Geisner—his emergency was over—and he wanted to get back to work. I hit the button to call him back, and stood outside at a railing looking out at an enthusiastic waterfall that disappeared behind the skating rink down below.

"Laura," Dave answered. "Where are you?"

"Where the hell did you go?"

"I had a casualty. I told you."

"That woman in the snow was hurt: broken ribs, maybe frostbite and you just took off and left her."

"Laura. There was a bad collision on the racing hill back there. That takes precedence. Anyway, I left you with them. So how bad could it have been?"

"Yeah, you left us down in that valley with no cell reception, so I had to leave them and ski out for the patrol, and by the time I got back they were gone."

"So, what's the problem?"

"That woman was hurt! Their tracks went straight downhill into the trees."

"Did they get out?"

"I never found them, though I did find one of their gloves. I suppose they must have."

"Then like I said, what's the problem? She was probably just shaken up. Happens all the time. Once she's up and gets something to eat— did you give her something to eat?"

"I gave her something to eat. The problem is if you'd stayed for two minutes to help her out of the snow, you'd have realized you already had a casualty. Matt and Janis were probably at that pileup in two minutes flat. Instead, I had to leave those women, and now they're gone. They were your responsibility, too."

"Look, Bailey, once that dark-haired one stood up and got her breath, she probably realized she was fine. Just pulled a muscle in her side. So stop freaking out and get down here and help me. You said you'd give me a day. My day's not over."

"Yeah, Dave. Whatever."

"Yeah, Dave. Whatever," he mimicked me. "Like I said, you still owe me half a day."

"Where are you?"

"In my office."

"I'm at the Crystal Palace. I'll head over. But ask around if anyone's had a call about those two. The blonde's name was Alexis."

"And the other one?"

"I don't know."

"The first thing you're supposed to do is get their names."

"Well, I didn't."

"Obviously. See you in twenty or so." He cut off the call. I stood there looking at the waterfall and feeling guilty.

―――

By the time I got to Dave's office in the concrete block ski patrol building, he was up and raring to head back out on the mountain. He'd spent the last half hour or so inside warming up and cooling his heels. I peeled off my gloves and fixed myself a cup of powdered hot chocolate, then took off my helmet and parka.

"Did you ask around about the two women?"

"I know how to do my job, Bailey. Of course, I did. Nobody's heard or seen anything."

I melted back into the chair in Dave's cluttered mess of an office. "Good. Guess I can stand down from red alert."

He smiled at me and shook his head like I was such a jerk.

―――

A half hour after the lifts closed, we started skiing all the way down from High Camp, the big building where the cable car emptied out. It had been a long, bitter cold afternoon of looking at snow pack, pondering over signs of early melt, and talking about low-cost snow management features the new owners could put into place this summer. Things like snow fencing around certain slopes and moving snow around differently early in the season. The more I looked at the signs of early melt Dave showed me, the more confused I got. In the back of the resort, on Granite Chief, the highest of the five mountains that make up Squaw Valley, channels were cutting down under solid snowbanks. I wished I had some insight into what was going on.

I could barely move my hands they were so cold. The temperature must have been in the single digits, and the wind ripped so hard that, standing at the top of a headwall, I pushed off and launched myself into space, spread my arms, and found myself suspended, skis pointing straight down a steep aspect and the winds holding me still; snow pinging off my face like a sandblaster. I had to duck into a crouch to cheat the wind and get moving. Snow was coming down so thick I could barely see. The wind twisted the falling snow into a blast coming down hard and sideways.

As we reached the village main meeting area between the Funitel and the Red Dog chair, a volunteer patroller came over and told Dave that some people had just reported their friends missing since around lunchtime.

"Over there." He pointed over to a group of well-heeled people below us on the main promenade through the village.

Dave and I stepped out of our skis and walked down off the snow towards the group. The volunteer told us they were lawyers from San Francisco, and they'd been skiing most of the day, but since 11:30 a.m. or so they hadn't been able to locate their colleague Alexis and her friend Jennifer.

Hearing the name "Alexis" knocked me into slow motion. It felt like I'd been expecting this all afternoon. We walked up to the group, two men and a woman. The volunteer introduced Dave as the head of the Ski Patrol.

"What's going on," Dave asked. "Give me the whole story."

A tall man stepped forward. He was dressed in expensive ski clothes, and had a long aquiline nose.

"I'm Sean Flaherty." He put forward his bare hand and waited while Dave pulled his mitt off to shake. "I'm the Managing Partner at Reed, Martin and Smith, San Francisco Office. We made plans last night to meet up for lunch, or coffee, at the Crystal Palace at 11:30. Our colleague Alexis Page and her friend Jennifer—what's Jennifer's last name?" He twisted around to look at a striking petite blonde standing beside and behind him. She too wore top-of-the line ski gear. Neither of them looked like big skiers because everything they wore looked brand new.

"Fellatorre," she answered.

"Yes, our colleague Alexis Page and her friend Jennifer Fellatorre never showed up for lunch. And maybe that's not difficult to believe in a place like a ski resort. But we've never heard from them since. Alexis' phone just rings and rings. Doesn't go to voicemail. It just rings."

Dave didn't say anything, just shifted his eyes from Sean's face to the ground in front of his feet. What in the hell was he doing? He just stood there.

Before the moment turned from awkward to angry I stepped forward and asked, "Would any of you happen to have a picture of the women?"

A man dressed in street clothes with curly graying hair stepped forward and thumbed through his iPhone for a minute, then handed it over to me. I already knew what I was going to see, so I was ready for it. I looked at the picture of the uppity blonde and her dark-haired friend, arms around each other's waists, grinning and all dressed up in sparkly cocktail dresses. It was them.

I angled the phone over towards Dave. He took a look. He still said nothing, so I turned back to the group of lawyers.

"We came across your friends this morning around 10:30. Jennifer had fallen in deep snow, and they'd been trying to get her out for a while. We asked her if she was hurt, and she said she wasn't. And just then, Dave got a call for a serious casualty. So he left. I got her up out of the snow and gave her some food and water and some hand warmers. There wasn't any cell reception where they were, so I had to ski out to get the ski patrol for them. Anyways, when I got back, they were gone. I guess they skied out on their own."

"Why did Jennifer need the ski patrol if she wasn't hurt?" Sean asked.

"By the time I'd pulled her out of the snow, it wasn't clear whether she was hurt or not. Her ribs hurt. So I thought perhaps she'd cracked a rib or two. I asked them to please stay where they were and wait, but, as I said, by the time I got back they were gone."

"Where was this?" Sean continued, his color rising as he spoke.

Dave finally joined in the conversation. "Over on Snow King Mountain. Off in some deep off-piste-snow."

"I don't get it," the blonde said. "What the hell were they doing there? Jennifer is a beginner, maybe at best a beginning intermediate."

"Alexis said she'd taken Jennifer there to give her a chance to ski in powder," I told her. "But it wasn't powder. It was heavy, deep snow. But Jennifer said Alexis had been following after someone she knew. And I think they were both in way over their heads."

I let that hang in the air for a moment.

"I did find one of Jennifer's gloves."

"So you just left them?" Sean shouted at Dave. "You just left them there?"

"The one in the snow, Jennifer, said she wasn't hurt. So I left them with Laura. I had a more serious casualty call."

"Then where the fuck are they now?" Sean asked.

"Where are they staying?" I jumped back into the conversation in an attempt to cool things down.

The man with the curly graying hair, the one with the iPhone, said, "Squaw Creek."

"Have you checked there?"

"We've called."

"Maybe they're in the bar?" the blonde said.

"Jennifer, the little dark-haired one, right?" I asked.

"Yes," Sean said.

"She might have been hurt. The Medical Clinic is just over there to the right. You might check there."

"Knowing Alexis, we should check the bars and the casinos," the blonde said. She pulled on Sean's arm. The group turned and walked away without even looking back at either of us. Finally, the man with the curly gray hair looked back and said, "Thanks."

Chapter 4

FRIDAY, APRIL 1, 5:00 PM,

"**W**ow," I said, as I watched them walk off, and not in the direction of the Medical Clinic. "They seem like a nasty bunch, but I'm sure they're worried about their friends."

I couldn't shake the feeling something terrible had happened.

"Lawyers," Dave said. "San Francisco lawyers. What do you expect? They are, after all, BayAryans."

I had to laugh at that. "I'm going to go check at the clinic, see if the women have been there. Think you should call your brother?" Dave's brother, Burt, served as the Sheriff of Placer County, where Squaw is located.

"Nah," he said, "Do you?"

I stood there for a minute in the middle of the courtyard walkway thinking. My head itched, so I took off my helmet and fluffed up my hair to get some air through it.

"You check the Clinic," he said. "That's a good idea. But beyond that, their friends aren't worried, why should we be?"

"I'm nervous about that tree well."

"You said you saw tracks out, right?"

"I did. But I'd like to go back and check."

"It's almost dark, and dumping snow. If they still haven't showed up, we can take another look in the morning. As it stands, I'm officially declaring it too dangerous to head back there now."

"No caves in the area? No mines?" I thought of Aspen, which is littered with old silver mines. On average, once a year someone falls in one and can't get out. If they're lucky, they're found before they freeze.

"Laura, they're somewhere warm and cozy kicking back cocktails. You check the Medical Center, if they haven't seen them then those women are officially off my plate."

I looked up at him and grimaced, certain he was not going to like what I had to say. "Dave, please do me a favor and call Burt."

He stood for a moment staring at me through heavy eyelids. He looked exhausted. After a long pause, he turned away and muttered, "Oh for fuck's sake. Check the clinic and then come over to my office." He climbed back up onto the snow to retrieve his skis, then clicked in and skated over behind the Red Dog chairlift toward the ski patrol building. His rigid posture revealing what he thought of my idea with every move he made. Or maybe I just imagined it.

Inside the tight confines of the Medical Center, an old construction trailer with tacked up sheetrock walls, and cheap indoor, outdoor carpet, I walked past the last casualties of the day. An older man with a scraped up face, and a boy with what looked like a broken arm. I asked the receptionist, a freckle-faced young woman who could barely keep her eyes open, if she had seen anyone resembling Alexis and Jennifer.

She tilted her head to the right, where I saw through a curtain an older woman with a cranky expression attempting to wiggle off the exam table and get standing with the aide of a pair of crutches. A miasma of pain floated around her. She wore a matching set of pink, flowered long underwear. The woman made her slow way past me towards the restroom. The patients left in the waiting area took a glimpse then looked away.

"She's the only female casualty we've had today."

"Thanks," I told the receptionist and got out of that trailer full of misery as fast as possible.

=

Alpenglow, the last lavender light of day, hung between the trees like a fog, as I followed after Dave, retrieved my skis, clicked in, and skated over towards the ski patrol building. Heavy grooming cats were already up on Red Dog moving on up mountain, their headlights cutting intermittently through the snow.

I heard Dave long before I saw him. Only this time, he was yelling into a cell phone instead of his sat phone, which lay silent on his cluttered desk. The whole office was stacked high with printouts of weather, snow reports and gear.

"It wasn't an avalanche!" he shouted into the phone, the same way he'd been shouting into that big sat phone all day.

Dave snapped shut his old clamshell phone and turned to face me. "He's not coming over."

"So I gathered. Is he sending someone?"

"No. He says wait and see if they turn up tomorrow. It's too early for a Missing Persons Report. They're probably at some bar. He said exactly what I've already told you. Exactly the same thing. And thanks for putting me through that. One thing I love is getting yelled at by that idiot. Just like my ex."

"I'm sorry."

I had never met his brother, but I had met his ex-wife Felicia, not a likable woman. "What was your funny saying from the Army about not getting married?"

He laughed, "Yeah, that was from Viet Nam. A service joke, I guess you'd call it."

"What was it?"

"Don't bother getting married. Just find a woman you hate and buy her a house."

We both cracked up about that. "You bought Felicia such a nice one."

"Didn't I?" He said with a big grin. "And I couldn't have found a woman I hate more."

I nodded, still laughing, "But she sure was good-looking."

"Still is," he said. "Still is."

This may all seem kind of a jaded take on marriage, but most self-described ski bum types don't seem to be able to keep a good marriage going: not enough money, too much time on the mountain, no incentive to do anything but ski all day, all winter. Many of them migrated to the southern hemisphere for the summer to follow the snow. They worked as helicopter ski guides, or lift operators. I guess it was like most people who are obsessed–there was no room for another person. A lot of marriages fell by the wayside, though there were certainly many great ones. Matt McCoughlin, for instance, had a great marriage and two well-adjusted kids. My friend Aldous Moore and his wife had been married happily for over fifty years.

Getting Dave to laugh had shaken him out of his foul mood, and I felt like I could leave.

"I'll see you Dave." I said as lifted myself up out of the wooden chair and headed for the door.

"Be on mountain tomorrow?"

I nodded yes. "I still need to see if we can ski out the back of Granite Chief, and now I've got to know if those two have turned up."

"Give me a call when you get here in the morning, and I'll tell you what I've heard."

We said goodnight, and I headed outside into the bitter cold, and the dark. Dave still had hours of work ahead of him before he'd be heading home.

===

In the parking lot I began digging out the rental car from over a foot of snow that had settled on top. I brushed off enough snow with my sleeve to be able to get the driver's side open and unearth a snow scraper out of the side pocket. The whole time I stood brushing the snow off the car, I was thinking about the ride back into Truckee, and the fact that there was nothing to eat at Rita's, for sure the furnace would be off again, and even if I could skip dinner again, I was yearning for a glass of wine.

I was still thinking this over as I finished clearing off the car and climbed inside, turned on the engine, and sat back to watch the pros clear the snow.

Where I parked that morning was called the Far East parking lot. And at the top of it stood Mount Carnetti Glacier where all the snow removed from Squaw parking lots was dumped. Dan Carnetti being the man in charge of snow removal for the resort. I sat and watched as a two story high dump truck backed up through the pounding snow onto Carnetti glacier. Right then the glacier was about a hundred-feet long, thirty-feet wide, and thirty-feet high. The big truck backed up the long snow ramp beeping and then moving slowly down the length of the glacier. The truck finally stopped backing up, and the beep, beep, beep, stopped. With a huge swoosh of packed snow, the truck emptied its load and pulled forward.

I noticed they were starting a new area because the truck dumped its load right onto the pavement behind the glacier. That would build all night and by morning it would be how high? Twenty or even thirty feet? Thus the glacier grew all winter. The truck's headlights shone into a wall of fat snowflakes, even though the temps were low. This indicated there was a mix of cold and warm air. Which meant it was going to get ugly out later that night. The truck drove off into the night, and the whole area lapsed back into darkness.

I pried my feet out of my wet ski boots, and slipped them into some cold Ugg boots, stepped out of the car, and walked back into the village looking for dinner and a drink. My ski clothes were damp and cold after the long day, but I had nothing else to put on. I needed to remember to bring some jeans and a sweater with me tomorrow.

Back on the main promenade through the village, streetlights were burning with a muted glow through the filter of dumping snow. Only two other people were out and about, both of them moving at a determined pace, with their heads down to avoid the blast of white. The temperature had continued its daylong descent, and judging by the way the snow squeaked beneath my boots, it must have been around zero. I ended up at Mamasake's, a Japanese restaurant, because it was the first open restaurant I saw. There was an affectionate couple making out at one end of the bar, and a man sitting by himself at the other end. The rest of the place was empty, so I crossed the restaurant to get as far away from the door as possible, and took a seat on the booth side of a long line of tables.

I adore Japanese food, so I felt ridiculously happy to have ended up there. I wanted to do a little victory jig, but the guy sitting by himself at the bar had swung his chair around and sat smiling at me, so I didn't. My parka, hat, and gloves all got dumped on the seat next to me, as a twenty-something, heavily tattooed waitress made her way over. She had dyed black hair cut asymmetrically, and a big gold ring through the septum of her nose. How can someone think that's attractive? All it signified to me was she wanted someone to hook a leash onto it and lead her back to the barn.

She gave me a big smile, despite my nasty thoughts, and looked out the windows over my head.

"What a night," she said. "You still have to drive somewhere?"

"Back to Truckee."

"Me too," she said, making a face. "Ready to order?"

"I'd like a big glass of Chardonnay. By the time you get back, I'll be ready."

"What kind? Here's the wine list."

"Don't care. A house wine?" No one will ever accuse me of being a wine snob. I like the way cheap wine tastes, within reason, as well as the way fancy wine tastes. My interests lay in the way it makes me relax into a warm puddle inside.

She turned on her heel and headed for the bar. Nothing on the menu sang to me, and it was almost more effort than I could muster to read it. By then the waitress was back putting down a coaster and setting a large pour glass of wine in front of me.

"Any suggestions?" I asked her.

"What're you in the mood for?"

"Something hot and a lot of it."

She smiled again, looking incongruously sweet and young for a woman with so much bodywork. "On the mountain all day?"

I exhaled and nodded. "I'm beat."

"A noodle bowl? Soba noodle soup? Maybe with rice and veggies and tempura of shrimp or chicken or tofu? Sound good?"

"Sounds perfect. Soba noodle soup and the shrimp, please."

"Shouldn't be long," she said and headed off towards the kitchen.

The winds howled outside. I took a big gulp of the wine and leaned back against the upholstered booth. I could feel the wine burn in a delicious way all the way down, and a second later a smooth rush of warmth and ease flooded my limbs, as the alcohol entered my bloodstream. There's a reason those Saint Bernard dogs in the Alps carry flasks on their necks.

The restaurant door flew open, and two men walked in. One was slender and a little stooped, and the other was obviously a big guy. They were so bundled up, I couldn't see anything else, but the slender man unwrapped a scarf from around his face, and I recognized my friend Aldous Moore. He turned back to the big man behind him, who didn't look familiar, and said something then scanned the room. I raised a hand and waved.

Aldous walked straight over to me, and I stood up just in time to be swept up in a hug.

"I didn't know you were here. Why didn't you let me know?"

"I knew I'd see you," I told him. "There's no being at Squaw and not running into you." Aldous and his wife Margaret are my oldest friends. At seventy-four and seventy-six respectively, they're the oldest people I'm friends with, and I've been friends with them since I was eleven, making them my longest friends, too. Aldous still worked as a part-time ski instructor after retiring ten years ago from serving thirty years as the head of the Squaw Valley ski school.

He kissed both my cheeks, then released the embrace and took both my hands in his.

"Mike," he called, and the big guy walked over to us.

"Laura Bailey, my co-worker Mike Bernese. Mike, Laura Bailey, snow scientist."

We shook hands. Mike had a grin stretched across his face, and his hand was strong and warm. He pulled off his parka, shaking off a coating of snow, and hung it on a hook. Then he brushed his big hands over his hair, knocking a melting veil of white onto the floor. Mike had clear blue eyes, an easy smile, and straight graying blond hair that was long on top but Squaw regulation collar length in back.

I smiled back, thinking of course I'd meet this guy right now at the end of a fourteen-hour day, with my hair a big ball of frizz, and wearing dirty, wet ski clothes. Well, I told myself, he might as well see the real me.

Mike didn't seem to mind.

"Laura, what a pleasure. I've heard all about you from this guy." He gestured a thumb at Aldous.

"So what are you doing here?" Aldous asked.

"I've got some equipment problems at the snow site, so I'm heading back in Sunday to see what's going on. Dave Geisner asked me to come in a day early, look at some early melt, and talk snow management. So I spent the day skiing with him."

"Looks like it was a long one."

"You could say that."

Just then the waitress came over to Aldous, "Your take-out's ready."

"I'm going to have to run, Laura. But have dinner with us before you leave town. My poor wife will be fading away if I don't get her some food. From what she's told me, she's had a hell of a long day too. Once 80's closed, nobody gets any time off. Certainly not doctors." Margaret Moore still ran a bustling pediatric practice in Truckee.

I kissed his cheek and hugged him again, noticing how thin he'd grown.

Aldous headed over to pay for his food at the cash register near the door, then waved again on his way out.

Mike gestured to the seat opposite me, "May I join you?"

"Please," I told him, and I could hardly believe it, but I was blushing.

He slid into the chair—graceful for such a big man—"So you're the snow scientist I've been hearing about? Not what I expected."

"Is that good or bad?"

He laughed, throwing his head back, and relaxed into the chair.

"Neither. Both. I don't know. This has been such an insane winter. We're all exhausted. It. Has. Never. Stopped. Snowing. A couple weeks ago, I had to leave my truck in my driveway in Truckee, walk out to 80, and hitchhike to work. Never had to do that before."

The waitress returned and said, "Hey Mike. What can I get you?" She rested a hand on his shoulder and gave him a big smile.

He turned to me, "Have you ordered?"

I nodded yes.

"OK...uh...," he paused. "How about a Sierra Nevada. Soba noodle soup, and stir fry veggies with tempura shrimp and white rice."

The waitress, "Ky-rah" her nametag read, "Hometown, Juneau, AK" nodded towards me, "She's pretty much getting the same thing. Should I bring a big platter, and you can share?"

"Sure," I said. "As long as he doesn't eat it all."

Ky-rah cracked a smile, then spun on her heel towards the bar.

Mike leaned forward towards me, "So as the kids say, give me your story."

I laughed, "Where to begin?"

"Single?"

"Absolutely. You?"

"Definitely. Ever been married?"

"Close once, but no. You?" Rolling my stiff shoulders, I reached for my glass and took a sip, trying to relax. How in the hell had it come to pass that this guy was single? I was thinking, please don't let him be an adrenaline junkie like so many ski guys are. I couldn't stand to lose another one.

"Divorced just once. No kids. One dog. Still friends with the ex, and I think that's always a point in anyone's favor. If you're interested, she'd be happy to write a letter of recommendation."

I laughed and went to take another sip of wine, only to find I'd already emptied my glass. He had high cheekbones, a gray stubble of beard, and a sexy down-turning mouth beneath a straight, finely etched nose. Not classically good-looking, but more of a rugged Viking type.

Ky-rah returned with Mike's beer, and slipped another glass of wine in front of me. "On the house," she said. "You look like you could use it. Anyways, I heard you say you're helping Dave Geisner check the snowpack. So if you're working for free, it's the least Squaw can do."

She moved away before I could respond.

I looked up and met Mike's eyes, "Not that I don't want it, but I still have to find my way back into Truckee tonight." The wine was irresistible, and I took a sip. "Oh well."

"Where you staying?"

"Do you know Rita Chambers? She's a friend of mine from Aspen, and she has a house on West River Street. I'm staying there. No food, almost no heat. But it's a place to sleep."

"I think I know the house. Did she used to be married to Dan Gilbert? It's kind of washed out pink with a derelict hot tub on the porch?"

"Yes and yes."

He laughed again. "I thought it was abandoned."

"She got it in the divorce, and won't sell it, won't stay in it, or keep it up either. She lends it anyone who wants to borrow it, otherwise it just sits."

"And Dan and his new wife tried to buy it?"

"That was never going to happen. The new wife is what ended Dan and Rita's marriage."

Ky-rah came back carrying a big tray loaded with our food. I was grinning like a monkey and feeling no pain.

We dug in and the conversation stopped. Ten minutes later, we both raised our heads from the ruins of our dinner, locked eyes, and smiled. I leaned back into the booth for a breather. Steam covered the restaurant windows, and I looked outside, and could just make out a world of snow. The restaurant and bar had emptied out. The bartender, Ky-rah, and the cook were closing up.

I pulled out my phone to check the time. It was 7:55, and I had nine phone calls, four voicemails, twenty-seven texts, and forty-eight e-mails. Who in the hell were all those phone calls from? On average I have maybe one or two phone calls a week, since most people text. Even if they want to talk on the phone, they text first to see if I'm available to talk, we agree on a time, and then talk. Nobody just calls anymore.

"Sorry," I told Mike, as I slipped my phone back into a pocket on the leg of my ski pants. "Did you hear a couple women went missing today?"

He shook his head, his mouth still filled with rice and vegetables.

"Dave and I came across them around 10:30. One of the women had fallen in the deep snow and, of course, couldn't get up. Dave skied off to a multi-person casualty, and left me with them. I got the one woman out of the snow, and it seemed like her ribs were cracked. I couldn't get any cell reception, so I told them to stay put, and skied out for help. When I got back, they were gone. Apparently no one has heard from them since."

Mike's brow knit, and all his good-natured camaraderie disappeared, "Where was this?"

"In the snow fields off Lake View."

"Around Montezuma?"

"Before that."

"Where'd they go?"

"I followed their tracks, from where I pulled the one woman out, straight down into the trees."

"So like up above the old stables?"

"That's what I was thinking."

"That's just forest–huge trees and cliffs."

"That's why it's so weird. I'm wondering if you have a tracking system on lift tickets? The one woman is from San Francisco, and she might have a season pass."

"Sure we can tell you if she used any lifts after you saw them. But that's only on season passes. Day passes, no way. Maybe they got disoriented. Straight down might have seemed like the path of least resistance."

"I thought that too: path of least resistance. Their tracks seemed to go straight into a big tree well, which was all filled in with snow on top of their tracks. But then tracks came out on the other side, and went right back into the trees. And I found one of the women's gloves there, kind of tucked away under a fallen tree. Just fifteen yards after that their tracks joined up with the cat track that cuts through there."

"The Western States Trail?"

I shrugged, having never heard of that.

"Weird," Mike said and leaned forward with his chin in his hand and a blurry far away look in his eyes. "I don't know—tourists generally don't know about that cut through the trees."

"I don't know what happened to them. I guess they got out. I'd like to get back up there and look at that tree well"

"Yeah." He nodded, staring at the beer bottle in his hand. "If they don't turn up. Which they probably will. After something like that most likely they headed to the nearest bar."

"That's what their friends seemed to think. Either a bar or a casino."

By then I was starting to really worry about the roads. Standing, I stepped over to a window and rubbed a clear space on the glass to look out onto the main promenade. Snow seemed to hang suspended outside the window. I turned back to face Mike.

"I better get going. The roads are going to be hellacious."

He stood up and raised a hand to Ky-rah for the bill. I already had my wallet out and pulled out some cash.

He looked from Ky-rah to me. "You're not going to let me pay for this."

I shook my head no.

"OK. Next time though."

A giddy chill fluttered up my spine. I was such a teenager. He said "next time." There was going to be a "next time."

We settled up with Ky-rah and headed outside into the storm.

Mike walked close beside me.

"Where're you parked?"

"Far East lot. Right in front of the glacier."

"Let me follow you back into Truckee. My truck's great in snow. What're you driving?"

"I've got four-wheel and snow tires. I should be fine."

"But I'm following you."

"That would be wonderful. Thanks."

A biting wind coursed down the walkway between buildings. Snow fell in swirling flurries around us, and the streetlights spilled out dull circles of light on the snow covered pavers. Wood fire smoke mingled in with the snow in a fog.

We reached my car first, and after brushing off two or three inches of new snow, I settled into the cold leather seat and started the engine, as I waited for Mike to bring his truck around. The seat heaters began ticking up the temperature under my legs and rump, while the defroster blew icy air onto the windshield. I started scrolling through the phone calls. All of them were from Tim Schneider. What the hell? I was sure he wanted me to referee his latest tiff. That guy can't get along with anyone. In front of me a huge dump truck began beeping as it backed up the long ramp leading to the top of Mount Carnetti glacier. It's headlights drilled into the falling snow in dull pencil-shaped beams. I lost sight of the truck in a sudden swirl of snow. Somewhere off in the distance, a snowmobile engine revved as it headed up the mountain. The dump truck, still beeping, backed up to the end of the glacier, and dumped its load of snow onto a thirty foot wide snow berm that was already a couple feet high, and with a grinding of gears slowly began to pull forward. Once again, the mountain of snow lay in front of me invisible in the darkness. Just then Mike pulled up in a dark pickup truck with huge grippy tires. I rolled down my window.

"Ready?"

"Ready," I replied, sliding my phone back into the pocket on my calf, easing the car into gear, and pulling slowly forward behind Mike.

Chapter 5

SATURDAY, APRIL 2, 7 AM

I awoke the next morning in a fugue state, aching from head to toe. Seemed like I should be happy, having met the first guy since Peter I could imagine being interested in. I thought that would never happen to me again. I got out of bed and looked at myself in the bathroom mirror. I felt worse than I looked. Not that I looked great, just the normal me.

I picked up the remote and turned the TV to the local morning show, "What's Happening In Tahoe." A dark-haired guy in his late-twenties with a deadpan demeanor detailed the street clearing efforts of St. Pud, South Truckee Public Utilities Department.

"St. Pud should have all area power back on by 11:30 this morning. Hail St. Pud!" A surge of gratitude filled me, when I realized how many people didn't have power.

A minute later, he started giving the weather for the area, then launched into a humorous litany of weather for the country.

"By Tuesday, the cold front approaches Detroit. A lot of opportunity in Detroit. You should move there." I sat on the worn pink bedspread transfixed by the good-looking guy's deadpan delivery. "Seven degrees at Squaw's High Camp right now, a high of fourteen expected for the day. Winds currently gusting on top up to thirty-five miles an hour, and expected to top out at seventy later this afternoon. Like your mother said, "You should dress in layers." Don't bother with sunscreen. There won't be any sun. Great day for vampires."

My phone interrupted the show. It was Dave Geisner.

"Where are you?" he shouted in my ear. "The lawyers are looking for you."

"Dave. You don't need to shout. I can hear you just fine."

"Shit. Sorry," he said, in a normal tone of voice. "I get so used to yelling on that damn sat phone."

"What's going on?"

"The dark-haired one, Jennifer. Her husband's been calling from back east, and he'd like to talk to you."

"Why me?"

"You were the last one to see her."

There were a lot of things I felt like saying to him. Like for instance, "Yeah, thanks to you!"

Instead, I just said, "I'd like to look at that tree well again before I talk to him. That way I'll have something to tell him besides how much I want to look at the tree well again."

"If it's safe. After the snow we got last night—"

I wanted to cut him off quickly before he had a chance to say no. "On my way. Be there as soon as I can get through."

"89's open. Chains or four-wheel with snow tires, the usual restrictions. Are you covered?"

"My rental has four-wheel and snow tires. I'm good. On my way."

⸻

Luck was with me, and I got a parking spot right outside the Medical Center, which is as close as you can hope for. I parked and booted up then grabbed my skis, poles and backpack and walked down the main concourse between shops then climbed onto the snow of the big open area near the entrance to the Funitel. I clicked in and skated across the open snow to the ski patrol building.

Janis Murphy, looking cute in a fitted pink fleece, was on the phone just inside the door of the building. Cold seemed to radiate inward from the cement walls adorned with safety posters.

"Dave's out on mountain," she told me. "Not answering either of his phones."

"He called and told me to get over here, and now he's nowhere to be found?"

She shrugged.

Just then, Matt McCoughlin walked in carrying a tray of coffees followed by a college-aged woman dressed in street clothes and gold hoop earrings that hung down past her shoulders. She carried two pastry bags soaked with grease stains.

"Did you guys hear about the missing women?" I asked Janis and Matt.

"Oh, yeah," Janis replied. "We've heard. The husband of one of them has been calling all morning."

"Any chance you two might want to ski over with me to the tree well I found?"

"Sure," Janis said, and sprang up out of her chair. "Happy to. Tracy, you made it back just in time to man the phones."

Tracy looked less than thrilled.

"Come on, Matt," Janis said.

Matt cast a longing sideways glance at the coffee.

"You can nuke it when you get back," I told him.

The three of us headed outside. Though no one said anything, it was obvious all three of us wanted to get going before Dave got back. So we clicked in and pushed off hard downhill towards the Red Dog chair. We were flying by the time we reached the chair thirty seconds later. We cut the line and loaded up fast. On the ride up, I filled Matt and Janis in on the whole story of what happened after I got back and found the women gone. I finished by telling them how Dave didn't want me to go back to the tree well late yesterday, and I was afraid he'd feel the same today.

Once we skied past the glade where we came upon the women, I took the lead. Heading downhill into the thick forest of pine trees forced me to slow down and weave carefully between the trees. Every time I made a turn, my downhill ski nearly skidded into a tree well camouflaged with loose snow. This would never be a fun place to ski, and certainly no one but an expert should ever venture into this area. Why would the women ski into this mess? And if they started in and realized what a disaster it was, why didn't they turn around and climb out? Wasn't Alexis rumored to know the area? That reminded me, I needed to find out whether or not Alexis had a season pass.

Even with an additional two feet of snow on the ground, I recognized the tree immediately due to its size and the way it backed up to a nearby granite cliff. Fresh snow, like a thick comforter of white, lay across the ground around the giant Ponderosa pine. A heavy cornice of snow curled over the face of the cliff thirty feet above us.

"Not a great place to stop," Matt said. "The avie danger is through the roof right here."

"Maybe we should go back before we search the tree well and get some hand charges for up there," Janis pointed up to the cornice hanging above us. She strained to look straight up towards the top of the cliff.

"And bury anything we might find?" I said. "No, let's just be careful."

The snow had started up again, and the winds were howling. My handy thermometer zipper pull told me it was 12 degrees. When the winds fell still for a moment, it was so quiet I could hear the quiet music of the falling snow. Then I noticed a subtle but distinct smell of pinesap. For a few seconds, I sniffed at it to be certain.

"Did one of you break a branch?" I asked.

I opened my eyes and turned to Matt and Janis. They both shook their heads that they hadn't.

"Do you smell it?"

"I do," Janis said. "Where's that coming from?"

"I don't know," I said. "But I'd be interested to find out in case someone's been up here before us today."

"I'll climb up and check out that cornice," Matt offered.

"Let me go," I said. "Since it's my mission, I might as well be the one to do the dirty work."

I began sidestepping over to a grade leading up to the cliff face. At the bottom of the cliff, I stepped out of my bindings and began booting it up along the side of the rocks through waist-high snow.

It took ten minutes to climb thirty feet to the top of the rock face. It got easier after the first few steps because the terrain grew too steep to hold the snow. Matt and Janis had moved to the side, away from the potential trajectory of an avalanche. On top of the cornice, I grabbed hold of a sturdy branch above my head and hung on with both hands then began stamping on the snow with my boots. After ten or fifteen stomps, loose snow scattered and spilled in a flurry of white. I kicked and kicked at the harder, crusted-over snow beneath and then let go with one hand and began to beat my ski pole on the remainder of the old cornice. The snow remained solid beneath my feet.

"I think it's good," I shouted down to Matt and Janis.

"Come on down, then," Matt yelled up. "Let's take a look at this snow."

For a moment, I stood staring straight into the branches of the big tree. Between the twenty feet of snow pack and the thirty feet of cliff face, I figured I was fifty feet up the tree. The sharp scent of fresh pinesap reeked up here. Through the snow loading down the branches, I looked in towards the trunk of the tree and could see a cluster of branches that had been broken off. The fresh, white inner bark showed.

"This is where the pine smell is coming from," I yelled down to Matt and Janis. "There're a bunch of freshly broken branches up here."

"Probably happened when the tree dropped its snow load yesterday. Right?" Matt shouted up. "You said the tree had dumped wet snow load right down here?"

"That's possible." I grabbed hold of the branch of a tree behind me and leaned out closer to the pine tree. A big branch about ten feet in from me and just below the level of my feet looked like its bark had been rubbed off. I thought the branches did look like they might have broken when the heavy wet snow load of the day before fell. But this big branch, about the circumference of my thigh, looked like something rubbed over it. I could see that the fresh white inner bark ran about six or eight inches down the length of the branch and wrapped around a bit onto the sides. The damage to the bark hadn't begun to heal over or darken.

The rev of a snowmobile echoed up the valley we stood in. I could hear it winding from a ways off, growing closer then shutting off. A minute later, Dave came through the trees on snowshoes.

"What's going on?" he growled. "You guys couldn't wait a half hour for me?"

"Just doing some avie work, Dave, before we start digging," I told him.

I expected him to blow any minute and begin shouting, but he stayed calm and acted like he'd expected us to be there. He kicked at the snow.

"A lot of new snow on the ground since you were here yesterday."

As I stood on top of the cliff, hanging onto a branch and wondering when Dave was going to blow, I was also trying to figure out what happened. It seemed like someone recently, very recently, ran a line, like a climbing rope, over this big branch. And over towards the cat track, where Dave was standing, it looked like a faint impression of a snowmobile track buried beneath the snow.

"What're you doing up there? Quit stargazing and get down here," Dave shouted. "Let's take a look at this."

I climbed back down, skidding through the fluff on my butt the last six feet, and quickly clicked back into my skis to keep from sinking. Back beneath the big tree, I took off my skis again and lay them crosswise with the bindings down near where I imagined the tree well would begin on the side of the tree towards the cliff. Then I knelt down on my skis and began to gently brush the new fallen snow away. Once I cleared the new snow away from an area of about a few square meters, I pulled off my pit kit backpack and extracted my snow saw. Carefully, I cut snow then brushed it forward and away, so a two-foot pit wall of clean-cut snow was exposed.

"Look here," I told the others who were crowded around watching. I pointed at a layer of ice beneath an inch of crusty snow. "Something heavy came by here and compressed the snow. Maybe skis. But I think it was something heavier. Maybe a snowmobile drove up here last night"

"A snowmobile would have had a hell of a time in this deep snow," Matt said.

Dave hemmed and hawed, and finally announced, "Any kind of weight passing over that mashed potato snow we had yesterday is going to melt the snow and cause water to gush up. Then late in the day it got cold, so any powder coming down last night would have frozen into tracks in the snow beneath. There's no way to tell what packed these tracks down. Could have just been your two women skiing by here."

I disagreed. "It was already cold when we found the women. And it was several hours after that when the snow started up. So any melt the women's ski tracks caused would have long since frozen into the snow pack below, long before the snow started falling. Anyway, especially here in the Sierra, core snow tends to hold its own temp. The water on top would have frozen into the snow below, which would have held a steady temp, so no."

"Yeah, what the hell ever. I just tried driving a snowmobile up here, and it floundered every time I got off the cat trail."

"There're a bunch of broken branches up in this tree and a place where the bark has been rubbed away on a big branch. Come up here and take a look," I told Dave.

"It's going to take more than that to get me climbing up that cliff-face, Bailey."

That was obvious. I decided to drop it. I was going to have to do a lot more thinking about this before I tried explaining it to anyone, especially Dave.

"Don't you smell the fresh pine?" Janis asked him.

"So what?" Dave replied.

I pulled out a roll of red plastic ribbon I use for all sorts of things, and cut off a twenty foot length. On big powder days, I cut six foot lengths of it and tie it to my binding on each ski and tuck the rest into the top of my boots. That way, if I get separated from a ski in deep powder, I don't have to spend the rest of the afternoon looking for it. But my usual use for it is to mark layers of snowfall.

I moved all the way around the tree and lay the ribbon down along the layer of hard snow the new powder rested on top of. This way, if I needed to come back and check this place out, I'd have an easy reference to find the snow that was on top yesterday.

"What are you wasting time on now?" Dave snapped at me. "I want everyone out of here. Now. It's dangerous, and the more tracks you guys make skiing in, the more idiots are going to try skiing back here."

I didn't understand at first why he suddenly sounded so pissed. Then I realized it was because I didn't just take his word that the tracks I saw were from skis. He probably didn't appreciate that I contradicted his theory of the melted tracks merging with the new powder. He was the head of the ski patrol after all, and I had mouthed off and acted like the expert in front of two of his employees. Could have been more diplomatic, I guess.

"Maybe the compression you saw came from the tree dropping its snow load?" Janis said. "Such a huge tree probably dumped a couple hundred pounds of snow, at least, right?"

"I really thought I saw some snowmobile tracks over there towards the cat track," I said though I had a feeling it was a losing battle.

"Are you sure?" Dave asked.

"No. There's not much open land, just a few yards where I thought I saw tracks."

"Laura, accept it. There's no way to say what caused this ice layer," Dave pulled his glove off and ran his finger along the ice. "There're a lot of reasons this snow could be packed down."

"If we dig out the tree well we'll be sure—"

"I'm not okaying that from a safety standpoint. There's a tremendous danger of avalanche in here right now. We're in a canyon, it's nuking snow. We've got lots of fresh on top of old surface hoar, and an avie could cut loose from above in a dozen different places. I'm going to call this. It's not safe. And anyways, nothing happened here."

It was clear he'd made up his mind. Matt and Janis packed up their gear and began to ski out, but Dave stopped them.

"You two take the snow sled back down and meet up with us at the base of the Red Dog chair. I'm going to ski out with Laura."

I pulled a rag out of my pack and dried off the blade of my snow-saw, put it back into my backpack, slung it over my shoulder and hoisted it in place.

"Dave, promise me you won't send anybody else back in here. I've got a feeling about this tree well."

"Yeah. No," he said. "Can't do that. Especially not if idiots start following your tracks in. It's my job to make sure nobody dies in an avalanche at Squaw. I've got to hold to that premise. I know you can respect that." From the bite in his voice, I could tell he was still angry.

I nodded to him. It was snowing so hard that if no one had followed our tracks in by now, there were no tracks left to follow. With a backward glance at the huge pine, I followed Dave out through the trees. Some kind of scary shit happened there. In my heart, I knew it.

=

We found Matt and Janis waiting at the loading ramp of the Red Dog chair, a triple chair, meaning it's older and only holds three people per chair as opposed to the newer chairs that are both faster and hold up to eight. I rode up with Matt while Janis and Dave came up in the chair behind us with a volunteer patroller.

I'd known Matt and his wife Lorena for nine years. We met when I coached one of their sons on the university ski team in Fort Collins. And I had a world of respect for Matt. For twenty-five years, he had been the go-to guy for Tahoe area search and rescue. He was utterly fearless, with a resolve that never wavered. Matt had brought more people out, dead or alive, than anyone else in the area. In my opinion, Squaw Valley USA, Inc. made a huge mistake when they promoted Dave to the head of the ski patrol instead of Matt. But Matt lacked the political connections that Dave had. Matt's brother wasn't the Sheriff of Placer County. He was an alcoholic carpenter who drove a twenty-year old pickup and lived in a run-down trailer by the Truckee River. I already knew that Matt's opinion on Dave Geisner was the same as his opinion on Burt Geisner–an overall good guy but at times too quick to toe the company line, and at times too pig-headed to back down from his own pronouncements.

Just a glimpse of the frustration on Matt's face as we sat together going up the lift was enough to tell me he thought the latter of Dave's read of the Ponderosa pine tree well. He fiddled with his gloves, taking them off so he could adjust his helmet and dry his goggles. Once he got all settled, he breathed a big sigh and turned to me.

"There's no reason for those women to have skied into that forest. Doesn't make sense."

"Yet they obviously did. At least, yesterday, the tracks said they did. Skied into the forest and disappeared."

"So why is Dave acting like it didn't happen?"

"Maybe he's thinking skiers get in over their heads every day, and we both know, we all know, how most of them somehow make it out in one piece."

Matt laughed. "Which only encourages them towards more and greater stupidities."

"Ain't that the truth."

We lifted the tips of our skis and prepared to unload.

═══

Dave told Janis and Matt good-bye at the top. Why did he say he wanted us all to ride up if he wasn't going to talk to us? Maybe he just wanted a word with Janis, but they got stuck with the single volunteer riding up. In any case, Matt and Janis headed over towards the patrol shack, and I followed Dave down Red Dog Run, a racing hill that wound down the front of Snow King Mountain.

Dave sped down in front of me, going faster than normal within the bounds of a popular ski run. Rolling my skis onto their edges, I let my speed run, too, and soon I was flying down the steep turns of the mountain right behind him. My mind emptied. Nothing mattered but my next turn. I rolled my edges up higher to cut the cross section of my skis to nothing but a slender metal edge slicing through the snow at tremendous speed.

I moved up beside Dave, matching him turn for turn. If he felt the need for some macho pissing contest, I was not going to be the one who lost. I cut in front of him. Sailing over a mogul, I moved out and caught big air, flying twenty or thirty feet before my skis slapped back onto the snow. Landing in the middle of a mogul field forced me to flatten out my skis. You can't catch a rail, snow slang for riding your edges, in the bumps. I kept my speed up, cutting up against the side of one mogul and bouncing off to the next one, switching the angle of my skis in the air.

I burned through the moguls. I didn't know what his problem was, but, if it's with me, screw him. Since I got to Squaw, I had done nothing but try to help him. Being in the snow business did not make me everyone's lackey.

Nearing the bottom of the run, I began to bring my speed down as I moved in among people, finally coming to a stop right in front of the Funitel Building. Looking back up mountain, I spotted Dave still in the middle of the mogul field. A grin split my face–I smoked his mopey ass.

As I turned away from the mountain, I saw those lawyers hovering around dressed in street clothes. The tall one with the long thin nose—what was his name? Flaherty, something Irish, I couldn't quite get it—started marching towards me, and, when the other two noticed where he was headed, they followed right after him. Stepping out of my bindings, I stood waiting for Flaherty, Sean, that's it, to make his way over to me. He was slipping and sliding on the snow since he wasn't wearing any kind of mountain boots, rather flat-soled leather loafers. I was waiting for both him and Dave, and I wasn't sure which of them I dreaded more.

"They still haven't shown up," Sean said, as soon as he got within range.

"Sorry about that," I said, not knowing what else to say.

A third man I hadn't met previously came forward and joined the group. He walked up to me and held out his hand to shake. I pulled off my glove and shook hands.

"Nice run," he said with a smile. "You really tore through those bumps."

Like the other male lawyers, he was tall and lanky and looked fit. He had straight sandy hair receding at the hairline into two big Vs. He wasn't handsome like the other two men, but he had a likable face.

"Daniel Burdick," he said. "Another lawyer, I'm afraid."

"Guess you guys travel in pods," I said and smiled back at him. "Laura Bailey."

Just then Dave skied up and joined the group. Daniel extended his hand to Dave and introduced himself again. Dave didn't just give his name but added on "Director of Squaw Valley Ski Patrol."

"Were you up with your friends the whole time?" Dave asked Daniel.

"I have a condo over at Alpine. I've been staying there."

I noticed then he was the only one of the lawyers in ski gear, and the only one whose gear looked like it wasn't brand new.

"I guess you haven't seen hide nor hair of the women either?" Dave asked.

"I was just telling my colleagues that yesterday, I got up to Tahoe around 9:00 a.m., did some work at the condo, and I'm not certain, but I'm almost positive I saw Jennifer and Alexis walking to Alexis' car in the Crystal Palace parking lot then driving out. I park there so I don't have to fight the crowds."

"How do you get away with not being towed?" Dave asked.

"Never been towed yet, and I've been parking there for years," Daniel said, seeming pretty pleased with himself. "Jennifer walked like she was hurt, limping and kind of leaning on Alexis. They got into a black Mercedes SUV, so I assumed it was them. And this morning I noticed Alexis' car is gone. I know they were staying there. So—" he shrugged. "I assumed she was hurt and Alexis took her back to San Francisco to get some medical care before 80 closed again. I know Tahoe Truckee Hospital has great doctors, but Alexis—"

"Absolutely," Sean cut in. "Alexis is not going to let her friend have medical care that's less than the best."

"We have some of the best orthopedic specialists in the country," Dave said, stepping in closer to Sean. What's he going to do next? Punch him?

"That's not the point," I cut in. "The point is Mr. Burdick saw the women leaving, saw them get into Alexis' car and head out. Have any of you heard from them since then?"

"I said it looked like them. They got into a black, late-model Mercedes SUV, the kind of car Alexis drives."

Seemed to me it would make all kinds of sense for Dave to call his brother Burt and let him know what's going on. I also saw this wasn't going to happen because hearing what Daniel had to say had caused the corners of Dave's mouth to begin curling upwards in something that would shortly be a grin. I could hear him from six feet away thinking "Off My Plate!"

"Does this sound like something Alexis would do? Leave without telling any of you?" I looked each of the men in the face. They seemed non-committal, then I turned to the blonde looker, who seemed to be attached to Sean.

"It wouldn't be out of character for Alexis to do something like that." Her mouth pouted up into a moue, and I had a good idea what she and Sean had been up to all night, and it wasn't worrying about their colleague Alexis.

Was Dave ever going to say anything? Ask for their names and contact info? Tell them to let him know once they heard for sure that Alexis and Jennifer were safe? No. Apparently not. He was still moping because I disagreed with him about the snowmobile tracks, didn't take his opinion as the last word, or more likely because I kicked his ass skiing down. So I covered his bases again.

"Can I get everyone's name and contact info, so that if we hear anything we can let you know? And if you hear anything, you can let us know?

"Who are you?" Sean asked.

"I'm Laura Bailey. I'm a snow scientist doing some research and consulting work for Squaw.

Sean looked over at Dave who still said nothing but nodded in an affirmative manner.

"O-K–," he said, dragging out both letters. "I'm Sean Flaherty, Lead Counsel for Reed, Martin & Smith, San Francisco Office." He rattled off his cell phone, office phone, and e-mail address almost faster than I could enter them into my iPhone.

"This is Anna Strunk. A Partner at Reed, Martin & Smith, San Francisco." He gestured to the blonde on his arm who wore a big, gory fur coat. She was fit but didn't look like a woman into outdoor sports.

Sean continued, pointing to the good-looking man with curling gray hair—who, if the pinging of my gaydar was anything to go by, was gay. "And this is Dorian Stievquist, a Managing Partner at Reed, Martin & Smith, San Francisco. You can get their contact info from them."

They all seemed so tall huddled around me giving me their numbers. Even Anna Strunk seemed tall, but the day before she'd seemed petite. I looked down and noticed she was wearing above-the-knee black boots with five-inch stiletto heels.

"And Daniel you've already met," Sean continued. "Since we've pretty much figured out what's happened to our friends, I'll be adjourning to the bar at PlumpJack. If the rest of you care to join me after giving Ms. Bailey, Snow Scientist, your info, please do. He stepped down gingerly off the snow and headed to the left towards the cable car building and beyond that PlumpJack. 10:30 in the morning and they were headed for the bar.

Once they'd left, Dave came over and stood beside me for a moment not saying a word. I bent down, picked up my skis, and brushed the snow off them as best I could. He seemed frazzled by something about the lawyers: their worldliness, their money? I didn't know.

He cleared his throat, "Couldn't the heavy snow from the branches have packed the snow down instead of a snowmobile?"

For a second, I had no idea what he was talking about.

"Didn't you say people had skied by there?"

Then I realized he was still going on about me saying I saw snowmobile tracks. I shook my head. "No, Dave. I don't think just skiing past would make the tracks I saw."

"Lots of reasons that snow could be packed. You know, snow loads release at the most unpredictable times. Like the minute you're comfortable in a hot tub with a beer in your hand, a scientifically proven most likely time for a tree to dump its snow load on your head."

He was leaning forward on his poles, smiling up at me. I guessed this was as close to an apology as I was ever going to get.

I smiled back at him and shook my head, "Right. Sure. You got it."

Dave slapped my helmet good-bye and headed over towards his office. If both the ski patrol and Alexis' colleagues were satisfied with this explanation, who was I to doubt it? I didn't know either of the two women well enough to have any idea what they'd do.

Chapter 6

SATURDAY, APRIL 2, 10:45 AM

A couple minutes later, I was still standing holding my skis where the lawyers and Dave left me, lost in thought about whether I believed the story of the women leaving and going for medical care, when someone bumped my shoulder. Aldous Moore stood lined up beside me smiling.

"Earth to Laura."

In the bright light his skin looked drawn tight over his cheekbones and chin, and had both the hue and texture of old parchment.

"Hey there!" I answered. "What a nice surprise."

"What was all the commotion?"

Before I could answer, Mike came walking over from the ski school meeting area. He was wearing a ski school parka and pants, with a big sat phone like Dave's strapped to his chest. I guess that signified his position as the new head of the ski school.

"I hoped I'd get a chance to see you today," he said, and pulled off a glove and held out his hand. "Did I mention I took your friend's old job?"

"No," I said with a laugh. "But now I've put it together. I've heard nothing but good things about you from Aldous."

I, too, pulled off a glove to shake, but Mike took my hand in both of his, and held it for a minute.

"What was going on over here?"

"One of the lawyers from this office, where the whole bunch of them work, just said he thinks he saw them leaving, getting into the woman–Alexis'–car and driving off, and that the woman we came across in the snow seemed to be hurt."

"Was she hurt when you saw her?" Aldous asked.

"I thought she had a cracked rib or two. She was definitely cold and exhausted. I wish I hadn't left them."

"If anyone should have stuck with them, it was Dave," Aldous said. No love lost between those two.

"Look," Mike said, "Aldous has a private in two minutes, and I've got to keep things smooth at the ski school, but maybe the three of us could meet up for a drink at Le Chamois after the lifts close? Would you be up for that?"

His eyes shone with the color of the Tahoe sky on a bluebird powder day.

Aldous tugged at my arm. "A drink at 4:00?"

"I'd love to."

My crew would be arriving from Fort Collins late the next day, if the snow ever let up long enough for a plane to land and I-80 to get cleared off so it could be reopened. I still needed to get up and check out whether it was going to be possible for us to ski out the back of Granite Chief, or if we'd have to come around through the backcountry. It would be a long trek around hauling a couple sleds filled with heavy gear.

So I was back to worrying about what we'd find in the backcountry. Could Dave be right about the dirty snow? Of course, snow in a ski resort was a completely different animal than snow in the backcountry. Ski resort snow gets pushed around all over the place. But if expanses of untouched snow in the backcountry had dirt in it, it would say a lot both about human-induced climate change, and the melt coming earlier and earlier. It still didn't seem likely we could be dealing with dirty snow during such a big snow year.

As I walked into the Funitel Building through the two metal pillars that read lift tickets, I remembered I wanted to ask if Alexis had a season pass. I joined the line to the left, the I-want-to-sit-down-for-the-eight-minute-ride-to-the-top line, and stepped up behind a couple of young women when I heard a male voice call out, "Laura Bailey."

As I stepped into the Funitel, I saw one of the lawyers hurrying to make it into the same car. It was the guy with the curly gray hair—what's his name—some literary thing? He cut into the car just prior to the doors closing from the line that didn't mind standing all the way up along with two other local-looking guys. He was sans skis, I noticed.

He wore dark brown corduroy pants and a buttery-looking tan leather jacket, and hiking boots. Bending slightly forward from the waist, he put a hand over his collarbone and said, "Dorian Stievquist."

"That's right," I said. "No resemblance to Oscar Wilde's Dorian Gray, I'm sure."

He chuckled sarcastically. "Yeah. I've never heard that before."

"Sorry."

I sat down on the metal bench that ran all the way around, and Dorian sat next to me.

At midday, it wasn't so crowded. Two local girls sat opposite us in grubby end-of-season parkas, one fresh-faced and wholesome, and the other one all black eyeliner and piercings, blue hair jutting out from under her helmet. They sat jammed together texting away. Two guys stood in the middle lost in talk about what they'd be skiing next.

"I was hoping to get a private word with you," Dorian said in a low voice. "The ski patrol guy—what's his name?"

"Dave Geisner."

"Dave doesn't seem much interested in Alexis and Jennifer, so I want to mention to you that the three of us were staying at Squaw Creek, and I got a call early this morning from the manager who told me that the women's suite was broken into sometime last night. Apparently someone picked the lock, or had a passkey. They aren't sure yet which. But a maid found the door wide open at 6:00 am."

"Why'd they call you?"

"Both of our suites were on my corporate credit card. It's supposed to be an annual working retreat."

"Were things missing?"

"Well, that's it. The manager said their suite was empty. So I asked if they'd checked out, and she said no, but since their suite was on my credit card, that's not unusual. But then she also said they'd left some stuff in a safe deposit box at the front desk, and it's still there."

"Where are Anna and Sean staying?"

"I don't know why I'm telling you all this. I guess it's because you're the only person who seems to give a damn. Flaherty has a house on Lake Tahoe. A big estate." He straightened his spine, rolled his shoulders back, and raised his chin.

"A familial estate," he said in a funny voice, like some old upper-crust English butler. His gray eyes twinkled with humor.

"What estate?"

"I don't know. Ah, The Hempfield Estate, I think it's called."

"Outside Tahoe City?"

"Yes."

"So his mother's a Hempfield?"

"Yes, I believe most of the money came from Flaherty's mother's side of the family." Again, he said this in his upper-crusty voice.

"That explains a lot." As in why the guy had such a moneyed air about him. "So if it was a working retreat, why are you staying all over the place? When was the work going to happen?"

He laughed, "Well—"

"It wasn't really going to happen, right?"

"Anna and Alexis just made partner, and Alexis is having a lot of success representing a gas-drilling company back East, so it's really more of a celebration than a working retreat."

"But you call it a working retreat so the firm will pick up the bill?"

He looked away and tilted his head from side to side.

"What kind of law does your firm practice?"

"We're an environmental law firm. Which is sad because it means every last one of us wanted to do good when we began our careers."

"Just like the missionaries in Hawaii," I said. There was something likable about Dorian. He was an easy guy to sit and chat with, sort of the anti-Dave.

"Exactly. Yes. Exactly that. We all came in wanting to do good, and each one of us has ended up doing very well."

"How's Alexis to work with? I'll be honest, I found her prickly in those few minutes we talked. I was surprised to hear she's a lawyer. How's she get along with clients?"

"Our Alexis is a special case, and because of this she can act however she wants. Before going into law, Alexis earned a Masters in Biochemistry from the University of Pennsylvania. But she found the work boring. Well, mostly the low money bored her, I think. That and the lack of prestige. So she looked around and decided on law. She graduated at the top of her class, headed the best law review at Hastings, and, because of this dual background, she's a hot commodity."

"Even though you've done well, are you still doing good?"

"It's a dichotomy in the firm–some people end up working for the chemical or gas companies, and some people litigate against them. Reed, Martin has no trouble walking both sides of the street."

"You just follow the money."

"Wherever it takes us."

Looking behind us I realized we were just coming over the last rise leading up to the Gold Coast Building where the Funitel unloads.

"Do you happen to know if Alexis has a season pass?"

"She and Jennifer bought three-out-of-five-day passes from the ski concierge at the hotel. I walked them down to pick up the lift tickets."

We stood up in preparation for unloading as the Funitel rocked into the cement building.

"Where are you headed with no skis?"

"I heard about a bar up here with an amazing view over Lake Tahoe."

We unloaded, and Dorian and I walked forward a few yards, standing in the middle of the cavernous space.

"That bar's at High Camp," I told him. "There's no bar in the Funitel Building, just a restaurant, where I guess you can get a beer and a couple ski shops." We stepped outside the building, and, once again, it was snowing, and the wind blew a gale.

"Does that little gondola go to High Camp?" He pointed to a small gondola line running between High Camp and the Funitel.

"Nope. That thing hasn't worked in years—if it ever did. You need to go back down on the Funitel, then take the cable car up. If you're not on skis there's no real way to get to High Camp in this much snow. It's a half mile up that way." I pointed up a mountain of white.

He slumped with frustration. "This day just gets better and better." He shook his head and walked back towards the building to download.

"Just one more question before you go."

Swiveling around gracefully, he turned to look at me, raising his hands as if to ask "What? What?"

"What do you make of the story about Jennifer and Alexis leaving to get medical care? Isn't it odd they wouldn't say a word to any of you? And more than twenty-four hours later, still no one has heard from them?"

"I don't know, Laura. Alexis has a reputation for being wild. She certainly won't lose any sleep over worrying her friends. And Jennifer, I know her as well as you'd know anyone you'd eaten a couple meals at the same table with. By the way, what's a snow scientist?"

But he must have changed his mind because he turned away and stepped from the snow onto the rubber mats leading into the building.

"Never mind," he called over his shoulder. "Maybe you can explain that to me later."

He moved off into the building. I grabbed my skis and walked out farther onto the snow, then clicked in.

I felt relieved to finally get back to my work. I hiked a few yards to the Emigrant chair and headed up to the top of Emigrant Mountain. Emigrant, at eight-thousand-seven-hundred feet stands the third high-est of the five mountains that form a ring of mountains closing in Squaw Valley like an oblong bowl. Granite Chief is both the highest, at nine-thousand-fifty feet, and the farthest back in. I planned to get to the top of Emigrant, then ski down across a big open bowl to the vast Shirley Lake intermediate area. At the bottom of Shirley Lake, behind the Shirley Lake chair sits the chair for Granite Chief.

As I was heading towards the Funnel around the side of Emigrant, I felt my phone vibrating in my pocket. After a while, it quit, and I tried to enjoy the day, but it was nuking snow, which made for a seriously low-viz, snow slang for visibility, environment. The wind screamed up the mountain so hard I had trouble breathing. As I launched off the Funnel, it caught me full in the chest and face, pushing me backwards up hill, until curling down into a tuck, I managed to get out of the wind enough to start downhill. I needed to get over to Granite Chief, though at this point, with the way the snow was suddenly hammering down, I wasn't optimistic about either my crew being able to get in the next day or about 80 being open to make it up here if they did manage to get into Reno.

There wasn't another person in sight aside from the liftie, as I skied into the Granite Chief chair. My phone went off again just as I sat down. I fished it out and recognized the number as the Squaw Valley ski patrol.

"Yes?"

"Laura, it's Dave again. Sorry to bother you, but Richard Fellatorre, our missing Jennifer's husband, has been calling and wants to talk to you. I tried to tell him we have every reason to believe her friend took her to get medical care, but he's having none of it. Anyway, are you willing to talk to him?"

"Sure," I replied, though I wondered what I could tell him that Dave couldn't.

"Great. Hang up, and I'll give him your number."

"OK," I said and cut off the call.

A minute later, I realized that was a mistake since the wind was blowing so hard that the chair rocked sideways, and I wasn't going to be able to hear someone on the phone. A couple minutes later, passing through a quieter spot down among the trees, my phone rang again. The screen showed a number and, above that, "Philadelphia, PA." I jammed the phone right up against my ear inside my helmet.

"Yes? Laura Bailey."

"Laura Bailey, I'm Richard Fellatorre, Jennifer Fellatorre's husband. I've been told you were the last person we know about who spoke to my wife and Alexis, and I'm hoping there's something you can tell me to help find her."

"Alexis' colleagues seem to think that Jennifer was hurt and that Alexis wanted to get her better medical care than she could get here. And one of them, Daniel Burdick, said he thinks he saw Jennifer and Alexis in The Resort at Squaw Creek parking lot, getting into Alexis' car. But I guess you've yet to hear from her?"

"Would I be calling now, frantic, if I'd heard from her?" He paused for a moment. "I'm sorry. Please don't hang up. I'm desperate."

"I understand. I'm also worried about them."

"What happened when you came across her in the snow? What happened after the ski patrolman left?"

"I'm sure he told you that we hadn't been there thirty seconds when he got a casualty call about a big pileup. He asked her if she was hurt first. And she said she didn't think so. So he took off. I helped her up and got her on her feet. In the process of pulling her out of the snow, she felt a lot of pain in her ribs. I figured she had a cracked rib. She was exhausted and cold and miserable. I asked them to stay where they were. To not move. They were in a glade with no cell reception. So I went to ski out and get help. When I got back, they were gone. I was shocked. Jennifer had said there was no way she could go anywhere except on a toboggan. So I also felt confused."

"Did Dave have a phone he could have called for help on?"

"Yes. But your wife said she wasn't hurt. That's why he didn't."

"She was tired, exhausted you said, and somewhere she shouldn't be, and he wouldn't just call for a toboggan to take her down? I don't get it." The poor man sounded like he was bouncing between desperation and despair. Right then he hung on the despair end of the cycle.

The line hung silent for a moment as I racked my brain for something comforting to say.

"My daughter would like to talk to you. Will you talk to her just for minute?"

"Sure," I told him. I heard him calling, his voice echoing down the hallways of their house in Philadelphia, which I imagined as something with dark wood and long hallways, big rooms and floors covered with carpets from Asia. "Chloe! Chloe! Pick up."

"Hi," a small, breathless voice came on the line a second later. "My name is Chloe Fellatorre, and I want to tell you, Ms. Bailey, that I'm nine, and in my whole life I've never gone more than one day without talking to my mom. Even when I'm at camp, I talk to her every day." The girl's voice choked with tears, and she struggled for a moment before she could speak again. "Please help me and my dad. We're so far away. We just—we don't know what to do, and nobody wants to help us. Please help us." The girl's voice collapsed again into sobs.

My own sinuses were prickling, hearing the pain in her voice.

Through the snow, I could just make out the shack at the top of Granite Chief where the wind was going to hit like a sledgehammer, and I'd have to unload.

"Chloe, listen. I'm about to get off a chairlift in the middle of a blizzard. Let me get down somewhere protected, and we'll talk some more. I have your number on my phone. Let me call you back."

Just then the chair cleared the ridge of the mountain, so I never heard her response. I skied off the chairlift into a gale with my phone still in one hand. Zipping the phone back into my parka, I looked around. The mountain stretched out before me all windblown powder and dark looming pines. The lift shack disappeared from view fifteen feet from it, and there was no one in sight. Luckily, I kind of remembered the way down. But there certainly wasn't going to be any poking around on the back of the mountain to see if we could ski out. With visibility so low, I didn't feel like wandering off into the glades Granite Chief is famous for. And there wasn't going to be any stopping on the way down because if I couldn't see anyone, no one could see me either.

As I began my slow descent down the mountain, between the wind, the pounding snow, and the lack of visibility, I decided to call it quits. It was officially a blizzard.

The liftie at the Shirley chair told me to head in. They were shutting down the whole upper mountain, meaning everything reached by either the cable car or the Funitel, leaving open Snow King Mountain and KT-22.

Downloading to Base Camp in the Funitel, I wanted to call the Fellatorres back, but, since the whole upper mountain was shutting down, the car I rode in was packed. By the time I got back into the village and walked over to Starbucks, bought a hot chocolate and found a quiet corner, almost forty minutes had passed. I settled down in a chair, pulled my helmet, gloves and parka off, then hit redial.

Richard answered on the first ring. "I thought you'd stood us up."

"No," I grunted as I leaned down to unbuckle my boots. "Weather's a mess here, and they kicked me off the upper mountain. So it took a while. Sorry."

"Chloe and I are flying into Reno tomorrow night."

"Really?" I eased each boot off my freezing feet. "I hope you're able to make it in. It's a blizzard here. And I-80's been closed both ways since yesterday afternoon."

"I can't stay here and be this far away. And because of this, I have to ask you a favor."

"What can I do to help? By the way, look into taking Mt. Rose Highway in. Sometimes, when 80's closed, you can get up that way. Also look into taking 395 to 50, Spooner Summit. That's another possibility. Then you'd drive up here from South Lake Tahoe. Be sure to come around the east side of the lake. Around Emerald Bay, 89 is always closed in bad weather."

I realized I was jabbering. That's what I do when I'm nervous–either talk incessantly or laugh like a hyena. But I was able to catch myself.

"How can I help?" I asked again.

"Could you look into this a bit until we get there? I'm afraid those lawyers are going to head back into San Francisco and lock themselves up in their skyscraper, and, if I want to talk to them, I'm going to have to make an appointment for next month. They'll barely speak to me on the phone."

"I'll do whatever I can. But I'm a snow scientist from Colorado State University, not a private investigator."

"Who better than you? What about this tree well Dave Geisner told me about? Who better than a snow scientist to look into that? He said you weren't satisfied that nothing had happened there."

"I'm not," I told him softly.

"Shouldn't they be digging there? Looking for them?"

"I think so. But the weather is a huge factor right now. And I found out today that someone broke into their suite at Squaw Creek last night."

"What?" he yelled into my ear.

"One of the lawyers told me that this morning."

"What? They won't tell me anything. Please help me. You can see I can't do this on the phone."

"I'll do whatever I can. I promise. I'm supposed to be heading out into the backcountry soon with my team. But with this weather, I'm sure that'll be postponed by at least a day. Can I tell the lawyers I'm working for you? You'll back me on that?"

"Absolutely."

We hung up, and I sat there wrapping my hands around the warmth of the paper cup. Why wouldn't the lawyers talk to Richard? Why didn't Dorian tell anyone but me about the break-in? What was going on? If Dave had talked to Richard several times, why wasn't he worried about the women?

A minute later, a crowd of hard-core skiers flocked into the Starbucks. The whole resort had shut down due to the weather.

"Unless you live at Squaw, you better get going," one of the guys told me. "Highway Patrol is shutting 89 down as soon as they can move the last of us out of here."

I realized there was no way I could stick around until 4:00 to meet up with Aldous and Mike. Anyway, I figured they were wrapping up and getting ready to head home as well. I called Aldous and left a message on his voice mail that we'd have to plan on a rain check.

I got up, threw my cup in the trash, and headed back to Rita's.

ACT II

Chapter 7

SUNDAY, APRIL 3, 8:30 AM

The next morning as I turned off California 89 onto Squaw Valley Road, the clouds parted and revealed a cerulean sky. I took that as a good omen. Everything was gleaming white and bright, and the flow of cars heading into the valley quickened. It reminded me of what Aldous always said about Squaw–that it looked exactly like what comes to mind when someone mentions a big ski resort. I agreed.

The promise of a bluebird powder day was too strong a lure to keep anyone even close to the speed limit. Not much chance of a lucky up-front parking space with that crowd. I considered following Daniel's lead and parking at the Resort at Squaw Creek, but that parking lot had Tow Away signs posted everywhere—I wasn't willing to risk it.

I was directed towards the end of the Far East Lot but decided to try my luck up near PlumpJack. My Great Aunt Helen always used to say, "Drive slowly through any busy parking lot, and you're going to find someone leaving. The key is not to rush it." I decided to take her advice, and prowled the rows of cars for a couple minutes before catching someone ten rows in just climbing into their car. A minute later, the space was mine.

I hoped to find the lawyers milling around somewhere. The Tahoe morning show said 80 had been closed all night both east and west and wasn't reopening anytime soon. Driving in that morning, I saw that Donner Pass Road, the main drag through Truckee, was lined up all the way through town with semitrucks waiting for 80 to reopen so they could get back on the road. Hotels were overbooked, and coffee-shops, and restaurants were packed with people waiting to get out of Truckee. So I felt hopeful the lawyers hadn't left yet. Dorian seemed anxious to chat yesterday, so I figured I'd start with him.

I dressed in ski clothes in case I got a chance to sneak in a run back up on Granite Chief to see how conditions were on the backside, but I wore my mukluks, not ski boots. I didn't have high hopes for the safety of conditions in the backcountry, or for my crew being able to fly in. It wasn't a Level 4 avalanche day, but it was in the same zip code.

Around 9:30, I spotted Sean Flaherty, Anna Stunk, and Dorian Stievquist lounging in a corner of Starbucks. I hadn't expected to see them out and about so early. I made my way through the crowd to where they sat.

Sean saw me coming and smiled. "Our favorite snow scientist. You're going to have to tell us all exactly what that is." He spread his hands out to each side in what I read as a sarcastic display of happiness at seeing me. He was dressed in a burgundy cashmere sweater and black corduroys.

"Morning," I said. "Squaw Valley has asked me to look into the women's disappearance as an accident investigator, and I'm wondering if I could have a word privately with each of you since I know you're as concerned about Alexis and Jennifer as I am."

"Of course," Sean replied. "Anything we can do to help, Ms. Bailey."

"Dorian, can I start with you?"

All the open friendliness from the day before had vanished. He scowled as he made his way through the maze of chairs and feet to where I stood.

"Back in a minute," he told the others.

I led him outside and stood beside a roaring gas fireplace. Adirondack chairs reclined buried in four feet of snow in a homey circle around the fire pit. I continued to the left and into a covered walkway with a picnic table where I sat on the green wooden bench.

"So what do you want?" he asked. "And by the way, I don't believe for one minute that Squaw hired you as an accident investigator."

"Is that why you're all attitude today? Yesterday you wanted to talk to me. What's changed?"

"You don't have a legal right to question any of us." He dug a pair of brown leather gloves out of the pocket of the same cushy leather jacket he wore the day before, and pulled them on.

"Are you cold?"

"I'm fine."

"I spoke with Jennifer's husband Richard and their daughter Chloe yesterday, and he's asked me to find out what I can until they get here."

"Let's get this over with."

"I'm asking again whether you believe this story about Jennifer and Alexis leaving to get better medical care? Where do you think they are?"

"Have you been in the emergency clinic here?"

"I walked in to see if they'd treated Jennifer, but I've never gone there for care."

"I fell two years ago over on Shirley. Had to be brought down on a toboggan, and that's where they took me. Tore my ACL and my rotator cuff. They examined me, handed me my X-rays, made me give them three-hundred dollars for the X-rays and a pair of crutches, and shoved me out the airlock. I couldn't walk on crutches because both injuries were on my left side. They didn't care. Out the door. So tell me all about how great the medical care is in Truckee. And maybe the hospital in Truckee is excellent. I don't know. None of us know that. To us, good medical care happens in San Francisco, or maybe in Davis or Sacramento. And in Alexis' rush to get Jennifer to her idea of a good doctor, she might have forgotten about everyone else. She's not a thoughtful person. Not some sensitive, touchy-feely type."

"OK, thanks. Now it makes sense why they might not have wanted to get Jennifer medical care here. Yesterday you were telling me about Alexis' work. What does Jennifer do?"

"I don't really know. From what Alexis said, I know that they went to Penn together. I think Jennifer studied something to do with environmentalism and government science policy. Something like that. I think they both started out wanting to be environmentalists, and

Jennifer has stayed with it, and made something of a name for herself. My feeling is that Alexis maybe feels like she's abandoned their ideals when she's around Jennifer."

"How so?"

"As I said, Alexis works both sides of the street, and I think Jennifer is involved in anti-Marcellus shale drilling back east. And the only client Alexis is working with these days is a big Marcellus shale drilling company back East, Plains Drilling."

"But Jennifer doesn't know this?"

He laughed and twisted around scanning the plaza. "I don't think so. Alexis asked us all to act like we couldn't talk about work in front of Jennifer."

"Because she feels guilty?"

"Well," he laughed again. "Working for a fracking company is about as far from environmentalism as you can get."

"Why would a fracking company back east hire a San Francisco firm to represent them?"

"Our main office is in Philadelphia."

"I see. Let me get this straight. So I thought you said Alexis could pretty much work on whatever she wanted. Then why would she choose to work on something she's ashamed of?"

"Alexis loves what's she's doing. And right now she's in court all the time, which she loves, and she's challenged. She's happy. My feeling is she only feels guilty about it around Jennifer. Jennifer stuck with their early aspirations, and Alexis—" he searched for the word.

"Sold out," I said.

He twisted his handsome face into a rueful smile. "Pretty much." Reaching into his pocket he pulled out a BlackBerry and checked the screen.

"Is that a work phone?" I asked. "You had an iPhone yesterday. Maybe we could check the GPS on Alexis' phone and get an idea where they are."

"I've tried calling both her work phone, a BlackBerry like this," he held his phone up, "and her personal iPhone. They both just ring and ring. They don't cut to voice mail. Nothing."

"How could I find out about her work phone?"

"Talk to Flaherty. He can have the office manager give you the info on her phone. He could also tell you a lot more if you ask right."

"Ask right how?"

Dorian shook his head. "I can't tell you that. You're the one asking the questions. I just think you can piss him off, or you can get along. He'd know more than anyone else. He's closer to her than the rest of us."

"Romantically?"

He cocked his head to one side, "They've been off and on for years."

"But he's with Anna Strunk now?"

"Sean and Alexis were never exclusive."

"Anything else that might help find them?"

He wasn't telling me something. I could feel it. He was weighing in his mind whether or not he should say something. There was a far off look in his bluish-gray eyes.

"Anything at all?" I asked again. "What're you thinking about telling me?"

"Nothing," he snapped. He stood up and brushed off his pants. The moment had passed.

"Thanks for talking to me. When are you guys heading back?"

"Supposedly today, but 80's closed. So as soon as we can get out."

Dorian went back into the coffee house with me trailing behind.

Sean was the last person I wanted to wrangle with, so I approached the couple and asked if Anna would speak to me.

A dazzling smile spread over her face. "I'd be delighted to," she said, as she stood and made her way over to me, then looked back to throw Sean a smile.

We started wending our way through the crowd towards the door.

"I don't want to sit outside," she said. "It's freezing, and I don't want to get snow all over my coat."

"Oh right, because the little animals you took the fur from never got wet."

87

"The minks were dead long before I bought this coat."

She minced along behind me over the cobblestones on her high heel boots as I crossed the plaza to a restaurant serving breakfast. We found an empty corner table where we could sit and talk.

"Want anything?" I asked. "I'm buying."

"Just a regular black coffee. I hate Starbucks coffee."

I walked over a few steps to stand at the counter behind two young guys buying breakfast burritos, then paid for two cups of self-serve coffee, poured the coffee, and returned to the table.

"A napkin?" Anna asked.

"Right there," I said, pointing up front to the condiment counter.

Anna decided to go without. She turned her pretty face to me.

"You don't need to ask me questions. I'm going to tell you what I think. What I know. Don't waste your time digging up that tree well right now. Just hold off on any search. Anyways, if they did fall in your tree well, they're long dead by now. Peepsicles, right?"

"Peepsicles?"

Anna paused and gazed down to sip her coffee, then turned her eyes to look back up at me through her long and carefully coiffed blonde bangs—the old Lady Di trick, looking down to look up.

"I'm not a lesbian," I said. "Flirting with me isn't going to do anything but waste your time."

She turned her upturned nose up even more and began again, her brown eyes assessing my response as she spoke.

"My advice would be to spend your time checking the casinos. Alexis mentioned a couple times she wanted to go over to Crystal Bay to the Biltmore and the CalNeva. And it would be just like her to say, 'Jennifer, fake it you're hurt so we can ditch this crowd and go have some fun.' God knows that's what the two of us used to do. I don't know Jennifer, but this is not out of character for Alexis. She bores easily. And anything wild, she loves."

"What do you mean by wild?"

"Dangerous, exotic men, fast boats, fast cars. You know, WILD." Her hands fluttered in the air by her face as she spoke.

"Sorry. But we have different ideas of wild."

"What? Sleeping in the mud and cold and holding a hotdog on a stick over a damp campfire is yours? Then bunking down in a sleeping bag on the ground? Or the snow?"

I held my hands up, laughing against the onslaught.

"We aren't here talking about me."

She turned to smile at a male ski instructor coming in the door.

"But one more thing," I told her, "I thought Sean was Alexis' on-again-off-again guy, but here you're staying with him and looking all cozy. What's up with that?"

"Sean has been done with Alexis for some time. I don't know why Dorian told you that. Alexis is off partying somewhere. That's all I can tell you. Are we done here?"

She stood up and smiled again at the ski instructor, who stood in line grinning back. She was a natural flirt.

"Unless you can think of anything else to tell me," I said. "Anything I can tell Richard Fellatorre and his daughter when they get in today. By the way, Jennifer's daughter is nine and has never gone more than a day without speaking to her mother."

"Then it's about time, I'd say."

We headed towards the door with Anna still looking back and smiling at the ski instructor. I would have loved to have grabbed her shoulders and given her a head-snapping shake. Instead, I took a deep breath as we stepped outside.

"So Jennifer is off with Alexis being wild and glad to finally get away from the family? Is that what you're thinking?"

In the sunlight, I could see her beautiful skin. Her coat fell open, and I realized she was tiny, but, like an animal puffing up in the wild, she dressed to make herself look bigger. This woman was a primal mass of self-defense mechanisms. She definitely lacked the easy swagger of Alexis or the quiet self-confidence of Jennifer.

"I wouldn't hazard a guess as to Jennifer's state of mind. Happy family life is something I know absolutely nothing about."

She slapped her gloves in her hand and strutted back into the Starbucks. The glass door caught in the wind and slammed shut behind her.

Talking to these people was more tiring than lugging a fifty pound pack up a ten-thousand foot mountain on show-shoes. By the time I walked back inside the Starbucks, the lawyers were leaving. I wasn't sure I felt up to talking to Sean right then. Daniel, the only one of them in ski clothes, joined the group as they were walking out.

"Oh hi," he said when he saw me. "Dorian said you wanted to talk to us. Can I grab a hot chocolate, and we can talk for a minute?"

I sat down at a table. "Sure."

Dorian poked his head back in the door. "Daniel, when you're done, we're heading up to the bar at High Camp if you want to join us."

Before I could stop myself, I blurted out, "It's barely 10:00."

Dorian gave me a you're-not-my-mother look, and I wish I'd kept my mouth shut.

"Well, Ms. Bailey," he started, "We can't leave because 80's still closed, and, except for Daniel, we've all had it with skiing—I've had it ever since that fall on Shirley—so I am getting drunk." He stood in the doorway, leaning towards me. A crowd of teenagers squeezed into the store behind him. The bulk of them squeezed past me and crowded around the table behind where I sat waiting for Daniel. One of the kids talked so loud and so foul it was difficult to tune him out.

"Sure," I said. "Sorry. But with the way the sky's closing in, you won't be able to see Lake Tahoe."

"Were you born no fun or did snow science cause you to become this? This gorgeous—" he waved his hands in circles to illustrate his loss of words—"this attractive assemblage of flesh, attached to a prematurely dour spirit."

"Wow. I don't know whether to be insulted or complimented. I'm not always a big downer. It just depends on what kind of fun you're looking for, I guess."

Daniel came back to the table with a cup in his hand and his mouth stuffed full of muffin.

"What do you want to talk to me about?"

Dorian turned his back on us and left.

"I've agreed to help Richard Fellatorre look into his wife's where-abouts. He doesn't seem to think going off on a girl's weekend with no word to anyone is something his wife would do. I also spoke to their daughter, Chloe, who told me in tears that she's never gone more than a day without speaking to her mother. And I'm wondering if I should prod the ski patrol into digging up that tree well I'm sure you've heard about."

Daniel took a sip of hot chocolate to wash down the last of his muffin. "It's almost as if they've split up because this kind of behavior is the norm for Alexis. She's a wild woman–just ask her friend Anna what I mean by that."

The kids behind us kept up the din, intermittently jostling our chairs. The foul-mouthed one was still the loudest of the pack.

"But Jennifer," he mused, "it sounds like this is out of character for her."

We fell silent for a moment.

"What did Anna tell you?" Daniel asked.

"Just that she thinks they went somewhere to be wild—whatever she means by that."

"I see," he said. He rolled the muffin wrapper up into a ball, stuck it into his half full cup of chocolate and threw the wad in sort of the general direction of a wastebasket, which he missed and instead hit the loudmouth kid sitting behind us. The kid hurled off a string of obscenities. Daniel had aimed right at the kid. I saw it happen. The kid ended up with cold chocolate all over his parka and white pants.

"What the fuck, you motherfucker?" the kid yelled, and started moving towards Daniel.

"I didn't do that," Daniel said.

"I saw you!" the kid yelled.

Daniel stood up and leaned over the kid. He had easily a foot and forty pounds of muscle on the kid. "It was just an accident, kid. Wash it off."

Daniel turned his back on the kid and turned his attention back to me. "And next time don't be so loud or foul," he said over his shoulder.

The kid and his crew stood up and made their way out of the coffee shop amid lots of grumbling and foul looks.

"You did that on purpose," I told him.

"No, I didn't."

"But you did. I saw you. That was an asshole thing to do. You could have just asked him to keep it down."

He grimaced like he couldn't imagine why I was going on about such trivia. "Where were we? Oh. Talking about Anna. She didn't explain that to you?"

"No. No one has been very forthcoming with information. I don't know what you guys are trying to hide."

He gave me a wide-eyed, guileless look.

"I'm not trying to hide anything. Alexis is my colleague, and I'm always happy to help. I honestly don't think any of us know anything about where they've gone. If people aren't forthcoming, it has more to do with being private, I'd guess."

"Then be helpful and explain to me what kind of wildness Alexis and Anna like to get into."

"I don't think I'm telling tales out of school to tell you that they used to fly all over the country together to sex clubs in New York City, Miami."

"Really?" I said. "How interesting."

If he had told me they volunteered as test subjects for cholera studies in Africa, I could not have been more surprised.

"But why fly to New York? Surely there's plenty in San Francisco?"

"Notoriety, reputations, business."

"I see. To keep it quiet. But then why is it common knowledge?"

He rocked backwards on his chair and stretched languorously.

"Anna's big mouth. She found it all so exciting she talked. But this was a few years ago. Now, I don't think you'd get her to admit that ever happened. Not with the high-society, moneybags boyfriend she has now."

I realized he was talking about Sean. "Why is that causing people to not talk about Alexis and Jennifer?"

"Obviously, you need to talk to Anna again. There's a whole lot she isn't telling you."

"You tell me."

"I don't know. It's not mine to tell. Ask Anna again; maybe you can find out more."

We sat in silence for a minute. Something seemed off, but he wasn't giving me any more information. That seemed clear.

He stood up suddenly. "I want to get out on KT yet this morning."

"Yeah," I said, "here it's a powder day, and you're the only one in ski clothes. And what's more, ski clothes that don't look brand new."

"That's because I'm the only one who can ski."

"One more thing," I said, as he pulled on his helmet. "About your work BlackBerries. Is there any way I could have the service provider try and locate the GPS tracker on Alexis' phone?"

Daniel thunked his helmet with the heel of his hand.

"We should have thought of that! I'll look into that right away, and get back to you if I learn anything. And by the way, I didn't mean to throw my drink on that kid."

"Whatever you say."

He didn't like that, but he headed out the door, picked up his skis from a rack out front and started in the direction of the KT-22 Express chairlift, affectionately known by the locals as The Mothership, without a backward glance.

Chapter 8

SUNDAY, APRIL 3, 12:00 PM

Snow flurries turned into a bitter blast of needle shaped snow as I walked over to the Ski Patrol Building to talk with Dave. By the time I got inside, I was covered in a gauze of white. A wood-burning stove sat against one wall, but the heat didn't seem to radiate out more than a couple feet. Tracy with the lank blond hair and the huge earrings manned the phones.

"Dave in?" I asked her.

"Just stepped out for a minute."

I sat on a bench running along the wall to wait. A couple seconds later, Janis Murphy walked in, brushing the snow off her shoulders.

"Snowmageddon out there," she said with a laugh. "They're not getting 80 open till spring at this rate."

She flopped onto the bench next to me. "What're you doing here?"

"Waiting for Dave."

"Seems like you've spent a lot of the last few days doing that."

"Not too bad."

Tracy leaned over the counter towards us.

"Hey Janis, any chance you could man the phones, so I can take a smoke break?"

"Five minutes. That's it," Janis told her.

Tracy grabbed her smokes and high-tailed it out the door.

"I don't know about you," Janis told me, "but I sure as hell think we should be searching that tree well."

"Yeah."

We fell silent for a minute as Janis got up and moved around behind the counter to be ready in case a casualty call came in.

"How're you doing working with Dave?" I asked.

"Well," she paused for a second and shook her head from side to side like she was weighing her answer carefully. "There're a lot of things I think Dave does well."

"You can be honest with me," I told her. "I'm not an earpiece for Dave. He's old school. I know that and realize someone young and up and coming like you, or me, might have very different ideas about how to run things."

"Very different ideas is putting it mildly."

"How come you got a job under him? You're not even from here?"

"Just between us?"

"Absolutely."

"Dave retires in two years, and I'm hoping to get his job."

"Of course," I said. "Now it makes sense. I was wondering what a woman like you was doing—. Well, it all makes sense now. Good for you. I'm hoping that works out."

"We'll see."

The phone rang, and Janis got busy taking a casualty report. I got up and walked back to the bathrooms, and by the time I came back Dave and Tracy had returned, and Janis was geared back up and heading out to work. She swung an arm around me as I passed her and gave me a quick hug.

"What're you doing here, Bailey?" Dave asked as he shook off the snow from his parka and brushed a hand over his hair.

"Dave," Tracy interrupted, "you should just let me cut your hair right here. I cut all kinds of guys' hair. I can bring my scissors tomorrow and do it."

Dave looked at her like she was speaking Swahili.

"Can I talk to you for a minute," I asked him.

"Sure, let's go up to my office."

We started up the stairs while Tracy held a lock of her hair out from her head and made snipping motions with the fingers of her other hand.

Dave held the door for me and motioned me to the comfortable wooden visitor's chair.

"Is she coming on to me?" he asked the second he shut the door. "She could be my daughter."

"Grandaughter, Dave. She could be your grandaughter. And no, I don't think so."

He sat down behind his mess of a desk, pried open a drawer with his foot and leaned back with both his feet resting on the open drawer.

"Thanks for setting me straight on that. So what do you want to talk to me about? Fellatorre told me he asked you to poke around and see if you could find out anything. Have you?"

"Bottom line is no one has heard a word from either of them. Apparently, this is normal behavior for Alexis, but the opposite for Jennifer. I'm trying to find out about their phones. If we could get a fix on their GPS, that might be a start, but the lawyers aren't very forthcoming. I've got to talk to that Flaherty guy to see if he'll have his office give me the info I need for the phone. Or if they could do it. I won't know about Jennifer's phone until her husband gets up here. And with the weather and 80 being closed, who knows when that's going to happen."

"What do you think happened to them?" he asked, suddenly dropping his feet, leaning forward and slamming the drawer closed. "Where do you think they are?"

"I certainly don't think they're partying at some casino. And I don't believe they left to get better care for Jennifer. If that was true, we'd at least have heard from her by now. I think they never left the mountain that day."

"So what happened?"

"Met up with some kind of foul play? We've got to get back there and dig that tree well out. Something awful went down there."

"We can't go back there right now. We've had almost six feet of snow since we were back there the other day. It was dangerous then, and it's extremely dangerous now. I can't okay that. In fact, I want to get someone back in there to do some clearance work. The only thing stopping me is that some idiot might see the tracks and follow them in."

"If it does avalanche back there, it's not going to do any damage. Can we just leave it until conditions improve? Dave, please. I feel certain if we dig that tree well up, we're going to find out something. Hold off on sending anyone back there."

He shrugged his agreement to wait. The reason I wanted him to hold off so badly was because I was considering going back in there and seeing what I could find. I wouldn't be able to completely dig out the tree well on my own, but I suspected I could at least dig enough of it up to figure out what happened there.

"I think you should call your brother and tell him what we've heard. Maybe he'll want to get involved now that more time has passed, and he hears about Jennifer."

"I've asked him twice, and he's bit my head off both times. There's no evidence of foul play or misadventure, so he's not doing shit. Personally, until there is, I'm not doing shit either. As soon as we have something new, I'll call him again. Aren't Alexis' buddies worried about her?"

"They don't seem to be. They're a weird bunch, all kinds of love/hate things going on. This one went out with that one, who's going out with the other one. I don't get the idea any of them are going to be broken-hearted if something's happened to Alexis."

"Thhh," he breathed out between his teeth, shaking his head. "No matter where you go, there you are."

"Meaning?"

"Look at these people–all the money in the world, respected jobs, and they fuck their lives up as easily as us. I mean, the rest of us ski bums seem so good at getting married, getting divorced. Yet we've got nothing on them."

It wasn't clear where he was headed. So I sat nodding and trying to look like I understood what he was talking about.

He fell silent for a few seconds then met my gaze.

"I was thinking about you. How long ago did Peter die? Two years ago?"

"Three."

Did he have to go into this? I knew I couldn't go on forever telling people I didn't want to talk about it. But until I could talk about it and not start to cry, I didn't want to talk about it. We had three and a half good years living together. He was what Dave just described as a ski bum: he worked at various times as both a ski instructor and a ski patrolman. But he also worked as a boot fitter, a liftie, and a bartender. In summer, he worked as a rafting guide, a climbing guide or a carpenter. For what were probably the best four months of his life, he worked as a heli guide in Alaska. Then I came along, and he stayed closer to home. He was kind and funny and loving and smart and noble and loyal, and now he's dead and nothing will ever change that. I was not the only one who missed him; he had hundreds of friends who still talked about him every day.

Even three years later, the mention of his name choked me up. The image of him lying on the snow staring up at the sky dying will never leave me.

"Sorry," Dave said. "I don't know what I was going on about."

"It's OK," I told him. "It's ridiculous I still can't talk about it."

I got up from the chair. "I've got to go. I still need to talk to Sean Flaherty and Anna Strunk yet today—"

"The sex kitten."

I smiled. "You're such a guy, but yeah, she's the one. They're staying at Flaherty's family's place on Tahoe. You know his family owns The Hempfield Estate?"

"Jesus. That's where he's staying?"

"Yes."

"Deep pockets."

I said good-bye and started back downstairs. I waved to Tracy as I passed the desk, then pulled my parka and hat back on and braced myself as I stepped outside.

——

Passing the ski school building, I heard someone call my name and turned around to find Mike Bernese leaning out the glass door.

"Come in here," he yelled.

Happily, I followed his suggestion. He led me through the big empty front room, past the desk, and into the back through a room with a row of lockers and benches, racks for skis, and a waxing area set up with wooden tables, and all the paraphernalia for ironing a fast coat of wax onto skis. I followed him to the first in a row of private offices, as he shut the door behind us. Inside the room was lined with honey-colored wood paneling and a big window that looked out onto the ski school meeting area. The walls of his office were lined with posters from PSIA, the Professional Ski Instructors of America, listing dates and places for training sessions and safety posters. A green and blue carpet covered the cement floor, and an old wooden table spanned the width of the office serving as a desk. Two navy-blue upholstered chairs sat across from the table.

"Here, have a seat," Mike gestured towards a chair. "You look like you're freezing. Been out on the mountain today?" he asked as he sat down beside me in the matching chair.

"No. The way it's snowing and blowing I don't think you'll be open much longer."

"Just got a call five minutes ago that the Tram and the Funitel are shutting down. KT as well. Nothing left open but the beginner lifts and Red Dog." He sat down in the chair next to me, and leaned towards me with his elbows on his knees.

"Find out anything new about the missing women?"

"Let's see. They never checked out of the Crystal Palace, though they left stuff in the safe at the front desk. Their room was broken into. The back East one's husband asked me to see what I could find out. So I'm trying to help until he gets here, which is supposed to be tonight, but with the weather, who knows?" I settled into the chair and pulled my hair back, wishing I had a hair tie to get it out of my face.

Mike stared right into my eyes. "How are you doing with all this?"

"I feel sick I left that brunette on the mountain."

"What could you have done differently?"

"Her friend wanted to go for help. Maybe I should have let her."

"You can't second guess yourself that way. You did what seemed to be, and what I think was, the right thing. What good would it have done to get the other one stuck in the snow as well? It sounds like both of them were in way over their heads."

"I guess the big thing right now is trying to find the boss of the lawyers, Sean Flaherty. I've been trying to talk to him, but so far no luck. I also want to speak again with the blonde he's hanging out with. She's staying with him, at—get this—The Hempfield Estate."

"You're kidding!"

"Nope."

"I've wanted to see inside that place since I was a kid."

"Come with me."

"Really?"

"Absolutely. I can use the support. Those two scare me." I shuddered.

"Love to. I'm done here around four. Maybe we could catch some dinner afterwards?"

"Sorry. My crew's supposed to get into Reno this afternoon. And with the weather, who knows what's going to happen? Another time?"

"Sure. Turn me down. At least let me drive to Tahoe. We can pull your rental around to the Red Dog Lodge garage. It's covered. I know the manager there."

"Ehh," I rubbed my neck. "I've still got to drive back tonight. But I'll happily let you drive over to Tahoe City."

The warm room, my many layers of clothes, and Mike's presence all added up to a lot of heat. I was yearning to get back outside into that cold wind. Mike stood and walked with me back to the front door of the ski school. There he held out his hand to shake, which seemed oddly formal.

When I put my hand in his, he pulled me towards him and kissed my cheek.

"Sorry. Couldn't resist, he said, a grin plastered across his face."

"Behave yourself! See you around 4:00."

A young man in a neon green parka and red pants skidded up just then yelling, "Hey Bud! Bud!" and stopped abruptly, throwing snow all over the plaza where we stood. "I wanna talk to you!" he yelled looking at us.

"What Grappa?"

"Not you, her," Grappa said pointing at me. "I need to talk to her."

Mike stepped outside, and we walked over a few steps to where he stood at the end of the snow, kicking out of his bindings.

"Laura Bailey, this is Grappa McDermott, a local. Known him since he was a kid."

"So, Grappa," Mike said turning to him. "What do you want to talk to Laura about?"

Grappa McDermott looked to be around twenty-two, almost as tall as Mike, who's probably six-three, with green eyes and bleached blond hair poking out from under his silver racing helmet. He had a nice face, a tan, smooth-featured, likable face.

"I heard about those missing women. Well, it's a long story how I know this, but I hear you're asking questions about those SF ladies who disappeared. Right?"

Mike stood in the biting wind wearing just a thin base layer, and rubbing his hands up and down his arms. I turned to him.

"I'm going to go talk to Grappa. Meet you back here around 4:00?"

He squeezed the tips of my fingers, and headed back inside.

"Let's go somewhere and talk. I'll buy you something to eat. What do you want?"

We decided on a nearby pizza place and settled into a red leatherette booth, shedding clothes and snow around us in a flurry. A cute waitress came to bring us water and take our order.

"Hey, Grappa."

"Hey, Stell," he said, paying no attention to her. He ordered a large pizza with pepperoni and a Coke.

"You going to eat all that?"

"You want some?"

I nodded yes.

"I'll share."

The waitress left, and he turned back to me.

"So how do you know I'm looking for these women?"

He sighed and slumped forward, as if to show how weary he had grown of stupid questions.

"My Grandma Limoncello talked to Dave Geisner's ex-wife Felicia, and Felicia told Grandma that you're a snow scientist—which is so sweet. How can I be one? Seriously. And anyways, I told my grandma that I thought I saw those two SF ladies skiing down into the forest there towards the Western States Trail with some guy. And Grandma said I should tell you. So I saw you, and now I'm telling you. Right?"

"Let's start at the beginning."

He pulled his helmet liner off to reveal a shock of bleached white hair about three inches long that stuck out straight from his head once he mussed it up. Just then the pizza arrived, and he looked at it sideways, obviously wondering how long before he could eat if we started talking first.

"Go on," I told him. "Go slow. You can talk and eat."

He gave me a shy smile, looked embarrassed, and then dug in.

"So, I saw these two women stuck in a field of deep snow off to skier's left up before Montezuma. This must have been Friday. I was coming down in the fresh snow under the Far East Chair. I noticed them digging out for around an hour, and then came by and found them gone. I thought that one standing in the blue parka was hot, so I kept checking on her, wondering if I should offer to help her friend. But, you know, damn! I didn't want to get stuck there all day. That other one, the dark-haired one, didn't begin to know what she was doing."

He paused to inhale a slice, then wiped his mouth, took a chug of Coke, and turned back to me.

"So an hour or so after I first saw them, they were gone. Then farther on down, I'm shredding the glades and hitting some lines again under Far East, when I thought I spotted the blue parka again. So I tracked over that way a bit and saw the blue parka woman with the one who'd been stuck. And the one in black, she was skiing all wobbly, like I don't think she knew what she was doing in that mashed potato snow, first off, but then I think she was hurt, too. And some guy—a strong skier, but he's skiing wonky, like he had a bad tune on one ski or something—was leading them into, of all fucking places, the thick trees there. The forest. Which is no place anybody ever goes. Anyways, that's all I saw. It was nuking snow. And I'm not positive it was them. I think it was. Yeah, it was them. That sky blue parka. That's all."

He turned his full attention to the pizza.

"You didn't ever see them again?"

"Noooo," he sang in a jokey falsetto voice.

"Could you recognize the man if you saw him again?"

He stopped for a moment to ponder this as he watched grease drip down his hand.

"Not his face, I don't think. But I could probably recognize the way he skis. Funny on the one side—let's see, I guess his right side. But don't get me wrong—he was good. I could probably recognize that again."

"Thanks. That's the first break I've gotten. Is it OK to call if I think of anything else?"

He leaned forward and smiled at me. "Oh it's excellent if you call me. Please, go right ahead. In fact, give me your digits."

I exchanged digits with him, wondering if that was wise, and left him to finish the pizza.

Chapter 9

SUNDAY, APRIL 3, 5 PM

Built in the 1920s by San Francisco industrialist Jacob Alexander Hempfield, The Hempfield Estate covers three acres running along the north shore of Lake Tahoe just outside Tahoe City. A twelve foot wrought-iron gate runs the circumference of the estate, with a guardhouse where one could be allowed in either by a guard, or by the use of a keypad.

Neither of these were necessary, since the gatehouse stood dark and empty, and the twelve foot wrought-iron gates hung open. Mike simply drove his truck into the estate. We wound our way through the grounds, passing three small houses, all of them snowbound, before coming to a stop in front of the main house. The driveway must have been heated since there were only a couple inches of slush on it. Snow berms on either side of the driveway stood ten or eleven feet high. It wasn't until we stood at the massive, double wooden front doors, which rose to gothic arches, that we saw the spill of Lake Tahoe before us. We caught a momentary glimpse through the falling snow of the runs of Heavenly Valley cutting down the mountains twenty-four miles away at the far end of the lake. A long pier ran out into the lake with a minia-ture version of the main house serving as the boathouse.

"Wow," I whispered to Mike, and ran a gloved hand over the iron struts strapped across the doors at two foot intervals. "How tall are these doors?"

"Eighteen feet? Maybe twenty?"

There didn't seem to be a doorbell, at least nothing obvious. Finally, Mike spotted a coil of metal in the shape of a breast. He pushed the nipple, and a gong echoed through the inside of the mansion. Our eyes met, and we both shook our heads. We waited a minute, then Mike pushed the nipple again. Finally, after three or four minutes, the door opened a crack. Sean stuck his long, elegant nose into the crack.

"What are you doing on my property?" He swiveled his gaze to Mike. "Who are you?"

"Mike Bernese. Just here with Laura."

Sean squinted his eyes and gave us both a sideways look.

"I didn't see any No Trespassing signs, and the gate was open," I told him.

"OK," he said with a facetious smile, "consider this your warning. Please get off my property."

A blast of wind off the lake pushed the door open, and we got a glimpse of a dark foyer. Someone moved into my line of sight, and it took me a second to realize it was Anna Strunk. With no makeup on and wearing a set of red velour sweats, she looked like a girl. And I noticed again that she wasn't five feet tall and probably weighed well under a hundred pounds.

Turning my attention back to Sean, I told him, "The Sheriff's name is Burt Geisner here in Placer County. I've got his number if you'd like. Just so you don't have to look it up. But I guess you can always call 911."

Anna moved forward into the open doorway and put her hand over Sean's where he held the door. "Sean," she said, "it's the snow doctor. Let me talk to her for a minute." She spoke in the voice she might use to quiet an upset child. She turned to look between Mike and me. "What do you want?"

Sean remained standing in the doorway, glaring at me. Erratic wouldn't begin to describe his behavior. His dark eyes looked like they were all pupil in the late afternoon light. Maybe he was high? Once I thought of it, that seemed a reasonable explanation for the flips in his attitude. I was trying to look into what happened to his on-again-off-again girlfriend, his colleague and employee, so why was he fighting me?

"Can we come in?" I asked Anna.

"No," she said. "Ask your questions right here."

We stood in the settling twilight, wind howling around us and snow pelting down once again. "Daniel Burdick suggested I might talk to you again. That maybe you could help me get a better insight into Alexis—"

"That dick—," Sean started, but at a look from Anna he fell silent.

Anna backed up to stand further out of the wind and snow. "Alexis is a little wild. We talked about that already. A little—how shall I put it—maybe selfish at times. Daniel isn't fond of Alexis because she sometimes teases him. So if he can find a way to make public that Alexis is sometimes," she paused again, "injudicious in her behavior, that's probably what he's doing."

"Can you clarify what you mean by injudicious?"

Anna paused, apparently thinking about how to word it.

Sean surged forward and shouted in my face. "This has nothing to do with Alexis' disappearance or with you! I'm telling you right now, get off my property and do not come back, or I'll have you arrested for trespassing. I don't care if you're friends with the Sheriff!" He slammed the big wooden door in Mike and my faces.

As we turned and walked back to Mike's truck, he reached over and took my hand. It would have been a more tender moment if we both hadn't been wearing heavy ski mitts, but, even so, it was tender enough.

The ride back to Squaw passed in silence. Mike needed all his concentration to keep the truck on the road. We passed several cars that had slid off the road and landed in various stages of distress. I wondered how I was going to get the rental back to Truckee. Or whether 89 would be closed before we got a chance to try. Ice glimmered under the snow covering the road.

Back in the parking lot at Squaw, Mike pulled up behind my car. He leaned over me and opened the passenger door of the truck.

"Sure we can't catch some dinner together?"

"I'd love to," I told him. "But my colleagues are supposed to be getting into Reno soon, and I've got to find out what's going on."

"It's Level 4 avie danger in the backcountry."

"I know. I've been following it. But we've got to decide what's next. I'm sure you'll be seeing me around Squaw tomorrow."

"Excellent."

"So I'll see you then—"

"Yeah. But you'll also be seeing me in your rearview mirror all the way back into Truckee."

"You're going to follow me?"

He gave me a slight nod.

"You don't need to, but thanks. The car's been fine so far, but then there hasn't been all this ice."

The ice ended quickly once I made the left back onto Highway 89. But the road continued to be treacherous with snow and low visibility. The worst of it loomed up the mountain to our left in darkness. That stretch of road between Truckee and Squaw is famous for avalanches, and there's no avalanche patrol, few houses, and, in places, no trees to break the snow's path down onto the road and on into the Truckee River on the other side. If there is one way I don't want to die, it's in an avalanche roaring down onto me in the dark. Or just in an avalanche, period.

Once I pulled into Rita's driveway, Mike flashed his lights and moved on down the street. Just before turning off the ignition, I noticed the dashboard clock read 5:55 p.m. and 4 degrees. I walked onto the porch dithering about whether or not it would be worthwhile to shovel off the hot tub and see if it was running, but realized I had a bigger problem since there was still nothing to eat but Frosted Flakes.

As I stood in the vapor lock room, a narrow strip of hallway between the front door and the inside door designed to keep the cold out, and a place to dump your wet ski clothes, my phone began to play Kiss' "Calling Dr. Love." Tim Schneider entered the ringtone on my phone as a joke. I lowered myself onto a narrow strip of wooden bench, dug it out of my parka, and hit the green Accept button.

"Tim, where are you?"

"Sure as hell not in Reno."

"So where—"

"Still in Denver. They've been delaying the flight for hours and finally just cancelled it. So no heading out tomorrow."

"I figured as much. Loads of snow here. We've had over six feet in the last forty-eight hours. And it's not over. It just keeps hammering. Backcountry would be way too dangerous."

"I'll keep in touch then. I'll follow the weather here. And as soon as you think it'd be feasible, let me know."

"Will do."

"Are you going to stay out there? What're you doing?"

"There's no going anywhere right now–80's closed from Sacramento to Reno. The roads are atrocious. It's Snowmageddon."

"Take care then. Talk to you soon."

Once he cut off, I sat on the bench for a moment thinking, then browsed through my contacts and hit the number for Aldous and Margaret Moore. Aldous answered on the third ring.

"Aldous, what're you doing?"

"Margaret is nearly ready to put dinner on the table, and I'm opening a bottle of wine."

"Can I invite myself over?"

"You're always welcome, my girl. Come on over. Where are you?"

"Just five minutes away. But you go ahead. I'm going to get out of my ski clothes first."

"See you in ten minutes."

I knew they'd wait dinner for me. I kicked my black mukluks off and headed into the house. It took me two minutes to strip down out of my ski clothes, pull on a pair of jeans and a sweater, attempt to run a brush through my hair—I quickly gave up on that and bunched it back into a ponytail—pulled my mukluks back on, and headed out the door.

Aldous and Margaret Moore lived in a large affluent neighborhood of mostly second homes called Tahoe Donner. An eclectic grouping of homes made up the area, all of them looking out onto green spaces. Multi-million dollar mansions sat next to modest ski shacks. The area was famous for its amenities: miles of cross-country skiing, downhill skiing, tennis, golf, horseback riding in the summer, a beach on Donner Lake, pools, gyms. It was a lovely area. The Moores bought their house in the '70's, early on in the development.

The development was dreamed up by a bunch of rich Bay Area young men with counter culture inclinations who sat around wondering what they could do to make a difference. Tahoe Donner came out of their nightly cloud of smoke. It occupied several thousand acres of rolling mountainous area above Truckee, so it was high, up to seventy-six-hundred feet at the highest. It was also in a major snow belt. If I thought the snow levels around Truckee, Lake Tahoe and Squaw Base Camp were high, it was a dusting compared to Tahoe Donner.

As I drove along the well-plowed streets, I couldn't see the houses, buried as they were behind thirty foot berms. Nothing showed where a house sat other than the deep cut of a driveway into berms high enough to enclose the power lines. Snowbanks had swallowed the street signs as well. I had to pull over and plug their address into my iPhone to get the GPS to tell me when I'd arrived.

The Moores' street turned off a larger thoroughfare. The asphalt was covered by packed-down snow that rolled up at the width of the road to merge into twenty-or-thirty, or sometimes forty foot high berms. I'd never seen anything like it in Colorado. We don't get that kind of snow.

The Moores' driveway ran down steeply from the road. It seemed too narrow for a two-car garage. Apparently, their driveway had grown narrower as the winter wore on. Where was all this melt water going to go? The obvious answer seemed to be their garage. I stopped in front of the right-hand garage door and put the car in park. Their bear box—a metal, supposedly bear-proof, box used to store garbage the night before pick-up—at the end of the driveway had ten or fifteen feet of snow stacked at a precarious tilt on top. The walkway to their front door was gone–just a twenty foot drift of snow from the driveway to the roof. Pulling out my phone, I hit their number and told Aldous I'd arrived. Outside lights came on, and the garage door opened a minute later.

"Sorry about that," Aldous said, as he came out to greet me wearing a navy and red Scandinavian ski sweater and jeans. "I keep forgetting we've lost the use of the front door 'til spring. I left the front porch light on for you, but there's no way you could see that!" As I came around to meet him, he moved over and gave me a quick hug.

"Good to have you back in town." He nodded towards my car. "You may end up spending the night if this snow doesn't let up. We won't get plowed out again until around 6:00 in the morning."

"What's that?" I asked him, pointing at a large snow-blower.

He laughed, "Oh, that old thing?" and led me into the warm glow of the house.

Inside, I stood in the airlock, prying off my boots, and Margaret came over and pressed the warm skin of her face against my cold cheek.

"Hello, dear. What a treat to see you."

"Sorry to invite myself, and worse, come empty-handed. Afraid if I stopped at the Safeway, I'd never get out of the parking lot."

"We're always happy to see you anyway we can get you." Margaret smiled. "And we've got enough wine around to fill Lake Tahoe."

Aldous slipped my parka off as Margaret took my hand and pulled me along farther into the house, through the vapor lock door and into the warm interior, fragrant with the smell of roasting meat. She pointed me towards a Captain's chair at the wooden breakfast table in the kitchen.

"Sit here, dear. We could have been more formal and eaten in the dining room, but this is cozier."

Aldous set a glass of red wine in front of me and squeezed past into a corner chair. Dark glass walls reflected our images on two sides. Across the room, a rock hearth rose to the second-story-high ceiling, and a wood pellet stove glowed in its corner.

Margaret placed a platter of sliced roast beef with crispy potatoes and browned carrots on the table and sat down. She had been in such a whirl of motion since I arrived, it was the first chance I had to really look at her. Margaret, too, had lost weight and seemed even tougher and wirier than a year ago when I last saw the pair of them in Aspen. Silver, wavy hair hung to her shoulders, and she wore a lavender sweater and slender black pants. Her skin had a rosy glow and her eyes sparkled.

They had been married for fifty-one years and had grown to resemble each other in build and facial expressions. They never had children.

"I love children," Margaret told me when we first met over twenty years ago, "but never had any desire for my own. Luckily, I found a husband who felt the same way."

At nine or ten, when Margaret told me this, I knew that was the kind of man I was going to need as well. I'd never for a moment wavered in that belief.

"So," Margaret turned her dark blue eyes on me, "Tell me everything."

"Where to start? I was supposed to meet up with my team tonight, and tomorrow we were all going to head to my research site back in Granite Chief Wilderness."

"What were you going back there for?"

"I'm interested in this big snow year you're having. I set up remote sensors to transmit the data, but they've stopped working. I have no idea why. Maybe all the snow, maybe some kids went back there and messed with them. But I really want to get back and take some measurements on the snow pack."

"Like what?"

"Well, of course, the basics, like how much water's in it is always important for farmers and for hydropower, things like that. But at least at Squaw, we've seen signs of early melt. So that's what I'm really interested in. What's going on? Is there really early melt? What's causing it? That kind of thing."

Margaret balanced her fork on the edge of her plate, and folded her arms on the table turning her full attention to me.

"Why does this matter so much?"

"In this area, you get eighty to eighty-five percent of your water from snowmelt. So an extra month without snow is a huge deal. Since NorCal supplies so much of the water for SoCal, it's important. If there isn't enough water for LA, they'll be up here draining Lake Tahoe."

She shook her head and returned her attention to her dinner.

"Amazing," she said. "Truly, I have wasted my life. There was no such field as snow science when I was a child."

"You've had a wonderful career as a pediatrician. You're respected, kids love you, parents trust you," I said.

Margaret chewed a mouthful of carrot, then took a sip of wine.

"I'm certainly correct in saying, it's too late now."

"You have a great career," Aldous chided her.

"Has Aldous told you I've gotten a new job since I got here?" I asked.

"What's that?"

"I'm a private detective."

"I think he did mention something about that. How dreadful those two women disappearing. You don't think they just skedaddled off for some fun?"

"I don't think so."

"Who were these women?" Margaret asked "Aldous already told me how you went for help and returned to find they skied down into the trees. What else have you found out?"

Aldous poured the last of the bottle into my glass and turned his full attention to me. In the dim light from the chandelier and the pellet stove, he looked old. How fast our lives go by. How little time we end up spending with the people we love the most. I'd gone along thinking Aldous and Margaret would always be around. All I had to do was pick up the phone, and we could arrange a trip to Aspen, or a trip to Squaw for me. Somehow, without noticing it, I'd grown up, and they'd gotten old.

Margaret was still staring at me intently.

"The women grew up together in Philadelphia with both of them wanting to be environmentalists. They went to Penn together, and the one studied biochemistry and the other environmental policy. The one who went into science wasn't happy, wasn't satisfied maybe with the money? So she went to Hastings. So the other one, Jennifer, the one we came across stuck in the snow, went on to be a community activist against Marcellus Shale Drilling—especially one big company that's sort of at the forefront of all this drilling back East. And this is a huge deal back East in that area. But the lawyer, Alexis, works defending a Marcellus Shale drilling company. How funny is that? And apparently, Jennifer doesn't know what Alexis is doing. I guess Alexis is ashamed of it because she's not still the environmentalist they both dreamed of being."

"What company is Jennifer trying to stop?"

"Uh," I have to wrack my memory. "Oh. It's called Plains Drilling."

Margaret blanched, and fell silent for a second.

"I know the president of Plains Drilling," she said. "A horrible man named Seth Riordan."

"Oh my god, him," Aldous groaned.

"He has a place over at Alpine Meadows," Margaret continued. "I coached his boys when they were in Mighty Mites, the Squaw ski team for kids five to ten."

"That mess," Aldous said, and got up from the table and began to clear away our dishes.

"What happened?" I asked.

"Let's see," Margaret said, and got up from the table too. "This should help prod my memory. This happened, let's see—" She walked over to the hallway and opened a cupboard then returned with a big photo album. "I guess this was in—Aldous, how old do you think Jason Riordan is?"

He paused for a second, leaning against the counter with a dishtowel thrown over one shoulder. "He must be what? Twenty-five? Twenty-six?"

"And he was let's say nine or ten when the trouble started. So this started let's say 1994." A second later she came to the couch carrying three more big photo albums with the years 1994, 1995, 1996 on the binding. On the front, the leather albums were emblazoned with the caption, "Mighty Mites." Margaret laid them on the coffee table and gestured for me to join her on the green leather couch. I moved over and sat beside her. Flipping through the 1994 volume, she came to a stop and pointed me towards a page of photographs of young skiers in their speed suits beaming for the camera as they held aloft a big trophy.

She pointed to a boy who didn't seem to be sharing in the triumph.

"This is Jason Riordan. A sweet boy. Who definitely did not want to be a ski racer."

Aldous popped his head out from the kitchen. "Who didn't want to ski, period."

Margaret nodded and remained focused on the album.

"That's true. Didn't like to ski. Didn't like the cold."

She pointed to another photograph of adults grouped together with most of them wearing ski clothes.

"And this is his father, Seth Riordan. He was one of the parent volunteers for the end of the season race." She pointed to a nondescript middle-aged guy with brown hair and casual, preppy-looking street clothes. "Seth wouldn't accept that Jason wasn't a skier. His older brother Ryan loved to ski and for a few years was an adept racer. But Jason, no. More of a reader. Seth Riordan would not accept that. He rode that poor boy like a demon. I don't know how many times I came across Jason cowering in tears and his dad standing over him haranguing the poor kid."

"As if this wasn't enough, then he started in on us coaches. It was our fault he didn't like skiing. We weren't challenging him. And to be honest, a challenge to Jason was just getting down the hill. Any hill. We're all volunteer coaches. Nobody got paid for anything. The next thing I know he's trying to pay me to work extra with Jason. Or pay Aldous to train more with him. So that's fine. If he just wanted to pay for extra lessons or something, that would have been fine, but no, he wanted to pay me to always choose Jason first. First heat, first down any practice run, more time, better equipment.

It turned nasty. And that was when Aldous was the head of the ski school, so he had to tell Seth to back off, and that we weren't for sale. It had to be an even playing ground for all the kids."

"You even tried to convince him to let Jason quit the team, didn't you?"

"Many times. I tried to direct Mr. Riordan's energy elsewhere. But all that happened was he started trying to bribe other coaches and finally tried to bribe the judges. Either him or that man who worked for him, the ex-special forces guy. What was his name?"

"Yes, what was his name?" Margaret flipped through a few more pictures then moved on to a different album.

"Here he is." She pointed to a hulking man with a military type haircut shaved on the sides and enough sandy colored hair on the top to not quite see his scalp.

"He looks like a brute," I said.

"Actually," Margaret countered, "he was the nicer of the two. What was his name?" She shook her head in frustration. "I don't know. Aldous?"

"No," he said. "I can't help you with that."

"He ended up getting that sweet girl—what was her name, Shirley, I think—got her fired from the ski school, and from coaching, of course, because she told him Jason didn't want to ski, and shouldn't have to."

"The whole point of Mighty Mites was for the kids to learn to equate skiing with fun," Aldous told us. "So he asked me to fire her, and I told him to go to hell, so he went up the chain of command, and in the end Corning didn't want to fire her. He felt terrible about it, but the guy didn't give us a choice. His donations made the whole program possible in those days."

"A real pit bull," Margaret added, "but I feel bad saying that because it's a slur on pit bulls. Let me put it this way, he was tenacious. He got hold of something, and he would not stop."

"And he must have been pretty wealthy?" I asked.

Margaret rolled her eyes. "There didn't seem to be any limit to that either."

"Poor kid," I said.

"Jason moved away to New Zealand. I don't know what he does. He cut off contact with his father. I think he's in touch with his mother. I run into her occasionally. But I don't think Jason has anything to do with his dad."

The conversation fell off, and we all sat in silence for a moment. Then Aldous got up and returned from the kitchen with a tray of three plates, each with a slice of chocolate cake.

"Made this myself," he said with a smile.

"Did you really?" I asked, never having known him to cook.

"No," he laughed. "From our good friend Trader Joe's." A few minutes later, Margaret got up and excused herself, saying she still had some work to do and needed to be up early in the morning. She kissed me good night on the cheek and headed upstairs.

Having finished cleaning up the kitchen, Aldous came over and sat in a big overstuffed armchair that matched the couch.

"So what are Dave and Burt doing to help with this investigation?"

"Nothing," I said, "absolutely nothing."

"Why? What's their excuse for that?"

"I've only spoken to Dave. He's not exactly against the idea of digging out that tree well, but he says right now it's too dangerous to go back in there. And that's not completely untrue. It's pretty dicey back in there, and the weather isn't helping. He says until we learn something new, or there's some reason to believe foul play is involved, neither he nor his brother are doing anything."

Aldous didn't respond, just seemed to ruminate about that.

"I'm hoping once Jennifer's family gets here, they can file a Missing Person's Report, so at least that will be official notice to Burt that he needs to begin taking this seriously. Right now, I think they're both only too happy to think it's not their problem."

We moved on to discuss how much longer I thought there would be snow in the continental United States if nothing changed. Later, we talked about Aldous' memories of the 1960 Olympics at Squaw. He'd been in the Army and was sent to Squaw to stomp down the snow on the Men's and Women's downhill runs. This was in the days prior to grooming equipment.

Finally around 10:00, I realized I'd been yawning for the past half hour, and I stood up to take my leave. Aldous walked out with me to check the driveway, and we found the snow had stopped, leaving a dense quiet cold to the black night. An inch of snow covered the windshield of the rental car. I brushed it off with my sleeve and climbed into the driver's seat. Aldous leaned over and kissed my cheek.

"I'm grateful that we got to live in the time of snow," he said, then stepped back and waved as I backed out of the driveway and drove on out of sight.

=

Back at Rita's, the front porch light was off, and I felt certain I had left it on. Inside, I discovered the power had gone out, and the house had once again returned to its default state of freezing. Poor, unloved house. I grabbed the down comforter off the bed, lit a fire in the stove, and curled up on the couch in the dark, cold living room near the stove. Just as sleep settled over me, and the room started getting cozy, my phone rang. I saw it was Rita Chambers calling from Aspen.

"Hi Rita."

"Hey, how's it going?"

"Crazy snow here. And I've got a new job."

"Doing what?"

I went on to break down for Rita every detail about the women's disappearance. We talked it over, back and forth, for a while.

After working for eighteen years on the Aspen Ski Company ski patrol as a full-time, paid employee and member of a blast team, Rita wore out her knees by the time she was thirty-eight.

As she put it, "My Grandfather always told me to do things in moderation. But I didn't listen. I was too busy proving I could do everything a man could. And my poor knees paid the price."

Aspen Ski Company's health insurance would only pay for a knee replacement at the hospital in Aspen—which had a lukewarm reputation for orthopedics. Rita tried to get an exemption so her surgery could be done in Vail, a world-renowned center for this surgery. Most of the upper-level employees of Aspen Ski Company get the exemption and have their orthopedic work done in Vail. But Rita didn't get the exemption, and the surgery was done in Aspen with the feared result. Though she still got around, and was able to ski cross-country, she has never been able to downhill ski again. She still worked three days a week as a lift ticket checker on the gondola. Her resentment towards the Aspen Ski Company, like Aldous and Margaret's wine supply, could fill Lake Tahoe, which in places, was over sixteen-hundred feet deep. Only difference being, Rita's resentment could fill it several times over.

Once the room got up to 50 or 55, I could barely stay awake, so I begged off, and received exactly the advice I expected to receive from Rita.

"Don't trust gas company people, ski company people, or lawyers."

"Thanks. Sweet dreams to you, too." Somewhere deep down inside, in the darkest caves of my guts, I suspected she was right.

Chapter 10

MONDAY, APRIL 4, 8 AM

A telephone rang and rang, and no one answered. It took half a dozen rings before I realized the noise came from my phone, and I was the one who wasn't answering. I reached out from the cocoon of the comforter to the coffee table. The living room had reverted over night to its normal temperature of around 20 degrees. I didn't recognize the number on my phone, but answered anyway. I did recognize Richard Fellatorre's voice.

"Are you here?" I asked him.

"We got in late last night. Had one hell of a drive up, had to stop and buy chains and put them on in a foot of slush."

"You should have paid the guy $30 to put them on for you."

"We'd still be there waiting if I did that. But I followed your advice and got up over Mount Rose just before they closed the road. Listen, can you meet me for breakfast at the Resort at Squaw Creek?"

"Sure. But it's going to take me at least an hour and a half or so to get cleaned up and get over there."

He suddenly lowered his voice. "I'd like to talk to you without Chloe around, just so we can be frank with each other, but I don't know what to do with her. I don't usually—I'm not the one—." His voice trailed off, rife with pain.

"How about putting Chloe in the Squaw Kids program? They ski, but they do all kinds of other fun things–you know, go swimming, try cross country skiing–I don't know what all, but it's got a reputation for being a great program."

"We brought her bathing suit, but no ski clothes."

"In the lower level where you're staying, they have a rental shop where they rent skis and ski gear. Or there's a store right there, and you can buy her the clothes she needs."

"Not the one in the walkway, by the coffee shop?"

"Not unless you want to pay a fortune. The better place is below that, on the lower level. Get her outfitted, then take the shuttle over to Squaw, and look for the ski school. Ask for Mike Bernese. He's the director. Tell him who you are. Even though the program's begun for the day, he'll get Chloe in and get her situated. I'll call him as soon as we hang up and let him know you're coming. I mean, if you want to. I think being with kids her own age, and outside doing something active, might help get her mind off things."

"Thanks. How about if I call you once I get her settled?"

"Perfect."

We hung up, and I called Mike and left a voicemail asking him to explain to Squaw Kids about Chloe coming in late.

Picking up the remote, I went to turn on my "What's Happening in Tahoe" morning show, and only then remembered there was no power, which made life harder because I sure needed a shower.

I threw on a pair of corduroys and a sweater, and decided to bring along my ski gear as well. Who knew what the day held? I brought two parkas with me to Squaw–a red one and a green one. They're both equally—how to put it nicely—broken in? I decided once again to opt for the red one I'd been wearing ever since I got there.

At Squaw I walked around with a backpack full of bath gear wondering where I could take a shower. In Aspen, I often used the shower for the gym at Little Nell's, so I was thinking about that when I walked past the ski school and remembered the women's locker room there had decent-looking showers. I slipped in and asked if Mike was around, but learned from the woman at the front desk that he was out on the mountain dropping in on new instructors just to see how everyone was doing. I explained my predicament, and she offered me the use of the ski school locker room.

Richard still hadn't called by the time I finished my shower, so I took my time blow-drying my hair out smooth. Smoothish. When he still hadn't called after that, I even put on some makeup. It was at that point, officially, a cold day in hell. I figured I'd wasted enough time, so I headed over to Squaw Creek. I'd grab something to eat if he still wasn't back. If I'd had any idea what he looked like, I could have probably found him at Squaw Kids and given him a ride back myself. I headed out to the parking lot and drove the couple miles over to Squaw Creek Resort.

After buying a soy latte and a breakfast sandwich at the coffee-shop, I settled down in the enormous lobby of the four-star hotel to wait for Richard. I'd only been sitting a minute or two when he called and told me he was on his way down. What does an East coast magazine editor look like? I had all kinds of ideas–from the iconic, monocled and top-hatted figure from *The New Yorker* to a hipster dressed all in black with a fedora.

The lobby featured native stone. Big granite boulders came up through the floor near the main walkway through the grand space. A dozen or more intimate seating areas of leather club chairs and velvet sofas had been placed strategically, and huge carpets warmed up the vast stone floor. End tables featured chess and backgammon sets. A twelve-foot high fireplace blazed, and a three-story window looked out on an impressive view of the valley.

A man dressed in jeans and a black sweater, a little under six feet tall with a shaved head and round, wire-rim glasses, but no fedora, stood near the long stretch of front desk scanning the room. It had to be him. He had a round honest-looking face. He spotted me sitting on my own, looking at him, and headed right over.

"Laura Bailey?"

"Right."

"Richard Fellatorre."

He dropped into a chair near the corner of a couch where I sat. He looked exhausted and just shy of desperate.

"I got Chloe into the program you suggested. She wasn't happy about it, but she went. Took me forever to get her clothes and geared up. That's why I'm late."

"No problem. I just got here myself."

"Please," he said, "tell me everything from the beginning."

So I began telling him how Dave and I came across the women, how Dave left and I skied out for help. At one point, he leaned forward and pushed away the corner of coffee table that came between us, then bent forward with his elbows on his knees, giving me his rapt attention. It took me another five minutes to wrap up explaining to him everything I'd discovered—which wasn't much.

As I finished by telling him how Grappa thought he saw them skiing off into the trees with a large man, he put his head in his hands and shook his head slowly from side to side.

"I didn't want her going off with Alexis. But they do this several times a year. I never told Jennifer in so many words, but I don't think Alexis is much of a friend. She's too selfish to be a friend to anyone. But they've done this for the past twenty years. How can I stop that?"

"How old are they?"

"They're both forty-two. To be honest, and why shouldn't I be—" He looked up suddenly, and I saw that his dark eyes were filled with tears. "I don't like Alexis. Certainly don't trust her."

"You told me on the phone that their coming up here to ski was a last-minute decision. Why do you think they did that when Jennifer isn't much of a skier?"

"I don't know. Just that sometimes I think Jennifer acts differently around Alexis than she does around me, her family. We got married right after college, and Alexis went on to a much more exciting life. So when Jennifer's with her, she maybe cuts loose more than she would around me? I'm guessing this seemed to Jenn like another wild Alexis driven adventure."

There's that word "wild" again used in conjunction with Alexis.

He turned and scanned the lobby, then looked out the big picture window before turning back to me.

"What do we do next?" he asked me.

"I'd like you to talk to the Sheriff, Burt Geisner. He's the brother of Dave Geisner, who I was with when we came across Alexis and Jennifer."

"But I want you to keep working with me. Please. These people, these Geisners, have already proven to me they don't give a shit about my wife, and they'll do as little as they can get away with. I'll pay you whatever you need. $1000 a day? Is that enough?"

"You don't need to pay me. I was the last person we know of to talk to them. I want to help you find them. But I need you to talk to Burt Geisner. Once you file a Missing Person's report, the police will make sure they aren't in a coma in a hospital somewhere we haven't thought of. Or in jail. The police will take care of the basics we can't cover."

"So you'll keep working with me to find them?"

"Sure. Until I have to leave. I'm waiting for my crew to get in, and then we're heading into the backcountry to check my snow research site. But the way it's snowing, that's not going to happen for days. So yes, I've got a stake in this, too. We've got to find them. You can also pressure Dave Geisner to dig out the tree well, once it's safe to be back in that area."

"What do you think happened?"

I couldn't lie to him, but I also couldn't tell him that I felt in my heart they were dead. "I don't know," I told him. "I just don't know."

Tears kept rolling down his cheeks, and he dropped his head into his hands.

"Chloe and I can't stay here long either. We've got two boys back in Philadelphia. They're with Jennifer's parents right now, but I can't leave them—"

I nodded. I didn't know what to say. I felt so terrible for the guy.

"The few minutes I spoke with your wife, she seemed like a lovely person. Do you think she had any enemies? Anyone who would want to do her harm?"

He gave a bitter laugh.

"I'm sure the powers that be at Plains Drilling wouldn't mind if something happened to her."

"Tell me about what was going on there?"

"Jennifer is dangerous to that company—and not just Plains, all the companies involved in Marcellus Shale drilling in our area—but especially Plains because they're the main active company in northeast Pennsylvania. What makes her so dangerous is that she's smart, she's done her homework, she's well spoken. And I'm the editor of

Philadelphia Today, a magazine that covers current events in the region. We've published several articles for her group, and we have a large and loyal readership. So in the midst of a bunch of screaming voices hurling accusations this way and that, here's Jenn who has all the facts on the tip of her tongue, and she's quiet and eloquent. What she says hurts.

These guys are denying they've ever polluted farm wells, say. And here's Jennifer saying, 'Oh just a minute, how about the Robertson's in Dimock, say, where they found their water contamination rate at such and such level, and samples tested before your wells went in tested clean at a low parts per billion.' You know whatever. I'm not knowledgeable enough to just spout the data. But Jenn is. She doesn't get hysterical, she doesn't raise her voice, and she never stumbles on a fact. So she is dangerous."

"And this is already happening? It's not that she's trying to prevent it, it's already happening?"

"Oh yes," he gave another bitter laugh. "Just a little over a month ago, Plains Drilling had a huge well blow-out that shot fracking fluids hundreds of feet into the air and pumped out tens of thousands of gallons of this toxic-laden mess for weeks before they could stop it. It killed a pristine trout stream where Jimmy Carter used to fish every year. It took a little over two weeks to shut it down. And after that, people from Plains Drilling threatened Jennifer. I don't know exactly what was said to her, but she was shaken. Her partners seem to think the president of Plains, Seth Riordan, accused her of being involved in sabotaging that well. But you need to talk to my wife's partners at PAMSD: Pennsylvanians Against Marcellus Shale Drilling. Talk to LaTisha Cimino and Steve Diderowski. They can give you more specifics of what's going on."

He took a sip of his coffee, eyes still blazing with worry and frustration.

"I know that Plains has hired ex-military psychological operations people. And I know that somehow they've gotten the Department of Homeland Security in Pennsylvania spying on PAMSD and labeling them terrorists. I know that because PAMSD has filed suit against the state over being labeled terrorists. So things are pretty intense at home. But talk to Steve and LaTisha–they can give you the specifics."

He gave me their numbers, and I entered them into my phone.

"I'll get right on this," I told him. "You call Burt Geisner."

I wrote down Burt Geisner's number and handed it to Richard.

"Call the Sheriff and officially declare Jennifer and Alexis missing. Then call Dave and demand the tree well be dug up as soon as possible. You know, squeaky wheels and grease. I've got a couple people I need to talk to."

He straightened his shoulders, then blew his nose and stood.

"Excuse me for a minute. I'm sorry." He looked around flustered, like he didn't know what to do next. "Can I buy you another coffee?"

"Sure," I told him. "A soy latte would be great." I watched him walk over towards the coffee shop. He seemed relieved to have something to do.

A few minutes later when he returned and sat two coffees on the table between us, he seemed calmer.

He held onto my hand for a minute and met my eyes.

"Thank you so much."

We separated in the lobby. I left my coffee on the table between us and walked down to the parking lot. Richard headed back up to his suite. Hopefully to call the Geisners.

As I drove back over to Squaw, I wondered why I didn't tell him that Seth Riordan, the President of Plains Drilling, had a house here? It's not like he wasn't going to find out. Maybe he already knew?

=

The day had warmed up and people set up beach chairs in the parking lots near their cars. Sound systems blared, cocktails were mixed, and the smell of weed hung in the air. Dogs usually left in the back of pickups with the camper window up, or in cars with the windows open, wandered around the parking lot saying hi to everyone and peeing on things. Just outside of PlumpJack, I got lucky and snagged a parking spot. Sitting in the car, I tried first to call LaTisha Cimino then Steve

Diderowski. Both phones cut to voicemail. I hung up and climbed out of the car and started walking towards the ski school.

I thought to myself about why I was walking over there? Mike wasn't my partner. He wasn't my boyfriend. I couldn't run to him with every new detail. I resolved not to be clingy, even if I liked him—which I did--and he seemed to like me. I hadn't thought of a man in a romantic or sexual kind of way since Peter died. But I admitted to having some pretty graphic thoughts about Mike.

I plopped down in a patch of sunshine on a bench just outside the big concrete cable car building, and tried LaTisha Cimino again. This time she answered immediately.

I told her who I was, and about Jennifer's disappearance, which she knew nothing about. "Do you know anything about Seth Riordan or the ex-military guy who works for him?"

"Darnell Armstrong?" she said. "The person who can help you with information on those two is Steve Diderowski. He's keeps tabs on them. I work more on the media end of things. If you need a photograph, or archived news stories about them, I'm your girl."

"I'd love a current photo of both of them, if you have it."

She took my number and promised to text photos to me within five minutes.

"I think the world of that woman," she said. "I sure hope you're wrong about those two having anything to do with her disappearance."

"Me too," I told her, and we hung up.

I sat there in the sun for a couple minutes. It was the first time I'd been outside and warm at the same time since I got to California. My phone dinged, and I checked out the photos LaTisha sent. In a relaxed portrait shot, Seth wore a striped shirt with the collar open, and sat with a leg crossed ankle over knee, in an open, friendly sort of pose. He looked like the same white-bread rich guy he looked like fifteen years ago in Margaret's photo album. Only his hair was more gray, and he had on rimless glasses. If you saw this photo of him, and knew nothing else about him, you'd think he looked like a guy you'd be happy to sit and shoot the breeze with.

When I brought up the photograph of Darnell, I had to laugh. Compared to the old photograph Margaret showed me, he looked like a different person: he'd gone Western. His sandy hair had grown out to curl over his collar. He wore a dark brown or maybe black cowboy hat pulled low over his eyes, and a mid-calf canvas rancher coat with aqua and brown Tony Lama boots. He didn't look like any cowboy or rancher I knew. And having grown up in Colorado, I knew quite a few of them. He even had a rodeo belt buckle on his tooled leather belt.

"Wow," I whispered with a laugh.

I filed away the photos and tried Steve Diderowski again. He picked up just before his phone cut to voicemail. I repeated what I told LaTisha about Jennifer's disappearance.

"I'm very sorry to hear that," he said. "I have a world of love and respect for Jennifer."

"Do you have any idea who might profit from her disappearance?"

"Plains Drilling," he said immediately. "Their planned rape and pillage of Pennsylvania would be much easier and more profitable without her around. It's her voice that's kept the argument about an extraction tax alive. I don't know if you're aware of this, but our governor is bought and paid for by the fracking industry. He's staffed the environmental advisory boards with people from fracking, and he's the one leading the charge for natural gas companies to pay no extraction tax whatsoever in Pennsylvania. We'd be the only state with this kind of drilling with no taxes on it. And he's also fighting tooth and nail for a law that would override individual municipalities right to set their own zoning rules against fracking. For instance, no fracking within five hundred feet of a school, or a watershed, things like that. He wants frackers to come in and spread their filth any place they want. So Jennifer's voice has been the main thing standing between the frackers and the governor giving all our rights away."

"I had no idea. I mean I've heard about it happening in the East, and, of course, I'm familiar with it in Colorado and Wyoming, but I thought we'd learned something from the disasters we've had out West."

"Oh, we've learned a lot. But companies like Plains would just as soon we hadn't. And then we've got a governor who allows Homeland Security to spy on us and label us terrorists just because we say, 'Slow down, what's the rush. Let's be sure we do this the right way.'"

"Would you happen to know if Riordan is in the Tahoe area now? I heard he has a house here."

"Yes, he's owned his house there since 1986. The address is—." He gave me the address, as well as Seth's cell phone and home phone numbers. "He got into the Tahoe area on March 28th, by helicopter into Truckee Regional Airport from Reno Tahoe Airport where he left his company jet. He often does that since helicopters can usually make it into Truckee." He rattled this all off in a matter-of-fact voice, then lightened up a little when he said, "It's my job to keep track of the dick."

"Have you ever met him? What's he like?"

"He's a polite-to-your-face kind of guy. A little under six feet and in good shape for fifty-five. He's smart and charming when he needs to be."

"Thanks for all this. I'd also like to hear anything you can tell me about Darnell Armstrong. Starting with how good a skier he is."

"OK. But that'll take a few minutes. I've got to look it up. Can you hang on?"

"Sure," I said expansively. Then sat for the next few minutes wondering why the hell I said that. I felt antsy to get going, but I had no idea where.

Finally, Steve came back on the line.

"Darnell Armstrong is fifty-three. He was in the Military Mountaineering School. So I guess he's adequate on skis. Certainly adequate."

"Adequate?" I said. "Adequate in the same way Rolls Royce advertises that their cars engines are 'adequate?'" I asked.

"Probably," Steve replied. Apparently lacking a sense of humor.

"So Armstrong is ex-military then?"

"Yes. He had a long career in the military. He ended up in psychological operations, psy ops. But he was also in Special Forces for quite a while. Some kind of unit commander in Special Forces in Kuwait and Iraq. But he also served in South and Central America."

"Do you know much about his relationship with Seth Riordan?"

"He's been with Riordan for twelve years. Riordan made him head of security after a year. Fired the old guy and promoted Armstrong. I get the idea Armstrong is loyal to Riordan."

"Any idea why he's dressed like a cowboy?"

"Cowboy?"

"Any idea why he's dressed like a guy from New York City's idea of a cowboy?"

"It's a new look for him in the past year, year and a half. He used to be all ex-military. I guess I put it down to a mid-life crisis."

I laughed.

"I saw a photo of him in a past incarnation. Somehow he doesn't strike me as the mid-life crisis kind of guy. How about women?"

"He was married. Got a divorce about ten years ago. He has a daughter who is married now, and a grandaughter who's a year or so, maybe eighteen months old. I don't think he has lot to do with them."

"Where's he from?"

"Beckley, West Virginia. Coal mining town. Very poor. His father and older brother were killed in a mine collapse when he was four. His mother couldn't deal and turned to oxycodone, which I guess was plentiful and cheap around there back then. He went to live with a grandmother, who also died, so he ended up a ward of the state, lived in half a dozen different foster homes until he finished high school. Got to give him credit to rise up out of a life like that."

"Well, thanks for all this information."

"I hope it helps to find Jennifer," he said.

"I hope so, too."

Chapter 11

MONDAY, APRIL 4, 1 PM

The sky began clouding over as I spoke with Steve Diderowski. Just as we ended the call, snow began falling in clumps of snowflakes called graupel, which is never a good sign. Graupel in summer means thunderstorms coming soon. If you're up high in the mountains hiking, say in Colorado, graupel means run down mountain as fast as you can go. Lightning strikes above timberline are close-up and often way too personal. And those storms come in fast, just like this one.

I looked up mountain, and couldn't see the towers for the cable car. It had closed in that fast.

As I walked away from the cable car building, I spotted Mike carrying his skis over his shoulder. He looked tall and competent, and my heart sped up. He probably just downloaded in the cable car.

"Mike," I shouted.

He looked over towards me and a big grin spread across his face. As he strode across the plaza, I noticed for the first time that he had endearingly crooked teeth. His pointy cat incisors lapped over his front teeth. Which maybe explained his sexy downturned mouth. I'm not a fan of this trend of all kids having identical orthodontically straightened teeth.

"Hey there," he shouted over a sudden gust of wind. "Upper mountain is closing down just in time. This mess came in fast."

He fell in step alongside me, and we headed toward the Ski School.

"Just finished talking with Richard Fellatorre. He said you got Chloe in Squaw Kids."

"Yes." He smiled. "Nice girl. She's off swimming somewhere today. What'd you learn from Fellatorre?"

I filled him in quickly on what I'd heard from both Richard and from LaTisha and Steve.

"Did your crew make it into Reno last night?"

"No. That's on hold until the weather clears up."

"What a shame," he said, with a grin on his face.

"Any possibility you might drive over to Alpine with me once you're done with work, and I can try and talk to Riordan?"

"Sure," he said. "No problem. So no power last night?"

"No. Took a shower in the ski school locker room this morning."

"See. You should've taken me up on that dinner offer. How about tonight after we talk to Riordan?"

"I'd love to. Last night I crashed in on Aldous and Margaret. It turned out they both know Seth Riordan through Mitey Mites. Don't like him much."

As we neared the Ski School, and the big open space at the entrance to the Red Dog Chair and the Funitel Building, Grappa McDermott skied up and waved.

"Hey! Laura!" he shouted. "Wait a second."

He kicked out of his bindings and came trotting over to us in his ski boots the way only someone far younger than me can do.

"Hey, I just saw that guy again on KT. I think it was him. But far away. I'm pretty sure it was him because he's big."

He outlined the size of a full-grown black bear with his arms.

"And he skis wonky. Maybe he has a bad tune on that right ski?"

"Let's ski together tomorrow," I told him. "We'll just tour around and see if we can find him. Sound good?"

"Sure. That'd be awesome."

"What time?" I asked, figuring he probably sleeps until noon.

"Lifts open at nine," he said with a shrug.

"Ten's good," I told him. "Let's meet here, at 10:00?"

He looked back and forth between Mike and me. "Why do you suppose a guy led two women off to disappear into the forest, and is still hanging around here skiing?"

"I don't know," I told him. "Maybe he's trying to prove something to somebody."

"Maybe he just loves Squaw," Mike conjectured.

Grappa nodded, gave me a snappy salute, and turned back to his skis. Mike and I walked down off the snow.

It was an excellent question.

===

We drove through a world of white flowing towards us to split just before hitting the windshield. It was snowing so hard that trees loomed up like dreams out of the snow. Cars zoomed into view just a few feet from us, swooshing out of the white, then fading back into it.

I was glad Mike was driving. I don't mind snow-covered or icy roads, but this lack of visibility was beyond my comfort range. Once we reached Alpine Meadows, a family ski area tucked into a steep, avalanche-prone valley just behind Squaw, Mike cruised past the Riordan's mansion, then pulled into the parking lot of some condos while I dialed Seth's cell phone number.

He answered on the first ring.

"Hello, Mr. Riordan. I work at Squaw and I'm trying to help Richard Fellatorre look for his wife Jennifer, who's been missing off the slopes for a few days. I'm in your neighborhood and would like to drop by for a minute."

Seth agreed to speak with me. He gave me directions I didn't need, since we'd already scoped out the house, and we pulled into the main driveway two minutes later.

The sprawling dark wood and stone mansion had been built in the Old Tahoe style. A horseshoe driveway served as the main entrance. In the center of the horseshoe, we pulled up to a porte cochere buried in twenty feet of snow. Off to the right sat a three-car garage. Around the corner from that, farther off to the right, sat another wing of the house, and another three-car garage. A black Hummer H3 rested in the driveway in front of one of the garage bays. One of the garage doors was open, and I could see inside a couch and some chairs and a rug on the floor. Looked like some kind of an independent living situation for an older child.

Mike and I got out, and I rang the bell. An attractive woman with shoulder-length dark hair answered and ushered us in.

"I'm Ellen Riordan," she said with a warm smile. "I'm just getting you some refreshments, so come on in, then I'll be out of your way."

Inside the house continued the Old Tahoe theme with wood paneling, high ceilings with stripped log beams, and leather couches arranged around a blazing fireplace. Seth came in from a darkened hallway and took our coats. Both Mike and I bent down to pull off our snowy boots, then stepped into the great room of the lodge.

The house looked old, but the great room, kitchen, and dining room all made up one vast space, so the house probably had been extensively renovated in a style I'd often heard referred to by my Tahoe area friends as the Tahoe Cave.

Ellen came out of the kitchen carrying a wooden tray laden with cookies and translucent china. Mike stepped over and offered to take the tray. She passed it off to him with a smile and moved back into the big kitchen then returned carrying a silver carafe.

Ellen gestured to Mike to set the tray on a wood and copper coffee table. She placed the carafe next to it then stood beside her husband.

Ellen wore a camel wool skirt and matching sweater with a blue silk blouse. Her husband wore gray wool slacks and a navy sweater.

"Please sit," she said, directing this to Mike and me. We sat next to each other on a dark suede couch.

"Help yourselves," she told us.

I poured out two cups of coffee, gesturing towards Seth to ask if he wanted one, but he shook his head no with an almost imperceptible movement. Ellen hovered until we both took a cookie. A lemon wafer for me, and Mike selected a ginger cookie. After this, she excused herself and left the room.

Seth twisted around in his chair to watch his wife depart.

At the sound of a closing door, he said, "How can I help you?" He spread apart his hands in a seemingly gracious manner. "I'm terribly sorry to hear of Mrs. Fellatorre's disappearance. I'd heard two women were missing, but had no idea I knew one of them."

"I spoke to them about half an hour before they disappeared. In fact, Dave Geisner and I were the ones who came across Jennifer stuck in the snow. Dave left to attend to a multi-person casualty, and I got Jennifer up out of the deep snow, then skied off to get her some help. When I came back, the two women were gone, and no one has seen or heard from them since."

He nodded and made a tent with his hands in front of his chest.

"As I said, I heard two women were missing. But I heard they were from San Francisco. Jennifer," he paused. "How odd, but then I guess people come here from all over."

"I've heard that you're acquainted with Jennifer and her group PAMSD."

"PAMSD? His demeanor flicked from relaxed to suspicious. "Now who did you say you were?" he asked.

"Laura Bailey. I'm a snow scientist from Colorado State University. I've been working at Squaw Valley the last few days, and I've been asked by Jennifer's husband, Richard, to look into her disappearance."

"OK," he said, and nodded toward Mike. "And you look familiar. Who are you?"

"Mike Bernese. Director of the Squaw Valley Ski School."

"I thought I recognized you. You were the head of Alpine Meadows Ski School up until this year. Am I right?"

"Yes. I moved to Squaw this season."

"I remember your name. I've owned this house since 1986. Now listen," he said, obviously a man used to having people shut up and open their ears. "I'm all for an open and frank debate on energy matters. Jennifer and her group were sometimes strident, but I respect her as a well-informed, and well-spoken advocate for the environment. And many of the things she says are true. We've had problems. Fracking is a new technology. We in the industry feel it can be done safely, but I don't disagree with those who would like to see proof of that prior to bringing it into an area. But I want to make my position clear to you. I know Jennifer as someone who has seen her speak. I know nothing of her personal life. So why are you here?"

"I'm trying to speak with everyone who knew her, or perhaps saw her last Friday. And your name came up. I also heard she was suspected of sabotaging one of your wells at a delicate time. And I've heard that you and your spokesman Darnell Armstrong got into some kind of a contretemps with her."

Seth's white skin drained of what little color it had. He sat forward in his chair, then took a deep breath and willed himself to relax.

"It's true we suspect our well was sabotaged. We know it was. It's possible Jennifer's group was involved. Don't misunderstand me, we have certainly had our differences. As I said, she is intelligent, she does her homework, and at times that makes her dangerous to us, but I like to think, most times, we're of a like mind."

I could tell he was obfuscating, but not about everything. Like most people, he was spinning half-truths.

"Excuse me for a moment," he said, jumping to his feet, then he disappeared down that same dark hallway. A minute later, we heard raised voices coming from somewhere far off in the house. It went on for thirty seconds or so, then Seth came back and sat in the same chair.

"Excuse me," he said, and smiled. This guy made my skin crawl.

I took a sip of coffee, then set the delicate cup back down and leaned towards him.

"Was anyone from your company, anyone you know of, skiing at Squaw last Friday morning?"

I could hear muffled voices. It sounded like Ellen arguing with someone whose reply I couldn't hear. Maybe it was the son who liked skiing. What was his name? Ryan?

Seth sat up straighter in his dark green chair.

"Why do you ask that?"

"As soon as the weather breaks, we need to get in and dig out a tree well where we think perhaps the women fell. So the more people we talk to who have seen them, the better we know where to dig."

This wasn't quite the truth, but hopefully he wasn't as good at spotting an equivocation as I was.

"OK, that's enough of this. I'm a busy man. You need to leave now." He jumped up again from the deep embrace of his armchair.

"Ellen!" he called out. "Ellen!"

She came bustling into the room, wearing cheap terrycloth slippers, which seemed surprising. I guess I was expecting embroidered satin slippers or something.

"What?" she asked. And if I wasn't mistaken, there was a hint of irritation in her voice.

"Get them a card for Darnell and one for the law firm!" he snapped.

She moved off in another direction across the vast room.

"I'm sorry if I offended you, Mr. Riordan," I said. "I certainly didn't mean to."

He gave me a grim smile, and held out his hand.

"It's best if you deal with either Darnell Armstrong–he's the spokesman for Plains Drilling, but you know that–or speak to our lawyers in Philadelphia. It was a pleasure to meet you, Ms. Bailey, Mr. Bernese, but I don't believe we'll meet again. I hope you find Mrs. Fellatorre and her friend safe."

He gave us both a fleeting handshake.

By now Ellen had returned and handed me the business cards, hustling us along to the front door.

I glanced at the card on top and saw "Reed, Martin and Smith, Philadelphia Office."

"Mr. Riordan," I said. "You know both the women who disappeared. Alexis Page works for the law firm that represents you in Pennsylvania. Right?"

His face went blank. Completely blank.

"What a coincidence?" I said, smiling.

Mike and I sat down on a bench to pull on our boots, then donned our parkas, and Ellen hustled us out the big front door whispering, "I'm sorry for my husband's rude behavior. So sorry."

=

Once we climbed up into Mike's big truck, he fired up the ignition and got the defroster blasting. With his hands draped over the steering wheel, he stared straight ahead into the snowy windshield.

"I must have hit a nerve," I said, as I fastened my seatbelt and pulled it tight. "You know, in the past two days I've been ordered off the premises of more mansions than in my entire prior life."

Digging around in the side pocket, Mike pulled out the windshield scraper, stepped outside and made fast work of removing the half inch of ice and snow that had accumulated.

"I guess I just have the magic touch."

"In the past two days," he said, "we've pissed off more rich people than in my entire prior life."

He realized the side windows were also caked with snow and ice and climbed back out again to clear the remaining windows.

"That's not true," he said, sticking his head back in the cab. "Pissing off rich people is sort of a hobby. I've done it lots of times. You can't run a ski school in the Sierra without pissing off rich people, right and left. They're like gnats around here; swarms of them everywhere."

I chuckled and sank back into the warmth of my parka. The temp had dropped 30 degrees since earlier in the day when people were sitting in the parking lot smoking dope and soaking up the sun.

Mike climbed back in and put the truck in gear and pulled out of the driveway.

Half a mile up Alpine Meadows Road from the Riordan's house, we saw a wild chiaroscuro of headlights swirling off the snowbanks, and a second later made out a jumble of cars. Mike braked hard and slid sideways across the road. As soon as we slowed to a stop, I jumped out of the cab to see what was going on. Another car suddenly materialized out of the snow from behind and came straight at me. I ran and jumped over to the side near the big cliff shooting up at the edge of the road, and just then I saw a bright light up on the side of the mountain to my left, followed almost immediately by a tremendous WHOMP, and the thunder of an avalanche came roaring down and swept me up and away.

Chapter 12

MONDAY, APRIL 4, 11 PM

The first thing I noticed next was a banging headache, then a gray light seeping in through my eyelids. Apparently, I started making noises before I was even awake. Groaning, probably because my head felt like it was smashed apart. Then I heard someone calling my name. I felt a warm hand on my wrist, and someone prying my eyelids open and shining a bright light in my eyes, one then the other. That made my head explode: stars and fireworks went off inside my eyelids. Around then I realized it wasn't just my head that hurt: I hurt all over.

By then I could hear voices around me. Angry voices. I eased open an eyelid and through the haze saw Mike. He was shouting at someone to not do that again. Whatever *that* was, I didn't know. Felt pretty hazy about things at that point.

He leaned down with his face close to mine.

"Laura? Are you back with us?"

"Apparently," I croaked in a voice that sounded nothing like mine.

A grin spread across his face, starting with his eyes.

"Oh thank God," he said, and leaned down to kiss my cheek. "Thank God. Thought I'd lost you there for a minute."

"Let me examine her, and then I'll give you two some time alone."

A woman stood behind Mike. She had cropped brown hair and a no nonsense attitude that both comforted and scared me.

"Come on," she said, "come on." She moved Mike out of her way. "Out in the hall with you. Give me five minutes."

Mike gave my hand a squeeze, then moved away.

The woman, who wore a long, white doctor's coat, moved forward and raised my eyelids one at a time with her thumb.

"I'm Dr. McNaulty. How you feeling?" she asked.

"Like an elephant partied on my head."

"You have a concussion. That's going to give you a headache. Anything else hurt?"

"Everything hurts. Can I have some water?"

She held to my mouth a Styrofoam cup with a straw coming out of the top. "Easy, easy," she told me as I tried to raise my head. "Just a sip."

A sip is about all I could manage. My head sank back into the pillow, and the act of moving sent waves of pain rocketing up my spine and ricocheting around my skull.

"I think I'm going to puke."

"Breathe deep," she told me. "Deep breaths. You think that hurt? Vomiting is going to be a whole lot worse than that. Take deep breaths, and it'll pass."

Which it did.

She leaned over and listened to my heart through the hospital gown, then reached inside it and moved a stethoscope around, telling me to keep taking deep breaths.

"Think you can slowly roll onto your right side, but leave your head on the pillow? Don't try to lift it again, just slowly rotate."

I started to do that, and my whole left side felt broken. I gasped and froze.

"Yes," she said. "You have some substantial bruising on your left side. Keep rolling slowly."

"My right side hurts, too."

"You have some stitches on your right side. Just move slowly, and it should be fine."

Finally, I got far enough onto my right side that she could listen to my back. Once she finished, she said, "Why don't you try to stay on your side for an hour or so." She pushed pillows against my back to keep me wedged onto my side.

"How am I? What's the damage?"

"Do you know what happened?

"Avalanche."

"Yes. Luckily you weren't buried for long. But in the process of digging you out, some overzealous rescuers cut your right side up with shovels. So you have twenty-eight stitches in your right side. If your left arm hurts, it's from a tetanus shot. Your left side has substantial bruising sustained in the avalanche."

"But nothing's broken?"

"Let me finish. As you know, you have a concussion. I don't think it's too bad. But we'll get someone in here soon to give you a concussion test. Do you know where you are?"

"Truckee, I guess?"

"You're in the Tahoe Truckee Hospital. And your name?"

"Laura Bailey."

"What month is it?"

"April."

"OK, I don't think it's a severe concussion. But you've been banged around. You're in pain, and we'll get you something for that right away. Other than that, you have a broken left wrist. We're going to wait for the swelling to go down a bit, and then put a cast on it. Right now you have a brace. I think that's the extent of your injuries. We've done two abdominal scans looking for internal injuries, but we don't see anything. We'll keep a close eye on you for the next 48 hours. Looks like you were one of the lucky ones. Should I let your friend in?"

"Please."

"I'm going to send a nurse in with something for the pain. Should just be a couple minutes." She left the room.

I closed my eyes for a second, and when I opened them Mike was leaning down and looking into my face like he'd lost something there.

"Hey," he said. "How you feeling?"

"Sore. But glad to be alive."

"That's two of us."

"You're scaring me with that look on your face."

"Sorry," he said. "It's been a night."

"What time is it? How long ago did it happen?"

"It's about 11:00 p.m. Just happened a few hours ago. You were in the Emergency Room quite a while for them to run tests. They just got you into a room a few minutes before you woke up."

"I wasn't out that long?"

"You woke up in the car on the way to the hospital, but then you faded out again. And you've been in and out since then."

"What'd I miss?"

"You want the whole story?"

I waved him on with a twirl of my unbroken wrist.

"So when I got the truck stopped, and you for some reason leaped out of the cab—and I'm saying this in the nicest possible way—but when you leaped out of the cab like an idiot, I saw a light from what had to be a hand charge go off about a hundred feet up the side of that mountain. Followed immediately by what looked like a slab avalanche. That's a known avalanche spot. It's even posted. But this didn't happen by accident. I'm positive about that. So once you were swept up, the snow continued moving for ten or eleven seconds. And I knew the clock was ticking down for you. But, luckily, everyone there was a local and knew what to do. I kept trying to figure where you most likely were. Again, lucky you just got caught in the edge of it. You didn't get the full blast. So everyone comes running with shovels and avalanche poles. I'm thinking you're probably at the crux of some cars. The mountainside of the cars were buried, but the sides away from the avie were still clear.

"Then some kid home from Berkeley starts screaming 'Over here! Over here!' So a bunch of us go running over to where he's standing, and I turn a flashlight on where he's pointing, and there's a big hank of wavy blond hair sticking out of the snow. So we start digging like crazy. Most of us had avalanche shovels, but some people had regular shovels for getting their trucks unstuck. Anyways, I'm shouting for everyone to come in from an angle, so we don't cut you. It was pandemonium. Everyone wanted to get you out so badly. It took us four minutes and sixteen seconds to get your face clear. But you had your hands up against your face. And, honey, that saved your life. But you were unconscious. So we kept digging like crazy.

141

"Around then, some ski patrollers showed up, and they got every-body but me away, and then the three of us started digging more care-fully. And in another minute, we had you freed to the waist. You were sitting straight up with your legs out in front of you. Your head was rolling to one side in a way that made me sick to my stomach. It was like chipping away at granite, trying to dig that snow out. But we finally got you loose, so I picked you up and ran across the debris field to this woman's SUV, on the far side of the avie debris. Turns out she's a nurse. She wanted to stay with you in the back seat, so thank god she let me drive. I got you to the hospital pretty fast. Faster than most people make that drive."

The pain from, apparently, a bunch of shovel cuts on my right side, had gotten pretty intense, and where was that nurse? I eased back into the pillows and found that hurt, too.

"Will you, slowly, pull the pillows away from my back?"

Mike moved around the bed and eased them away from under me, so I could do a slow slump onto my back.

"Better?"

I started to nod, but that hurt too much, so I said, "Yes," instead. "Will you find out where the nurse is?"

He disappeared for thirty seconds, then came back in with a woman nurse on his heels.

"Not feeling so good?" she asked me. "Where do we hurt?"

"Head. Body. Everything," I told her.

She smiled sympathetically, and shot a needle full of fluid into a joint in my IV.

"This should help you start feeling better right away."

By the time she said it, I could already feel it easing through my wracked body. "Yeah," I whispered.

She smiled and bustled on out.

Mike reached down and rubbed my right hand, the one place I didn't hurt.

"So what do you remember?" he asked me again.

Talking felt like swimming in mud, but I tried to oblige him.

"Jumping out of the truck like an idiot, of course." I smiled all dopey at him. "Then I saw that car come out of the snow at me, so I leaped over to the shoulder, on the mountain side to avoid the car, and then like you, I saw a flash and heard it a millisecond later. And I thought right away it was a hand charge. But how did all the cars come to be piled up right there? Awfully convenient."

"I didn't hear this while we were digging you out," he said. "I had tunnel concentration at that point, but later the nurse, Gloria, told me the other guys driving said they'd had lasers shined in their eyes. Green lasers that blinded them for a few seconds. Long enough for the pileup to happen. We came up just after that."

"Jeez."

"Yeah," he said. "This wasn't any accident. So then what?"

"So of course I'm thinking, Great. I'm in avie without my beacon on, without my avalanche float. Nothing. So I'm trying to swim through that shit, which felt like setting up concrete. I'm trying to swim and stay as close as I can to the top, but when I felt it slowing down, I got my hands up against my face. That's all I remember. I was hoping I had up and down right. That's it."

What I didn't tell Mike was that I was feeling pretty close to Peter. Felt like he was right there. It seemed like there was a leisurely span of time for me to think about how I'd be seeing him again soon. My body sort of took over on the whole trying-to-save-itself thing, while my mind went somewhere else: to a bluebird day, on a mountain, with nothing but untracked snow in front of us, and Peter and me standing there on our skis looking down at the vast expense of snow, almost ready to push off. If I hadn't made it, I think we'd still be making turn after lazy turn down that mountainside together.

I realized then that Mike was still holding my right hand.

"How you feeling?" he asked, and leaned over to run his fingers down my cheek.

"Not bad now. Just sort of freaked out because that is the last way I'd want to die. No kidding. I'd rather be burned at the stake. What do you think happened? It seems pretty coincidental to me.

We get kicked out of the Riordan's house and POW. An avie hits only me?"

"I don't know," Mike said. "Can you rest now? You're pale. Don't you have a headache? The doctor said you took quite a blow to the head."

"I've got a headache, but that stuff she gave me works pretty well. It's not so bad now." I fell quiet for a minute. That peaceful place I found with Peter, as I must have been dying, seemed like it happened to someone else. Instead, I felt filled with shock at the tawdriness of the fact that someone did that to us on purpose.

"Get some sleep now. We can talk about this more in the morning."

I realized with a jolt this was what Alexis and Jennifer probably went through as they died somewhere on Snow King Mountain—probably in that tree well. Hopefully, they had their own happy places to ease off to with their own loved ones to comfort them as their bodies fought to stay alive.

"This is what happened to Alexis and Jennifer," I said to Mike. "I've got to find out what happened. I can't let this go until I know."

Mike stared at me for a long span of seconds without a word. "No," he said finally, "it's obvious you aren't letting go of this."

I raised my hands, and for the first time noticed my left wrist was encased in a navy-blue brace.

"Tell you what—see that recliner over there?"

He gestured at a tan armchair on the far side of the room. `

"If you're ready to sleep, I'm going to move over there. But I'll be right here if you need anything."

"Are you always such a good guy?"

"No," he said. "This is just an act for you."

ACT III

Chapter 13

TUESDAY, APRIL 5, 5:45 AM

I always imagined that a peacefulness descended and then shortly after that, you died. I lay awake in my hospital bed thinking about how schizophrenic it seemed, the split between my body struggling to live, and my mind already someplace else, someplace better. How sleazy that someone was trying to put me there, on the other side, with no thought or empathy towards my plans, my hopes, my future. These insights into my own near death experience filled me like a big weepy bowl of empathy soup for Jennifer and Alexis and whatever the hell it was that happened to them.

I thought of all the people who have come and gone through my life. The people I loved, the people I liked, the ones I didn't like at all. They were with me, and now so many of them were gone from my life. How many of those hundreds, maybe thousands of people could I even find today? How many of their names would I remember? We pass in and out of each other's lives. And there are so few people we manage to hold on to.

Richard and Chloe needed to know what happened to Jennifer. She couldn't just be another person who slipped away. And Alexis had a life; somewhere there were people who loved her, and who would lose some of the joy in their lives when they heard she was gone. The walls of the hospital closed in around me. I had to get out of there and find those women. Find out what happened. Any shred of hope I clung to that they'd turn up alive and apologetic, embarrassed at their thoughtlessness, had disintegrated. I knew they were dead. I just had to find out what happened.

Inside the hospital it apparently never got darker than twilight. My window looked out on a parking lot, and I watched as the inky blackness of night faded to the indigo of dawn.

Shortly after that, Mike stirred and woke up.

"You're awake already?" he said. "Need anything?"

"I'm good. Just thinking it all over."

"Any decisions?" He stood up, stretched, then walked over to the bed. I shook my head no.

"I'm off then to check out that avie site. I'll see you after work this afternoon. I'll call to check on you. See what you want for dinner."

"This," he added, "is how I get you to eat dinner with me."

We held each other's gaze for a long moment.

"I'll let you know what I find out tonight," he said. And then he was gone.

I pushed the button for the nurse. Now that I was more awake, I realized my head was killing me again.

After breakfast, another abdominal scan, and the exhausted Dr. Denise McNaulty's visit, then I was left alone around eleven.

The ringing of my phone woke me up. It was Dave Geisner.

"How you feeling?"

"I'll live"

"I heard it wasn't too bad. I wanted to give you a head's up that my brother will be taking over the case now."

"What?"

"Yeah. Daniel Burdick's car was towed from the lot at the Crystal Palace this morning, and inside they found the women's luggage. All their stuff. So the investigation's focused on him now. I guess things are about wrapped up."

"How'd his car get towed? He's parked there for years?"

"It's clearly marked as parking for guests only. Signs all over the place saying no ski parking, and you'll be towed if you do park there."

"But people eat there all the time. Shop there."

"You're supposed to have the valet park you if you're not staying there. It's clearly marked."

"That's just ignorant. How come his car was towed today? What did Burdick say about how the bags got there?"

"Nobody's talked to him yet. He hasn't been located."

I thought to myself that the Geisners were clearly a couple of lazy idiots.

"So Burt wanted me to tell you he's sending a deputy by to pick up everything you have on the case so far."

"I don't have anything to give him."

"Listen, Bailey, don't screw around. This is now an official investigation."

Choosing to ignore that, I pressed his weak side: "Have you found the missing women?"

"I can't comment on that." He sighed then in a resigned voice said, "but no."

"And even if his car was towed, why did they search it? Surely that's not SOP for tow companies?"

"You tell the deputy all your theories. I don't know every detail about this and that. I'm just relaying what Burt told me."

Clearly, whatever idiocy was at play here, he wasn't going to tell me about it.

"OK, Dave. Consider me told."

I went to disconnect the call, and at the very last second I heard him say, "I'm real sorry about this."

But it was too late to say anything in response. I'd already disconnected.

===

A half hour later, an large, absurdly young detective wearing what looked like riot gear poked his head into my room.

"Ms. Bailey?"

"Yes."

"Sheriff Geisner sent me to pick up whatever information you have on the Fellatorre-Page case."

He stepped forward into the room. He was probably twelve or thirteen. His Adam's apple bobbed up and down when he spoke like on a Saturday morning cartoon. I tried not to look. He had an oddly elongated head.

"You've wasted a trip because I don't have anything. I haven't written down a single word."

Drooping his big head in despair, the kid stared down at his feet.

"Have you learned anything you haven't written down?"

"Haven't learned anything," I told him. I've revised my estimate of his age up to seventeen-eighteen, which meant he's probably twenty-one or twenty-two.

"Ma'am," he said, "I can't go back to Burt—I mean the sheriff—and tell him that. He'll think I didn't even come by."

"You've got to have something?"

He nodded like a bobblehead and looked up at me hopefully.

"OK."

At that, the deputy pulled a leather notebook off his hip and took a chewed stub of pencil out of his pocket. He held it poised over the paper in his left hand.

"I think it's too early for the sheriff to close up the case and try pinning everything on Daniel Burdick. It might be him. But it might not. That's all I've got."

He met my gaze and nodded again.

"OK, Ma'am. At least that's something, but why do you feel that way?"

"I've come to think there are other suspects, too. Look into the company Jennifer Fellatorre lobbies against. Look into the company Alexis Page works for. Look into all the usual suspects–family members, things like that. Burt needs to consider who the actual victim was and who ended up being collateral damage."

"Thank you, Ma'am."

He snapped the notebook shut and hooked it back onto his belt, then settled his hands on his hips.

"Will you let me or the Sheriff know if you hear anything else?"

"Will do."

"How much longer will you be in the hospital?"

"Is that you asking or Burt?"

"Well, the Sheriff wants me to ask." He blushed.

"I don't know. Probably several more days."

I told him that in the hopes it would get Burt to leave me alone. I planned on being out of there way sooner than that.

"Thanks, Ma'am. I wish you a speedy recovery. I got caught in an avie on a snowmobile outside of Bishop a couple years ago. Thought I was a goner. I still wake up in a panic. It was the most awful thing I've ever been through."

"Thank you, Deputy. It was pretty awful."

He turned for the door, then looked back, "Ma'am."

I sank back into the pillows. "Ma'am?" When did I get that old? Is thirty really that old?

=

An hour later I woke up and found the sunlight streaming through breaks in the leaden clouds. The light coming through the pines outside my window filtered down at a tall angle like the light through stained glass windows in a cathedral, a splay of refracted colors on my white bedding. I watched it change, lighting up the top of one tree, then a few minutes later moving on to another. I felt relieved and happy to still be alive.

I checked my phone and found thirty-six e-mails. One of them was from my department chair, Lee Borders, back in Fort Collins. A guy I had always gotten along with well. I clicked on Lee's e-mail first.

Dear Laura,

What are you up to? I thought you were there to check on your snow station, but I just got a phone call from President Fredricks, and I NEVER get calls from that far up the food chain—asking me what in the hell you're up to. He received a complaint from one of the university's biggest donors that you've been harassing him, and what's worse, doing it in the name of the university.

151

I don't mean to be a hard-ass here, but Fredricks actually asked me whether or not you have tenure yet. Need I say more? So a word of caution–whoever it is you're pissing off, back-off. Apparently, this fellow already donated the funds for an endowed chair in geology, and is thinking of giving us a huge amount more for a big new science library. He's a big fish the president's had on the line for a while and apparently is hoping to land even more profitably, and you're in danger of screwing it up.

Don't tell me what's going on, I don't want to know, but whatever it is, knock it off and get back to work.

Lee

To say I was shocked would be an understatement. That bastard Seth. That lying bastardly bastard. Of all the schools with energy-production-leaning geology and mining departments, why did he have to give money to my school? But then why was I thinking he only threw money at my school? Obviously, giving judiciously here and there is a form of lobbying that works. I've just never run up against one of these big money energy guys before.

I laid back in bed thinking about it, taking some deep breaths to calm myself down. What was I going to do? I was going up for tenure next year, so was I supposed to back off, let him get away with killing whomever gets in his way? Alexis? Jennifer? Me?

What would the great aunts have done? Back off? Leave Richard and Chloe hanging? That's as likely as the witches in MacBeth getting frightened and backing off. That's a recurring image I have of the great aunts—indeed the Weird Sisters—and made even more appropriate by the way they used to stand in a circle around a campfire outside our cabin next to Big Thompson Creek, frying trout in a cast iron frying pan and harping at each other about how they were each doing it wrong: "You cook trout in pure butter." "It should be a mix of butter and lard." "Flip it now." "It's not brown enough yet." "Who wants burned trout again?"

And besides all that, the right and the wrong of the situation, I'm a scientist, and as a scientist, I'm curious as hell to figure out what happened.

Despite all this roiling around in my brain, I slipped off to sleep again. It had to be the pain meds.

When I woke up there was a voicemail from Mike saying he'd taken off work early, and asking me to text him with my dinner order. Nothing sounded good. Between being furious, in pain, and doped up, my appetite had left the building. Finally, I texted back "Spicy tuna sushi," just because it was my default lunch.

The smell of food woke me. The dark blue of the end of twilight had fallen among the trees of the parking lot.

Mike was next to my bed.

"Hey gorgeous! I brought food."

Leaning down, he brushed my hair aside to give me a kiss on the cheek.

"Here's your sushi." He rolled the bed table up from my knees to over my lap and set a tray of sushi and a pair of chopsticks in front of me. I pressed the button to raise the bed up into a sitting position.

"And here's my dinner."

He lifted a brown paper bag from the floor and began unpacking take-out boxes. He opened a big one and tilted it forward to show me.

"Noodle soup."

It was a miso broth with coiled ramen noodles and pea pods floating on top.

"Spicy tempura shrimp."

He tilted another box forward to reveal big prawns in a crispy coating. My mouth began to water. He opened another box filled with stir-fried vegetables.

"And, finally, sticky rice."

He opened the fourth container and set it on the bed table.

"Yours looks better," I told him.

"I think so, too. In fact, I thought what kind of a woman would order cold raw fish on a ten-degree day? And then it came to me: a woman with a brain injury. And since you have a brain injury, I thought maybe it would be wise to order enough of the good stuff for both of us." He grinned, pleased with himself.

"Did you also plan what you were going to say all the way over here?"

He kept on grinning as he stripped off his parka and hat.

"I sure did."

From another bag he began unloading plates, small cardboard bowls, utensils and packets of wasabi and soy sauce.

"So dig in."

Suddenly, I was starving.

A few minutes later, over the ruins of the meal, I told him about Daniel's car being towed from the Crystal Palace parking lot.

"He seemed like the one normal guy in that lot." He held up the last shrimp in his chopsticks. "Want it?"

"All yours."

I spun the tray of untouched sushi slowly in circles on the bed table.

"What reason would he have to kill those two?"

"From what Dorian Gray told me, Daniel and Alexis were up for partnerships, and Anna and Alexis got them. Maybe he was angry over that? And I guess Alexis teased him."

"He killed two women because Alexis teased him? What about?"

"Don't know. And since when is a car searched when it's towed for illegal parking?"

Mike's long-limbed body dangled over the edge of the small chair. His arms draped onto the bed table. My heart lurched at his awkwardness, his scruffy three-day growth of beard. I smiled and lay my cheek against his arm, and he put his arms around me and held me for a minute until I had to squirm away, the stretch in my left oblique excruciating.

"I guess I have to tell you what I found at the avalanche site?"

"Ah, yes."

"First off, I spoke with the guys involved in the original crash. I wanted to hear whatever it was they had to say about the laser. So the first guy, John Cummings, said the laser hit him in the eyes and blinded him. For a second he had no night vision. But what he did have was an ability to still see the laser, and he followed it up the mountain on the left."

"Where the avalanche came from?"

"Exactly. And then he saw it flash back, behind him, and that's when he hit the guardrail, and the pickup behind him rear-ended his car. So that's how the sequence of events went. Both drivers agreed on that. We pulled up, you jumped out, the car came up behind us and skidded into the berm to avoid hitting you, a whomp, a flash, and the avie started. Everyone seems certain that, until we stopped and you jumped out, there was no sound from the avalanche. And you were out there, what, not a minute? When did you hear the avalanche?"

"I was definitely out there before the sound started. So maybe thirty? Forty-five seconds? I ran out of the way of the pickup, bounced off the snow berm, and those guys were outside, on the far side of their vehicles from me. And then whomp. So what did you find?"

"I found tracks from skis with skins. The trigger point was a little over a hundred feet up from the road. And the tracks led right to the trigger point. There's a cliff face there, a rock face. Short and deep, very steep there. The avie went all the way down to the rock."

"Jeez," I said. "So that was a lot of snow. Snow pack had to be what, twenty, thirty feet?"

"More, since the snowblowers had really loaded up that hillside. It wouldn't have taken much."

I fell silent, fighting down the panicked "what ifs" as they rose up into my throat.

"So whether someone was trying to cause a catastrophe, or whether it was a direct result of our chat with Riordan, I don't know."

"How could someone have gotten so quickly from Riordan's onto skis and up that mountainside? I don't see how that would work? Even if someone else had been in Riordan's house, how could they have gotten there so fast?"

"They must have left before we did," he said. "And we did sit in the driveway for a while."

"I guess it's possible. I thought I heard Ellen arguing with someone while we were talking to Seth. And it looked like someone was living in that one garage bay. He might have had one of his henchmen do it. Darnell Armstrong was in the Army Mountaineering Division. I'm sure he has the skills. But is Jennifer's detailing the sins of this kind of natural gas drilling going to stop it? From what Jennifer's partners LaTisha and Steve told me, the governor of Pennsylvania is in the pocket of these big drilling companies. He's refusing to have an extraction fee on the gas removed from the ground—which would make Pennsylvania the only state with this kind of drilling without an extraction tax. He's fighting tooth and nail against additional safety measures. He even wants to bring in big refineries on a tax-free basis. So what damage is Jennifer going to do? She's an inconvenience. She's not stopping anything. Why would he bother with all the risks inherent in getting rid of her and then us, too, like this?"

"Maybe he thinks she can turn around public sentiment and put a cloud over his company's activities," Mike said, "not to mention the immense profitability."

I had to read more on this. That was something I could do from my hospital bed. Maybe Mike was right, and it was still in play and Jennifer's ability to turn public sentiment would be enough to pressure the legislature to vote against the governor's plan?

We sat in silence for a minute, then Mike let go of my hand, stood up and began to clear up the detritus of our dinner.

"Also, Dave Geisner told me a snowplow at the Tahoe Biltmore hit a black Mercedes SUV that turned out to belong to Alexis Page. It'd been there several days, buried in snow. That's why they hadn't found it earlier."

"Were the keys in it?"

"No. Locked up tight. They fingerprinted it, but that's all I've heard."

Outside, darkness had settled.

"The snow's finally eased up. Not supposed to start again until late tomorrow. I heard from Dave that he's planning to dig out that tree well tomorrow after the lifts close."

I bolted straight up in bed. "Really?"

"I don't like that look on your face."

"I've got to get out of here."

"What did the doctor say?"

"She hasn't said anything. But there's no reason to stay. They can either cast my hand, or I can go on wearing this brace. I'm just beat up, not broken. I've skied with a little broken wrist before."

"I don't doubt that," Mike said. "But no checking out until after you clear it with your doctor. Deal?"

"OK."

Once the dinner mess was cleared away, Mike laid down next to me in the narrow hospital bed for long enough for me to drift off.

I woke up a while later, and Mike carefully extricated himself, and gave me a big kiss that got my heart racing. He stood up and pulled on his outer gear, then left to go check back in with work.

=

Later that evening, I was lying in bed worrying and feeling guilty about those women. Why didn't I hike out through the deep snow and back onto the main slope and send someone else for the ski patrol? But I realized that would have taken longer than just skiing out.

It was 7:00 p.m. in Truckee, meaning it was 10:00 back East, but I decided to take a chance and call LaTisha Cimino. She answered right away and told me that little had actually been decided in Pennsylvania regarding Marcellus Shale drilling. The governor supported a plan that would override individual municipalities' laws regarding fracking: how close to residential areas wells can be placed, how carefully the settlement ponds have to be fenced off and lined, and he replaced the patchwork of regulations with an overriding set of state regulations that would take precedence. Of course, he had already made certain that the committee that set the statewide regulations was composed of people from the fracking industry. Also, no final decision had been reached on whether or not to institute an extraction tax. Though even some gas companies were coming out in support of a small extraction tax, the governor remained firmly against it.

"So there's still a lot Jennifer could do to cause Plains Drilling problems?" I asked LaTisha.

"Let me ask you this," LaTisha said. "If Plains isn't worried, why have they hired army psy ops people to sway public opinion on fracking? Why did the state Task Force on Terrorism label us terrorists? We've found some of their internal memoranda where they call PAMSD the number one terrorist threat to the Commonwealth of PA. Why would they do that if they weren't worried?"

Woman had a point. I thanked her, and we rang off.

Then I called Steve Diderowski again. He went into more detail about why Jennifer worried Plains Drilling.

"It's not so much what she's done so far," he told me. "It's more what she's going to do. In the midst of a crowd of screaming red-faced protestors, Jennifer's is the quiet, eloquent voice with all the facts. So when they try to lie about their record at public hearings, Jennifer quietly disputes what they say with the facts. And already judges have ruled in her favor on pre-trial motions."

Jennifer coalesced in front of me. Not only did I see her as a human being, but as someone out there doing good in the world. While Alexis remained an enigma. Who could fill in the details on Alexis?

I tried calling Burt Geisner, but he wasn't in, so I left a message asking him to call my cell.

Just then, Dr. Denise McNaulty came striding into my room with four students in tow.

"We have here a thirty-year old woman, who is very fit, and was caught up in an avalanche twenty-four hours ago. What should we be looking for?"

She got half a dozen answers ranging from internal injuries to menopause.

They went on for another minute talking about me as if I wasn't there.

"You all need to leave," I told them, but no one listened.

"You need to leave!" I said again. No response.

"GET OUT!" I finally had to shout, which left my head pounding with nauseating waves of pain.

"Get out!" I said again, more softly.

Finally, Dr. McNaulty turned around and looked at me, shocked. The students all stood frozen in space. She could tell I wasn't kidding, and shooed the students out of my room, then came back in.

"I'm terribly sorry," she said. "There's no excuse for not even acknowledging your presence."

I was furious and held myself back from screaming at her by thinking of how much it would hurt if I did.

"I want to check out," I told her, speaking rapidly.

"Now?"

"Right now."

"Listen to me for just a minute. I've been working for forty-eight hours straight since 80's closed and no one can get in to replace me. The students have been stuck here, too. They were supposed to be back in Davis two days ago. We're all trying to make the best of a bad situation. So I apologize for the way both I and my students acted, but I don't want you to check out tonight. Please stay, and we'll get a cast on your wrist. Then tomorrow morning, I promise I'll be in here early, by, say, 7:00 a.m. or so, and I'll give you one more check over, and then if all is well you can check out. Is that a deal?"

I was thinking maybe I had over-reacted a little. I held her gaze for a moment.

"From one mountain woman to another?" she said.

"OK. But you'll be here early?"

Her tired face melted into a smile.

Chapter 14

WEDNESDAY, APRIL 6, 6:30 AM

Dr. McNaulty proved true to her word and showed up at 6:30 in the morning, without her students, and looking more rested. She even handed me a coffee—a soy latte extra hot, what supposedly all the hard-core ski girls drank—and a muffin from Coffeebar, the best coffee place in Truckee.

"Thank you. I'm flattered I rate a soy latte."

"I've heard about you," she replied. "It's a peace offering." After examining my wrist, Dr. McNaulty said the swelling was down enough to put a cast on it and send me on my way.

While sitting on the side of the bed waiting for the nurse to arrive and cast my hand, I put on my favorite Tahoe morning show. This time the host was a joking man with a goggle sunburn, an untucked plaid shirt, Carhartt pants, and short-cropped hair—a well-known rock and ice climber. In reading the local news he mentioned a tremendous amount of unplowed snow on Donner Pass, something like thirty or forty feet worth, after an avalanche up there crossed I-80 in the night.

He then cut away to the blonde who played the straight woman for all the other jokers. Apparently, she wasn't ready because her sweater was unzipped down the front, showing a lot of black bra and cleavage, and this wasn't that type of show. She sat with her legs asprawl in front of her and her blond mess of hair in her hands, groaning.

"Too much Jameson's."

The scene cut back immediately to the goggle-tanned host.

"Whoops!" he said with a big grin, and launched back into a repeat of the weather.

Two minutes later, the same blonde came on again, this time with her sweater primly zipped into a turtleneck, bright-eyed and smooth-haired to give her update on happenings around Tahoe. The first happening she mentioned was that an avalanche had closed Highway 89 from Truckee to Squaw Valley in the early hours of the morning.

My cell vibrated on the bed table. A quick glance at the screen assured me Mike was on the line.

"Hey there, good morning. What's up?" I said.

"Good morning to you. You're sounding more like yourself. How you feeling?"

"Much better. Already saw the doctor and gotten the green light to get out of here."

"I assumed that'd be the case. Listen, I can come by and help you check out, but I was going to try and get Chloe over to talk with a friend of mine. He's a sports psychiatrist. But he's got kids himself, and he's also just a great guy. I thought maybe it would help her deal with the stress of what's going on."

"Good idea."

"Well, maybe, but are you going to be all right checking out on your own? I went by Rita's last night and picked up some clothes. They're in the closet there in your room, and I also had your rental car brought over from Squaw. It's down in the parking lot, to the far left as you go out the back door of the hospital."

"Of course," I told him. "Thank you. That was a lot of arranging for you to do. Can we meet up later at Squaw?"

"Absolutely," he said, and we rang off.

Turned out it wasn't easy getting out of the hospital without someone there to take charge of me. After wrangling with nurses for twenty minutes, Dr. McNaulty finally came by and signed my release papers, making it possible for me to head out under my own recognizance. On the front seat of the rental lay a worn left-hand ski glove. One of Mike's, no doubt. I hadn't thought that my own glove wasn't going to fit over the cast, but obviously he did.

In the closet of my hospital room I'd found clean jeans and a sweater, along with clean underwear and socks, but my red parka I'd been wearing ever since I got to Squaw hung in tatters from shovel cuts and a sleeve having been ripped off. Thankfully, the early morning air hovered around 30, so I got out to my car without freezing. I headed over to Rita's, where the inside temp was around 20, as usual, and changed into ski clothes, then grabbed my green parka, my skis, boots and poles and headed out the door for Squaw. I had some lawyers to track down. Hopefully, 80 would remain closed at least one more day.

Since Highway 89, which leads from Truckee to Squaw Valley, was closed, I was going to have to drive out Brockway Road on California Road 267 to the old biker town of King's Beach, and then around the northern part of Lake Tahoe to Tahoe City where I'd pick up 89 back to Squaw. It was going to a add good half hour of driving but also a gut punch of a gorgeous view of Lake Tahoe through the pines at the top of Brockway Summit. It also would take me near the Hempfield Estate. Maybe I could find Sean home alone. Anna couldn't be there with him all the time, could she?

====

The long driveway into Hempfield Estate lay covered in four or five inches of slush. I pulled up into a circular parking area next to the main house, and parked next to a silver Audi TT Roadster, a low-slung piece of engineering. Audi's are notorious for being terrible in snow since their clearance is so low, and I personally wouldn't buy a convertible if I lived in Tahoe. I walked up to the front door. The way the house was situated, you only got the full view of Tahoe at the front door.

The view staggered me. Low leaden clouds reflected a deep silvery blue on the water, making the whole twenty-four-mile-long expanse of Tahoe look like an underwater cave.

I rang the doorbell and heard it gong mournfully inside the mansion. After a minute, I pounded on the big wooden door, like a peasant begging entrance at the castle gate. The wet wind off the water reminded me I was just out of the hospital. It blasted me in a way that suggested maybe I should be back at Rita's in bed.

A pale, sleepy Anna Strunk opened the door. Seeing her face in daylight without makeup, I realized again what amazing translucent skin she had. Apparently, on her face, neck, and cleavage, at least, the woman had not one pore.

She looked at me with genuine surprise." I heard you got caught in an avalanche. What're you doing here?"

"I want to talk to you some more about Alexis. I can't get a picture of her in my mind. I've heard a couple times that she was interested in some new guy. Maybe a client? Do you have any idea who that is?"

Her face hardened over, and she snorted a laugh. "I'd hardly call him 'some new guy.'"

"Well, is she seeing someone?"

"No one you could visit dressing the way you do." She gave me a nasty once over to include my entire wardrobe.

I clasped my hands over my chest, "You got me—aside from my ski clothes, it all comes from Costco. But then where's the shame in that? So aside from your friend Sean Flaherty, you must mean Seth Riordan?"

That took her aback. Apparently, she had no inkling I'd be able to put together her innuendos. "I heard you were over at his house, bugging him about something. I can't figure you out."

"Likewise. You don't seem to fit in with all those upper-crust types you work with. And I don't mean that as an insult. You seem tougher and more pragmatic than your colleagues. You don't come from that same cushy background as Alexis, Sean, and Daniel, do you?"

Anna opened the door further and stepped outside, up close to me. She was four or five inches shorter and had to look up into my face.

"You're damn right I'm tougher than the rest of them. I came from nothing."

"Are you from the East Coast like Alexis and Jennifer?"

"Hardly! I'm from a lovely place in the East Bay, Pittsburg. Know it?"

"I know where it is."

"Then you probably also know what an armpit it is."

"I've heard. Does your family still live there?"

I asked this, but I didn't think she had any family. She was more like me.

"Family?" She shook her head. "Do you mean the father I never knew, or my heroin addict mother? I lived in sixteen different foster homes from the time I was seven until I turned eighteen."

"Sixteen different homes?" The number staggered me.

"Well, that's putting an ironic twist on the usual definition of 'home.'"

"That must have been hard. I also lost my parents at seven."

She brightened, and a brittle smile blossomed on her lovely face.

"Let's have a sleepover and do each other's hair and talk about how hard it was."

The smile cracked and fell away.

"Save the pity," she went on. "It made me tough. And that's why I'm the new partner, not Daniel."

"What kind of relationship do you have with him?"

"Not bad before, not much worse now."

"Is there anyone at the firm he doesn't get along with? Anyone here?"

"Well, Alexis. I told you that."

"But Alexis was expected to make partner. So why Alexis?"

"Oh, it's not that."

"Then why?"

She smiled and turned her gaze to the lake. "I'm done talking about this. I've been cooperative, and now I'm done."

"One last question—" I called after her.

She swiveled around and fixed me with an evil eye.

"Does Seth Riordan know Daniel Burdick?"

She looked taken aback, then quickly collected herself. "Fuck you," she said quietly, and closed the big door in my face.

Back in the car, I started the motor and waited for the seat heaters to tick on. So Seth Riordan was the client Alexis was talking about. That was who she said she'd seen and wanted to leave Jennifer on the mountain, injured, and go chasing after. And, evidently she wanted to use her sexual powers to keep him pumping in those billable hours to the firm where she had known she'd soon be a partner. Or maybe she just found his aura of power attractive. Ick.

I had no trouble imagining Alexis and Seth as a couple. Could he have also been the guy who came back and led them off into the trees? She was probably his main legal counsel in Pennsylvania. It made perfect sense. Two Brahmins joining forces, each with a secret agenda. Alexis wanted Seth's money and power. Seth wanted to get rid of his nemesis Jennifer. Made all the sense in the world. But then why did Alexis end up dead, too? Was she simply collateral damage? Or was there a reason for him to get rid of both of the women?

On the way back into Squaw, I peeled off to the left towards The Resort at Squaw Creek and parked in the lower lot to take a look around. I hadn't been in this lower lot for years. Across Squaw Creek a lone coyote nosed along the banks of the creek where the snow had melted. The lower lot was pretty bare bones parking: iced-over dirt with no parking spots delineated, just a big dirt lot on two different levels.

A lot of local cars were parked there; the vehicles were adorned with all kinds of Truckee license plate holders and Squaw stickers, "Keep Tahoe Blue" and "West Shore, Best Shore," as well as Tahoe area apartment and condo parking permits. Some of the vehicle owners probably worked at the resort, but there were a lot of locals parking there to ski, no doubt about it. I even spotted half a dozen pickups with the camper windows flipped up and big dogs in the back waiting for their owners to return. Again, could be employees, but most likely locals parking for a day of skiing.

There didn't seem to be any kind of an identifying sticker to differentiate between guests, locals, and employees. Every twenty feet big signs stated that the parking lot was for guests and employees only. All other vehicles parked in the lot would be towed. But I didn't see anything to differentiate between the groups.

While I poked around, a Subaru station wagon almost as old as mine pulled up and parked, and two obviously local guys got out, grabbed their boots out of the back, and sat on the tailgate of the car booting up, then grabbed skis and poles out of a Thule on the roof. They walked around to the right, past a couple loading docks, then the pool and hot tubs and around to the area where guests can ski out to the Squaw Creek Chairlift. By doing this, they avoided passing the parking valets and walking through the massive lobby—which would identify them as locals parking in the lots below.

So why was Daniel's car towed and searched when all kinds of locals were still parking their cars here illegally and without ramification? It almost seemed to me that Daniel had been singled out. Somehow, someone had some inside knowledge about Daniel. Either they wanted to set him up, or they knew he was guilty. But guilty of what? He certainly struck me as a smart guy. If he had killed Alexis and Jennifer, why would he have robbed their suite and stowed their gear in his car? His car that was parked illegally in the lot of the hotel where the women stayed? It made no kind of sense.

I trudged up two flights of stairs to the main entrance to the resort. My legs felt weak, and my whole torso ached. My head pounded out the rhythm of my heart.

At the front doors of the hotel, I asked a young, fresh-faced valet if anyone knew about the red Escalade that was towed the day before.

A weather-beaten man in his sixties came over and joined us. His nametag said "Wes, hometown Tahoe City, CA."

"Was your car towed?" he asked.

"No. But a friend's was. I'm just wondering what happened. The lower lot is obviously filled with local cars. They can't all be owned by people working here."

He leaned in close to me.

"I don't know what the hell that was about. I really don't. Out of the blue, the manager just told us every car parked in the lower lot—-except for employees and guests who listed a car when they checked in—were going to be towed. They towed over thirty cars. What the hell? We had guys working here, Nathan in the bar downstairs, his car didn't start so he drove his girlfriend's. It was towed. Now today we're back to letting locals park."

"What do you think was behind this?"

"I have no idea. No idea."

"What's the manager's name?"

"Stephany McClary."

I held out my hand to shake and slipped him a five. "Thanks."

He smiled and nodded, then turned back to the podium to fetch a set of keys.

I walked into the lobby and stopped at the long stretch of front desk and asked to speak with Stephany McClary.

"Is there a problem?" the woman at the desk inquired. "Something I could help you with?"

"No. I'd like to speak with Ms. McClary, please."

I gave the front desk clerk my name, and after ten minutes or so of cooling my heels in a cushy velvet chair staring out the three-story glass window at Squaw Valley, Stephany McClary stood in front of me holding out her hand. She was a middle-aged blonde with a lot of sun damage, brusque, and all business.

"Ms. Bailey?" she asked. "How can I help you?"

I smiled and shook her hand. "I'm going to remain sitting, if you don't mind. I'm just out of the hospital."

Her diamond hard façade melted a bit, and she sank into a velvet chair like mine across a corner of the coffee table from me. "Of course. Please stay right there. How can I help you?"

"First, let me introduce myself. My name is Laura Bailey, and I'm a snow scientist from Colorado State University. It was Dave Geisner and I who found the two missing women in the snow. I left to get help, and no one has seen them since."

She nodded.

"You know about this?"

"It's a small place. There isn't much that happens that doesn't make the rounds. As you probably know, they were staying here. But how are you? I know you were caught in that avie over on Alpine Meadow Road the night before last."

"A little worse for the wear. But overall, I'm fine. Just now I'm trying to help the husband of the woman from Philadelphia, Richard

Fellatorre. I'm trying to help him figure out where his wife is and what happened to her. So naturally, I'm interested—"

"To hear about how her luggage ended up in the back of that Escalade, right?"

"Exactly. The man staying here with them, Dorian Stievquist, told me how their room was broken into. What I'm interested in is why all the cars were towed the other day?"

She leaned forward and continued in a low voice. "I wasn't told to keep quiet about it, so I'm willing to tell you that the Sheriff asked me to have them all towed."

"Really? Any idea why?"

"No idea. But it must be something to do with those missing women. Believe me, we weren't pleased to have to do that. People were furious. I don't think I should say anymore about it than that."

"Burt asked you not to?"

"He did. But I told him I had to be able to tell people he had us tow the cars, or we'd lose a lot of business. So because of that I feel I can tell you."

The hard business visage closed down over her face once again, and it seemed obvious I wasn't getting any more information out of her. So I thanked her, and, with some difficulty, pulled myself free from the clutches of the chair and headed back outside.

Sitting in the Murano in the lower parking lot, I watched the same coyote still slipping along the edge of the creek. He pounced from three feet up on some unsuspecting mouse: all four paws landing at once. I sat wondering why Burt had all the cars parked illegally in the lower lot towed, and somehow while doing this Daniel's Cadillac was searched, and, lo and behold, there sat Alexis' and Jennifer's luggage. Seemed like Burt knew he'd find the women's luggage there.

As much as I dreaded it, I was going to have to talk to Burt Geisner and find out why that car was searched and whether or not any other cars were searched as well. Was it a drug bust? Had he gotten word that drugs were stored in a car there? I added that to my mental to-do list along with talking to Flaherty, Burdick, and Riordan. I also needed to find Darnell.

I wished I felt better. My head was splitting, and I regretted not taking the time in Truckee to get over to the Rite Aide and fill my prescription for painkillers. As I drove into Squaw Valley, I was thinking that maybe I should call Darnell. Ellen did give me his business card and told me to call him if I had any further questions. I also wanted to find out when Dave was going to dig out that tree well and see what was there.

After days of lucking into convenient parking spots, I drove around for ten minutes and finally ended up parking twenty rows back in the main Squaw lot. It was a ten-minute trudge in ski boots—carrying skis and poles—that I would rather not have had to make into the main village. As it happened, I barely made it and eased down onto a couch in the covered breezeway near the Starbucks. In a newsbox for the *Tahoe Times,* a headline caught my eye. "Video Released of Woman Who Disappeared While Skiing at Squaw Sabotaging Gas Well." I lurched off the couch and grabbed one of the last copies:

Philadelphia PA: Plains Drilling today released surveillance video of the sabotage of a natural gas fracking well in Eastern Pennsylvania. Plains Drilling's President, Seth Riordan, states that the video clearly depicts Jennifer Fellatorre, Press Secretary of Pennsylvanian's Against Marcellus Shale Drilling (PAMSD), in an act of domestic terrorism sabotaging the gas well by placing a small explosive at its base. The blast caused carcinogenic laden fracking fluids, used to lubricate the release of natural gas trapped in the shale, to shoot hundreds of feet in the air and heavily pollute a formerly pristine trout stream. The release of fracking fluids resulted in a total kill of all aquatic life in the stream for several miles downstream. It took two weeks to cap the well and stop the fracking fluids from leaking into the Wissahickon Creek Watershed. The exact chemicals used in the fracking process remain unknown due to the Industrial Secrets Act. Plains Drilling estimates millions of dollars in environmental clean up costs.

Fellatorre and a San Francisco woman, Alexis Page, disappeared on March 31st while skiing at Squaw Valley. No trace of the women has been found since that time. Police continue to look into their disappearance.

Digging into a pocket of my ski pants, I pulled out change to buy the *USA Today*. Inside it ran the same AP article. Strange timing. It made Seth and his minions seem even more guilty.

Richard had moved with a bullet to the top of my must-talk-to list. It was an ambitious day for someone who, thirty-six hours ago, was as good as dead.

Richard answered on the first ring. He told me I'd find him in the bar at PlumpJack. Ten minutes later, I sidled onto a stool beside him in the stone grotto of the bar and ordered coffee. He sat nursing a Bloody Mary.

A small girl of about nine with long dark hair pulled back into a frizzy braid sat at his side, resting her hand on her father's arm.

I leaned across him to the girl and stuck out my hand to shake.

"You must be Chloe. I'm Laura Bailey. We spoke on the phone."

She shook my hand with a solid grip, her small hand damp and callused.

"Ms. Bailey, I'm so happy to meet you."

"Call me Laura," I told her.

My heart stopped when I looked into her face. It was a porcelain portrait of her mother's: fine features, dark eyes, a delicate pink mouth.

"Their Bloody Marys are exceptional," Richard said. "Much better than the coffee. Can I tempt you?"

"I'm just out of the hospital. Don't think it'd be a good idea."

"I told Dad it was too early. How are you Laura?" Chloe asked a look of concern creasing her pale face.

"Oh yeah," he said "Sorry. There's so much going on my head is spinning. How are you?"

"Fine. Just a bit battered up. I held up my brilliant purple cast which enclosed all but my the tips of my fingers and ran up nearly to my elbow.

"Chloe, I thought you were talking with a psychologist today?"

"He's a psychiatrist, and I already talked to him. I think I should stay with dad today."

I smiled at her. I felt kind of guilty going into my questions about her mother in front of her, but if her father thought it was appropriate, who was I to second-guess him. I knew next to nothing about kids.

"Do you know anything about this?"

I laid the *USA Today* on the bar folded open to the article about Jennifer. They both scanned the article without touching the paper.

"She expected some kind of an attack. Didn't know where it was coming from, but she was expecting something along these lines," Richard said.

"So you don't think she did this?"

He looked at me, his face wavering between shock and rage.

Chloe pressured his arm with her small hand, as if to quiet him down, then turned to me. "My mother would never do anything like that. She believes in peaceful means."

"Are you kidding me?" Richard said, raising his voice and shrugging off his daughter's hand. "Of course, she didn't do this! She would never do anything to hurt the environment, put people out of work. She doesn't operate that way. You want to know who did this?"

He picked up the newspaper and waved it towards my face.

"Plains Drilling did this! They sabotaged their own well so they could make this fake video with some look-alike hired hand and use it against Jennifer and her group. Come on!" He pleaded with me. "They even had PAMSD labeled a terrorist organization. They won't stop at anything!"

"Are you aware the police found Jennifer and Alexis' luggage in the back of one of the lawyer's car?"

"Yes. What's going on?" he asked.

"That's what I'm trying to find out. Out of the blue every car illegally parked at Squaw Creek was towed. The lawyer's car among the many, and then they searched his car. Since when is a car searched when it's towed? So many things aren't making sense."

"I know you think she's dead," he mumbled.

I saw no point in denying it.

"I hope I'm wrong," I told him. "I really do. Living in Colorado, I've seen the ruin of fracking up close. I know how important the work she's doing is. I won't quit until we get whoever did this. Until we know what happened. I promise you that."

I left the bar with the look of shock on Chloe's face burned on my retinas. It obviously hadn't occurred to her that her mother might not be coming back. I cursed Richard under my breath for putting his daughter in the position to hear that.

The cold air felt like a welcome bracer after the gloom of PlumpJack's bar. Dave Geisner came up next on my list. I clicked into my skis near the Funitel Building and skated over to the ski patrol building. Tracy managed the desk and the phones. She wore chandelier earrings that hung down below her shoulders.

"If you're looking for Dave, he's on mountain," she told me.

"Could you call him for me. See where he is?"

She had obviously taken a bit of an attitude towards me. With a huff, she called, and, though I could clearly hear every word he said, she clicked off and turned to me, enunciating as you would to someone hard of hearing.

"He's. On. Granite. Chief. He'll. Meet. You. At. The. lift. Shack. There. If You. Want. To. Ski. Over."

"O.K." I told her. "I'll. Go. Meet. Him. There."

Dave sat on a lawn chair just inside the lift house chatting up the cute girl standing a few feet away seating people on the Granite Chief chairlift. Between chairs, she raked to keep the snow level on the loading platform. She looked mighty pissed. Dave had a reputation of scouring the mountains of Squaw, trying to sneak up on lifties or patrollers smoking a joint. He would get right up in their faces and sniff them. Then he'd ask anyone around to give an opinion on whether or not they smelled like reefer.

The liftie, "Laurie, hometown Stevens Creek, WA," met my gaze and tilted her head towards Dave.

I smiled sympathetically.

"How's it going?" I asked her.

Again she tilted her head to one side. She had fat blond braids, blue eyes, and a goggle suntan.

I stepped out of my bindings and ducked between two chairs, swinging past to join Dave in the lift house, sitting in a white plastic chair beside him.

"So this is what an avalanche victim looks like?"

"If they're lucky."

He looked abashed.

"Oh, god, sorry."

"It's fine. It's fine," I told him.

`Yeah. And you've got a concussion so that counts for nothing."

"And this," I smiled and peeled off Mike's big ski glove and held up my hand, the top of my cast peeking out of my parka sleeve.

"Sorry that happened to you," he said, and seemed to soften. "I'm so happy they got you out in time."

He leaned forward and put an arm around my shoulders and gave me a hug.

"So, can I dig out that tree well this afternoon after the lifts close?" I asked.

"Burt hasn't said anything about it."

"But wouldn't this be your jurisdiction? Come on, Dave. Jennifer left that glove for a reason. She didn't just drop it. We've got to know what went on there. The families need to know."

He sighed and stretched his feet out in front of him, partially blocking the door.

"What would you need?"

"A snowmobile, a few people, maybe you, Mike, Matt, and Janis, some shovels. That's all."

"All right," he agreed reluctantly. "Let's aim for after the lifts close this afternoon. Weather's supposed to hold today. Let's meet at the bottom of Red Dog at 4:00."

I jumped up and bumped his shoulder with my cast.

"Thanks, Dave," I told him. "See you at 4:00."

Riding up in the Shirley Lake Chair after talking to Dave, I got a whole six-seater chair to myself and decided to try calling Daniel. I realized I had no idea where he'd been through all this except that he had his own condo over at Alpine Meadows. His phone rang and rang, and neither went to voicemail or picked up.

Sean, however, picked up right away.

"My favorite snow scientist!" he said. "What can I do for you?"

"Can we get together and talk?"

"I'm in the tram on my way to High Camp for a drink. Care to join me, and we can talk there?"

"Sure," I told him. "I'll be there in ten minutes or so."

———

Sean radiated high spirits. His cheeks were flushed from fresh air and cold, and he appeared dressed in his usual elegant casual: velvety burgundy corduroys and an oatmeal cashmere sweater, with a silky light-blue shirt underneath. When he spotted me walking down the stairs towards the bar that looks down over Lake Tahoe, seeming to jut out over the precipice of the mountain, Sean jumped up, kissed my cheek, took my parka, admired my cast, and asked what I wanted to drink. All seemingly in one breath. Without waiting for an answer, he ordered a Ramos Fizz and a Sierra Nevada.

While waiting for the drinks, he talked non-stop about how much he loved Lake Tahoe. This segued directly into a lot of details about the 1964 Riva Ariston twenty-two foot Chris Craft wooden boat he bought last summer. Then I heard about how it's all original except that he upgraded to a 350-block engine, just to give it a bit more oomph. He showed me pictures on his phone of a gleaming wooden boat of two-toned wood and aqua-trimmed upholstery.

"What would something like that cost?" I wondered out loud.

He laughed. "You shouldn't ask me that," he told me. "Not really—" he drifted off for a moment. "But I paid $145,000. Of course, that doesn't include the new engine or any of the work I had done. I had fresh varnish and well—." Again, he gazed off into nothing.

"Looks good in your boathouse, I'll bet."

"Yes," he said, "it does."

I was trying to follow Dorian's advice and catch this fly with honey. But the more I smiled, the more frenzied the look on Sean's face, and the more grandiose the stories grew. He was flying on something.

The bartender set the drinks on the bar, and Sean peeled off a hundred from a thick roll of bills and took the beer and the Ramos Fizz—which I only realized then was for me—and led me over to a booth overlooking the lake.

With exaggerated care, he set the drink on a napkin just in front of me.

I gave it a skeptical look. "What is this? Christmas morning?"

He smiled and shook a scolding finger in my face, like I hate you, but I'm trying to be nice.

"Where's Anna today?" I asked him. "Back at the house?"

"I don't know where she is. She got a call a couple hours ago and took off." He swung his arms out to cover the entire view of the valley and lake.

"She's out there! Enjoying life. Living magnificently."

He was definitely high.

"Can I ask you a few questions about how Alexis and Daniel get along?"

"They hate each other. Well, I'm not sure Alexis hates Daniel. Maybe 'disdain' is a better word. She has nothing but disdain for him, and she makes it clear."

"Anna said she sometimes teased Daniel."

"Teased? Try tortures. She rides that poor guy senseless."

"About what?"

"You know that self-help guy—." He puffed his chest out and held both arms up in a victory salute, 'Just take it!' That guy? What's his name? Baskin Robbins?"

"I know who you mean. Has business people walking on hot coals? Daniel follows that guy?"

"He does. Makes him sort of a laughing stock, but Daniel eats it up. He's spent probably fifteen grand on classes just in the last year. So Alexis rides him about that mercilessly."

"How?"

"Questioning his sexuality. About exactly how he 'just takes it.' That kind of juvenile stuff."

"So is this why Daniel and Alexis don't get along?"

He thought about it for a while, twitching around in his seat, his brown eyes all black iris. Finally, after thirty seconds he blurted out, "Nobody really likes Daniel."

"Why?"

"Hmm. Daniel's different from the rest of us."

"How so?"

"Daniel is just past a clinical narcissist."

"And what's that? A sociopath?"

He threw back his dark head of hair and laughed for a minute, then leaned forward and whispered, "Someone better looking than you."

At first I understood him to mean someone better looking than me. But then I realized he meant each person finds anyone better looking than herself, a narcissist. A joke. I get it—finally. I smiled.

He laughed uproariously when he realized how long I took to get the joke.

Other people in the bar turned to look at us, and to find out what was so funny.

"What's just past a clinical narcissist?" he asked.

I was thinking, "you?" but remained silent.

He whispered, "A psychopath."

"What about Anna?"

"Anna's smart; she's sharp. There's nobody she's behind."

"But not cut from the same cloth as the rest of you."

"Not sure I want to go there," he said, and took a long swig of beer, draining the bottle. He leaned in towards me confidentially, "One more thing."

I got a whiff of the warm sour reek coming off him. "What?"

"I found Alexis' laptop in Anna's stuff at my house."

"Really? Any idea how it got there?"

"I don't think Alexis put it there. But there were some photographs on that laptop that someone in Anna's position might find—" He paused. "Troublesome."

"Will you tell me about the photographs?"

"Let's just say they aren't the kind of thing she'd want to get around."

"Her and Alexis at sex clubs?"

He took a quick sip of his empty bottle of beer to hide his surprise.

"Who told you about that?"

I smiled.

"You say they're damaging to Anna, but are they just of Anna? Because what I heard is that Alexis was her partner in crime."

He touched his tongue to the side of his mouth, hesitating.

"Well, their situations are different."

"How so?"

He grimaced, and let the question hang for handful of seconds.

"I don't want to get into that."

I'd obviously hit a brick wall, so I decided to switch tracks, as long as he felt chatty, I wanted to keep him going.

"How do you think Anna got hold of Alexis' computer?"

"It seems obvious to me. Why isn't it obvious to you?" He caught the bartender's eye and gestured for another beer.

"Are you saying Anna stole it?"

"Wasn't Alexis and Jennifer's suite broken into?"

"It was," I agreed. "But why do you think Anna did that? Why would she take that kind of risk?"

"She probably would have done anything to keep me from seeing those photos, which I saw years ago anyway. Alexis showed them to me ages ago. She thought they were hilarious."

Playing the naïf seemed to be working, so I kept it up.

"Why do you think she didn't want you especially to see the photos?"

"Let's just say I think she's a great deal more serious about me than I am about her."

"Oh, I see. You think she wanted to marry you and have babies, live at Hempfield Estate forever?"

One side of his mouth twisted into a wry smile. Whatever he was flying on when I arrived had apparently started to wear off. His exuberance was gone, replaced by something close to irritation.

The bartender brought his beer over and, glancing at my untouched Ramos Fizz, asked if I'd like something else.

"Glass of water, please," I told him.

We sat in silence until the bartender returned with my water.

"So where do you think the women are?"

"I have no idea,"

I took a big sip of water and pulled my helmet back on.

"Thank you for talking to me. I appreciate your candor."

"Laura, if you're in the Tahoe area this summer, give me a call. I'd love to take you for a spin on my woodie." He grinned.

I smiled and nodded, attempting to keep the horror off my face. "Wouldn't have thought I was your type."

"There's some cachet in your extreme athlete vibe. More than enough to make up for your sartorial choices."

I slid on my parka, picked up my gloves, and headed up the steps to the door.

=

OK. After talking to Sean, I knew that Anna broke into Alexis and Jennifer's suite in order to steal Alexis' computer. But how then did their luggage end up in Daniel's car? Did Anna put it there? And if so, why? And why did she steal Alexis' computer? She must have felt strongly about it to take a chance like that. She must be aware stealing digital images is more difficult than simply wiping them off one computer. Did she even feel desperate enough about Alexis to kill her? Maybe she really did want to marry into Sean's big money world? But if Alexis and Jennifer were lodged in that tree well, Anna wasn't the one who put them there. From what I had heard, she can barely ski. Who was it that told me Anna couldn't ski, and was it true? She certainly looked fit as hell.

Somehow, I couldn't buy her wanting to marry into big money and have kids. No way.

I realized it was Daniel who said none of the lawyers except for him skied well. I needed to talk to Dorian again. Maybe he could set me straight on some of these details.

First, though, I needed to meet up with Dave and the crew he'd gotten together to help dig out the tree well.

Chapter 15

WEDNESDAY, APRIL 6, 4:30 PM

Mike, Dave, and I took the Red Dog lift up and skied down to the tree well as Matt and Janis took separate snowmobiles up. Together we reconnoitered the area and discussed the cornice hanging from the rock face above us.

After a few minutes of discussion, Matt and Janis buckled into snowshoes, and climbed up to the cornice on a much more roundabout path than the way I had climbed up. It took them twenty minutes to reach the top. During which time Dave, Mike and I argued about how best to proceed. Dave acted like I was hell-bent on killing us all with my reckless disregard of avalanche danger. I wondered why he seemed so resistant to digging out the tree well.

I was hungry, tired, and hurt all over. The headache had faded, but my sides were killing me. My left side was a deep bruising ache. The muscles on that side occasionally spasmed and left me gasping for breath. My right side burned from the cuts and stitches. I wanted to get something to eat, then take a pain pill, get out of my clothes, and lay down.

But that was only a self-indulgent dream. What I really needed to do was get this crew digging.

Janis and Matt reached the top of the cornice then wiggled into climbing harnesses, secured themselves to a Jeffrey pine at the top of the cliff face, and beat the cornice down with their ski boots and poles. Once the fresh snow on top of the cornice released, they threw a rope attached to a grappling hook into the branches of the big tree and pulled until the tree dropped the last of its snow load. We stood around hemming and hawing for five minutes until Dave finally declared the area safe enough to begin digging. Then Matt and Janis carefully climbed back down to join the rest of us.

After passing around shovels from the back of the snowmobiles, we all began to dig. After twenty minutes, we'd dug down far enough that my red plastic ribbon showed up all the way around the big tree. By this time, deep shadows lay across the valley where we stood, and the daylight was fading fast.

I grabbed a shovel and a whisk broom out of my pit kit. "Guys, let me take over from here."

Everyone stepped back, and I moved to the side of the tree where I saw the tracks pass by, and began carefully scooping away snow. Once I'd dug out a semicircular pit a little more than a quarter of the way around the tree and about three feet down, I began to find what looked like bits of blood in the snow. I kept digging, and down another three feet I found a wrapper, like from a candy bar. It was so packed with snow that at first it was hard to tell what color it was. Then I realized it was green and gold.

"What is it?" Dave asked.

"It's the handwarmer for one of Colorado State University's ski teams. I gave it to Jennifer Fellatorre before I skied off to get help."

Everyone fell silent.

I reached down as far as my arm would go and felt around, and, sure enough, I pulled up Jennifer's other glove.

"What's that over to your right, Laura?" Mike asked.

I crawled along the edge of the circle, and found a hunk of colored ice still partially buried. I dug around it, then took the whisk broom and gently brushed away the last of the snow that filled the curved mold of an ice mask.

I had never dug anyone out of an avalanche.

I'd never seen such a perfect delicate mold of a human face buried in snow. There wasn't a body. Just an ice mold that had frozen over her face when her warm skin and breath met the snow jammed up against it. Somehow, it had been ripped off.

But there it was: the eerie death mask of Alexis Page. Blond hairs fell away from the sides and makeup tinged the cheeks flesh colored.

Here and there translucent scraps of what looked like wet tissue paper clung to the ice. It took a second to realize it was skin. The bulges from her eyes were rimmed with black and blue eye shadow.

I'd forgotten exactly what she looked like, but there she was again, reminding me. There were even fake black eyelashes that had come off in the ice to complete her mask. Bright lipstick and scraps of skin delineated her mouth.

Silence filled in among the trees, the snow, the cold settling down, the falling dusk. No one said a word.

Alexis died when her warm breath and skin melted the snow smashed up against her face. The melting snow refroze and formed the ice mask. It suffocated her. It must have been dislodged when she was pulled from her icy grave.

I kept digging. Another foot down, and I realized I was scraping out an ice mold that two warm bodies compressed and melted into the loose snow that had been protected by the canopy of the Ponderosa pine. I brushed the snow slowly, carefully, tenderly out of the cavity of a hip, a shoulder. A clump of Jennifer's long, dark hairs were stuck in the bottom of the mold where they'd been ripped from her head.

I heard something, and looked up to find Mike leaning down and reaching his hand to me.

"Laura," he said. "Come on. It's enough. We know they were here now. Come on. You're exhausted."

I turned back again to stare at the outline of where the bodies had been. Mike jumped down into the pit beside me and pulled me up to my feet.

"Come on," he said. "It's enough."

He lifted me up high enough so I could scramble out of the pit. Matt gave me his hand and pulled me to the surface. The snow had soaked through my pants, and I was wet and shaking. I turned around and took in the blood, the ice mold of two bodies hanging upside down in the tree well: the hair, the blood, the ice mask, the hand-warmer wrapper. They had been here. Had died here.

"I'm getting there, Jennifer," I thought. "I'll be there soon."

"So what the hell happened to the bodies? It's obvious they were here, so where'd they go?" Dave asked.

"Somebody pulled them out," Janis Murphy said. "I guess that explains the rope burns you found up in the tree, Laura."

I turned to look at her. "Did you see them when you were up there?"

"Oh, yeah. Someone threw a rope over that branch. That's what made the marks on the limb. The murderer probably climbed up there, knocked the cornice onto them to bury them. Then later on climbed back up, threw a climbing rope over the branch, tied it to their feet, and hoisted them out."

"That would take a hell of a lot of strength to lift a frozen body straight up that way," Matt said.

"There was a snowmobile up here," I insisted. "Like I told you, I saw snowmobile tracks over towards the cat track. They tied the rope to a snowmobile and pulled them out one at a time."

"That's how Alexis' ice mask got torn off. But then what?" Mike added. "Where are the bodies now?"

"It'd be tricky loading up two frozen bodies onto a sled," Dave said.

Mike grimaced. "Whoever it was would've had to snap a lot of limbs to get two frozen bodies to fit."

"So what exactly do you think happened?" Dave asked looking at me.

"My theory is someone who knew at least one of the women led them down into these trees. It had been warm, the wells had melted open way down, maybe fifteen or twenty feet. It wouldn't have taken much to tip someone over into a tree well back in here. Especially someone unsteady on their skis to begin with."

"They're practically self-burying once they're hanging upside down by their skis," Janis said.

"Sure," Mike agreed. "The more they struggle, the faster they bury themselves."

"Absolutely," I went on. "And with two of them, they may have struggled hard enough to get the tree to dump its snow load. If not just kick some snow over the bottoms of their skis and climb up that rock face and knock the cornice down. It looked like it had just fallen when I first got here. If the tree hasn't dumped its full load, get it to, and they're buried. I must've skied right over them."

Mike put an arm around my shoulder and hugged me up against his body. "But they were dead by then. Let's get out of here before it's completely dark."

I wasn't at all sure they had been dead. There was probably air down there, most likely their hands were free so that when the snow got dumped on them they might have been able to protect their faces, given themselves some time. I guess the ice mask from Alexis' face disproves that theory for her, but Jennifer could have still been alive. I bet I was here less then fifteen or twenty minutes after they went in.

I gave myself a shake and sucked it up. The pain from my realization, the pain from my injuries. From realizing what happened to them and how horrible that must have been. How overwhelming their fear and panic.

Janis and Matt quickly roped off the entire area with yellow caution tape while the rest of us packed up the shovels and rope onto the two snowmobiles. I sat on the back of one of them.

"I'm not skiing down," I told Dave. "I don't care what your rules are." For liability reasons, no one is allowed to ride on ski patrol snowmobiles except for ski patrollers.

"You've earned it." Dave climbed onto the snowmobile in front of me. "Let's all meet up at The Chamois. We can talk this over," he said.

=

We all settled into a table in the noisy old Squaw Valley Loft Bar at Le Chamois—The Shammy to the locals. I sat wedged in between Mike on my right and Janis on my left in a booth that ran the length of the bar. Dave immediately got on his cell phone and called his brother Burt and told him what we'd found. He had to shout into the phone to be heard over the racket in the bar.

I tried to call Richard and found myself flooded with relief when his phone cut to voicemail. I left a brief message asking him to call me back. I ordered a glass of Chardonnay, but never touched it and gulped down a glass of water instead. I faded out amidst the swirl of conversation and the rowdy crowd at the bar. I was trying to make sense of what we discovered. And then it all swirled around and became crystal in my brain. I stood up.

"Laura, what is it? Are you OK?" Mike asked.

I looked around into each of their eyes and quietly said, "I think I know where the bodies are." I sank back onto the wooden bench and turned to Dave. "Where do you guys leave the keys to the snowmobiles at night?"

After a couple minutes of discussion, Dave and Matt admitted the keys are sometimes left in the snowmobiles since people are out on mountain late at night and early in the morning. Though that certainly was not the policy.

"So on the night the women disappeared, no one would probably have noticed a snowmobile gone missing for a couple hours?"

The three ski patrollers agreed chances were good it would have gone unnoticed.

"So that night, I left your office right around dark, Dave. I'd parked in front of Carnetti Glacier. I got into the car and sat there taking off my ski boots and thinking there wasn't anything to eat at Rita's. It was pounding snow at that point. While I was sitting there, I noticed a truck backing up the snow pile and dumping snow on a new area of pavement. Right on the blacktop. Anyways, I was starving, so I went into Mamasake's, and that's where I met Mike and Aldous. Mike and I had dinner, and he walked me to my car. He wanted to follow me into Truckee because the roads were hellacious. So I sat waiting for him in my car, and I noticed the new area of snow dump was already about three feet high all along the back of the glacier. So three feet deep and about thirty feet wide. Then as I sat waiting for Mike, I remember hearing a snowmobile winding up mountain. Groomers were already heading up KT, and I remember wondering who was heading out on a snowmobile at that time of night."

"You think it was the murderer heading back to dig up the women?" Janis asked.

"I do now. Yes. What time was that Mike?"

"Maybe 8:00, 8:30? It was nuking snow that night. So he took a couple hours say to get the women out of that tree well and onto the sled—and it pounded snow all night—" Mike fell quiet.

I looked around the table. Everyone sat deep in thought, parsing it out.

"Nobody would be taking a snowmobile out in that kind of snow so late at night." Dave looked around the table into everyone's face. "Well, so where are they then?" he asked.

Janis got it right away.

"Dave, Laura's saying they're in Carnetti Glacier. They're wherever in the glacier they started adding onto the night of March 31st when the women disappeared. They've been there since that first night they went missing."

"Right. They're at least three or four feet up from the pavement," I told him. "Probably towards the middle. Or at least well in from the sides."

Dave looked thunderstruck. Stunned. But to his credit, he got over it in a flash and jumped up.

"Then we've got to call Dan Carnetti. Get him out here. I've got to call my asshole brother again."

This time Dave walked out of the bar, his cell phone in hand, so he could be sure to hear better. But then he turned on his heel and came right back in and walked up to the table.

"Wait. Let me get this straight–so he just dumped the bodies on top of the new snow and let the dump trucks bury them? Wouldn't the drivers see them?"

"Maybe he knocked a little snow over the bodies. But the way it was dumping that night, even if he'd just thrown them there and left them, chances are no one would have seen anything."

"Jesus," he said, and headed back outside.

Mike asked the waiter for the bill, and the rest of us sat silently until the waiter returned with the tab. We settled up and then followed Dave outside where we found him in the middle of the walkway screaming into his cell phone. When he spotted, us he held the phone away from his mouth.

"Carnetti will be here in a few minutes," he told us. "My brother might take longer. He seems to think you're full of shit, Laura." He looked at me and shrugged as if to say, What can I do? Then he turned back to the squawking voice in the phone. "That's right I'm talking about you, asshole!"

=

An hour later, Dan Carnetti and some of his snow-blowing crew had joined us, as well as a deputy sent over by Burt Geisner. We had two car-sized snowblowers and one two-story sized snowblower. We'd gone back and forth, over and over, where we thought the new line of snow was dumped on March 31st, and we were ready to begin digging into the cement-like snow of the snow pile.

Digging started at 11:05 p.m. The big snowblower came in and bit out a yard-wide path from the side of the glacier. We all moved in for a close look under the glaring blast of klieg lights that had been brought in to light the scene. No sign of the women, so the two-story high snowblower moved in again and took another yard-wide swipe from the side of the snowpile. Again, no trace of human remains. The driver wheeled around for another swipe, and, after the third swipe, we saw hanging out of the edge of the new cut what looked like tatters of black material.

We moved in with shovels. It was Jennifer. Jennifer Fellatorre. Her dead body.

Janis, Mike, and I started scraping away the snow until we could see all of her. She lay about ten feet in from the side and four feet up from the pavement. A torn aluminum blanket was twisted around her torso, and her legs encased in black ski pants thrust straight out into the snow. Her hair was frozen straight out from her head, and she had a black burn on her chin that went all the way through to bone.

"Probably from the snowmobile exhaust," Mike said. We dug out her body until it was completely free of the ice and lay it on the cement next to the mountain of ice and snow.

Then we stopped, and all bent over her broken body.

"Her hair froze upside down," Janis said.

Jennifer's arms were crumbled at her side.

"She's just a bag of bones," Dave said

I wish he hadn't said that because it was too apt. Her body lay broken and misshapen within the blanket and her clothes. Her face and neck were burned scarlet from the cold, or from having her ice mask ripped off somewhere between the tree well and here. Her bare fingers, torn and tipped with jagged, long red fingernails, looked like witches' hands.

I felt almost unable to stand looking at her. It was obvious she didn't die right away. She struggled and tried to claw her way out of the death pit she'd tumbled into. I had skied right over her. And maybe could still have saved her. I knew Mike was probably right in saying they were both dead by then, but a niggling thought kept rolling through my head, what if they weren't?

It was just too awful.

I looked over at the young deputy Burt had sent over. His mouth was hanging open like he'd be losing his dinner any second.

I put a hand on his sleeve. "You better call the sheriff. Tell him we found the first body."

He looked up from the ruins of Jennifer's body. "I guess so," he replied. "I guess I better."

We left Jennifer where she lay and moved past her to continue digging. Matt, Janis, and three snow-removal guys were doing the heavy lifting while the rest of us stood back, scouring the snow for hints of Alexis' blond hair, or bright blue parka. It crossed my mind that Burt Geisner should have some forensic guys out doing this, but, since no one mentioned stopping, I kept my mouth shut and watched with everyone else for signs of Alexis.

A half hour later, we uncovered Alexis' body. She was face down in the snowbank, her legs twisted around each other like licorice sticks in obvious spiral fractures. The murderer must have broken her legs to fit her onto the snowmobile, and then they dragged over the end of the sled, twisting. Her body was in much worse shape than Jennifer's. When Dave rolled her over, everyone gasped, as her face was ripped clean of skin. The muscles of her face stood out in frozen relief. Jagged shreds of skin from her throat peeked out of her blue parka. Apparently, when the ice mask ripped off, it took the skin with it. It didn't seem like there was much skin on the ice mask. Somewhere, somehow, the skin of her face was torn off clean. Her teeth looked huge and were a porcelain white grinning out of her skull. One eye glared up at us, and the other hung deflated out of its socket. Her blond hair was ripped back neatly from the front of her skull. Maybe the skin came loose after the ice mask came off and caught in the treads of the snowmobile? There was no blood on the snow around either of the bodies.

Just then Burt arrived with three police cars, flashing lights and wailing sirens. He stepped out of the lead car and ordered everyone away. I, for one, was more than happy to move aside and let his team take over.

"Let's get you out of here," Mike whispered. "You look all in."

"I am. I'm exhausted, and I hurt, but I've still got to make one last stop to talk to the Fellatorre's."

"Let's go," Mike said. "I'll drive you. What do you say to going to my house afterwards? It's warm and there's food there. Rita's house is freezing, and you said yourself there's nothing but Frosted Flakes."

"Sounds good."

We got into his truck and pulled out of the parking lot. I checked my phone again to see whether Richard had called me back, but he hadn't. I noticed it was 3:07 in the morning as we pulled out of the Squaw Valley parking lot. I tried Richard's phone again, but it cut directly to voicemail. Most likely he'd turned it off for the night, but I left a message anyway, saying I was on my way over.

I don't know what it was–the stress of having to tell to Richard and Chloe, or my body rebelling–but I started having muscle seizures that radiated out from my spinal cord to wrap around my ribs on each side. I could barely get a breath the pain was so vivid.

"Did they give you any pain pills?" Mike asked, when he saw me blanche pale with pain on the seat next to him.

"I have a prescription, but I didn't get it filled."

"I've got some Vicodin left over from my last crash. I'll give you one of those when we get to my place."

Mike pulled up to the valet service and told the man who opened my pickup door that we'd only be fifteen minutes or so.

"Give us a break," he told the valet. "Can we just leave it right here? We've had one hell of a night."

The valet took one look at me struggling to climb out of the truck and said, "Sure, Bud. I'll leave your truck right here." He helped me out of the truck and over to the doorway into the lobby. I dream-walked through the vast lobby and past the long front desk back outside and through a walkway of shops over toward the building where the condos were. Luckily, Richard had given me his room number when I first met him in the lobby of the Crystal Palace. And even luckier still, I remembered it.

I knocked as softly as something you hear and aren't certain you actually heard. A couple seconds later, Richard opened the door dressed in navy blue and white Penn State sweats. He looked dreadful, and obviously hadn't been asleep.

He stepped out into the hallway as soon as he recognized us. "I got your voicemail," he said immediately. "I just didn't have the heart to call you back. Pretty sure I know why you called, why you're here. Sorry for not asking you in, but Chloe's asleep. Let's let her rest."

"Sure, sure," I said. "I just wanted to be the first to tell you that we found your wife's body, and Alexis'. I'm so sorry. I'd hoped it would end differently, end better."

He raised his gaze from the floor of the hallway to my face. He looked drained beyond grief. "What happened to them?"

"Earlier this afternoon, right before I called you, we dug out the tree well, and found evidence that they'd been there, and had died there. Positive undeniable evidence of both of them having been there. About an hour later, I just sort of put it together where the bodies were, where they most likely were. The night they disappeared I was parked right in front of that big snow dump in the parking lot, and thinking back, I realized I heard a snowmobile heading up mountain in the midst of a wicked snowstorm. Anyways, I put it together and figured they were likely in that big snow pile in the parking lot. We found them there."

"Did they suffer? Did Jennifer suffer much?"

"Her body—well, she has a lot of broken bones, but they happened after she died. She froze to death in the tree well. I don't think she felt much pain, if any. I'm so sorry."

He stood pursing his lips and squinching up his face in an attempt to fight back tears.

"I've gotta go," I said. "I'm all in. I'm sure the sheriff will come by and speak with you first thing in the morning."

"Of course," he said. "You look—well, you look like you're in a lot of pain. Thank you for coming by and telling me yourself."

I nodded. There wasn't anything more to say. Mike and I turned and left.

I woke up as the truck rolled to a stop in his garage. Mike hurried around the cab to open my door and helped me into the house. My side was hurting so badly I could barely put one foot in front of another. The spasm passed, and I went all dreamy like a woman freezing to death curled up cozy on the snow.

Mike handed me a white pill and a glass of water. I gulped it down and felt him pulling off my snowboots, and wrapping me in something warm.

All I remember after that is when he slid me between the sheets in his bed and turned out the light.

ACT IV

Chapter 16

THURSDAY, APRIL 7, 7:45 AM

I was awakened by the smell of coffee and something wonderful I couldn't quite figure out. Bacon. I love bacon, but it's an indulgence I rarely give in to. Opening my eyes I found sunlight streaming into the room from above my head. Two big brown eyes stared soulfully into mine, and a golden retriever snuggled up along the left side of my body. I buried my fingers in the dog's sun-warmed fur. The room had a beamed ceiling that formed an A high overhead. The windows above the bed streamed in light in swaths across the room, and dust motes twirled lazily in the sun.

Lying motionless, nothing hurt. So I stretched tentatively and found everything felt better. A luscious bed, a good night's sleep, and waking up to a bluebird day with a dog at my side made not only an improvement in how I felt, but in my attitude as well. The guilty gloom from the previous night seemed to have lifted. At least we'd found them. We knew how they'd died. They were no longer just two women who were here and then weren't.

Giving the dog a shove, I roused myself out of bed and found I was wearing a frayed flannel shirt and my underwear. Bless Mike's heart. Over the end of the bed hung a pair of clean gray sweatpants and some red wool socks. I pulled those on and padded into the adjoining bathroom.

Outside the bedroom door a study was tucked into a loft: a wooden desk with a computer on it, a black leather mid-century reclining chair with a matching footrest, and bookshelves that ran low against the narrow arc where the ceiling met the floor. Downstairs in the great room

"Good Morning Lake Tahoe" was on the television with the deadpan host, my personal favorite, dutifully reciting the weather. Sunlight streaked into the living room, and two big tan suede couches faced the television with an enormous square coffee table in between, and off to the left, on a floor to ceiling river rock hearth, perched a wood-burning stove, the window lit with flames. It must work well because the big room felt cozy.

Back beneath the loft, Mike stood in the kitchen, wearing a sky blue T-shirt that made his blue eyes glow with light.

"Morning."

"Morning," I said. "Where did you sleep? That has to be your bedroom up there." I pointed up towards the ceiling.

"In a guestroom," he said with a smile. "I want you fully awake the first time I get in bed with you."

"Me, too." I laughed, embarrassed to realize how much I wanted that to happen, wanted him. I turned to look out onto a deck and beyond that a green space of tall fir and pine trees covered in snow. A hot tub bubbled away on the deck.

"I started that thing up thinking it might feel good after all you've been through."

"What a wonderful house. Is it yours?"

"Mine and the bank's."

"You bought this after your divorce?"

"I did," he said giving me a wary eye. "Connie got our old house. Why?"

"It's a lovely house. But it has a certain masculine ambiance."

"What do you mean by that?"

"Well, you know, the white walls, the lack of curtains. Don't get me wrong, I love it." I turned my attention to the food. "Whatever you're cooking smells amazing, and I'm starving. Is coffee ready?"

He pointed over to a coffee pot on the counter behind him.

"Mugs are up there." He pointed to a cupboard above the coffee pot, then gestured to the skillet he tended. "My buttermilk pancakes. You won't find a better pancake anywhere. They're so light you have to put syrup on them or they float off the plate. Can you grab the syrup? It's in the microwave."

As we finished up breakfast, Mike poured us each another fresh cup of coffee. I looked around for a clock and found one on the microwave.

"8:30–do you have to work today?"

"No, I have Thursdays off."

The air seemed warmer around us, a bit thicker maybe, and I sensed a physical hum. I wondered what to make of it.

Around 9:00 Mike got up to clean the kitchen. He reached across to take my plate, and his arm brushed against mine. Yes, definitely a physical hum. I couldn't help but notice the sheen of burnished skin from his forearm to his wrist. His skin weathered by the elements. It seemed especially masculine. It had been a long time since I'd noticed a man's physical attributes.

"Want to jump in?" he asked nodding towards the hot tub. I felt my cheeks warm, and I hoped I wasn't misreading the buzz in the air.

"Yes."

"What're you going to wear?"

"You just look the other way."

A warm smile eased across his face, and his eyes gleamed.

"No," I added. "I mean now."

He turned away slowly. I stripped down, then slid open the glass door onto the deck, not without a bit of effort since the door seemed to have frozen up.

"Are you going to put a bag over your hand?"

"No," I said, wishing I'd thought of that prior to getting naked. "Can you throw me a dish towel?"

He did, and I wrapped it around the cast.

Another inch or two of snow had sifted down since Mike had shoveled the deck earlier in the morning. I tiptoed across it and stepped into the tub. It felt like absolute heaven.

For a second. If only I could let my left arm drop into the water. If only the hot water didn't burn the cuts on my side like iodine. The seats were down low enough that I had to twist my left side up or sit with my arm propped up on a cupholder.

Mike came out and slid into the tub wearing nothing and not a bit shy about it. His body ran smooth and hard with a scar on his stomach and another cluster of them around his left knee. I felt a little catch in my breath seeing him naked and powerful so near to me while I felt a little less than my normal self. At the same time, I sensed we were headed somewhere. The heat in the water seemed to echo the heat in our bodies.

He chuckled when he realized my predicament, and, taking my left arm, braced it on his knee. I closed my eyes and finally was able to sink into the hot water. The mountain air smelled of pine trees and cold. I felt myself fill with anticipation and noticed in a sidelong glance that Mike was feeling similarly. I felt another spread of warmth unfurl in my lower belly. I'd piled my hair on top of my head, held in place with one hairpin, but strands were slipping down. Mike slid his hand into my hair and turned to me, lowering his face to mine. I moved across the distance between us, and we kissed. His lips felt warm and wet with the spray from the spa, and I played a little biting at his bottom lip and giving it a soft tug. It was part pleasure and part awkwardness as my left arm pointed straight up and rested on his shoulder. I reluctantly dragged my lips away from his and looked into his eyes.

"You aren't comfortable. Are you?" he asked.

I shook my head. I could feel our skin touching below in the water, limbs close and wanting to be closer.

"You probably shouldn't even be in here with stitches. Did they say anything about that?" He leaned forward and nipped at my earlobe, sending a chill straight down my spine.

"I don't know," I said. "They gave me pages of instructions to read. I didn't read them."

"If we keep this up we'll be spending the rest of the morning in the hospital getting you a new cast." And with this he pressed himself closer to me and kissed below my ear, right on the pulse throbbing in my neck.

We gingerly helped one another out of the tub. Once my feet were on the ground, he pulled me to him, wrapping a towel around us as we kissed again Then we dashed together across the deck and upstairs to Mike's bedroom where he flung the towel away from us onto the floor.

We turned the morning inside out and outside in again. Three times.

===

By noon we had parked in Mike's designated up-close parking spot and headed off to look for Dave. We found him in his office, yelling into his phone. Holding the phone away from his head, he gestured to chairs.

"More bad news," he said.

He cut the call off a minute later.

"Heard from my brother a few minutes ago that some kids hucking it off a cliff in Tahoe City just came across a woman's body buried in the snow above Commons Beach. Her purse was with her, and the driver's license belongs to Anna Strunk. Those kids were filming each other catching air off that cliff; otherwise, she would've been there until spring."

My ears rang with shock.

"I can't believe it. I just talked to her yesterday."

"Yeah, well, you better tell Burt that," Dave said. "I wish they'd get 80 open so these lawyers can get out of here before they finish killing each other off. Let them do that back in the city."

"Where was this exactly?"

"Across the street from The Blue Agave, about halfway down the cliff."

I envisioned the walkway above Commons Beach and the spectacular views down the length of Lake Tahoe. A fifty-or sixty-foot ninety-degree cliff led from the walkway down to the park and beyond that the beach.

Wind screamed around the building. Dave spun in his chair to look out the window, then turned to look at a radar picture of the weather on his computer.

"Another storm coming in. Great."

"You think the lawyers are killing each other? Did Burt say that?"

"He did find the women's luggage in that Burdick guy's car. And nobody's seen him since." He looked defiant for a second, then it faded. "I don't know what the hell's going on."

I leaned back into the molded wooden chair and propped my elbows on the arm rests, folding my hands across my waist.

"I agree they seem a ruthless bunch. But then so does Seth Riordan. Even though she made it difficult, I liked and respected Anna."

"Lay out your thoughts for us," Mike said.

Pausing a moment to order them, I twisted around in the chair, then began to talk. "OK. Here's my thinking. There are three suspects: Seth, who'd have been after Jennifer for the ongoing trouble and expense she's caused him. In that case, Alexis was probably collateral damage, but then she was Seth's lead counsel. So who knows what their dynamic was. Add into this the fact I just learned that Alexis was apparently having an affair with him. Maybe he wanted her out of the way so his wife wouldn't hear about it? Though I doubt that. He doesn't seem to me like he'd care much about Ellen's feelings. Or maybe he wanted to break it off, and she didn't want to? On the lawyer side, there's Sean Flaherty. He says Anna wants him badly enough to break into the women's suite and steal Alexis' computer just to get back some photographs that might be worrisome if he saw them—though Sean claims he already saw them years ago. Meanwhile, Anna Strunk didn't seem all that interested in Flaherty. Her interest in him seemed to have more to do with getting his job.

Finally, there's Daniel. Alexis apparently humiliated him in front of everyone else repeatedly. And Anna got the partnership he was in line for. The women's luggage was in his car. Flaherty claims Anna broke into the women's suite, but the evidence points towards Burdick breaking into their suite. If Burdick did it—and he is the only lawyer who claims to be a skier—then Jennifer was probably just collateral damage."

"That's going to seem way too flimsy for Burt," Dave said. "You've basically got nothing."

"Seth has a genuine reason to want Jennifer out of the picture," Mike said. "He has the motive, the means, and access. Laura got hit by an avalanche—someone set off on purpose with hand charges—as we left his house. His guy Armstrong, who is a skier, had just gotten into town when that happened."

"You're not going to sway Burt away from thinking Daniel Burdick did it. And I gotta say, I agree with him," Dave said.

Mike's phone rang, and he looked at the screen. "I've got to take this," he said, then he stepped out into the hallway. Dave and I sat there staring out the window as wind gusts howled around the building. Outside the window the world went white for a few seconds, then gradually the pine trees appeared as dark smudges through the falling snow.

Mike poked his head back in. "I've got to get over to the ski school for a few minutes. Minor emergency."

"I should go, too," I said, then quickly stood up and gave Dave a wave good-bye.

I parted ways with Mike with a quick kiss at the ski school office and headed over to the small village market overlooking the parking lot. My head was killing me, and once again my whole body ached. I wanted to try taking some Advil as opposed to another one of Mike's Vicodins. Being clear-headed seemed a necessity if I was ever going to figure out what was going on. Once in the store, I decided to buy a few things for Rita's house. At this point, I realized I was never going to get to the Safeway, so I picked up a decent bottle of Chardonnay, some bagels and cream cheese, a couple of pieces of fruit, and a big bottle of water.

As I walked out and started back to my car to drop the groceries off, I noticed a big man in a black hat in the wine store next door. He wore a red patterned coat made out of some kind of horse blanket. It had to be Darnell Armstrong. Ripping open the bottle of Advil, I spilled two pills into my shaking hand, swallowed them with gulp of water, squared up my shoulders, and walked inside.

I marched right up to him.

"Darnell Armstrong?"

He turned. Though he'd grown his sandy hair out from the military crop in Margaret's photo to a collar length cut, he hadn't lost any of his no-nonsense military bearing. He was a good-looking man—and huge, six-four or five—with a solid build and a capable air of athleticism about him. He stared at me with his head cocked to the right.

"I'm Laura Bailey."

He responded with a warm smile. "The snow scientist." He extended his hand. "You don't look bad for someone who just caught a ride in an avie," he said. We shook hands. As big as he was, I appreciated that he didn't crush my hand to show me how tough he was.

"I got lucky. Do you know anything about that?"

"Avalanches?"

"No, that avalanche."

"Only what I heard."

"Have you heard about Anna Strunk?"

"Who?"

"Another lawyer for Plains Drilling. Very pretty blond woman?"

"High heels? Beautiful skin?"

"That's her."

"No. Nothing. What about her?"

"Her body was found this morning buried in snow on the side of a cliff in Tahoe City."

"I'm sorry to hear that."

"Poor Anna. She came from nothing and worked hard to get to where she was." I paused and looked him straight in the face.

Though his face didn't move, the defiant pleasantness drained out of his features along with the color. Carrying a couple bottles of wine, he headed over to the cashier and paid.

I said, "You didn't know that about Anna? Yes, Anna Strunk grew up in Pittsburg, California in the East Bay. Well-known armpit. You didn't know she grew up in foster care?" I asked him again. "Not the good kind of foster care where a child lives for years with one loving family. Not that kind. The seventeen homes between the ages of seven and eighteen kind."

"Riordan said she was another trust-fund girl."

He turned his flat brown eyes to meet mine.

"Riordan lied to you," I told him. "Maybe he lied because he thinks you and Anna are the same. You were a ward of the state, too, weren't you? You're part of that sub-class that doesn't matter to someone like Riordan. You're not human to him."

Darnell's brown eyes faded almost black as the light drained out of them.

"Not like Alexis Page and Jennifer Fellatorre," I whispered.

He went completely still and didn't say a word for a few long seconds. Then he cleared his throat and spoke softly.

"I don't know what you're implying. If you've got anything else to say to me, make an appointment."

He spun around on the heel of a worn cowboy boot and took the stairs to the parking lot in two giant steps, like someone with no knee issues whatsoever. He strode from the stairway to his monstrosity of a black Hummer H3, climbed in, started it up, and roared off. I thought about running to my car and following him, but then what? Instead I watched as he sped away, heading out on Squaw Valley Road.

Hopefully, that would shake things up at the Riordan household—even just a little.

By the time I got back to Mike's office, the emergency had been resolved, and he was ready to go. I told him quickly about my encounter with Darnell as we walked towards his truck.

"Pretty interesting," he said, "that both of them were in foster care."

"Yes," I agreed. "I need to find out about what Armstrong's experience was. I think Anna had a really miserable time being bounced around, or maybe molested. Why would a kid move around that many times? She claimed it made her tough. I believe it. It's interesting how Armstrong reacted when he learned about Anna also growing up in foster care. My guess is, like her, he wasn't a kid who could fit into somebody else's family."

"Really? This isn't feudal England. Do you really think people care that Anna or Darnell grew up in foster care?"

"I think there are people out there who do. Some of them I'm afraid are mixed up in this mess."

"Who would think less of a person because she's an orphan? I'd find her more impressive because of it. Jeez. Where to now?"

I clasped his hand in mine, ski glove to ski glove. In a flash I remembered Peter saying that he felt sorry for anyone who didn't have a hand to hold. I was feeling pretty good about holding Mike's ski mitt as we walked down the pavers of the main courtyard.

"So where to?"

We reached his truck and climbed inside, out of the wind and snow.

"I'm going to call Flaherty."

As Mike cleared the snow off the windshield, I dialed Sean's number. I told him I'd like to talk a little more about Daniel Burdick. He said he was home and asked me over. He sounded drunk and tired.

Sean greeted us at the door in a navy blue velour bathrobe, his hairy chest bared beneath it. He seemed expansive and jittery as he invited us inside and escorted us through the cold great room with wood-paneled walls and vaulted ceilings painted a gold and red scroll between the beams forty feet overhead. He led us into a small den with a roaring fire in the fireplace, and pillows and blankets arranged in a nest on a tufted red leather couch. Trays of food and glasses were scattered around on the desk and on a long, low table in front of the couch. A space heater filled the empty space beneath the desk. Probably the only room in the mansion he could keep warm.

He brushed the clutter off the couch and motioned Mike and me towards leather wing-back chairs across the coffee table from him.

As we sat, he jumped up again and crossed the room to a bar I hadn't noticed as we walked in. The room felt claustrophobic with heat, and the wall of built-in bookcases, and the clutter.

"Can I get you a drink?" he asked, as he poured himself three fingers of scotch.

Both Mike and I said no thanks.

He must have been coked up again. Must have started up as soon as he invited me over. Almost like I made him nervous, and here I thought he was making me nervous. At least he didn't drive me to do coke in order to get up the nerve to talk to him.

"I'm sure you've heard about Anna?"

"Yes. Yes," he said. "The sheriff came by and told me. A brilliant young woman with all her life in front of her."

"And about finding Alexis and Jennifer's bodies?"

"Yes, Sheriff Geisner told me that, too. Quite a day yesterday."

He took a sip of his drink and stared into the fire.

He seemed bored, all slouched down on the couch with his long legs sticking straight out in front of him and a pair of navy and red plaid flannel boxers showing under his robe.

Almost as an after thought, he said, "I gave the sheriff Alexis' computer. He took all of Anna's stuff, too."

I looked over at Mike. He pushed his hands forward as if to say, go on, go on.

"Can you tell me more about your relationship with Anna?"

"It's none of your business," Sean said. "I don't have to talk to you." He paused. "But I don't mind answering."

No doubt. This guy was chatty as hell when coked up. He sniffed and rubbed his eyes.

"It was casual with Anna. Just a casual thing. I asked if she'd like to stay with me, here, instead of at the Crystal Palace. She said sure. There had been sexual tension between us for years, so I thought why not?

"Now, I don't know her thoughts, but it was my feeling that when she saw this place, when she got to know me better, her feelings grew more serious. I don't know this for a fact. We had yet to declare our troths. Well, I had no plans to, she—well, I don't know and now never will. Smart woman, lovely woman, but damaged. But then aren't we all?"

He seemed sincere. He liked her, had no future plans with her, and she died.

"Are relationships among partners at your firm encouraged?"

He laughed. "No. But none of us are the hand-holding, going-steady types. So for us blowing off some steam in this way was common. Fairly common."

"How about you and Alexis?"

"We were a couple a few years ago. At least I thought we were. Then I came to my senses. Alexis didn't want a regular relationship. She was lovely, funny, sexy, wild, but she could be a bitch from the seventh circle of hell. Controlling like nothing you've ever seen." He laughed. "Oh my god." He shook his head. "If she wanted to get married, the only husband who could stand her would be someone with no spine. A puppet. And, of course, that's the last thing she'd ever want. What's the saying? The world is full of strong women with weak men who are looking for strong ones?"

"And you were the weak guy?"

"I was the strong one who realized it'd never work. We hung out, had some fun, but after a while what we mostly did was butt heads. So it wasn't going to happen."

"Who do you think killed these women?" Mike asked.

"I don't know," Sean said. "I really don't."

"Enemies?" I asked.

"Alexis has enemies lined up around the block. I'm sure there'll be a parade in San Francisco when the word gets out. But as for enemies of Jennifer, I don't know."

"But who do you think would want to kill Alexis?"

He shook his head and looked around the room with hard, glittery eyes.

"So were either Alexis or Anna having casual sex with Daniel?"

He paused. "No," he said, and ran his hands through his hair, picked up an exquisite verdigris lost-wax casting of a reclining hippo off the coffee table and seemed to consider the weight of it in his hand. "No, no one I know of was fucking Daniel."

"Not part of the crowd?"

"Not really," he answered.

"I wanted to ask you more about what you said the other day about Daniel. Were you serious when you called him a psychopath? Do you think he could be responsible for all this?"

"If you want to know more about Daniel, you should talk to his brother back East. I've never really seen Daniel do anything out of line. But the firm always does background research on prospective hires, and some of the things I learned about him were troubling. Talk to Joshua." He grabbed an old black desk telephone. "I've already told him someone might be calling. I'll dial him up and leave the room, so you can talk to him."

Leave the room to go do a few more lines no doubt.

He dialed, and, after a short wait began to speak, "Josh, it's Sean Flaherty. I have here someone who would like to speak to you for a minute about your brother. I told you there've been some problems here in California." He paused and listened for a minute. "Sure," he said. "Maybe this afternoon." And handed the phone receiver to me, then left the room, followed by Mike who closed the door behind him.

"Joshua Burdick," a man's crisp voice said on the line. "Who's calling?"

"My name is Laura Bailey, and I'm working for Richard Fellatorre. His wife Jennifer was murdered here at Squaw Valley, and I'd like to talk to you about your brother, mostly just to clear him as a suspect."

"You're a—what? A private eye?"

"I'm a snow scientist helping the husband of one of the murdered women. I'm consulting with the police here."

"Now what's he done?" His voice sounded tired, not angry, but maybe resigned—aggressively resigned.

"You probably know what's going on from talking to Sean. Two women disappeared. We found their bodies in a big snow berm last night. So I'm trying to get background information on everyone involved in the case. One of the women worked with your brother. I understand that you love your brother and don't want to say anything against him—"

"No," he interrupted. "I don't love my brother."

"What is your relationship then?"

"My relationship is I'm wary as hell of him, and I'd rather be on the opposite coast."

"Really?" I asked. "I'm surprised. Of all the people he works with who are here now–five I've talked with–Daniel seems the most approachable."

"I don't recommend you ever try crossing him. He's fine as long as everything's going his way."

"Could you explain what you mean by that?"

"Just a minute. Let me take care of something."

He put me on hold and, thankfully, silence, not muzak, filled the minute I was left hanging.

"OK, I'm back. So—" his voice sounded exhausted, the aggression gone—"here are a couple examples of what happens to people who cross Daniel. In the first one, I was fourteen and Daniel twelve. Our parents had a summer house in Maine when we were kids. For maybe two weeks I'd been planning a bike ride from my parents summer house to a beach some twenty-five miles away. Sounds hard to believe maybe, but this was a huge deal to me. I was going with two friends. We planned everything. My dad drove us over the route again and again. And, of course, no cell phones, my parents not being early adaptors of anything. We knew where we'd stop to eat; what we'd do if someone had a flat; we were prepared. So the last night before we were to take off at the crack of dawn–our dad's away–Daniel convinces my mom that he needed to come along. He's twelve, my friends and I are four-teen. Big difference. But Mom says if I don't take him, I'm not going. Again, Dad's away. He would have stuck up for me. So in the process of a big family pow-wow over this, I called Daniel some things I shouldn't have. I don't even remember what now. Typical kid insults. But he ran to his room crying and saying he didn't want to go on my dumb bike ride, and I was ecstatic to be rid of him.

"So our house sat on top of a big hill with a sweeping view of the whole area down to the ocean—really lovely. And that next morning on the first steep descent away from my parents' home, riding with my buds, my front tire blew out, and I was thrown over the front of my bike and into a guardrail. I broke my collarbone, four ribs, and my right arm. Daniel was the perfect brother all the rest of the summer while I recuperated–kind, solicitous. My dad found a small nail in my front tire. Who knows how it got there? I never trusted my brother again. I, who probably knew him better than anyone, saw that, in his eyes, he won." Joshua paused and let the phone line hang empty.

"You want to hear another story?"

"Go ahead."

"Skip forward ten years. Ten years with several other less serious but similar mishaps. I'm twenty-four; Daniel's twenty-two. I bring a girl-friend home from college for Thanksgiving. The family's all atwitter because this has never happened before. So at some point, the day after Thanksgiving, my girlfriend and Daniel have a set-to in which she gets really upset with him. But they seemed to make it up. At least Daniel didn't seem to be holding a grudge. I'm not so sure about the girl; she didn't seem to get over the incident.

"Two days later, coming home with my girlfriend from a late night out, I hit an oil patch on the private drive leading up to my parents' house—their main house in Boston. I hit an oil puddle, and the car skidded sideways and rolled down an embankment. This time I was fine, but the girl was killed. Someone had emptied two quarts of motor oil on the road. The cans still lying there. Daniel was home in bed when it happened.

"But you thought he'd poured the oil on the road?"

"No doubt in my mind."

"Did you tell anyone?"

"My father. The police. It didn't make any difference. My mother at that time was still sticking up for him. And there wasn't anything to prove he had."

"You just felt you knew. Couldn't these have been coincidences?"

"He was my brother. I knew what he was thinking. I could read his actions. And the thing is, the accidents have never stopped. Do you want to hear about his ninth-grade math teacher who flunked him, and soon after found her dog gutted on her front porch? So maybe one thing, two things are accidents, but not a lifelong trail. When people are mean to Daniel, they suffer accidents. They some-times die."

"Can you tell me about something specific?"

"When he first passed the bar, he worked for two years as a Public Defender in the Bronx. Apparently, he and one of his earliest clients got into it. Well, the client got into it. You know the type, no impulse control. He thought something, he said it or he did it. Unfortunately, he said what he was thinking to Daniel. The next day, he died of ana-phylactic shock after eating chili with peanut butter in it. The guy was a scumbag, but he was allergic to peanuts. They only found this out when they cut him open for the autopsy. No chili or peanut butter was ever found. No one had any idea he'd eaten it or where he got it. Yes, Daniel had access to him. But so did a whole lot of other people. He was an indigent, and he died. Who knows?"

"Like I told you, Ms. Bailey, people who are mean to Daniel often suffer accidents. Maybe he just has really strong, good karma. But I walk on eggshells when I'm around him. And I say nothing that could be construed as an insult."

Almost as an afterthought, he added, "All these things I think he does to get back at slights are petty kid things, you know? I've often wondered how much of this shit he's pulled that didn't turn out? How many times has a tire not gone flat? Or went flat, but not on a hill? The car went slower than usual? How many of his schemes just fizzle out?"

All I could think about was that cup of chocolate he'd thrown at the loudmouth kid and then swore he hadn't until I doubted what I'd seen.

We hung up a moment later after I thanked him for his honesty. I couldn't help thinking he had these stories down pat. He'd told them time after time, trying to get someone to listen. I didn't know what to think. Sibling rivalry? Or the backstory for my avalanche? Or Anna's body in a snow bank, tossed off a walkway like a candy wrapper?

Leaning forward I rested my elbows on the burled wood of the roll-top desk—shouldn't this thing be in a museum somewhere? My head reeled. Maybe I shouldn't have been helping Richard put together what happened. I was obviously not much of a judge of character. I'd thought Daniel and Dorian were the two nice ones. What was I missing about Dorian?

I walked out into the cavernous vault of the main room. What a depressing old place. Seemed hard to believe there was ever a family living here with kids tromping in sand and screaming as they played.

Mike stood against a bank of floor-to-ceiling windows looking down across a snow-covered lawn to the lake. Sean lounged on a blue velvet couch staring out towards the lake as well. The view looked cold enough to drop the temperature in the big room a dozen degrees.

Sean turned to look at me and met my gaze.

"Do you believe him?" I asked. "Has any of this kind of stuff happened since you hired him?"

"There's no proof. Just innuendo. He's worked for me for ten years, and nothing exactly like this has ever happened before." He took a thoughtful sip of his scotch. "Well, nothing that could be proved."

"It's happened now."

"Again, there's no proof. Yet, anyway."

"I need some specifics. You're implying there were things that couldn't be proved. Like what?

Sean pulled a small, brown bottle out of the pocket of his robe, spilled out some coke onto his hand, and snorted it right in front of us.

"What do you want to know? About the ADA who called Daniel out in front of a whole courtroom causing the judge to give him a verbal spanking, and shortly after that the ADA went missing? How would that help you?"

"How about Anna Strunk, who would have been missing for several more months if some kids hadn't been fooling around on a cliff and found her. There are parallels!"

"Yes," he said bowing forward from the waist in a sarcastic gesture. "There have been incidents. People's dogs have disappeared. Their kids have gotten hurt. Shit just happens. But here's the thing: people's dogs disappear, and people's kids get hurt who've never heard of Daniel. It happens every day!"

"You knew this about Daniel, and you hired him. Anna might still be alive if you'd told me this earlier!" I shouted into his face.

Mike came over and held my shoulders, like he thought I was going to beat Sean up or something. Not that I wouldn't have liked to.

"I've known the guy ten years!" Sean shouted back at me. "I never saw anything like this in him. When Alexis gave him shit, he'd shrug it off. She never disappeared."

"Until she did."

"How was I supposed to know it'd come to this?"

"Let's go," I told Mike.

We stomped across the great room and out the front door, slamming the heavy Gothic door behind us.

=

As we were driving back into Squaw, the snow started up again.

"Oh good," I said. "More snow."

Mike asked what I learned from Joshua Burdick, and I gave him the rundown of our conversation. Afterwards, he drove through the snow in silence for a few minutes. The snow became a whiteout as we passed through Tahoe City and past the walkway above where Anna's body had been found.

"It sounds like that avalanche you got caught in would be exactly the kind of crap Burdick would pull," Mike said, as he made the right onto Highway 89.

"My money's still on Seth, and his charming henchman Darnell. We had just left his house. How would Burdick have known that?"

"If he'd been following us? You didn't get in an argument with Burdick, did you? Call him names." He said it as a joke.

I didn't say anything.

"You didn't! Tell me you didn't!"

"Well, I kinda did. He threw his drink all over this kid, and though he said he didn't, he obviously did it on purpose."

"So you called him out?"

"Well, I definitely told him I didn't believe him."

"But you didn't call him any names?"

"Does 'asshole' count?"

Mike laughed a really sarcastic laugh and shook his head.

"Sounds like Burt Geisner has his money on Burdick."

"Yes," I agreed.

"Are you going to go argue with the sheriff? Get him off Burdick's back?"

I thought about that for a while.

"No. Having Burt on Daniel Burdick gets Burt out of my way for a while. Burdick is plenty able to afford a lawyer in the meantime. Apparently, he knows a few."

"So, what's our plan? Today's my day off, and I want to help."

"I'm thinking that Darnell Armstrong and Daniel Burdick are supposedly the only real skiers in this group. And assuming they're stuck up here like everyone else, where better to find a skier on a powder day than on the mountain?"

"So we're gearing up, and we're just going to ski?" His profile lit up with a grin.

"Why does that make you so happy?"

"Because I have not spent nearly enough time skiing with you."

We changed in the ski school locker rooms and went over to KT-22 Express—The Mothership—along with a hundred or so of our closest friends. It took ten minutes to get up close to the front of the line. Every one in line was amped and chatting about which lines they'd already skied and which they planned on hitting. Two different guys tried to hand us energy drinks.

Mike and I were both in the singles line—waiting through the regular line would have taken forever—when someone yelled, "Hey Mike, Laura!" and I swung around to find Grappa McDermott and a bunch of his buddies.

"Ride up with us!" he shouted. His buddies split up so that Grappa and one of his friends could ride up with Mike and me. Grappa shuffled around so that he sat next to me, and his friend sat next to Mike. Both Mike and I wound up on the outside of the chair.

"I've been wanting to talk to you," I told Grappa as we loaded up. "Still think you could recognize the guy you thought you saw the two women with?"

"Dude," he shouted and grabbed my arm. "I heard about finding those bodies! What a horror that must have been! Frozen solid and in the buff. And I heard they had all their skin ripped off! And Carnetti Glacier was soaked in blood!"

"That story has certainly evolved in the telling. No one was in the buff. And all the skin that got pulled off came from your girlfriend, and that happened when her ice mask came off. No blood. So could you recognize him?"

"Well, maybe. I'd have a better chance if I saw him skiing." I told you, he turned wonky on one side. Like he had a bad tune on one ski."

My spirits rose as we headed up over the fabled terrain of KT.

"How'd you get the name Grappa?"

"Long story. It started with my Grandma; she lives with us. We're Italian. Well, my dad's Irish, but the rest of my family, on my mom's side, is all Italian. You'd never guess it, but my real name—." He looked at me expectantly.

"What?"

"Luigi. Can you believe it? Luigi McDermott. My folks must've been hitting the bowl. So, anyway, my grandma loves Limoncello. I mean, loves it. She makes it herself and puts it on everything. I mean, everything: in her coffee, on ice cream, as an afternoon drink, in lemonade. Anyways, she loves it so much that, when I was little, I started calling her Grandma Limoncello. And it caught on with the family, so that soon everyone started calling her that. They still do.

"So, sort of as a joke, to get back at me for giving her that name, she starts calling me Grappa because one time, when I was little, I tasted some really good grappa, and I liked it. You know, grappa the Italian brandy? Very strong! I thought it was good on ice cream. So she got everyone to call me Grappa."

What a nice, normal family this guy must have.

"So how old are you?" he asked.

"Too old for you."

"No, really."

"I'm thirty. How old are you?"

"Twenty-four."

I'd thought he was a little younger.

"Why aren't you in school? You're a smart guy. You should be in college."

"Nooo," he sang in his funny falsetto voice. "The mountains are my college. Living here, being in the mountains, they school me every day of my life. I could never leave. Anyways, until I met you, and heard about you being a snow scientist, I never heard of anything I'd want to be—that I'd go to college for anyways."

The top of KT approached. On a big rock outcropping, rising up to the left from the top of KT, an iron eagle stretched wide its wings in honor of a well-loved local guy who died on a mountain in France a couple years ago.

The four of us unloaded and skied straight back where we looked down on Alpine Meadows in the valley behind us.

"So were you really caught in an avie?" Grappa asked me.

"Yes," Mike told him. "She really was."

Grappa had his helmet off, adjusting something. I looked at his smooth tanned features and his calm green eyes, his platinum hair smashed to his head.

"Tell you what, Grappa. My colleagues are coming in from Colorado as soon as the weather breaks. We're heading back to my snow site behind Granite Chief to do some work and take some readings. It's so people can plan how much water we'll have from the snow pack for farming and hydropower, things like that. We'll snow camp, or maybe dig snow caves, and be out for three or four days. Maybe you'd like to come along and see what kind of work I do. I'll even pay you a little if you help us lug equipment in. Mike's coming along." I turned to Mike and smiled, having never even mentioned it to him before. "Aren't you Mike?"

"If that's an invitation, I accept."

Grappa looked back and forth between Mike and me, a big excited grin smeared across his face.

"I'd love to! Are we going back on snowsleds?"

"Old school. AT skis and skins." AT, meaning all terrain.

"Better yet," Grappa cried. "Perfect!" He pulled his helmet back on.

"So, I'll be in touch with you, hopefully tomorrow, about checking out this guy I'm looking for. Leave your phone on and be sure to answer if it rings. OK?"

"When you give me the orders, Boss, I'm gonna come flying," he said, and gave me a snappy salute. He skied off to join his buddy on the climb up to the top of Eagle's Nest toward a death-defying run called Freebird.

Mike skied over next to me and put an arm around my shoulders. "I can't imagine skiing that again."

"Not if I didn't have to," I agreed.

====

We blasted down the east face of KT together, running neck and neck in the soft snow. Three or four inches of powder lay in the gullies, the rest of the mountain having been blown bare down to the hard pack. We took the Red Dog chair back up to the top of Red Dog and came down in the unmarked field of snow beneath the Squaw Creek chair. We carved slow sweeping turns in the powder, then rode up on our edges when we came back onto hard pack. We grabbed the Squaw Creek chair and, since we had it to ourselves, cuddled up and made out on the ride up like a couple of teenagers.

As we neared the top, Mike turned around suddenly to look down mountain behind us, and said, "Isn't that Burdick?"

The chair lurched then swung from Mike's sudden move so that it took me a second to get twisted around to look behind us and down. Sure enough, there in the deep snow of the off-piste powder fields, I could see Daniel tearing it up, hooting and hollering. The guy was good. At first I was jolted by the coincidence and wondered what he was doing over there. My thoughts spun to a thousand old "Law & Orders" where the criminals keep looping back to the crime scene as helpless to stop themselves as salmon returning to their spawning grounds.

"Guess he didn't learn the lesson," Mike said, still twisted around in the chair watching Daniel ski beneath us.

"What do you mean?"

"He's still parking at the Crystal Palace. It's almost 4:00. The lifts are closing. Where else would he be heading?"

I realized he was right. The ski day had run out.

We unloaded and skied over to the side of the run. I called Grappa and asked him to meet me at the top of the Squaw Creek Lift the next morning at 10:00. I had a suspicion he'd recognize either Daniel or Darnell. I just had to find out which one of them.

Grappa said he'd be there.

A wonky tune on a ski may not seem like a big deal, but even experts can have their edges tuned and end up flailing on the snow, wondering how they could have forgotten how to turn right overnight. That's why most serious skiers like to care for their own skis. It's subtle, but a degree, or a half a degree in the bevel on your edges can make the difference between a struggle and a smooth glide. Or there could be a curl of metal on the edge that wasn't smoothed down. The reason it's so tricky to realize when you've got a bad tune is it could be a million other things. You could need to stretch, your ankle or knee could be sore, your boot liners may have started to pack down and you no longer have a tight enough fit, the snow could be weird, the layers of your ski could be coming delaminated. Or you could just be lacking the mojo. If you're having a bad day, it's almost impossible to immediately say why.

I turned back to Mike and caught him looking at me, probably wondering what in the hell I was doing standing there gazing into space.

"Sorry," I told him. "Ready?"

"Let's take our time skiing down," he told me. "80 isn't going to be opening for a while yet. Those lawyers aren't going anywhere."

Chapter 17

THURSDAY, APRIL 7, 5:00 PM

"**I** want to talk to Seth Riordan again," I told Mike when we got back into the truck, "and if possible Darnell Armstrong."

"Why don't we surprise them," he suggested, "and hopefully that won't give them time to plan anything injurious to our health."

"Good idea. It's harder to say no when we're standing on his doorstep."

We drove over to Alpine Meadows, joining the hordes leaving Squaw at the end of the ski day. As we snaked our way out of the valley my phone rang. It was Richard.

"Laura," he said. "Chloe and I were wondering if you'd join us for dinner. Maybe Fireside Pizza?"

"Sure," I told him. "Just a second."

I put the call on hold and asked Mike if he'd like to have pizza with the Fellatorres later.

"Absolutely," he said. "That Chloe is a great kid."

I took a glimpse at my watch. It's 5:00. "How about 6:30, Richard? Also, is it OK if I bring Mike Bernese?"

I heard him asking Chloe and getting an excited, "Sure Dad!" in response.

The bulk of traffic exiting Squaw Valley turned left, towards Truckee and I-80. Since 80 was closed, both into Reno and up over Donner Pass and on into the Sacramento Valley, it seemed surprising to see most of the traffic still turning left. Where were they headed? We turned right and drove a short distance down Highway 89 to the turn off for Alpine Meadows.

We turned off the main road and meandered down the lane the Riordans lived on. A black Hummer was parked under the porte cochere, which still looked on the verge of collapse under twenty feet or so of snow. Darnell was there. The snow draped so low in a deep elastic swag over one side it nearly touched the ground. With no idea what I was going to say, I took a series of deep breaths as Mike put the truck in park, killed the ignition, and set the parking brake. Then we got out and climbed the steps to the front door.

I rang the doorbell, and a few seconds later Seth Riordan's wife peeked through the watered glass in the front door and swung the door open.

"Ms. Bailey," she said with a warm smile. "How lovely to see you well. We were terribly sorry to hear about your accident. In fact, we sent you a card and a small gift, but were told you'd already left the hospital."

She turned to Mike. "How nice to see you again, Mr. Bernese. Welcome."

Apparently all memories of how our last visit ended had been banished.

"Let me take your coats," she said. I peeled off my parka and gloves, and she took them away.

Ellen looked elegant in a gray cashmere sweater and skirt and a single strand of dark silvery pearls. I realized again I was too old to wear nothing but ski clothes from late-October to the end of March. I was a slattern next to her, but I resolved not to let it bother me.

Mike decided to keep his coat on.

"Come in, please."

With a gentle pressure on my elbow, she ushered me toward a stuffed armchair covered in dark paisley velvet.

"Please sit. Mr. Bernese, maybe over there?"

She gestured towards a leather chair across the coffee-table from me.

Mrs. Riordan sat in a worn green velvet chair at the end of the coffee table, in between us.

"I wondered if your husband is around?"

"He is. He's just finishing up on an overseas conference call on Skype." She quickly went on. "Can I get you coffee or tea? Or perhaps something stronger? How about a glass of sherry? Or a beer, Mr. Bernese? Can I call you Mike and Laura?" She seemed nervous the way she was chattering.

"Of course," we both told her.

"Please call me Ellen. About those drinks?"

We agreed on a sherry and a beer. I don't know why I agreed, as I'm not a sherry fan. I followed Ellen to the kitchen, a surprisingly old fashioned room with dark French tile counters and backsplash. Diamond shapes of contrasting French country tiles were set over the old industrial stove. A rack of well-used copper pots hung over the center island. I had expected granite and stainless steel like every other McMansion I'd ever been in. I guess this house predated McMansions.

"What a lovely kitchen."

"Thank you. Most people find it dark, but I love it because it's Old Tahoe." She moved deftly, laying out a tray with grapes, crackers and cheese, then setting two crystal sherry glasses on the counter. "Can you handle this tray, Laura? Along with the bottle?"

"Of course."

I picked up the tray, and she took a beer and a mug from the refrigerator. Then I followed her back into the great room.

I couldn't tell how old she was. Seth was in his mid-fifties, and his wife seemed both older—in her gracious mannerisms—and younger in how effortlessly and gracefully she moved. Her face was a placid mask that barely moved when she spoke. She could be forty, she could be sixty. She had obviously had work done, expensive work, as there was nothing of the burn victim about her, with the shiny, fragile looking skin—the look so many plastic surgery enthusiasts end up with.

Once we were seated again, I couldn't stop myself from asking. "Ellen, do you do Pilates?"

She smiled and looked surprised.

"I do. I grew up in New York City and got into it because I danced ballet. I actually took lessons from Romana when I was younger. I've kept up my study all my life. Do you?"

"Yes. I suspected from the way you move."

We sat there smiling at each other like idiots. I'd love to dive into asking her all about Romana and the New York Studio. Maybe she even knew Joseph Pilates, but since I suspected her husband tried to kill me the last time I left there, that chat probably wasn't going to happen.

"Is Darnell Armstrong staying with you? I thought I saw his car outside."

"He is, yes. But he's out skiing today. What time is it?" she checked her watch. "Oh yes, he should be back soon."

"It's ski in, ski out from here?" Mike asked. Their house sat quite a ways from the base of any Alpine run, so it seemed odd.

"Well," she said with a little laugh. "For Darnell it is."

"Laura," Ellen turned her full attention to me. "Please tell me about your work. It sounds fascinating."

So I told her about my work.

Ellen had the ability to focus in a way that made me feel there had never been a more fascinating person in her living room, and certainly no one doing any more worthwhile work. We talked for five minutes or so, and by the end of that time I still had no idea what lay behind the placid beauty of her face. I got the feeling she wanted to tell me something, but maybe she felt inhibited by Mike being with us, or maybe something else held her back. Whatever it was, she never told me.

I was just explaining how we now have less snow in the Sierra, and because of that less water, when her husband walked in, and she abruptly stood and headed into the kitchen.

"How nice to see you again, Dr. Bailey." He stepped forward and stuck his hand out to shake. I shook his hand, and then he turned his attention to Mike. "Mike, good to see you again." He gave Mike a much more manly shake than the one I got.

"We were sorry to hear about the avalanche. I'm glad to see you're up and around."

Just then Darnell walked out in red plaid ski pants and a black Kjus parka. Those parkas cost around two grand. I'm sure they're nice. Everyone I've ever talked to who owns one swears they're worth every penny. They have the rep of being the Macs of ski wear.

Ellen handed her husband a heavy tumbler half filled with clear liquid and handed Darnell a bottle of Heineken, then asked if anyone needed anything else.

Mike and I declined.

"Then I'll give you this," she said and handed me a glossy lavender envelope and a silver box with a matching lavender bow. "Just a little thing. We sent this to the hospital, but, as I said, you'd already checked out."

I thanked her and she smiled, met my eye for an instant, then turned and left the room. Darnell set his beer on the coffee-table and stepped towards Mike.

"Are you here to harass Mr. Riordan?"

"I don't think so," Mike replied. "But we would like to speak with him."

"It's fine, Darnell. Ms. Bailey—I'm sorry, Dr. Bailey, Mike, please have a seat," Seth said. He turned to me. "What can I do for you?"

"I'd like to talk to you about the timing of the release of the video you claim showed Jennifer Fellatorre sabotaging one of your wells."

Darnell started to say something, but Seth shut him up with a flick of his hand.

"We have a private security company to guard our wells in contested areas. And that certainly qualifies as a contested area. The security company took the video, and I assume they released it. If not them, then I have no idea who did. It wasn't my firm. We merely stated who was on the film. I'm not pleased with the timing of its release. People might construe it as making my company look bad. Or suspicious."

I jumped in and cut him off.

"Maybe it makes Plains Drilling look bad, but not as bad as it makes Jennifer Fellatorre look. And it doesn't show any footage of Plains hiring ex-military psy ops people to spy on Jennifer's group, or pressuring politicians to declare her group terrorists. Get enough publicized incidents like that, and it would make Plains look bad."

Seth cast a quick sideways glance at Darnell. They seemed surprised I knew all this.

"Jennifer's group refuses to consider how carefully we drill these days," Riordan said.

"We've learned from our mistakes," Darnell added. "Our drilling brings in jobs, it brings in low cost, clean fuel for the entire country—"

I ignored him and turned my attention to Seth.

"I was reading up on this kind of drilling while I was in the hospital. And I see that it takes about a million gallons of water to frack one well, once. And that on average a well can be fracked about eighteen times. So that's eighteen million gallons of water for one well. And of course, you now have thousands of wells in just Pennsylvania. After the fracking process, most of this water is lost in the ground where it returns to the groundwater, polluting that, or the water that comes back up is so dirty it can never really be cleaned. Where do you think all this water is coming from? I'm a hydrologist, and I don't see where it's going to come from."

"Of course, we have many qualified hydrologists working for us—" Seth began.

"And they tell you there's enough water to support this kind of profligate waste of water?"

"Of course, they do."

"Then I'm here to tell you, they're wrong. They're working from old historical models. Because we don't get enough precipitation any-more to support that kind of water usage."

He looked shocked that I had the gall to tell him this.

Darnell unzipped his parka and shifted from foot to foot, uncertain what to do.

Seth smiled and spread his hands out expansively.

"I welcome a frank and honest debate on the issues surrounding hydraulic fracturing. I genuinely do. And that's why I valued Jennifer Fellatorre's voice. She was a smart woman, God rest her soul, and she gave us the opportunity to bring this debate to the public. As the governor of Pennsylvania is well aware, this is a debate we can only win once the public gets the straight facts."

I couldn't sit through his line of bullshit. I turned to meet Mike's eyes, and he gave me a warning glance—don't go crazy on him. I kept trying to take deep breaths, but the back of my head was tingling, and the hairs on my neck, I'm sure, were sticking straight out.

Finally, after a minute or two, I stood up and leaned over him where he sat on the couch.

"Three women are dead! And all three of them had close ties to either you personally, or to your company. Many people don't think that it's really Jennifer Fellatorre on *your* video—that it's a fake you set up—"

A big kerfuffle arose. Darnell lurched forward and grabbed my arms and jerked me backwards and away from Seth, who leapt to his feet and shouted at me.

"Get the hell out of my house! How dare you imply that—"

Then Mike jumped forward and chopped Darnell's wrists in a way that forced him to release his grasp on my arms. He then jumped in between Darnell and me, and they stood there snarling at each other.

I leaned around Mike and yelled at Darnell.

"Is your boss going to have you try killing me again?"

Mike pushed me back. Apparently not thinking that was a great idea.

All the time this was going on, Seth was yelling, "Get out of my house! Get the fuck out of my house! How dare you!" over and over.

A minute later, Mike and I were standing looking at each other outside the closed front door with the noise of it slamming shut still echoing in our ears. After a shocked handful of seconds, Mike started to smile, and I smiled back at him and started to laugh.

"Did you see Riordan's face?" Mike asked. "And did you notice the hair growing out of his ears? I mean, come on? Who just lets that happen?"

We were both laughing. But he laughed so hard he could barely speak.

"His wife hates him, or she wouldn't let him go out like that. She hates him."

The laugher died away along with the adrenaline from the fight, and we stood huddled together in the cold and the dark.

"I left my parka and gloves. And that present. Damn. I really wanted to see what was in that package. I never got a present from a billionaire before."

"I don't think there's any going back," Mike said.

We started laughing again at that. Since the temperature hovered around five degrees, and I stood there with only a thin sweater on, he wrapped an arm around me, and we headed for the truck. Lucky Mike for keeping his coat on, and his gloves in his pockets. On the way back, I kept thinking about what Mike said about Ellen hating her husband. He might have been onto something.

We made it back to Squaw around 6:15. I did some quick shopping for gloves, ski pants, and a new parka, then hurried over to the restaurant where the Fellatorre's and Mike sat ensconced in a wooden booth near a roaring fire. I hung my shopping bags and my new parka on a hook at the end of our booth, and slid in next to Chloe while saying hello to everyone.

"Did you order yet?" I asked.

Chloe shook her head. She looked tired and sad, but not overly so. In fact, I was surprised how well she seemed to be holding up. Her dad hadn't been faring so well. He hadn't slept in a while.

"Have you heard from Burt Geisner?" I asked.

Richard nodded that he had. "Chloe went to Squaw Kids today, and I had to go over and identify the body. There's going to be an autopsy tomorrow morning, and then when they release her body I guess I'll have to arrange to have it shipped home. I've also got to plan a memorial. Now I'm thinking maybe I'll have her cremated here. There certainly isn't going to be a viewing. It was—"

"Enough said," I cut in. I didn't want him going into detail about it in front of Chloe. Though he probably already had, gauging from the look on her face.

"How's Squaw Kids going?" Mike asked Chloe.

"It's OK, but I'd rather ski with you guys."

"Look what you've done," Richard said, attempting a smile.

"I don't want to go home. I want to stay here and ski," Chloe stated adamantly.

"You have to do well in school, so you can afford to live in a place like this and ski every day," I told her. "Skiing isn't cheap."

"You and Mike ski every day, Dad said." She slumped down and stuck her lower lip out. "Are you guys rich? You don't look rich."

My heart pinged again when I realized how much the girl favored her mother–the same delicate features, dark curling hair and pale skin.

"I'm certainly not rich, and I don't get to ski *every* day. Most winters I teach college students. And let me tell you"–I leaned down towards Chloe and bumped my shoulder against hers—"that's not as much fun as skiing! But I also worked hard to get a job that fits me so well—a job where I don't really have a boss, and I get to do what I love."

Chloe roused enough from her pout to take a sip of her Coke after the waitress slipped it in front of her. "What do you do?"

"I'm a snow scientist. Which means I study snow: how much there is, how much water is in it. Things like that."

She slumped back down, apparently not impressed.

I leaned down and whispered in her ear, "Doesn't Mike look like a big Viking."

She perked up and wiggled taller in her seat. "Like Leif the Lucky?"

I nodded.

She looked at him, twisting her head around to catch the angles of his face.

"But he doesn't have a beard. I think Mike looks like a Bernese Mountain Dog. And his name is Bernese, and he lives in the mountains."

We laughed about that for a second.

"Have you spoken with Seth Riordan again?" Richard asked.

The waitress appeared just then and asked if we were ready to order. After a moment of discussion, we ordered two pies, one veggie and one with mushrooms and pepperoni.

"I did. Well, we did," I told Richard once the waitress left. "We got in another big argument. Darnell was there, too, this time."

"And what do you think?"

"I'm getting there," I told him, and let my words settle in the air between us. "Another day or two, and I think I'll be satisfied that I know what happened. Until then, I'm not discussing it. Just as I wouldn't bounce around half-baked ideas in my science work, I'm not doing it here either."

Richard's face flushed with anger, and he took a long pull on his beer. "And how does the death of this third woman change things?"

"I don't know. I have suspicions, but until I'm certain I'm keeping them to myself."

As we stood outside in the cold saying good-bye, Richard's irritation hung in the air because I wouldn't tell him my suspicions. But that's why they're called suspicions. I wasn't sure yet.

Chapter 18

THURSDAY, APRIL 7, 9:30 PM

My headlights burned tunnels through the sifting snow. Mike followed me into Truckee, then flashed his lights good-bye as I made the right onto River Street. Nine o'clock had come and gone by the time I pulled the rented Nissan into the driveway at Rita's. Mike had asked me to spend the night at his house again, but I needed some time and space to think. Inside, the furnace had once again conked out, and the house had settled where it was apparently comfortable, at 24 degrees.

After a few minutes of my fiddling with the furnace–the pilot light had burned out once again–the furnace groaned out above freezing air. Despite the cold, I stripped out of three layers of ski clothes and threw them into the washer with some laundry soap. I then ventured into a back bedroom that hadn't been over 25 degrees since fall, and, with a big metal screw through the floor, I turned the water back on for the house; it couldn't be left on out of fear of frozen and burst pipes. After five minutes or so, the water in the shower warmed up enough for me to step in. It took forever to bathe and wash my hair with one hand. But the good thing about that was by the time I finished, I finally felt warm.

After drying my hair and weaving it into a side braid, I put on clean sweats, started the washer, and jumped in bed—the only warm place in the house—aside from the shower. After booting my computer, I went online and found another e-mail from my department chair, Lee Borders. Seth must have tattled on me again. As a kid, I always felt disgusted with tattletales, a feeling I hadn't yet out grown, and since I wasn't backing off anyway, I deleted the e-mail without reading it. I figured I could always fall back on ski bumming if my university career went away. Maybe Mike would give me a job? Or Dave Geisner?

I tried to find the video of Seth's well being sabotaged. All I could find were ten and fifteen second clips on youtube of a dark-haired woman, who looked like Jennifer, placing a small package at the base of a well then turning to run.

I tried calling Steve Diderowski, but his phone cut directly to voicemail. As I listened to LaTisha Cimino's phone ring, I realized it was past 1:00 a.m. back East. Oops. I hung up, but a couple seconds later my phone rang, and it was LaTisha Cimino calling back.

We said our hellos and talked for a few minutes about finding the women's bodies, and the memorial Richard had mentioned briefly at dinner for Jennifer in Philadelphia. At my first chance, I brought the conversation around to my reason for calling.

"I've been trying online to find a longer clip of the woman they're saying is Jennifer, but I haven't been able to get anything but the ten and fifteen second clips they're running on air. Could you help me with that?"

"I have the full video," she told me. "I'd be happy to put it up in Dropbox for you."

"What do you think about it?"

"Watched it several times now, and they did their homework. It looks like Jennifer. And that's coming from someone who knows it isn't her!"

"I'm going to wait until I get the video and make sure it runs before I hang up. Am I keeping you up?"

"Naw," she said. "Now Jennifer's gone, we've been working even harder. Though we do have almost a hundred new volunteers. The idea that Plains might have been behind her death activated the community."

A few minutes later it showed up in Dropbox, and I downloaded it, then clicked on the video to make sure it ran. It did.

"By the way," she said. "I have some press photos of Armstrong and Riordan at a charity event at the Philadelphia Museum of Art a couple weeks ago. Any interest in seeing those?"

"Definitely!"

"I'll get those off to you. They came as hard copy, so I'll have to upload them first. But I'll get them off as soon as I get them uploaded."

I thanked her, and we said good night.

Propped against pillows in bed, I watched the video, which ran for nearly twelve minutes.

I picked up my phone and called Richard. He answered just as it started to cut to voicemail.

"Sorry to call so late," I told him. "But can I come over?"

"Now?"

"Right now. Make sure Chloe's up, too. I'll be there in half an hour."

===

In the living room of the Fellatorre's suite, I plugged my laptop into the back of the flat screen TV.

"Have either of you seen the entire twelve-minute clip?" I asked.

"I've only seen the short clips that played on the news," Richard replied.

Next to the television, a gas fireplace raged, and the suite felt as overheated as only a ski lodge in winter can be—miserably hot. I stripped off my parka and then my sweater, too. Richard turned off the fireplace by flicking a switch, then opened a window at the far end of the narrow corridor of living space.

"I'm hoping you guys will see something that'll make it clear whether or not it's Jennifer on the video."

In her flannel PJs with cartoons of women on skis in various stages of falling, Chloe curled up at my side on the couch. For the next forty-five minutes, we ran the video over and over. Finally, Chloe asked me to stop it at a certain spot. I found the spot and ran through it in slow motion for her. The video was shot at night, but the area around the well was lit with bright lights that threw distinct black shadows.

"Can you magnify it. Right there?" she asked.

It was a section of video, ironically, from the fifteen-second clip they'd been running on television of the dark-haired woman bending down to secure a small package at the base of the dark outline of a well.

The woman was reaching out her right arm to place the package on the ground. She wore what looked like a raincoat. Soon she would twist a little to her right and secure the package; at that time, she had have her back to the camera. In the clips Chloe found interesting, she was in profile.

On my laptop, I found the spot in the video and pulled a couple screen grabs while Chloe climbed behind me on the back of the couch, directing me as to exactly which ones she wanted. Her hands rested on my shoulders, and her chin was propped on my head. Her physical presence and the touch of her body felt tender to me.

Then I heard her gasp.

"There!" she shouted in my ear. "There! I knew that was not my mom!"

She pointed to a small tattoo on the woman's inner right wrist.

"See that heart? My mother never had any tattoos in her life! I knew mom would never do that!"

She jumped around in front of me and looked into my face, her sweaty little hands on my cheeks.

"That woman with the bomb is someone else."

===

Midnight was long gone by the time I turned down West River Street and found a black pickup parked in the driveway at Rita's. Light glowed through the bungalow's curtains and wood smoke drifted up from the chimney. I parked on the street, beeped the horn, and ran up the driveway to the front porch stairs. Mike opened the door and stood framed in the swath of yellow light pouring out into the dark from the doorway.

"I know you told me you needed time to think, but I couldn't stay away. Where've you been?"

"I went over to the Fellatorre's to look at the clip of the Plains video they say was Jennifer."

It all came out in a jumble as I jumped up into his arms, and he lifted my feet off the ground and swung me around into the house, slamming the front door behind us with his foot.

"Just a minute," I said, extracting myself from our embrace. "Let me show you."

I turned on my laptop and brought up the e-mail with the video LaTisha sent me. Mike came in with a beer in his hand and sat beside me on the worn gray couch. "Look! It was Chloe who spotted this tattoo on the woman's wrist. She said her mother didn't have any tattoos, wouldn't have any tattoos."

"What's that?" he asked, and pointed to the e-mail from LaTisha.

"Jennifer's partner sent me these. They're of Riordan and Armstrong at a charity event a couple weeks ago."

"Let's take a look," he said.

I scrolled up the first photo. The photograph showed Seth in a tuxedo, standing on the steps of what must be the museum. Fat granite pillars flanked him, and behind him loomed a stone building. He stood talking to someone below him on the stairs and out of the picture. A shapely blonde stood on his far side, wearing a clinging black dress and sky-high heels. I scrolled up the next picture, and it was of Seth standing with a champagne flute in his hand and the same blonde close up against his side. She stood looking into his face and laughing. The photo was obviously taken inside the art museum. Paintings hung on the white walls, and a crowd of affluent-looking people in formal wear milled around with drinks in their hands. A shadow fell over the blonde's face; her head thrown back in laughter. The third photograph was of Seth and Darnell, both of them in tuxedos, both with empty hands, and they seemed to be engaged in a heated discussion.

In four of the seven photographs, the blonde stood close in and intimate at Seth's side. All the photos seemed to have been taken at the same event.

"Show me what you found on the video," Mike said.

I brought up the blown-up screen grabs, and showed him the tattoo.

"Now blow up some of this woman. Here, this one."

He pointed to one where the blonde was reaching across Seth towards a tray filled with champagne glasses.

"Who is this?" he asked. "Is this Alexis?"

I enlarged the photo as much as I could without it going blurry. It neither was or wasn't obviously Alexis.

We looked through the pictures again until we found one where the blonde's right wrist showed. In this one, a hand-size black evening bag dangled from her wrist. I cropped the picture down to just her wrist, and blew it up.

"I thought it was the strap from her bag, but that's the same heart tattoo," I said. "This is the woman from the video."

Mike leaned in close, squinching up his eyes. "No. This isn't a heart. It's an infinity sign. Though I can see where you'd mistake that for a heart. Let's look at the screen grab again."

I brought it up, and, sure enough, the tattoo was an infinity sign, not a heart.

"So this is the woman—" Mike started and trailed off.

I tried blowing up other pictures of the woman's face. I was able to enlarge the one of her next to Seth on the front steps of the museum. Once it was enlarged, I lightened it up enough to realize with a start that it was not Alexis Page, whom I expected it to be. It was Anna Strunk.

"So let me get this straight," Mike said. "The sex kitten played the role of Jennifer Fellatorre in that video?"

"I think that's it. I think she did. So what does that mean?"

"I guess it means she was having an affair with Riordan, not Alexis," Mike said.

"Then who did Alexis see ski past?"

I thought back to that day on the mountain over a week ago.

"Alexis said she saw a client she'd like to catch up with. Then Jennifer said they had followed him into the deep snow. You know, now that I think about it, Anna said Alexis liked dangerous exotic men. There's nothing dangerous or exotic about Seth Riordan. He's white bread."

"Then who? Maybe Daniel Burdick? Sounds like pushing those two into a tree well would be within his norms of behavior."

"But he's not exotic. And Alexis had nothing but disdain for him. It's got to be Darnell Armstrong. For a rich girl from Philly, an ex-special forces guy like him, with a menacing presence—that's exotic."

"I guess it makes sense then that Anna was in the way—"

I leaned over and kissed him.

"You're a genius! That's it, of course—their motive for killing Anna! After she made the video, it was fine as long as she and Riordan were lovers. But there's been some kind of a falling out, obviously. She's sleeping with Flaherty. Something has happened between them, and, once that happened, she became a liability. We need to call Burt Geisner and see whether or not there's a tattoo on her wrist."

"It's 1:00 in the morning. Truckee isn't your big city. We're not a 24/7 kind of place. I think that can wait until morning. She isn't going anywhere."

Mike closed the lid of my laptop and kissed me, and suddenly the cold, drafty room heated up.

We made our way into the bedroom, dropping a trail of clothes, like breadcrumbs, along the way.

Chapter 19

FRIDAY, APRIL 8, 8:15 AM

When I woke and took a look at the clock, what I'd imagined to be 6:00 a.m. was in fact 8:14. Overnight, while Mike and I slept curled up in post-coital bliss, the world around us went white again. Opening the lace curtains, I found snow and ice had sealed over the windows. I blew on the glass and wiped the frost away with a finger to see outside, and found a solid wall of snow. Ferns of frost twined across the cleared glass as fast as I could wipe it clean.

Overnight the house had reverted to its normal temperature of below freezing. Right around 23 or 24 degrees. Leaping from foot to foot, on the cold wood floor, I leaned over and gave Mike a shake.

"Better get up. We've overslept."

I jumped back onto the bed and pulled the hair out of his eyes, so I could stare into his face.

"It's still dark," he groaned, pulling the covers over his head.

"The windows are snowed over. Come on. It's 8:15."

He sat bolt upright. "What? Damn! Where's my phone?" Ten minutes later, we were on the way out the door, and then after shoveling eighteen inches of snow off Mike's pickup and my rental, we headed to Squaw in separate cars.

"Hey Laura," Grappa McDermott answered his phone. "What's up?"

Some kind of a high-pitched grinding noise whined in the background.

"Just a sec," he said. "Hold on."

I did, and in a second or two the noise stopped.

"Sorry. Making a smoothie. What're you saying?"

"I'm running late. I'm just driving in, but I've got to make a couple stops before I get on mountain. Any chance you could head up to the ski patrol shack at the top of Red Dog and keep an eye out for our guy until I get there? I'll call Matt and Janis on Red Dog and let them know to expect you."

"Sure, Bud," he told me. "That's cool. But the lifts aren't open yet."

"Right. When they open. I should be there by—I don't know. But will you help me out?"

"Indeed!"

"Cool. See you in a bit."

Richard answered on the second ring.

"Yes, Laura. What?"

"Mike and I are on our way over to talk to you guys. Could you hold on for a couple minutes till we get there?"

"We're already on the shuttle over to Squaw. Where do you want to meet us?"

We agreed on the Starbucks in Squaw village. Using my in-car-no-hands-involved Bluetooth, I called Mike to let him know.

The Village at Squaw was still in the process of digging out. And it was packed, this being a bluebird powder day. I had to park way out in the back of beyond, and catch a ride in with Mike to his close-up parking spot. We elbowed our way in through the crowd, since the massive snow dump of the previous night had delayed lift openings so patrol teams could finish up blasting. So it was just Mike, me, and ten or twelve or thirteen thousand powder fiends.

It took a while to locate Richard and Chloe in the Starbucks. But they had found a little foot-wide black table way in the back, and three chairs, so we cut through the crowd to join them. As much as I'd have loved a coffee, the line running out the door and down the walkway all the way to the bathrooms stopped me.

Once settled into the third chair, I showed Chloe and Richard everything Mike and I figured out the night before. Chloe, her dark hair in messy braids I felt sure she did herself, looked over the pictures of Anna carefully and asked me to let her use my computer. I did, and she pulled up an art app and used it to color Anna's hair dark. A hushed wave of shock settled over us all when we realized how much she looked like Jennifer. The glowing skin, delicate features, no wonder Seth chose her to play the role of Jennifer.

I leaned over and gave Chloe a hug.

"You are so smart!"

Richard agreed as he leaned over and kissed the top of her head.

"But what does this mean?" she asked me. "Do we know who killed Mom?"

"It's just one more piece in the puzzle. But it won't be long now--days not weeks, maybe just hours. Be patient a little longer, sweet thing."

She fought back the gloss of tears welling up in her eyes.

There was nothing more to say. I packed my laptop into my backpack, and we all wiggled through the crowd to get outside.

Chloe looked adorable in pink overalls with duct tape on one knee, and a silver parka.

"Can I walk over to the ski school with you?" she asked Mike.

He took her pink ski glove in his hand.

"Bye, Dad," she said. Then, almost as an afterthought, she hugged her dad.

Mike gave me a kiss and said, "I'll be able to get away in a couple hours."

"I'll come by your office."

Richard, wearing a new electric blue parka, and gray ski pants, said he'd be in PlumpJack, and started walking over to the right.

He turned and looked back at me. "Thanks," he said. "I guess."

"I don't see how hitting the bar at 9:00 in the morning is going to make anything better."

He didn't reply but continued walking down the promenade.

The parking lot was treacherous with ice, and it took me nearly fifteen minutes to make it back to the rental. I drove out against the steady flow of two lanes of traffic heading into Squaw and turned right onto Highway 89 into Tahoe City. The valley widened going this way, with the Truckee River spread out wide, clear and emerald green on the right, and the banks of the river pillowed deep with snow. On the left, steep granite cliffs towered over the road, the gray stone colored vividly with lichen like a piece of abstract art. In places, the snow berms along the road were high enough to enclose the power lines, and huge pine trees drooped beneath heavy loads of snow.

In Tahoe City, I drove almost all the way through town before parking in front of a coffee shop advertising free wi-fi. Once settled into an empty corner, I pulled my laptop out of my backpack and booted it up. I had to organize my thoughts so I could figure out what I still needed to know. I'm a scientist. Use the scientific method, dummy! I started listing what I knew, suspected, and needed to find out.

- Jennifer was a continuing & mounting source of trouble for Plains Drilling.
- Alexis found out Armstrong & Riordan were going to be at Squaw over the weekend and arranged it so she'd be there as well.
- Anna Strunk played the role of Jennifer Fellatorre while she sabotaged a Plains Drilling well in a video Plains Drilling made.
- Anna Strunk & Seth Riordan were having an affair. For how long?
- Then why was she sleeping with Sean Flaherty? To make Riordan jealous? Was it that oldest of revenge motives?
- Alexis Page & Darnell Armstrong were having an affair (?)
- Daniel Burdick had a long history of revenge acts just like pushing those women into the tree well, or throwing Anna Strunk over the cliff or burying me.
- Why did Burt Geisner have Daniel Burdick's car towed, & how did the women's luggage get in it?
- Was it just a coincidence the cars were towed at the CP that day?

- Were Daniel Burdick and Seth Riordan working together?
- How did Alexis' car end up buried in snow at the Tahoe Biltmore?

Burt Geisner had yet to call me back. He had yet to speak to me for that matter. I tried his cell number, which his brother gave me, and once again it cut to voice mail.

"Hey Burt, It's Laura Bailey. I've got some information I'd like to discuss with you."

What else did I know? Margaret said Seth was not a great skier back when she knew him. But that was ten years ago; he could be now. Whoever led those women down into that deep snow was an expert. Can I assume that the man who led them into that deep snow in the first place was the same man who led them down into the trees and ultimately to their deaths? I was betting it was the same person, but I had no proof—not yet.

Daniel and Darnell were the two experts in the bunch.

I packed up and did a U-turn in the middle of the road, then headed back to park in front of The Blue Agave. Mexican Food with Altitude, the sign out front said. It's in one of the oldest buildings in Tahoe City, The Tahoe Inn. It's an old log building painted pale blue with a low sloping roof and a split rail fence across the front.

After crossing the road to the lakeside, I found a way in through the snowbanks to the walking path some sixty or seventy feet above Lake Tahoe. Down below sat the bathhouse for Commons Beach, a sturdy brick building.

Usually, a black metal railing prevents people from getting into the walkway by crossing Highway 28—which in summer is bumper to bumper traffic all the way through Tahoe City–anywhere except in designated crosswalks. Just then only an occasional vehicle rumbled down 28: a bus, a contractor's pick-up, a car filled with teenagers headed out to one of the ski resorts.

The black railing that ran along the street side of the walkway stood enclosed in a berm of snow six feet high and about two feet wide, running in width from the shoulder of 28 to the edge of the walking path. The walkway had been kept plowed clear down to the cement, and ran about three or four feet wide. The path was completely hidden from the view of people driving past, unless they drove a semitruck, as well as hidden from anyone walking on the sidewalk on the other side of the road. The only way through the snow berm lining 28 was at the crosswalks, of which there were about one per block.

I had wondered how there would have been enough privacy to kill Anna here, but I realized the snowbanks between the footpath and the road gave a lot of privacy. Shoulder-high snowbanks were also built up on the lakeside of the path, where a fence usually stopped people from attempting to clamber down the cliff. So whoever killed Anna had to also be strong enough to heft her up into the air to shoulder height and push her out over a four or five foot thick snowbank.

Standing inside the snow berm at the crosswalk nearest The Blue Agave, I looked back at the businesses across the street. There was the restaurant, a motel, and, fifty feet past that, across a driveway into a small shopping plaza, on the second floor there was a vacation rental company. Farther down 28, on the lakeside, was the Fire Department.

In the Mexican restaurant, I asked if anyone noticed a black Hummer H3 parked in the area last Wednesday afternoon.

A harried-looking waitress said she thought she remembered a big Hummer parked in front of the windows, and customers were complaining they couldn't see the lake, but she wasn't sure if that happened on Tuesday or Wednesday, and she thought it might have been earlier, around noon.

After leaving the Mexican restaurant, I crossed the driveway to the small shopping center and climbed up a steep set of stairs covered in dirty blue carpet, and turned left. There was a counter inside the small office of the vacation rental place where people picked up the keys to their rental houses. No one manned the desk. I looked back into the office and realized it continued back for two more rooms, and the final room overlooked the street, the snowbank on the other side, and beyond that Lake Tahoe.

"Hello?" I called out. "Hello?"

Two big fuzzy dogs poked their noses around the corner of the front room, gave me the once over, and lay back down.

"Just a minute," came a muffled voice.

A toilet flushed, and ten seconds later a dark-haired man came out of the door to a bathroom on my right.

"Busted," he said. "What can I do for you?"

"I'm Laura Bailey. I'm helping the husband of one of those women who disappeared at Squaw last week look into what happened. I wonder if by any chance you noticed a big black Hummer parked outside last Wednesday afternoon."

"Right. Follow me," he said, leading me back farther into the office, to the room overlooking the lake. It was a big empty room with a filing cabinet and a folding table as a desk. The makeshift desk sat over to the left of the window and out of the line of sight I had when I first came in. His view of the whole scene was even better than I'd originally thought.

"That's a terrible thing," he said. "Pretty shocking finding them buried in the parking lot. Let me check here—last Wednesday . . ."

He began leafing through a date book.

"Last Wednesday. . . Wednesday."

He found the page he'd been searching for and tapped it with his right index finger.

"Last Wednesday, I got here around 2:00, and, yes, there was a monster of a black Hummer parked down this way a ways."

He pointed to the left.

"I remember because I thought at the time it's not exactly the California Tahoe way. Right? Pollute our chunk of paradise by driving a planet-raper like that? I was surprised when I saw Cali plates because I'd naturally assumed it was a Nevada car. I'm sure it was from the Bay Area. What can I say? The outsiders are ruining this place."

He paused a moment and stared out the window towards the lake.

I was thinking he certainly picked a strange line of work if that's the way he felt, but, not wanting to antagonize him, I kept my mouth shut.

241

"And then I saw something else. I don't know if this is part of what you'd be interested in, but, since you asked, I saw some tall gentleman, wearing a big black hat, and—" he paused.

"A big blanket coat?" I asked.

"No," he said and shook his head. "I think he had on a Canadian Tuxedo, you know jeans and a jean jacket?"

He apparently found that pretty funny. I smiled back at him.

"But anyways, a blonde drives up in a silver Audi, a little one, like a sports car, and gets out and talks to him. I saw them walking away together."

"Towards the Hummer?"

"Yeah," he said as if he wasn't sure. "Well, over that way." He shook his hand towards the left again. "But they started out talking all friendly and sweet. He kissed her cheek when she first got out of the car. But then it got kind of heated. After that, I can't tell you. I got busy, and I never saw them again. But I do remember it was Wednesday because that was the day I got in late."

"Did you notice the Hummer leave?"

"No," he shook his head. "Never gave it another thought. Should I have?"

I had no answer for him.

"Thank you for talking with me," I told him, and headed down the stairs to the street.

—

Sitting in the rental, waiting for my seat to heat up, I stared across the road at Lake Tahoe shimmering blue and flashing splinters of silver off the ripples in the water. I was thinking that the only soft chink in the armor of Plains Drilling seemed to be Ellen. I'd love to have a chat with her without her husband around. I decided to take a chance and dialed her home number, hoping she'd answer. On the third ring, she answered the phone. I acted like nothing happened the last two times I visited her home, and dove right in.

"Hi Ellen, it's Laura Bailey. I'm sitting looking at Lake Tahoe, and it's just gorgeous today with all the fresh snow. Have you been out yet?"

"No," she said. "Not yet. I have Pilates at noon, so I'll see it then."

"I lost the card you gave me with Darnell Armstrong's number on it. Do you by any chance know where he is today?"

"Seth headed out early. He had business in Reno and choppered out of Truckee around 7:00. Darnell took Seth to the airport and said he was going skiing after that."

"Do you know where?"

"Oh," Ellen said, with a laugh. "Darnell only skis Squaw on powder days."

"Thank you," I told her.

"Where are you? In Tahoe City?" she asked.

"Yes, I'm heading back to Squaw."

"Please come by the house and pick up the present and your parka and gloves."

"Wonderful. I'll be there in ten or fifteen minutes."

"I'll put some fresh coffee on," she said. "I'll see you soon."

Pulling out of Tahoe City, I instructed the car to dial Grappa's phone number.

He answered immediately

"I've seen the guy! The dude who used to have a wonky ski, but has obviously had it fixed or pulled another set of arrows out of his quiver cause he ain't skiing so wonky today."

"I'm on my way, Grappa. But I've got to make one more stop. So it's still going to be a half hour or forty-five minutes. Keep an eye on him, but don't do anything crazy like trying to follow him. OK?"

"Sure. Later." The phone beeped and went dead.

A few minutes later, I pulled between the massive snow berms in the driveway of the Riordan's home off Alpine Meadows Drive. My phone chimed for a text, and checking it I found a message from Mike:

Ready when u r–letz go sex ma-Chine~ xox

I texted him back.

K. B there soon <3. xoxo

I'm a sex ma-Chine~ huh?

As I climbed out of the car and made my way across the hard packed snow of the driveway, I wondered how many homes the Riordan's owned. The driveway was slippery as hell. I wished I'd worn my mukluks. The Ugg boots I wore scored a zero for traction.

Ellen Riordan waited for me at the door. She was wearing a pair of gray yoga capris and a pink and white paisley hooded top and fat-soled snowshoes with her skinny white shins protruding above. She looked kind of goofy.

"Come in, come in," she said and ushered me out of the cold as she shivered and rubbed her slender arms.

"You're not a cold-weather person, I guess?"

"No, I'm no skier. I'd rather be in Arizona right now. Though I love the Tahoe area."

"Do you have a home in Arizona, too?"

She had laid out a tray of delicate cookies, porcelain cups, and saucers.

"Let's sit here and be casual." She pointed me towards a dark wood bar stool at the kitchen island.

Once the coffee was poured and we were both seated, she took a sip, then looked me in the face. "Yes, to answer your question, we have a lovely home near Sedona."

"That's beautiful country."

"It is," she said tentatively, like there was more to the story, but she didn't want to get into it right then.

"Do you spend much time there?"

"Ah," she stalled grasping for words. "I used to. I don't go there much any more. My husband still visits his friends there, but for me— just a lot of bad memories."

She left it at that, but I thought I got her drift: Anna wasn't the first or last.

"Do you know Daniel Burdick? He works for the same law firm as Alexis did, and he has a place here at Alpine."

She thought for a moment, then said no.

I believed her.

"I'm curious as to whether or not you ever met any of the three women who have died in the past week?"

She paused again. "Yes," she finally said. "I met Alexis Page several times. Seth brought her over to our place in Philadelphia. They'd work."

"She was his main legal counsel in Philadelphia?"

"Right, her firm was. But she was Seth's main liaison."

"And the other women?"

"I certainly heard an earful about Jennifer Fellatorre—I should say I overheard an earful about her—but I never met her."

"I met her briefly," I said. "Right before she died."

"And what was your impression?"

"I liked her. Alexis—not so much."

"I never cared for Alexis. An overly aggressive young woman, I found. Spoke to me like a servant in my own home."

Once I took another sip of the coffee, she seemed assured that her hostess duties had been fulfilled, so she continued her train of thought.

"I'm sorry you had to be the one who spoke with them last. The last we know of, anyway. It must be a burden for you."

"I have to figure out what happened to them. My feelings of guilt over leaving them—combined with meeting Jennifer's daughter Chloe who's here in the Tahoe area with her father. She's a wonderful girl. Just lovely. She's nine and smart and funny, yet still a child. I feel ill for her."

Ellen winced at hearing about Chloe.

"And how are you coming with the investigation? Is there an end in sight?"

"It's coming along. But there seems to be a few brick walls I keep running into. A lot of people with something to hide."

"Name one for me."

"OK, Burt Geisner. He won't even talk to me. He's a major brick wall. I don't know if you heard this, but that Daniel Burdick I was asking you about, his car was towed from the parking lot at Squaw Creek, where he's parked for years, and not only towed but searched, too, which certainly can't be standard procedure. And Jennifer and Alexis' luggage was found inside. That seems too coincidental. So I've been calling and calling Burt to ask him why he had those cars towed, and why Burdick's was searched, but I've gotten no response."

Turning away from her gaze I looked out the kitchen window. There wasn't much to see as a heavy overhang of snow had curled down over it, and snow had drifted half-way up it from below.

Ellen turned slightly in her chair and followed my gaze out the window.

"In another week, I won't be able to see outside at all. I think I'll lose my mind when that happens. I feel claustrophobic not being able to see out the windows—just banks of snow everywhere I look. Our second-story bedroom window is drifted over for heaven's sake."

"Even if you don't like to ski, you should find some other outdoor winter sport. It would help if you could spend a couple hours outside every day. Breathe the fresh air, get some sun on your face. How about ice skating? You look like an ice skater."

She looked back into my eyes, a sad smile on her face. "In another life." She seemed to muster her energies. "If you'll indulge me for a moment, I'd like to show you something."

I nodded okay.

"I've tried to live my life a way that I won't end up lying on my deathbed feeling ashamed of the decisions I made. There are certain loyalties I cannot betray, even though perhaps I wish I could. I don't know what happened to these women. If I knew that, I'd feel compelled to reveal that information to the proper authority. So I can't help you there. But things I do know that perhaps could point you in one direction or another I will show and tell you what I feel I can without betraying my own mores. In regards to Burt Geisner, I can give you some information that would help you to understand his behavior, but I don't have any information that would help you find who killed these women."

"OK," I said, having no idea what was coming or exactly what she meant.

"I'd like your assurance of discretion. I'm trying to give you some background." She looked up at me, obviously waiting for me to agree.

"All right," I told her. "It's just background. Just between us."

"My husband was a supporter of Sheriff Geisner's re-election campaign. He was a supporter of his first run for sheriff. I wouldn't say they're friends, but they know each other well, and speak often when we're at the Tahoe house."

That explained a lot. "What kind of support? Financial? Political?"

"Both probably. I'll look around and see if I can find some kind of details for you."

"You said that Alexis was around a lot, but did you ever meet Anna Strunk?"

Her face hardened, and she stood and indicated by her body language that our chat was over.

"I can't say any more. It's been lovely getting to know you a little Laura. But I have to get going, and there's nothing more I can say except that Seth and I were raised Catholic, so I never believed that divorce was an option. I wish I had been able to but—"

She left for a moment then returned a second later carrying a silver Nordstrom's bag that she handed to me.

"Here are your things, Laura. I hope we meet again under better circumstances. I feel we've had a meeting of the minds. But if you'll excuse me—"

Once again I was sent packing.

On the drive over to Squaw, I called Mike, and asked him to meet me with our skis at the Funitel, so we could get up mountain to meet Grappa. We arranged to meet in fifteen minutes.

After speaking with Mike, I texted Grappa—while driving, I'm ashamed to admit—and told him:

On my way. Taking the Funi in 15. Meet where?

A text came back twenty seconds later:

Heya, top of silvi chair in 30. Take the tram.

I got a close-up parking space right outside the Medical Center—left by a deep powder casualty forced to head home early no doubt. The silver Nordstrom bag sat beside me on the front passenger seat. My parka lay on top, and, pulling it out of the bag, I found it had been cleaned. That was embarrassing. I opened the lavender envelope and read the card. It was a get-well card, with lilacs on the front. Inside in a spidery hand was written:

Dear Laura,

Best wishes for a speedy recovery. I hope this small gift tells you what I cannot bring myself to say.

Sincerely, Ellen Riordan

Inside the package was a sterling silver picture frame with green velvet backing, and a fancy script LB engraving near the bottom of the frame. Inside the frame was a picture of Seth Riordan in a tropical setting on a beach with azure seas and palm trees. He wore some kind of resort-wear shirt and shorts, and in his lap sat a drunk-looking Anna Strunk wearing nothing at all, stark naked, smiling for the camera and holding up a tropical drink.

I turned back four little silver flaps that held the frame together and pried off the green velvet backing. On the back of the photo in red ink was written:

St. Kitts, 2008.

So their affair had been going on for at least a few years. That made me really curious as to why Anna was staying with Sean and parading around with him dressed in a mink coat and over-the-knee boots with five-inch heels. Tell me it wasn't something as inane as trying to make Riordan jealous by showing him how quickly she could move on to the next mega-bucks guy. And this one younger and better-looking than him, though I doubt he was richer.

Her death started to make a kind of sense. Maybe Anna wasn't even thinking about the video she made. But when Riordan saw she'd betrayed him with Sean, he could easily have assumed she'd surely betray him further by revealing what she knew about the video. Maybe she wanted him to leave Ellen, and in the end he couldn't for the same reasons Ellen couldn't. Ellen said they were Catholics. Then again, maybe Anna told Riordan that if he didn't leave Ellen, she'd reveal her part in the video production. However it worked out, she obviously didn't realize exactly what her lover was capable of.

Chapter 20

FRIDAY, APRIL 8, 11:20 AM

Mike stood some twenty yards from the front of the Funitel at the ski school meeting area. He wore his blue Squaw Ski School parka and pants and the big satellite phone of authority strapped to his chest, milling around talking and joking with instructors and students as they queued up for classes. He disengaged himself from his colleagues when our eyes met, and walked over to wait as I climbed up several steps from the walkway onto the snow.

"Hey, Babe," he said, and wrapped me up in his arms and gave me a big kiss. This garnered a lot of attention from the crowd.

"That was a bold statement," I said, with a laugh. "We need to meet Grappa at the Silvi chair."

"OK. Let's head over to the tram."

We walked to the side of the Funitel building where he picked up both our skis, slinging a pair over each shoulder. I took the poles and followed him down off the snow and over to the cable car building. I felt sort of embarrassed, sort of useless, having someone else carry my skis. I followed behind like the good sport I am, trotting along and carrying the girlie poles.

We lucked out and had a cable car almost to ourselves, so I got a chance to fill him in on everything I'd learned since we split up earlier.

At High Camp, Mike unstrapped the satellite phone, stripped out of his official parka and pants, and nonchalantly stood in the middle of the big open space in his long black compression underwear and a fleece before pulling on a pair of bright green pants and a yellow parka from the locker he kept there. No one was supposed to wear Squaw Ski School gear, he told me, unless they were actively involved in Squaw business, so he dressed quickly, then we headed outside.

We clicked into our skis and swept down to the top of the Silverado chairlift. Silverado is the most recent area at Squaw, and the whole immense area is served by one ancient chairlift. The entire Silverado area, larger than most entire ski resorts back East, is for experts only.

At the top of the chairlift, Grappa sat plopped on a bench, leaning up against the lift shack and chatting with the liftie who sat next to him. Grappa had on a white parka that looked like a Jackson Pollock painting, a crazy web of black lines spotted with yellow, red, and blue drops of paint.

"Hey, Grappa," I yelled, and he spun around on the bench, his whole face lighting up when he saw us. "Mr. Mike, Ms. Laura!" He said something quickly to the liftie, and skied over to us. Once I got a whiff of him, it became clear what they'd been up to.

"Don't let Dave Geisner catch you!" I shouted to the liftie. "That guy's got a nose for it."

"Yeah, don't I know?" the liftie said back.

"Don't worry, Bud," Grappa told him. "Laura Bailey's cool!"

"It's Mr. Mike I'm worried about," the liftie said.

"You should be," Mike yelled over at him. "Put the dope away and get to work."

The liftie smiled, looked relieved, and jumped to his feet and started shoveling snow onto the loading ramp.

We skied on past the chairlift along the ridge of a mountaintop to drop into Silverado. Since this was such wild country, you dropped in via a series of gates with seven being the easiest; we decided to drop in at Gate Three.

"How did you figure our bad guy would be here?" I asked Grappa.

"It's totally out of the way. No one skis here but experts, and it's got more territory than most whole resorts. This is where the untouched pow is today."

Mike and I took our time skiing down behind Grappa. He took every opportunity to become airborne, banking up against perpendicular walls to bounce off and flipping back down onto the snow cat track we followed. We were all alone, just the three of us as we moved through shin-deep snow. We carved down into the vast white canyon of Silverado, dotted with color only from protruding rocks or the occasional tree.

Watching Grappa ski inspired me to do things I don't normally do. Like flying off a cliff face fifteen feet into the air and bouncing off a fat puff of snow to go airborne again, this time feeling so exhilarated I did a spread-eagle—throwing wide both my arms and legs. At thirty, I'm too old for flips—except maybe on special occasions.

I caught up with Grappa, and he streaked past and skied into a narrow shoot between big granite rocks. He moved straight down the narrow strip of snow and flew out airborne at the bottom, rocketing far out into the air. Slowly, elegantly, he spread his arms wide, and with his legs tight together, drew his head back and did a slow back flip, crossing his skis as he hung upside down into an iron cross as he arced up through the air. He landed on his feet in a wave of snow and seemed to sit on the back of his skis, but reappeared skiing fast ten yards below. He twisted back to look up at us and waved his arms in a triumphant V.

"Don't be too impressed," he shouted. "I've practiced flips there all winter!" His wild laugh echoed down the canyon.

Mike skied up beside me, and we looked at each other and shook our heads.

"Do I need to do that, too?" Mike asked "Cause first I'm going to need some practice."

We laughed as we picked up our speed cutting through the knee-deep powder and flying down the steep face of the canyon behind Grappa.

Mike cut in front of me and rocketed out into the air off the sheer face of a granite outcropping and bounced off a fat puff of snow, went airborne, hit another mushroom of snow, and flew out through the branches of a pine tree to land in a fat whoosh of powder, invisible for a few seconds until he, too, came shooting out the bottom of the powder cloud.

We were living, right there, right then, in that moment—the three of us. There was nothing better, nothing more. We did amazing things on skis, as if gravity didn't apply to us. We caught huge air in places other skiers would barely launch off the ground. Skiing behind Mike and Grappa, I marveled at the way they interpreted the terrain, the things they judged possible.

I felt thrilled to be there. Inspired by their joy, their true passion for skiing. Their commitment to the moment, the day, the lines we skied.

On the way back up in the lift, we sat smashed together doing what people always do after a run like–that talking about the run we'd just skied. Our spirits soared as we rode up in the chair, nobody thought about Alexis, Jennifer, or Anna. For those few minutes, we had a break from all that pain and loss.

Then suddenly, Grappa rotated in his seat, and said, "That's him. Right there." We watched as Darnell dropped into Silverado.

"That's him," Grappa said again in almost a whisper. "That's the guy I saw those two women follow down into the trees, over there where nobody ever skis."

The lift continued on for some ways, and when we finally unloaded, we turned around and flew back into the canyon towards a wild mountainside called Katmandu and past that China Wall. At the top of Katmandu, we watched as Darnell cut his way down the nearly vertical face of China Wall.

We all stood motionless, watching him ski.

After a stretch, Grappa said, "That's him for sure. He's doing it again. See how he turns a little wonky on that right leg? I thought he had a bad tune on that ski, like it was grippy. But no, I see now that leg is tweaked. Something's a little off. And he was skiing fine yesterday. Maybe that only happens when he gets tired?"

"Guy knows his way around," Mike said.

"Let's follow him," I said, and, not waiting around for an answer, I pushed off the steep headwall of Katmandu. "We should invite him to lunch," I yelled back.

Half way down, Mike came up along side me. "Is that a good idea? What're you going to say to him?"

"I have no idea," I told him, and picked up speed down the steep, wild incline with Mike floating along behind me on my tails.

As we caught the chair at the bottom of the canyon, I pulled out my phone and dialed Darnell's number. We watched him, six empty chairs in front of us, fumble to dig out his phone.

"Hey, Darnell," I said, sounding perky. "Will you meet me for lunch at High Camp? It's past noon."

"Oh," he said, then paused. "I'm not skiing today. Otherwise, I'd have been happy to."

"That's funny because I think you're a few chairs in front of me."

Darnell jerked around in his chair, his skis swinging out to one side, to look 180 degrees behind and down the steep incline of mountain.

I waved.

"OK," he said. "Maybe I am skiing. Just didn't want to talk to you."

"But you're the man Riordan told me to talk to."

"Let's head to High Camp," he said, not sounding happy about it.

"See you in a few minutes," I said ending the call and putting my phone away. I loved my new ski pants, but there's no pocket on my calf for my phone. I missed that about my old pants.

"Will you guys come with me?" I asked.

"Sure," Grappa said.

"We're not going to let you have lunch by yourself with a guy we think killed three women," Mike added.

A few seconds later, we unloaded, then started off across a long open meadow heading over to High Camp. We followed along behind Darnell, way ahead of us.

The restaurant and bar at High Camp seemed to spill into Lake Tahoe. Walking down the stairway when you first enter the restaurant, you have to grab the railing so you don't tumble in. By the time we tromped in, shaking off snow and pulling off helmets and gloves, Darnell had already ensconced himself in a half-circle booth facing out over the valley below and past that Lake Tahoe, and in the direct glare of the sun. It had to be 75 degrees in the restaurant, but coming in from the cold, it felt more like 90. The three of us stood around the booth unsnapping chin straps, shaking loose from parkas, gloves, fleeces, sweaters, and unzipping turtlenecks, until we finally got down to our base-layers and slipped into the booth.

Darnell sat watching this three-way strip tease with a coy smile on his face. He was wearing a red base-layer shirt unzipped to his breast-bone with a few reddish hairs poking out from underneath. All of our faces burned crimson from the cold and the sudden heat.

The restaurant was a cafeteria, but no one made a move towards food.

"Grappa," I said, "you're the closest to the outside, would you get us all some water?"

He jumped up and jogged up a flight of stairs like he was wearing tennis shoes instead of ski boots.

"So what did you want?" he asked, looking back and forth between Mike and me.

"I want to get your opinion on something," I said as I dug around in my parka for my phone. I showed Darnell the blow-up of the picture of Seth Riordan and the woman with him at the reception.

He gave it a glance. "So?"

"Do you know who this woman is?"

"No."

"If you look closer, you'll see it's Anna Strunk."

"OK, maybe it is. She's counsel for our firm."

"But now look at this." I brought up the screen grab from the video and showed him the woman, then the blow-up of her tattoo. "If you look at these women carefully, you'll notice they both have the same infinity sign tattoo on their inner wrists. These two women are the same person, and definitely not Jennifer Fellatorre, who never had a tattoo."

Next, I pulled out the photo of Anna from the reception in Philadelphia, the one where Chloe colored in her hair.

He shrugged again. "OK. She looks like Anna. But she also looks a lot like Jennifer Fellatorre."

He flipped back to the picture from the reception. "This doesn't mean it wasn't Jennifer Fellatorre dressed up to look like Anna."

I couldn't wrap my head around what he was saying for a minute.

"What? You're saying that Jennifer dressed up to look like Anna and went with Seth Riordan to a reception? That makes no sense at all."

"I'm saying Jennifer dressed up in the video to look like Anna Strunk pretending to be Jennifer. Just so she would be mistaken for Seth's mistress."

"Including a fake tattoo?"

I couldn't help it. I gave him an eye roll and exhaled loudly.

"What was your relationship with Alexis?"

Just then Grappa returned with four big glasses of water and proceeded to distribute them around the table. Mike put his hand on my leg and squeezed, signaling me to take it easy.

"Alexis represented a legal firm Plains does a lot of work with."

"I know you were having an affair with Alexis."

He glared at me, refusing to admit I had anything on him. So I shifted around to attack him from a different angle.

"Well, you and Riordan certainly read Anna wrong. She may have looked like a doll, and pretended to be a doll, but you two found out the hard way that she wasn't a woman you could push around. She was probably tougher than you and Riordan put together. What'd she threaten to do? Make public her role in the video? Or did she just tell Riordan she'd had enough? So then what? Did he send you into Tahoe City to what? Meet her? Talk some sense into her? Take care of her? You know somebody saw you? A guy who works in a vacation rental office on the second floor, near Blue Agave. Saw her drive up, and saw you kiss Anna on the cheek. Saw the whole thing go down. You killed her, a foster child just like you. Everything she had she earned, just like you did. I'm surprised, that's all," I told him. "Alexis I understand. She was in the way, and she was just another trust fund girl."

Darnell said nothing, just leaned back against the booth and stared into my eyes. His dark eyes and slab of face had no affect. I didn't feel a bit intimidated by him.

We all sat silently for a long moment, the quiet hanging heavy in the sunlight, and the heat streaming in from the big windows.

"Excuse me for a second," Darnell said, and stood. He'd been sitting at the other end of the booth from Grappa. He headed downstairs for the bathroom, leaving behind his Kjus parka, fleece, gloves and helmet.

I sat there feeling sad and somehow responsible for Anna and her short, brutal life. Anna was orphaned at the same age I was. But she didn't have a clutch of old women reaching out to break her fall. I turned to look at Mike, and something hard jabbed into my leg. I lifted up Darnell's parka, and found I was halfway sitting on a light blue Snow Angel CamelBak, a woman's CamelBak. Flipping it over, I unzipped the flap where you insert a hand warmer to keep it from freezing up, and pulled out a green and gold hand warmer from the Colorado State University ski team.

I looked up at Mike and Grappa. "It's the CamelBak I gave Jennifer Fellatorre."

I felt so in shock I was having trouble figuring out exactly what that meant. "Why would he keep this?"

"Poor kids don't throw anything away," Grappa said

"Get your stuff," Mike yelled. "Let's go!"

All three of us leapt up and began pulling on gear as we raced outside.

We clicked into our skis and skated around the corner of High Camp towards Broken Arrow in time to see Darnell disappearing over the rim of the mountain.

I shouted at Grappa. "Go get Dave and Burt Geisner. Tell them what's happened and where we are. Get Dave to send help!"

"No," he shouted. "I'm coming with you!"

"I need you to go back and get help. NOW!"

He skidded to a fast stop and turned around.

"OK. I get it," he yelled after me.

Next we saw of him, he was skating back up towards High Camp as Mike and I ripped over the lip of the mountain and down after Darnell.

I caught up to Mike and skied along side him.

"It's clear where he's headed," Mike shouted.

We watched him head to the left, into ungroomed snow. Soon all three of us waded through crusty thigh-deep snow. We moved out of the deep snow in a few yards.

Darnell was heading down the Tram Face—which is permanently out-of-bounds, death-defying territory. Most of the Tram Face, which runs directly under the cable car, is comprised of towering glacier-polished boulders jutting up into perpendicular rock faces with a few narrow chutes of snow between the rocks, and lots of huge cliffs.

I took a deep breath, gulped, and swallowed painfully, then pushed off past the point of no return starting down Tram Face after Darnell. I roused a senate of ravens that lifted off the carcass of a marmot to scream and circle around on air currents as I passed, and then a second later Mike riled them up again.

Darnell stopped at the top of the first cliff and looked back, spotting us.

"Stop! Wait a minute!" I screamed at him.

Somewhere he'd picked up a chartreuse parka that his long arms poked out of like chopsticks, and a pair of baby blue gloves.

As I headed down the steep incline following in Darnell's tracks, I felt a jolt from the snow beneath my feet and heard a loud boom. I spun around and looked up mountain to see a crack spreading horizontally across the face of the hard, crusty snow above me. A slab avalanche in which a whole big area of snow triggers and begins moving downhill in one piece was breaking loose fifty yards above me. Mike skied above it, looking down at me in horror. I took it all in with a glance, then turned my skis straight down hill, as fast as I could go. I I angled over to the left as the roaring sound of the snow grew louder until it drowned out everything, even thought. Nothing mattered but getting out of the main thrust of snow. The crumbs of the avalanche caught me and took me over a rock face and down ten feet or so. I landed on crusty snow, which I broke through into five or six feet of softer snow below. I lay on my stomach with my skis sprawled out behind me and my arms out to my sides, hung up by my poles. The snow locked in around my body, and I couldn't move, my mouth and nose filled with snow. With each breath, I inhaled clumps of ice and melted snow. Tossing my head side to side to free a breathing space, I tried to fight down the rising terror of being trapped again for the second time in a week.

I felt a pressure on my ski boot, and then a hand pulling on my leg.

"Not my foot," I tried screaming into the snow. "My face!"

The snow muffled the sound to a whimper. Hands worked their way up my body and finally brushed the snow from under my face and scooped away a path to breathe. I took a huge gulp of air and twisted my head around to look into Mike's blue eyes, the same cerulean as the sky behind him.

An electric grin lit his face.

"You OK?"

"Yeah."

"Scared me," he said. "All I saw was one tail sticking up."

I lay stretched out face down just under the crust of snow, having sunk no deeper than a foot or so. In two minutes, I was out and clicking back into my right ski that came loose in the fall.

"Did you see where Armstrong went? Was he buried?"

Mike shook his head and leaned forward on his poles, peering over the edge of the rock face just in front of us. "Sorry. I was watching you."

We made our way carefully down through a series of six five-foot high cliff jumps towards the debris of the avalanche. After two more short jumps, we came to the field of avalanche snow and began to work our way around the big chunks of tumbled snow. The avie ran down another forty feet below where we stood and into a cluster of huge pine trees.

"Since we see no sign of him, most likely he was swept up, and dumped right there in front of the trees," Mike said, pointing at the pines below us. "That's the most likely place."

We continued to comb back and forth over the avie field for another minute.

I looked up from the rough snowfield and on down the mountain. Over fifty feet to the left, and below where we stood, I saw Darnell sitting on a rock outcropping. His left arm hung limp at his side, and from behind looked longer than the other one. I whacked Mike with my ski pole and pointed down mountain to the left, then put a finger to my lips. We crossed over, clear of the avie debris, and begin to ski down to Darnell.

Hearing a wisp of voice, I turned and looked up the rock face, three figures were waving arms and ski poles. Straining to pick out their voices through the wind blowing up from below, I realized they were screaming, "Stay put! Stay put!'

Ignoring them, together we edged in closer to Darnell, who seemed not to have heard the shouts from the ski patrol. Twice we had to jump down a ten or fifteen foot cliff. But I knew, we both knew, the big jump lay straight in front of Darnell: The Tram Rock, a sheer cliff that dropped down at least a hundred feet, maybe a hundred-and-fifty. I tried to hurry towards him, but in a way that wouldn't put either Mike or myself in more danger than we were already in.

When we were still a hundred feet or so of steep incline and hard crusty wind-slab snow away from Darnell, he struggled to his feet. I realized then he was still in his skis. Something very bad had happened to his left arm or shoulder.

"Wait!" I shouted. "We just want to talk to you!"

Twisting around, he looked at Mike and me for a long second and then sat back down.

A few seconds later, I moved up to just a couple yards from him, and my skis skidded sideways on the icy, sunburned crust of snow leading up to the Tram Rock cliff. I managed to stop just as my bottom ski began slipping out towards the cliff. My uphill ski lurched ahead and hit rock, bringing me to a bone-jarring stop that deposited me onto the ground where I skidded a few feet over ice-hard snow that had melted in the heat of the day and frozen overnight a hundred times since the onset of winter. Nothing soft lasted up there. Anything not frozen had long since blown away. I sprawled awkwardly with both skis still on, and my body stretched out behind some rocks. Darnell swiveled around and looked at me with a face as devoid of emotion and color as the rocks he sat on.

"You again," he said.

"What happened to your shoulder?" I asked, as I gathered myself together and managed to maneuver up onto the rocks Darnell sat on, but far enough away, I hoped, that he couldn't reach over and give me a shove towards the edge, which loomed a few steep yards in front of us.

He shook his head, his good right arm gesturing to the rough passage below. "I'm fucked," he said. "Just fucked."

He turned to face me, and the color and emotion seemed to reanimate his face. "What do you want with me? I haven't done anything that wasn't justified. That Alexis bitch was nothing but demands. Nothing but threats. And Jennifer Fellatorre just wouldn't stop. She was relentless. She would've never stopped."

His sandstone-colored hair swirled wildly in the wind.

"You left a nine-year old girl with no mother. You did that. And what did Anna ever do to you? What did Jennifer do?"

He smiled. "Not asking me what Alexis did?"

I mirrored back his shrug. "I have no idea. I get the impression she wasn't a pleasant person."

"She deserved everything she got."

"But what about Anna?"

"Once Riordan dumped her, she swore she'd tell everyone about the video. That he couldn't do that to her. She'd make him pay."

Wind came up from below in a gale, a solid wall of air. His eyes dripped tears that froze on his cheeks and off his chin in a tiny icicle. It was bitter cold, and he wore nothing but what looked like a kid's parka, with nothing on his head. I recognized the frostbite that leached the tops of his ears white.

"Anna. I regret what happened to her. I feel—well, it doesn't matter now."

He swiveled his head around slowly to face me. "After Riordan lied to me about Anna, there was one more person on my list. You want to get to the bottom of all this, you'll find it in the Martis Flats. That's where this ends. If you hadn't–"

Sudden voices spilled out behind us. Darnell looked over his shoulder in a jerk and spotted the three ski patrollers coming off the final jump towards us. Mike skied towards us just a few yards away. A quick, steep traverse over wind-blasted ice and snow, and they'd be on us.

Darnell grabbed hold of my cast at the wrist and jerked me toward him, then launched himself down the steep run to the edge of the cliff. Flinging myself backwards, away from the cliff onto the steep, iced-over snow of the granite mountainside, I tried to dig my edges in to break my slide.

As I twisted the cast loose from Darnell's grasp, my pole wound around his arm, and I heard a loud snap before the strap broke loose, followed a heartbeat later by a stabbing pain in my already broken wrist. Ignoring the pain, I tried to dig my fingers into the snow to halt my inexorable slide. I gave up on that and managed to grab hold of a pro-truding rock. For a moment, I stopped, gasping and holding onto the rock with my broken left hand. My wrist couldn't hold, though, and the rock began to slip from my grasp. In four feet I'd be following him off the cliff. The snow covered the rock face in a thin, icy veil where I lay.

At first Darnell looked good in the air, stretched out over the tips of his skis. Then his right arm began to windmill frantically to keep his balance; his left arm hung long and useless at his side, blown back behind his body by the wind. He began to fall the rest of the way down the hundred-and-fifty-foot cliff in a tumble of skis and limbs. Then one ski blasted away from his body and shattered against the sheer face of the cliff.

Still struggling for purchase on the rocks, I watched him land head first in deep snow. Finally, I brought my slide to a halt and managed to get a firm grip on the rocks with my right hand. I felt sick for Darnell. I could feel his panic and his struggle to breathe, the way he lay unable to move and breathing in snow particles with every breath. But I was not going to jump off that cliff face after him.

Mike skied to my side, braced his skis on the topside of some rocks, and helped lift me onto my feet. Together, we began to slowly make our way down over to the far left of the Tram Chute, one small jump after another. The ski patrol followed behind, still occasionally yelling at us to stop.

Finally, we reached the place where I saw Darnell go into the snow. The only sign of him was the tail of a ski jutting up from the snow at a crazy angle. We began to dig frantically for his face. A minute later, the ski patrol arrived, and all four of us dug out a trench along what we hoped was the length of his body, aiming for his head: to get him an air passage, get his face cleared of snow. But having gone in headfirst from such a height, it took a lot of digging.

Twelve minutes after I watched him dive into the snow, the ski patrollers pulled him out, unconscious, but with a pulse. I caught sight of the ice mask completely covering his face. He had no breath left; the ice had seen to that.

The patrollers broke the ice mask off Darnell's face and begin CPR, and a wash of color slowly rekindled in his face. He lay on the snow breathing peacefully, but still unconscious. Mike and I filled the patrollers in on why the chase started. They called Dave Geisner at the top of the Tram Face.

A few minutes later, three more ski patrollers arrived with a small yellow plastic sled, and they began preparations to get Darnell loaded and get half a dozen ropes tied onto the sled.

Just as they were ready to head out, Darnell began to wake up and throw his head around frantically. He thrashed and moaned and made everything take longer. Though he didn't seem to be cognizant, he was awake. By the time they got him stabilized as best they could on the small rescue sled, Dave Geisner had arrived.

"Jesus, Laura," he said and hugged me. "I asked for a couple hours of help looking at some dicey snow, and now you've got the whole resort as your own personal bitch."

He shook his head and banged Mike on the back. "Glad this turned out the way it has. Don't get any ideas about skiing the Tram Face again. This could've gone a lot of other ways."

I looked at him like he was crazy. "As if!"

Finally, they had Darnell lashed securely onto the small sled, his head and neck stabilized in a web of ropes and canvas straps. He wasn't awake, but he continued to struggle against the ropes.

The big cliffs were all behind us, only a handful of five-six-and-seven foot drops remained to relay Darnell down. Around 3:00 p.m. we started down mountain, two patrollers roped in as a brakes and two skiing in front.

Mike, the rest of the patrollers, and I followed behind.

It took another hour for all of us to wind our way down off of the mountain and into Base Camp to the waiting rescue team and an ambulance. At some point, unnoticed along the way, Darnell died from internal injuries. He bled out.

Chapter 21

So, finally, Burt Geisner wanted to talk to me. Wanted to talk to me so badly, he couldn't wait for my old cast to be cut off, new x-rays taken of my arm, and a new cast to be put on, but needed to come harangue me in the hospital waiting room in Truckee. I was in no mood to take one minute of shit from him.

Burt Geisner was a big man, like his brother, and had the same hard gut—though his was much larger than Dave's—and the same brick red face. I couldn't imagine what his blood pressure must be, somewhere up in the stratosphere.

"You're out of your jurisdiction here, Burt," I told him, leaning back, in a position I hoped looked casual, in a chair in the waiting room. Mike sat on my right, holding my good hand.

"If you start giving me any grief," I went on, "I'm calling the Truckee Police, and the Nevada County sheriff." Truckee lies within Nevada County, whereas Burt was the sheriff of Placer County.

"You're out of line, Bailey," he protested. "All this happened in my jurisdiction."

"I've been trying to talk to you since an hour after the women disappeared, but you never returned my calls, never picked up, so if you want to talk to me now, I want the sheriff of Nevada Country present as well as someone from the Truckee Police."

"You got a problem with me?"

"You mean beyond the fact that you're buddies with Seth Riordan? Probably bought and paid for by him. Beyond that fact, have I got a problem with you?"

His hazel eyes glossed over hard. "What's that supposed to mean?"

I realized my mistake too late. Shouldn't have said that, not to make excuses, but I was frustrated, exhausted, hungry, and ached all over. But I had told Ellen Riordan I wouldn't reveal what she'd told me about her husband's support of Burt Geisner.

"I've called you two, three times a day ever since those women disappeared. I was hired by Richard Fellatorre to look into what happened to his wife—"

"Doesn't mean I can't throw you in jail for withholding evidence." He paused to run a hand across his hair. "OK, OK," he said. "What do you want? You want to wait to talk to me once you've got the new cast on?"

"I'll talk to you once I'm done here, and with Mike Bernese and your brother present. You don't trust me; I don't trust you."

He stood glaring at me.

"Either that or I'll call a lawyer. I happen to know a whole bunch of them. Better yet, though, as I said, let's have some outside law enforcement present."

"Bailey," he said, "you're not accused of anything. I just want to find out what you know about this mess. That's all."

"Then let's all sit down together. Mike and Dave have been part of this from the beginning."

Unlike you, I wanted to say, but thought better of it.

━━

Around 8:00 p.m., and I sat around a conference table in the ski school with Mike, Dave and Burt Geisner, and the same deputy who visited me in the hospital. For once, it was not snowing, and the moon lit the plaza outside the long stretch of plate-glass windows. A woman named Jennie, the head of promotional programs for the ski school, brought everyone water, and asked what else we'd like. That scared me. I wasn't feeling up for an all-nighter.

"Is there any chance we could get some takeout? Some sushi? Or a veggie pizza?" I asked.

Turned out I wasn't the only one starving, and everyone but Burt placed an order for pizza or sushi. I ordered both as a reward to myself for not asking for a glass of wine.

Sitting there, waiting to get started, I realized again how profound it was to be with a vital person who was alive one moment and dead the next. I kept thinking about Darnell. He killed three women, yet I mourned him. I felt sad for the childhood he endured, sad for the way Seth Riordan duped him. The way he acted like Darnell was from a sub-human caste. Darnell seemed genuinely shaken over the similarities between Anna Strunk's life and his own. Of course, I didn't know him, but he seemed like an ordinary mountain guy who liked to hunt, fish and ski. Kind of a redneck. Kind of a good-ole boy. Only a spec-ops-type-good-ole boy. Without that childhood, without Seth Riordan, would he have still been a murderer? I couldn't stop wondering what he meant by saying if I wanted to really get to the bottom of this, I'd find it in the Martis Flats.

Burt finally stopped whispering to his deputy, who pulled out an iPad. I had my laptop in front of me already booted, as well as the silver framed picture Ellen Riordan had given me face down on the table.

"Let's get started," Burt said. "Laura if you'd walk me through what happened?"

"OK, a week ago last Friday, April 1st, Dave and I were skiing down under the Red Dog chair when we came across two women—"

"For Christ's sake!" Burt blurted out. "I know this shit! Tell me what I don't know!"

I had to take a deep breath to keep from saying what I wanted to say, which was Burt, you lazy, crooked, jack-ass—

"How am I supposed to know what you know and don't know? You've never seen fit to return one of my fifteen or twenty phone calls to you."

Dave stood up.

"OK, let's calm down. Burt–Laura's right, you've never talked to her, so you're going to have to put up with hearing things you already know. Laura, let Burt ask the questions. We're all tired here. I know the

three of us who came down the Tram Face today are *really* tired. Good?"
Dave turned to look at each of us, and we nodded our agreement.

"Laura, please go ahead."

"Since you know all about the women disappearing, I won't bore
you with that—"

The door to the conference room opened, and Jennie walked in
with the food. Burt looked ready to spit nails since it was obvious there
wouldn't be anymore talking until Dave, Mike, and I had eaten.

By 10:30, I had Burt convinced that Darnell killed the three women
over problems connected with Plains Drilling. But nothing I said
would convince him Seth Riordan had anything to do with it. Not the
pictures of Anna Strunk naked in his lap or with Riordan at the gallery,
or the matching tattoo on the woman in the video. He admitted that
Anna Strunk's body had an infinity sign tattoo on her inner right wrist,
but that was as far as he'd go with the idea that Riordan had involved
her in making the video. Though he did accept the fact that Riordan
and Anna had been having an affair. The best I could do was to pry
him off the idea that Daniel Burdick had killed the women.

For me, Burt's refusal to even consider Seth Riordan a suspect was
just further proof of how crooked he was. Obviously, Riordan had the
motives to get rid of all three of the women: Jennifer for the ongoing trouble and expense she caused him, Alexis because of her realization that Riordan had set her friend up to be the fall guy for an
environmental disaster—the blowing up of his own well—and Anna.
Poor Anna died because she had the audacity to not be eternally grateful to Riordan for being her lover, and had instead broken up with
him. Seemed to me that was the final thing that pushed Riordan to
the brink. A low-life like her had broken up with a guy like him. He
couldn't take it. I didn't for one minute believe the version he'd sold
to Darnell, and apparently Burt Geisner, that he'd broken up with her.

Burt finally admitted that it was Seth Riordan who asked him to
have the illegally parked cars at The Resort at Squaw Creek towed. We
also discovered Daniel Burdick's car was searched because the passenger door had blood smeared on it. Tests had revealed it to be coyote

blood. In a flash the image of that lone coyote roaming Squaw Creek by the lower parking lot came to mind.

"Who put coyote blood on Burdick's car?"

"Armstrong probably shot one and smeared the blood on the car," Burt said.

"Or got blood on his hands," the deputy put in.

"Then why was it on the passenger door?" Burt responded, his face pumping redder by the second. Like his brother, the guy could not stand to be crossed on anything.

"Who cares how the blood was smeared on the car? It doesn't matter. What matters is why it was on his car, who put it there, and how the women's luggage got in his car," I shouted at Burt.

He slumped back into his chair, and turned to stare at me with surprise all over his beefy, red face.

After a pause of five seconds, I calmed myself down enough to add in a lower voice, "And why would Armstrong, on his own, shoot a coyote and smear the blood on Daniel's car? That doesn't make sense. If it was Armstrong who did it, he did it because his boss told him to."

Burt thought this over for a few seconds, rotating his heavy white coffee mug slowly with a forefinger.

"Burdick had to have been in league with Anna Strunk," he finally said. "You told us how Anna wanted to get the porno off Alexis' computer. She was probably having it off with Burdick, but since he didn't break into the suite, Anna did. I'm not charging him with anything right now."

"I don't think Anna cared anything about those pictures. If there even were any pictures. That was years ago."

"Then why did—" he checked his notes. "Why did both Dorian Stievquist and Daniel Burdick tell you they were an issue?"

I had to think about that for a moment. In my head, it was clear why Dorian, Daniel, and Sean as well, thought those pictures were an issue, but in reality they didn't mean much to Anna. It took me a moment to understand and verbalize why I thought that.

"Anna was a different kind of person than the rest of those lawyers. She didn't come from money. She came from nothing and worked her way up. And whereas to us that might not seem like a big deal, or it might seem impressive, I think some of the lawyers never forgot it for an instant. Alexis could do something like go to those sex clubs, and it was no big deal. She was just blowing off steam. People saw pictures of her and laughed.

"But when Anna went, I think both Flaherty and Riordan, and maybe others, maybe Dorian, thought to themselves, or said to each other, it figures. She's trash. She came from nothing, and she's reverting to type. And I don't think anybody cared more about that than Seth Riordan. Maybe it didn't even matter to the lawyers. But it mattered to Seth Riordan. And I think it especially came to matter when she broke it off with him. I think that was a blow to his ego that pushed him to get even with her. Then I think Darnell realized how expendable Anna was to his boss—this woman he had probably professed to love. He realized how expendable he, too, would be. And maybe it seemed to Darnell that they would be expendable most of all because of their common backgrounds. Darnell told me flat out that Riordan had told him Anna was just another trust fund girl like Jennifer and Alexis."

I looked around the table and tried to gauge if people followed what I was trying to say.

Realizing how hardheaded Burt was being about who was at fault and who wasn't, I realized right then and there it would be best if I kept trying to nail Seth Riordan on my own.

By midnight we were all standing out in the parking lot saying goodnight. I could barely keep my eyes open, so Mike suggested I leave the rental in the Squaw parking lot overnight, and ride back into town with him.

As I climbed into Mike's truck, Burt came around to stand in the lee of the open door.

"Bailey, if I hear about you bugging Riordan, I'll have you arrested. I don't want you going near him. Got that?"

A slow grimace spread across my face.

"Sure, Burt," I told him. "No worries."

Chapter 22

SUNDAY, APRIL 9, 6:00 AM

The next morning Mike left around 6:00 a.m. for work. I lingered on in bed barely registering his departure. Ten or fifteen minutes later he returned and set a soy latte from Coffeebar on the bedside table along with a muffin. He leaned down and kissed me, so I pulled him down on top of me for a few seconds. He'd brought so much of the cold in with him, though, I pushed him on his way.

"Thank you, thank you," I told him, "but you're freezing cold."

"Give me a call or drop by in a couple hours. Let me know what's up," he said, and headed back out the door. A few seconds later, I heard the slam of his pickup door and the engine's low growl.

Since the furnace apparently did not putter out overnight, and the house was warm for once, I took a leisurely shower and blow-dried my hair as I tried to figure out what to do next. Nothing presented itself except for going back to Ellen Riordan.

Around 8:30, I gave her a call.

"I was just going to call you," she said. "I found something you need to see. Maybe we could meet someplace? I need to get out of this awful house."

"Sure? Where?"

"Have you had breakfast?"

"Just a muffin."

"Let's meet at the Log Cabin Café, in King's Beach in forty-five minutes. Know it?"

I was surprised. The Log Cabin is a dive on North Beach Blvd. The food is amazing. Breakfasts are stellar, but it looks like a dump from the outside—a dirty yellow log cabin, not a place most people would drive past and think, "Oh, let's eat there!"—and while it's clean inside, it's crowded and noisy. But if Ellen Riordan wanted to meet me in one of the primo breakfast dives in all North Lake Tahoe, I wasn't going to say no, since she's the person I most wanted to speak to that morning.

Forty minutes later I pulled onto the rutted ice of the dirt parking lot and found an open spot in the back. Inside, Ellen Riordan sat waving at me. She wore a grey sweater with black velvet trim around the neck. As I fought my way through the crowd over to her table, she stood and took my hands in hers, leaning across the table to place a soft kiss on my cheek. She smelled amazing.

She looked surprised when she saw my new bubblegum pink cast.

"Broke it again yesterday," I told her. And with a start it occurred to me to wonder whether she knew about Darnell. And if she did know, how did she feel about it?

Sinking down into my chair, I freed my hands from her soft, cold clasp and looked into her eyes. Before I could say anything a fresh-faced young waitress appeared and poured coffee, then took our orders. Ellen ordered the regular Eggs Benedict, and I asked for chilaquiles.

Once the waitress hurried off, I started again. "Did you hear about Darnell Armstrong?"

"I did," she said, and dropped her gaze to her coffee. "Poor Darnell. Burt Geisner came by yesterday evening and told me about the whole thing."

"Yes."

I couldn't think of anything to say. I didn't want to get into telling her how badly I felt about his death, or about Anna's death and Jennifer's, and Alexis'.

"What did you want to give me?" I asked instead.

"First, I want to explain something. Seth never came back from Reno yesterday. I called the helicopter company, and they said he never kept the reservation he held from Truckee to Reno yesterday morning."

"Where do you think he is?"

"Usually, I'd assume he's holed up somewhere with one of his girl-friends," she said slowly. "But I know that Anna, who he's been crazy about for the past several years, severed their relationship recently."

"How do you know that? Darnell told me that Seth broke it off with her?"

"I know that because he's been my husband now for thirty-five years. When he breaks up with one of them, he's happy. He's got a spring in his step. He buys me trinkets. He promises that's the end of it, and it won't happen again. None of these things happened this time. Instead, he's been in a rage. I think he's felt like the world is crumbling around him. I think he knew what a mess things were turning into and left Darnell behind to face it."

"So what do you think about Anna's death?"

She fell silent for a moment, warming her hands around her coffee cup. After a silent minute, she looked up at me, suddenly more certain of herself.

"I'm finished with all of this. All of it. I never dreamed this day would come, but I'm divorcing Seth. Even though we're Catholics. Even though I promised—" She spoke slowly, rambling, not really certain how the words were going to string together. There seemed to have been a profound change in her thinking since I saw her the day before.

Again, she fell silent for a long moment.

The waitress arrived, and with a bustle of activity put a plate swimming with artery-clogging Hollandaise sauce and fried potatoes in front of Ellen, and eggs scrambled a brilliant orange with chili sauce and tortilla chips in front of me, then quickly refilled our coffee cups and hustled off towards the kitchen.

"Why now?"

She picked up a fork and twisted it between her fingers absently. This seemed like an awfully private conversation to be having in such a public place. A guy sat so close to me our elbows practically touched every time he took a bite.

"Well," Ellen sighed heavily. "I find I can no longer keep his secrets."

She paused and took a bite of potatoes, then picked up her knife and cut a piece of English muffin, Canadian bacon and egg through the pale yellow veil of sauce, and raised it to her mouth.

I sat silently and waited for her to go on, thinking to myself which secrets?

"Or bear his lies," she said finally "And when a marriage reaches that point, I believe it's as important a time to get a divorce as when one can no longer be faithful. We both should have known years ago that it was time to divorce."

I couldn't wait or keep myself quiet any longer.

"Which secrets? Are you talking about the murders of Jennifer Fellatorre, Alexis Page, and Anna Strunk?"

"I don't know anything definitive, but I can tell you that when Seth heard from Darnell that Alexis and her friend Jennifer were coming to Squaw, and apparently Darnell arranged for that to happen, I overheard Seth tell Darnell that here was his chance to get rid of two problems at once."

I leaned forward listening to her voice, which registered barely above a whisper, but, upon hearing that, I collapsed against the wooden back of my chair.

I knew it, but hearing it made it seem like I hadn't really known it until then. They baited Alexis to come up to Squaw, knowing how hot she was for the piece of strange that was Darnell, and then laid the trap, and the two idiots skied right into it. Maybe only Alexis was the idiot. Poor Jennifer didn't ski well enough to do anything but tag along behind her life-long friend.

"And as for Anna—" She paused again then looked up and met my eyes. "What else makes sense but that Seth was furious? She probably knew some of his secrets—I don't know what. I'm not a lawyer like she was, but I know he has business secrets he'd do most anything to keep from being made public. I imagine she knew some, and once she'd broken up with him, all the trust he had in her ended. With Seth, you're either with him or against him. There's no middle ground. My guess is he used that as an excuse to have Darnell fix this problem for him, too. Thinking anything else would be delusional."

"So what I found for you—" she paused to reach down to the floor for her handbag and pulled out a piece of paper that she unfolded once and lay on the table in front of me—"is this."

It was a photocopy of a check from Plains Drilling International, Inc. for $200,000 made out to Burton Geisner's General Re-Election Fund, and dated last October 12th.

Neither of us said anything for a long stretch of seconds. Ellen stared at me. I stared at the photocopy.

"Will that help you?" she finally asked.

"I don't know," I said after a pause. "But I think this is a huge deal."

"What will you do with it?"

"I'll take it to the sheriff of Nevada County, and the Truckee Police, but what if they've been recipients of your husband's largesse as well? Maybe I should call my friend Lars Addison in Aspen and ask him for advice. He's the sheriff of Pitkin County. I'm pretty sure your husband hasn't gotten to him."

"Don't be too sure." She laughed sardonically. "Well, probably not."

"It seems like a huge sum for a small local campaign."

She looked at me, surprised at how gullible I was.

"Local campaigns here don't even have advertising budgets. No one has run against Burt Geisner in the last two elections. It's a bribe, pure and simple."

My mind churned through the implications. Did this bribe imply coercion or a pass on anything Seth and Darnell might do? For example, Burt appeared genuine last night in his belief in Seth's innocence. However, I never believed him that Seth was innocent. Did the others?

I sat pondering the morality of Ellen's behavior. She knew from the get-go that her husband and Darnell were planning some kind of a trap for Alexis and Jennifer. If she'd been forthcoming about that information, Anna would probably still be alive. It seemed to me she was almost an accomplice to all three murders. I also saw how trapped she felt, torn between loyalty to her husband and coming forward and turning the bastard in.

Still, I liked her. I empathized with her. She had molded herself into the old-fashioned model of a wife, and she was trying to break free from the way she was raised, the mores of her childhood. Seemed like a lot of people spend their whole lives doing that. It's something I see in my students' eyes all the time, the dawning realization that perhaps the stuff their parents have fed them all their lives wasn't right, or true.

Ellen finished every bite of her breakfast. I was still too stunned to make much headway into mine. The orange chili sauce hardened, and the tortilla chips turned to mush.

When the check arrived, Ellen grabbed it and took my left hand where it rested on the table.

"I've had a lot of disappointments," she said. "But haven't we all. I've been disappointed in my son, my husband, and I think I let that hold me back. I felt like our family was so fragile and damaged that the least breath of fresh air would disperse it like dust. I want to thank you," she said, "for giving me the strength to take this step, this long overdue step. I realize now what I should have known all along–there are worse things than having a family break apart. That night you came over and told me about your work, and I saw the passion you had for your research, the good you were doing in the world, and right then I started thinking about leaving. I couldn't drift through life any longer. Your strength made me stronger. So thank you."

I almost choked up, not accustomed to having such raw emotion laid out in front of me this way. Which son was she talking about, I wondered? The only thing I could figure is she must have meant the way Seth pushed away Jason.

"Your resolve gave me the backbone to do what I need to do. I'm putting the house on the market immediately. I don't care what Seth says. And then I'm looking for another house in Tahoe. My house."

=

Later that afternoon, after getting my friend Lar's advice, I called the sheriff of Nevada County, Coy Billings, and explained to him about

Burt Geisner's refusal to pursue Riordan. I drove into his office in Truckee and explained the whole story, showing him the photocopy of the $200,000 check. Coy Billings was short, stout, and looked strong as hell. He had an easy smile, a big laugh, and a thin sweep of short blond hair. I liked him immediately.

After talking with him for ten or fifteen minutes, he called the Truckee District Attorney, Tom Simmon, and Captain O'Reilly from the Truckee Police. Captain O'Reilly showed up in under five minutes. He seemed stressed and in a rush. He drank coffee and sat talking quietly with Coy while we waited for the DA. It took Tom another ten or fifteen minutes to arrive. He was a robust, trim man in his sixties with a mop of white hair and the florid face of an outdoorsman.

The rest of them wandered off and left me sitting in an overheated room waiting for another half hour until one of the District Attorney's from Placer county, who worked out of the Tahoe City office, arrived, and everyone was ready for me to explain it all again.

The Placer County District Attorney, Randy Jenkins, bustled into the room carrying a stack of binders, which he thunked down onto the table. It took him a while to get settled, but he finally did, and once again I explained it all, start to finish.

After that, they all left the room to make some phone calls, and finally returned almost ninety minutes later to sit across from me and explain that there would be a Grand Jury investigation into Burt Geisner's actions as well as the actions of Seth Riordan. They would commence proceedings to have Burt Geisner suspended immediately. I was going to have to come back to testify in front of the Grand Jury along with Ellen Riordan. Apparently, the grand jury only met once a month, and it wouldn't be on the schedule until May or June.

Randy Jenkins said at one point that they'd found corroborating evidence in e-mail correspondence on Alexis Page's computer that Anna had been the woman in the video, not Jennifer. I figured Anna must have stolen it in an effort to get rid of that evidence.

Everyone at the table kept wondering and guessing about where Riordan had gone to ground. They finally decided to make inquiries before going public with the fact that he was a fugitive. He might show up any minute. Or they figured, he could be anywhere by then: Rio, Barcelona, the Alps. Anywhere.

I couldn't stop thinking that if he missed that heli flight out of Truckee the day before, how'd he get out? The roads were all still closed then. What'd he do–take a snowmobile to Reno, snowshoe out? I kept thinking about what Darnell said–that if I wanted to get to the bottom of this, I'd find the answer in the Martis Flats. I can't explain why, but I left that part out of the story. It seemed too vague to be useful.

It was 4:45 in the afternoon by the time I made it back out into the bright mountain air. It was a warm day with a cloudless indigo sky, the low sun throwing long streaks of shadow. Interstate 80 had finally opened in both directions for the first time since I arrived way back in the early hours of April 1st. There was no snow in the forecast for the next ten days—for whatever that forecast was worth—hopefully we'd get through at least two or three days without any more precip. I didn't know where to go or what to do. I knew I should call my colleagues back in Fort Collins and tell them to get packing. Tomorrow morning early I should get up onto Granite Chief and see about the possibility of skiing out the back to the snow station. I sat in the car for a minute thinking about all the things I needed to do.

=

Around 5:00 p.m. I headed west on Donner Pass Road and stopped at a sporting goods rental store where I picked up a set of snowshoes, and before I knew it I was driving out Brockway Road to the Martis Flats.

The Martis Valley, called the Flats by locals, covers seventy square miles of largely flat land, beginning north of Lake Tahoe and running up past the California/Nevada border. The valley includes Truckee Airport, part of Northstar Resort, and Lahotan Golf Club as well as open plains running along Prosser Creek and Martis Creek, both of which emptied into the Truckee River. There were several small lakes in the area as well as Martis Creek Reservoir, a larger lake that was built in 1972 to reduce the risk of flooding down below in Reno, Nevada.

All this information I knew via my interest in the politics of water. And a lot of California water politics had played out in this valley. But I didn't know much more than that. The Martis Flats I was familiar with was the big stretch of flat land I drove through every time I took Brockway Road, otherwise known as California State Route 267, from Truckee over Brockway Pass to King's Beach on Lake Tahoe. So that was the practical knowledge I had as I headed out to Martis Flats that late afternoon; it was a huge field surrounded by a bowl of mountains, with a couple small lakes off to the east, and a bigger lake to the west which was surrounded by an upscale housing community. There was a place offering glider rides on the eastern side of the Flats, and on the west a popular hiking trail that was also a good place to spot wildlife. The parking lot for the hiking trail was off the road on the right, heading towards Lake Tahoe, as I was. That's pretty much everything I knew.

Except the fact that when I had heard locals talking about Martis Flats, nine times out of ten they were talking about the hiking trail. And Darnell was no more a local than I was, so I doubted his knowledge of the area ran deeper than mine. And I didn't think he shared my interest in water. Though I'd have bet money he had a keen interest in wildlife, mainly in killing wildlife.

The sun sank below the mountains of Northstar Ski Resort just as I pulled the rental into the parking lot off of 267. Another ten minutes, and it would have been too dark to find it. The lot hadn't been plowed, but enough big cars and trucks had driven in and out that it was barely passable in the Murano. The four-wheel drive whined into gear as I drove down a steep pitch over the packed snow and ice to the parking area. I left the car in the middle of the packed snow, not willing to risk pulling into a parking spot I'd be unable to back out of later.

Full dark settled as I sat on the tailgate, strapped the snowshoes on, and pulled on my pit kit backpack. Luckily, shortly after that a fat white moon rose up over the mountains towards Reno. If it wasn't full, it was close. I grabbed my ski poles and set off following a couple sets of tracks. It crossed my mind that I'd read in *The Tahoe Times* that there had been recent mountain lion sightings in the area, but I pushed that worry back as the least of my problems. Twenty minutes later, I could see almost as well as in daylight.

It was rough going as at least ten feet of packed snow lay on the ground. The top six inches had been softened up by the warm day. So every third or fourth step my snowshoe would sink into the snow up to my knee. There hadn't been much traffic, a few cross country ski tracks worn into parallel ruts, and off to the side some marks from snowshoes. I paused to listen to the night sounds. The path led over a humped-up place rising up into the air five or six feet, what must have been a bridge, and then ran down low and parallel to a creek. I paused there. The traffic sounds faded, and the hoot of an owl came from somewhere near by. A few bare willows grew along the creek buried ten feet or so up their branches. A big black shadow whooshed by, and I felt the breeze from the owl's wings against my face.

After that, everything fell silent. The moonlight lay bright on the snow with the only noise the gurgling of the creek. The moment ended as my eyes grew more accustomed to the night and made out a dark shape way up ahead, strewn out on the snow. It was difficult to judge distances in the moonlight, but I picked my speed up to a trot. It looked like a crumbled blanket on the snow, or maybe a sleeping bag. My mind immediately made sense of it as teenagers trekking out here to find a private place to hook up, and in their hot pursuit leaving the blanket behind. No doubt somewhere in Truckee right then a parent was demanding to know where the damn blanket went?

Five minutes later, I reached it, way off the hiking trail, maybe a hundred yards or more, and, even standing over it, I couldn't make sense of what I was seeing. I pulled out my phone and brought up my flashlight app, turned it on the dark patch on the snow, and realized only part of the dark patch was material; at least half of it was something wet and dark. I grabbed onto the material with two fingers and tried pulling it over. I could make out enough to see it was a human body, still partially clothed, but most of it was just raw meat. What I'd thought was a blanket were shreds from a dark wool overcoat. By the light from my phone, I discovered my hand was covered in blood.

A sudden scrape across the crusted snow caught my ear, and I shined the flashlight app around over the moonlit snow. Over to the north, towards a small cluster of brush, a pair of yellow eyes stared back at me—motionless—and the scariest part was how far up off the snow the eyes were. They probably came up to my waist. It had to be a mountain lion or maybe a bear. Let it be a bear. But with the rough winter, most of the bears were still tucked up snug in their dens. The eyes stared back at me, and once I moved the light away, I still saw them in the moonlight. My heart pounded painfully as I fought to calm my breathing. Mountain lions can smell fear from a mile away—an adrenaline aphrodisiac. What did I have with me I could use as a weapon? Slowly I began to ease my back-pack off and unhook my avalanche shovel.

My phone's xylophone ringtone went off, scaring the bejeezus out of me and electrifying the night. Mike's face lit up the screen.

"Hey," Mike said. "Thought you were dropping by?"

It took a second before I could calm down enough to speak.

"Laura?" he said. "Laura are you there?"

"Uh," I started. I fought hard to keep the panic out of my voice. "I'm a little over a mile or so out on the wildlife trail at Martis Flats. I just found a bloody mess; I think it's a body. Can you help me out? I've got a mountain lion for company."

"The wildlife trail?"

"Yeah."

"What can I do?"

"Call Coy Billings, the Nevada County sheriff, and get out here as fast as you can."

"Do you have any light?"

"Um, my flashlight app. That certainly isn't scaring it away. A couple flares."

"Light a flare and back slowly away from the body. That's what it wants. Don't bend over, or you're prey. Just get away from the body and let the cat have it. I'm on my way."

As I waited for the troops to arrive, I lit a flare and moved a dozen yards away from the bloody mess. I started looking more carefully at the tracks leading from the hiking trail to where I stood. The body had been dragged over to the depression where it lay, leaving a long streak of blood all the way. I'd tromped all over it; the forensic team was going to love me. The gore I saw when I looked under the coat had to have been a face once, a neck. No sign of feet or legs poked out beneath the overcoat. I wasn't about to take another peek to see where the feet were. My brain, my eyes, struggled to make sense of it. My guess was the mountain lion, or maybe a pair of them, had gotten a hold of the body, and dragged it off somewhere more private where they could feed and return. I probably chased it—or them—away from dinner.

Every time I run into a big, wild cat, I'm always shocked anew at how cat-like they are. This mountain lion was no exception. I could hear him occasionally hissing in the dark: first to my right, a few minutes later to my left, then the soft pads on snow behind me. I spun around, fighting back the panic. If I panicked and ran, that cat would have me on the snow in a heartbeat. I wished like hell that Mike would get there. I only had one flare left. After that it was going to be the mountain lion and me with a sharp-tipped avalanche shovel in my hands.

It was my guess that I was standing thirty feet from the remains of Seth Riordan.

"You'll find the end of the story in Martis Flat's," Darnell had said right before he jumped to his death. "You'll get to the bottom of it there." I didn't feel certain anymore what his exact words had been.

The ringer of my phone went off again.

"I'm in the parking lot. You didn't leave much room for anyone else."

"I didn't think anyone'd be out here this time of night."

"Did you use snowshoes?"

"Yeah."

"I'm strapping mine on right now. Where are you?"

I reached into my pit kit, pulled out the last flare and struck it. "See me now?"

"I see evidence of you. What's the cat doing?"

"I moved away, like you said, and now I think it's circling around closer to the body, and keeping an eye on me. I caught a couple more glimpses of it after I lit the first flare. It's one big-ass mountain lion, maybe a pair of them. Occasionally, he hisses at me. You know, it's been a hell of a day."

"Tell you what–let's have a quiet dinner after this?"

"Sounds good. But seeing as most likely I'm standing over Seth Riordan's mutilated corpse, my guess is dinner is a ways off."

Ten minutes later, he stood next to me staring down at the remains of a dark woolen overcoat. He'd brought along a bright flashlight that lit the scene dramatically. The red on white motif had been overdone. It reminded me of a fairytale gone wrong. Snow white and rose red. We could see tracks from more than one big cat all over the place.

"How in the hell did you know he was here?" Mike asked.

"I guess that's going to be the question of the evening, right?"

He exhaled in a manner that implied that was obvious.

"I remembered today that when Darnell was sitting on that rock next to me, right before he jumped, he said that if I wanted to get to the bottom of this to go to Martis Flats. Or maybe he said if I wanted to find the end of this, I'd find it in Martis Flats. There was so much going on, and I was trying to talk to him, to get him not to jump, yet to find out why all this had happened, I forgot that he'd said that."

"How did that lead you here? I mean, the Martis Valley is a big place."

"I know. I just took a guess. Aside from water politics, all I know about the Martis Flats is this place. And Armstrong was no more a local than I am. So I guessed this was all he knew of it, too. Driving through, this is all you really see."

A few minutes later, the police arrived and called Mike's phone for directions out to the body. A dozen people showed up with banks of lights and a folding white canopy to erect over the scene.

Coy Billings was the first to arrive.

"Damn it, Laura!" he said when he saw me. "Why in the hell didn't you tell me about this? You know how bad this looks, you coming out here on your own? Is this Riordan's body we're looking at?"

"I don't know. Believe me, please, I wasn't expecting to find a body. I really wasn't. And once I realized that's what this was, I didn't touch a thing. I just thought it was a blanket."

The anger flickering across his face made me feel sick. I had liked him from the moment I met him. Now he looked like he wanted to skewer me.

"Jesus! Look at these cat tracks. Is. It. Seth. Riordan?"

"I don't know. I think a couple mountain lions have been at it. One big one has been circling around since I got here. The last I saw him, he was over that way." I pointed to the north.

Coy bent down and started to pull back the cloth.

"It's not obviously human," I told him. "Only that it's dressed in what's left of men's clothes. And as I said, I only turned it over enough to realize there was a body."

He dropped the fabric and turned back to face me. I demonstrated for him how I'd delicately lifted a corner of the fabric with two fingers.

"But you assume it's Riordan?"

I nodded.

"Are you going to tell me the information you had that led you out here right after talking to me?"

"I didn't have any actual information. I just remembered something Darnell Armstrong said in passing right before he flung himself off the Tram Chute."

"And what was that?"

Billings' anger seemed to recede. Still, I realized I had to measure every word I said or he'd be hauling me off to jail in Riordan's place.

"I don't remember exactly. There was a lot going on. He said something like, if I wanted to see how this ends, then it ends in Martis Flats. But I'm not sure that was exactly what he said. He just mentioned the words Martis Flats. That's all. I started thinking about it, and thought I'd come out here and look around. I mean, obviously, Martis Flats is a big place. But this is the only part of it I'm aware of as a non-local, so I came here."

"What were you expecting to find?"

"I don't know. Not a body."

"Maybe a map? Or a golden widget that would spin around in your hand and magically find him for you?"

"Now you're just being nasty," I told him.

"Laura, you're making me feel kind of nasty," he said with a reluctant smile. "Why didn't you mention this?"

By then the forensics team swarmed the area. Camera flashes went off like strobes, and Mike and I got hustled over fifty feet outside the ring of lights.

"Wait here!" Billings told us. "Don't move. Bernese, I should arrest you, too, just for hanging out with bad company."

Finally, some ninety minutes later, he let us trudge back to the parking lot where my rental had been thoroughly parked in. Happily, Mike had left his truck parked along the shoulder of 267, so we were able to head out for that late dinner.

I'd only gotten away from Billings by reducing my story with every repetition. In the end, all I'd admitted to was that Seth had said the words, "Martis Flats." Thankfully, Mike hadn't chimed in that the story I told him had been a bit different.

Lesson learned. The police can be picky about where my job ends and theirs begins.

By the time we'd been excused from the scene, we had overheard some of the techs saying the dead man's wallet held ID in the name of Seth Riordan.

Apparently, Darnell made a quick stop just five minutes from the Truckee Airport and lured Seth out on the snow and to his death. He hadn't died quickly. He'd been gut shot and left.

It seemed like what I'd said to Darnell about Anna's past and how her lack of breeding had made Riordan see her as disposable, subhuman, meaning he must have seen Darnell that way as well, had led straight to this bloody path in the snow. I didn't know how badly I should feel about that. Right then, this whole miserable mess seemed more than I could wrap my head around. How had a few days of skiing in the mountains around Squaw Valley turned into this blood-soaked snow in Martis Flats? Brother. Teaching college kids about hydrology never sounded so good.

We rode a mile or so back in towards Truckee in silence. Mike pulled into The Rock, an area of business near the airport, in the Martis Flats.

"Drunken Monkey Sushi," he said. "Best Japanese food in the Tahoe area."

He turned to me prior to climbing out of the truck.

"I know you're feeling guilty about not giving Coy the head's up before heading back in there. But think about this. He'd been gut shot—a really slow way to die—chances are Riordan wasn't dead when that cat found him. They can smell blood from a couple miles away. Armstrong shot him, what? Yesterday morning? And that cat had already dragged him more than a hundred-and-fifty yards off the trail. If you'd waited around and hemmed and hawed and told the police, and they'd taken their own sweet time believing you, as they have every step of the way in this mess, nothing would've been left of Riordan by that time. He'd have never been found until some poor kids out playing one day came across some bones hanging from a tree. Or maybe he'd never have been found at all."

He leaned over and kissed me until my knees went weak and my heart pounded in the cage of my chest.

I moved my body in snug against his. I could feel the heat emanating through his ski clothes.

"We can skip dinner and head back to your place," I whispered.

"Let me feed you first."

We went in and had dinner. No man had ever worried about me getting enough to eat before.

Chapter 23

SUNDAY, APRIL 10, 9:00 AM

By special request, I ended up back in Coy Billings' office the next morning.

He didn't seem as angry towards me as he had the night before, but some of the friendliness from when we first met had evaporated. He was Mr. Business this time around. The DAs from Nevada and Placer County both showed up twenty minutes after I arrived, and we rehashed everything that had taken place out on the Martis Flats.

I stuck to my story that all I really remembered was Darnell mentioning the Martis Flats, and finally they set me free. I'd have to return to testify for a Grand Jury the first week in May.

It was 4:00 in the afternoon by the time I got out of there. They'd made sure to not give me any further information beyond the fact that an autopsy had confirmed the corpse was Seth Riordan. He'd suffered a single gunshot wound to the abdomen that had missed any vital organ, and left him to slowly bleed to death out on the snow. I felt safe in assuming he'd gotten on Darnell's last nerve. A bite, most likely from a mountain lion, had severed his jugular, and that's what killed him.

I figured if Riordan's autopsy was already finished, then the women's autopsies must be done as well, but, if they were, nobody shared any information with me.

As soon as I got out of there, I gave Mike a call. I hadn't even noticed how low I was feeling until I heard his voice.

"Let's get together this evening," he said.

"Sounds good. But let's stay at Rita's if it's okay with you. I need to get back to thinking about my own work, and it'll be easier for me to start getting organized there. You and Grappa coming along into the backcountry changes what we're going to need."

"Sure," he said. "That's fine. I can help you."

"Good. Let me be in charge of dinner tonight."

"Absolutely," he said with a laugh that seemed to imply both disbelief and discomfort. "But give me a general idea of what you're making."

"Mexican."

"Got it," he said. "See you probably around 7:00."

We hung up, and I sat in the car thinking this meant I was going to finally have to hit the grocery store. I headed down Donner Pass Road to the Safeway. The entire shopping plaza was hidden from view behind a long bank of thirty-foot high snow berms. I picked up a couple rotisserie chickens, corn tortillas, a couple bags of chips, a couple cans of refried pinto beans, lettuce, jalapenos, and the makings for a huge batch of fresh red salsa. As I headed out of the produce section, I spotted a net bag of five ripe avocados and grabbed them too.

Mexican was about all I knew how to make.

Sitting in the rental in the Safeway parking lot—a zoo at the best of times, but with people able to finally get out and about more easily it was chaos—I tried Richard's number. It rang and rang and finally cut to voicemail. I left a short message saying I'd like to speak with Chloe and him prior to their departure.

I started up the rental and figured I'd head back to Rita's and try getting in touch with my team when my phone rang. The Bluetooth picked it up, and my post doc Tim Schneider's voice came through the speakers.

"Hey, Tim," I said. "How's Fort Collins?"

"It's been good here all along. Looks like we've finally got a break in the weather where you are."

"Yes," I said, "When do you think you guys can head out?"

"When do you want us?"

"The backcountry snow needs to compact a bit, and I've got to round up provisions, get over to UC Davis, and check out a couple things. How about you guys fly in early the week after next, and we'll head out early Thursday or Friday?"

"It is done, Memsahib."

We talked for a few more minutes about the specifics of who was bringing what, then hung up.

It felt good to get my own life back, even temporarily.

I figured tomorrow I'd check out conditions on the backside of Granite Chief early, and after that I'd start picking up provisions for the trip. I could get online and check out what new research papers were up. Perfect.

Back at Rita's, the furnace had once again given up, and the inside temperature hung around 30 degrees. I changed out of my jeans and fleece and put on a pair of black corduroys and a pale blue sweater. After running a brush through my hair, I weaved it into braids. It was the best I could do. I promised myself once I got back from this trip to the snow station I'd buy some new clothes from a real women's clothing store. Not from Costco. I slipped around to the back of the house to climb underneath and jiggle the dying furnace back to life.

Deboning the chickens and chopping the veggies for salsa felt normal and relaxing after the hellish rush of the past few days.

At 5:45 the phone rang, and Richard's name and number came up.

"Richard, how are you and Chloe doing?"

"Pretty well, considering. It helps to know what happened to Jennifer and why. Listen, Chloe and I are all packed up to head out early tomorrow morning. I wondered if we could drop by to thank you?"

"Now?"

"Perfect."

"OK," I told him, and gave him the directions. "And if you guys haven't eaten, I'm making Mexican."

Turning my attention to the avocados, I mixed up a big bowl of guacamole, and in a cupboard found the perfect black lava bowl to scrape it into. I set out a wooden bowl filled with chips, and a bowl of salsa and the guacamole.

＝

Twenty minutes later, Richard stood at the door looking clean and rested for once. I invited him in with a wide sweep of my arm. Chloe came bustling out of the car a second later and smiled at me. Her red puffed-up eyes and big mess of hair were in stark contrast to her father's demeanor.

"Hi Chloe," I said. "How're you feeling?"

Tears welled up in her eyes, and I saw then that she held a hairbrush in one hand.

"I'm fine. But I just can't get my hair to work. Mom always did it—"

"That's something I can help with," I promised, hustling her inside. "Hand me that hairbrush and sit right here."

I motioned to a chair at the kitchen table, and she sat in front of me. Her hair was a rat's nest. It took me a couple minutes to realize that the messy braids I saw a couple days ago were still in there, only they'd been surrounded by frizz and were close to becoming dreadlocks.

"Get me a comb," I told Richard and pointed him towards the bathroom.

I began the laborious job of combing through her dark hair.

Richard sat in a chair across the table from his daughter, apologizing that he didn't know how to help Chloe with her hair. He didn't even know how to braid hair, or anything else for that matter.

I acted like it was no big deal, but I could tell he'd never spent much time with her doing anything, let alone braiding her hair.

"Are you two going to be OK?" I asked. "Who's going to braid your hair?"

"Well," Chloe said, "Dad and I talked about this. He said there're only so many hours in the day, so I can pick what's most important to me. Taking me to soccer, and coming to games, going to piano recitals, hanging out with me, or braiding my hair. I picked hanging out and coming to games and recitals."

"Still, who's going to do your hair?"

"I'm getting it cut short when I get home! I've wanted to cut for a while, but mom didn't like the idea. Now I'm getting it cut!"

"Great. You guys are going to do fine."

"Will you walk us through what happened, from beginning to end?" Richard asked.

It took me a few seconds to think through how to begin.

"Alexis Page was having an affair with Darnell Armstrong. Or maybe it wasn't an affair, maybe they'd just started seeing each other—"

"Having sex," Chloe chimed in.

"Yes. I think that was pretty much it, having sex."

Richard added, "From what I understand after talking with the police, the legal firm has a yearly retreat for each office to build teamwork and to celebrate the new partners' promotions. Alexis hadn't planned on going because of Jennifer's visit, but apparently she was talked into coming up."

"By whom?"

"Darnell Armstrong. The police found e-mails from him asking her to come up since he'd be up here, too. My guess is Riordan was behind that?"

"But the rest of the lawyers had planned to be up here?" I asked.

"It's an annual thing. Everyone is urged to come."

"OK. So to continue, Seth Riordan's wife heard him saying to Armstrong that it would be an opportunity to get rid of two problems with one accident. Meaning Alexis and Jennifer. Her being up here was a happy coincidence for Riordan, and I imagine that put the whole scheme in motion."

"What about Anna Strunk?"

"Anna and Seth had been having an affair for a couple years. Apparently, a serious affair, for Riordan anyway. Anna broke it off with him, and his wife said he'd been spinning out of control recently. I don't know if that was because of her breaking up with him, but my guess is that had a big effect on his behavior. Remember, Anna was the woman pretending to be Jennifer in the video. By now I'm sure the police or the DA has spoken to the video team and has proof of what went on there. What I know is that Anna impersonated Jennifer. They actually looked a lot a like: petite, delicate features, beautiful skin. You saw the picture Chloe colored in. So once Anna broke it off—"

"Riordan didn't trust her anymore," he cut in.

"Exactly. Ellen Riordan said with Seth it was all or nothing. You were on his side or you were against him."

"So why did Armstrong kill him?"

"I think Armstrong felt loyal to Riordan for some reason. I don't know why. But he killed Alexis because she'd made herself a problem for them. He killed Jennifer because he knew she was a problem. And with Anna he was just sort of going along with what his boss wanted. When I told him about Anna's background being just like his, and maybe Riordan thought them both disposable, Armstrong became unsure of his boss. Riordan had told him Anna was another trust fund girl like Alexis and Jennifer. After that, I guess, he didn't trust Riordan anymore. He'd lied to him. And like his boss, with Darnell you were either in or out. At that point, Riordan became out. Armstrong also realized, I'm sure, that his boss was doing a runner. Leaving him to take all the blame. So he killed him."

"Painfully, from what I heard," Richard said.

"There's no doubt about that."

I hated to have all this discussion going on where Chloe could hear it, but she sat playing a game on her dad's iPhone, and munching on chips, so I decided to go ahead and ask about her mother.

"Have you heard anything about the women's autopsies?"

"Yes, Alexis suffocated and Jennifer froze to death. No pre-mortem wounds, which is a huge relief to us. Jennifer had two cracked ribs, as you suspected when you met her, right?"

"Yes. And her finger's—"

"Yes, and her fingers." Richard finished speaking and let that hang between us. Hopefully, Chloe didn't realize by that we meant her mother hadn't died right away.

About the time we finished chatting, I had finally gotten Chloe's hair combed out and woven into tight French braids.

"These should last you a few days."

She swiveled around in her chair and put her arms around my waist, pushing her head in hard against my ribs. She was killing the big yellowing bruise on my side, but I stroked her head and hugged her back.

"Thank you," she said. "Thank you."

Just then, Mike came in the front door bringing a wave of cold air into the kitchen with him. He shed parka and gloves as he moved into the room, where he paused long enough to put a brown paper bag on the counter.

Chloe let go of me and leaped up from the table and headed over to hug him.

"Hey, what are you doing here?" he asked with a smile. He swooped her in his arms and lifted her up level with his face so he could get a look at her braids.

"We got Laura a present!" she shouted. "You guys are going to really love it!"

Chloe and Richard stepped back into their boots, then pulled their parkas on and headed outside. A couple minutes later they returned carrying a huge frame backwards into the kitchen. As they turned it around, Chloe shouted, "Tah da!"

It was a set of four eight-by-eleven inch photographs of Squaw Peak taken from the Gold Coast Building: a bluebird sky and a whole mountain of untracked powder. A good four inches of green matting filled in all the way around so that the frame was probably three feet by five feet.

Chloe pointed to two tiny red dots of ski patrollers out blasting the mountain after a big snow.

"Do you like it? Do you like it?" she asked.

"It's beautiful," I said. "But how am I going to get it home?"

"This one isn't yours. It's just for show. The photographer's going to make you another one and mail it to you. I just wanted this one to show you. Do you love it?"

"It's beautiful," I told her. "What a great idea for a present. I love it."

She beamed at me. "Is it okay if maybe I write you sometime. Will you be my Facebook friend?"

"Absolutely."

"Let me pay you for your time," Richard said, pulling out a checkbook.

"No. It was my honor to be able to help you guys figure out what happened. I'm so sorry for your loss. Are you going to be OK?"

Chloe nodded her dark head.

"I think when my mom left her glove where you'd find it, she was leaving us a message. She was saying good-bye."

"I think you're right," I said. "I think she was."

By this time, Mike had stripped out of his boots and snow pants, grabbed a beer from the fridge, and sat on the couch in the living room. He pulled off his wet socks and warmed up his feet by rubbing them for a moment, then he got up and started a fire in the cast iron stove.

As Chloe and her dad carried the photograph back out to the car, Mike hugged me. "Are you loving that?" he asked.

"It's good. But I've no idea where I'm going to put it. Wall space is at a premium both in my apartment, and in my tiny house in Aspen. Do you want it?"

He smiled and took a swig of his beer. "I see that view every day."

We both laughed. "It's the thought," I said.

"Guess what I brought?"

I raised my eyebrows.

"Margarita makings."

"Excellent! Will you bartend?"

"Let me get changed. I'm wet and cold."

Mike headed off into the bedroom carrying a black bag of his gear.

For the next hour we drank margies and ate chips as we talked about a wide range of topics. It felt like how normal people must live. Mike kept the margaritas flowing for the adults and kept Chloe topped off with her virgin Margarita of lime-juice, sugar and soda water.

Just as I put dinner on the table, Richard wandered over to the living room, fiddling with his phone, and then a minute later called out.

"Hey come here! Let's look at this! Laura, can you boot your computer?"

I turned on my laptop in the living room. LaTisha Cimino had sent us both a video. The e-mail header read, "A new Riordan."

I pushed the play button. It was a human-interest segment, an ad or maybe something from the local news, about the Plains Drilling Marcellus Shale Bass Fishing Tournament in Pittsburgh, Pennsylvania. The announcer said the segment was taped that day. Different pro fishermen spoke about how great it was going to be to get a chance to fish for bass on the three rivers of Pittsburgh. The camera did a long pan of the three rivers lining downtown Pittsburgh. It was obviously a gorgeous spring day with everyone dressed for warm weather.

After a minute or so, the camera cut to a blond man who stood on a platform in front of a banner for the tournament—next to a gorgeous blonde in a gray suit with a short skirt and sky-high heels. The announcer introduced the man as Jason Riordan, new president of Plains Drilling, and continued to introduce the woman as Plains Drilling's new publicist. Jason smiled and turned to look directly into the camera.

"As the new president of Plains, following the death of my father, I'm pleased to have the opportunity to continue his legacy of environmentalism. And there's no better way to do this than announcing a project close to my father's heart, the Plains Drilling Marcellus Shale Bass Fishing Contest. There are no fishing contests on dirty rivers!"

The woman beside him then said a few words about how appropriate it felt for Plains Drilling to be sponsoring a fishing tournament since so often hydraulic fracturers are said to not care about the water quality.

"This tournament proves how much Plains Drilling cares about the quality of water in the areas where they drill."

Jason thanked her with a smile and stepped forward to the microphone.

"This country desperately needs the clean energy that comes from the hydraulic fracturing process. Clean natural gas. Plains is sponsoring this tournament because we want everyone in Pennsylvania to know how much we care about the environment, about clean drilling practices. Our drill bits go down into the shale inside of three layers of protective casing."

"It's not the drill bits that are causing the pollution. It's what happens once their toxic brew gets loose in the rock," I said, shaking my head with disgust. "This is so misleading."

"Plains' newly promoted head publicist, Karen Winters"–he put his hand on the blonde's back—"suggested to my father that we sponsor this fishing tournament over a year ago, and it's finally come to fruition. There are no fishing contests on dirty rivers! And I've just signed a ten-year letter of support for this contest. Hydraulic fracturing means clean water! Not just today, but always!"

The meager crowd of twenty or so people applauded.

"Today's the day we come clean about hydraulic fracturing!" Jason yelled and took Ms. Winter's hand and raised it up in his.

"Jesus," Richard said, "what a load of crap."

"He had the son who supposedly hated him already in the wings," Mike added.

"I wonder if his mother knows he's been working for his dad for a while," I said. Then I remembered her saying how she'd been disappointed by both her husband and a son. I guess she did know.

"Did my mom change anything?" Chloe asked in a tiny voice.

"She sure did," Mike started. "She made people more aware of what's going on with this kind of drilling."

"And she provided leadership in the struggle against this kind of reckless environmental destruction," Richard said.

I squatted down so I could look her in the eye. She had to understand how important her mother had been. "And sadly, Chloe, the fact she was murdered by a man who owned one of these drilling companies is going to show people just exactly how far they're willing to go to stop people from knowing the truth about what they do. It's only because of her that people know how they had your mother's group declared terrorists."

A sad smile stretched across her face. "So she did some good." She said it as a statement, not as a question.

Chapter 24

MONDAY, APRIL 18, 8:45 AM

Backpacks were loaded, sleds packed, skis skinned, and Tim Schneider, Manfred Heimler, Sarah Wilkins, Mike Bernese, Grappa McDermott, and I milled around at the top of Granite Chief, ready to head down into the backcountry. We were actually teasing each other about who had Randonee skis and who had Telemark skis. Mike, Sara, Grappa, and I were on Randonee skis with Dynafit bindings. Tim and Manfred were on Telemark skis.

Randonee skis are mostly a setup for bindings that leave your heel free when climbing, but the heel can lock in and then be skied pretty much like normal Alpine gear on the way down.

In Telemark skiing, the heel is always loose. In turns, the inside knee drops low, and the inside ski drops back, creating stability.

Needless to say, each style of skiing has a cult-like following. Grappa was telling people that he had a bumper sticker on his car that said "No One Cares that you Tele."

"In fact," he said with a straight face, "it is one of the most popular bumper stickers around Tahoe. I do not know why."

The real reason why is because Telemark skiers have been known to go on and on and on about how bored they are with normal Alpine skiing. So they need the technical aspects of Tele to keep them interested.

The Tele skiers both drew breaths in order to ream him out.

I jumped in. "It's fine for Manfred. He's European after all." Telemark skiing originated in Telemark, Norway.

Mike, Grappa, and Sara started laughing.

"Let's get going," I said. "No one style of AT skiing is better than the other."

We had four sleds loaded with new equipment for the snow station, and each of us struggled under the weight of forty-fifty and sixty-pound backpacks.

As Tim and I did a final run through of the equipment list, Dave Geisner skied over from the Granite Chief Chair.

"Laura," he shouted, waving a pole at me even though I stood staring right at him.

"Finish up going over the inventory with Sarah," I told Tim, and skated over to meet Dave.

"Just wanted to say good-bye. I guess you'll be heading back to Colorado after you get back. Right?"

"Yes, I'm pretty anxious to get home."

"Thanks for—" he paused and kicked at the snow with the inside edge of his right ski. "Well, thanks for keeping me on it. It wouldn't have been great if a few weeks from now a foot came sticking out of the melt from the snowbank."

"No. That wouldn't be good for any of you."

"No."

"How's your brother doing?"

"He's stressing. But he keeps on day by day. It looks like he'll be headed to prison. Federal prison probably. Hopefully it won't be too long, a couple years. I never did like the asshole."

"I'm sure you have some complex feelings about it. No matter what you say, it can't be easy seeing your brother going to prison. Any idea yet what the charges are going to be?"

He shook his head. "Have to wait for the grand jury indictment to know that. You'll be back for that in early May, right?"

"Yeah."

"You talk to Ellen Riordan, right?"

"A little."

"Did she have any idea her son was working for his dad? I just remember that kid hated his dad so bad he moved to the other side of the world to get away from him."

"Seth had recently told her. I think that was one of the big issues going on between them. She had hoped Jason would stay out of the family business."

"But the big money pulled him in."

"It did. But then he'd studied minerals and law in New Zealand. Had already passed the bar in Philadelphia by the time Ellen found out he was in the States. So it seems like he'd been planning this for a long time."

"Next thing he'll be out here skiing."

"Don't laugh," I told Dave. "He's buying the house in Alpine from his mother."

"Jesus."

We let that hang in the air between us for a time."

"So, Dave, well—we've got to get headed out—"

"I know, I know," he said. "Give me a hug. I probably won't be seeing you again."

I drew back and looked at him quizzically. "Why do you say that?"

He sighed. "I'm worn out, Laura. This is my last year as the head of patrol. And after this, I'm going somewhere warm for a while."

"Who's taking over?"

"It's time someone else gets a shot at running this place, and with the new owners and all, seems like this is the time."

"Have they hired someone to take over?"

"They've got a short list. But I'm pushing for Janis Murphy. She's young. She's got the skill, the drive. I think she'll do a great job."

He held out his arms, and I slid forward so our bodies were side by side, then I hugged him.

"Be careful back there," he said into my hair. "Got your sat phone? Avie transponders?"

"Transponders hell," I said. "We're all wearing inflation bags, too."

Avalanche inflation bags have CO_2 cartridges that go off if you're caught in an avie to expand into big balloon-like wings, which, hopefully, will keep you at the top of the snow. They're designed on the biggest-potato-chips-float-to-the-top theory.

"Glad to hear it," he said, and gave me a last squeeze before letting go.

I stopped and turned back to face him. "You know, I didn't believe you about the dirty snow until I had my team pull up the sat images from last December, January, and February. Prior to the start of this big train of storms, there was dust blowing in on the prefrontal gusts."

"Really?" he said, and grimaced, then gave a laugh.

"You bastard!" I yelled at him. "I would have come gladly if you'd just asked. You didn't need to lie to me."

"Sorry about that, I'm a jerk. But I didn't think you'd come out unless it was about something directly in your field. And I just had to know what was going on with that early melt."

"That is so uncool."

"I said I'm a jerk. We never really decided what was going on with that melt. What with all these murders and crap."

"Yes, that did put the brakes on the snow science. But then it turns out you just thought you were lying to me."

He looked either confused or skeptical.

"Here's how I figure it. There is no real relationship with temperature and melt, but there is a strong linear relationship with dust. Dirty or clean? That is the question. And the sat imagery shows us, the early season snow was dirty. And that is going to control the steepness of the rising limb of the hydrograph. Dirty snow is going to melt sooner."

I spun around and started skating back to my team. I raised a mitt up over my head and waved good-bye without looking back.

"OK. You got it now, Dave. My scientific opinion. You're an asshole!" I yelled.

His laughter echoed across the mountain.

=

That evening, Mike, Grappa, and I were strewn out on snow platforms built up around a campfire. The platforms were raised a foot off the base snow and covered with plastic tarps, then piled high with mats and finally sleeping bags. It was a mild, clear night with just a sliver of new moon. The Milky Way threw a brilliant streak across the sky.

My crew was still over at the snow station, a hundred feet above us, arguing over what we'd be doing first come morning–installing the new remote sensors, or putting up a light-emitting-diode-weather indicator I was able to snag with grant money from a friend at UC Davis. It's a neat device that measures the light scatter from falling snow crystals. The scatter and scintillation, or the sparkling or twinkling, of the light beam is related to the size, shape, and fall speed of the particles. So with this information, we know how fast and heavy snow falls, and the accumulation rate. Hopefully, this will give us more accurate remote insight into not only how much snow, but how much water the snow holds.

But Mike, Grappa, and I were more concerned about the stars, the moon, the creak of snow settling around us, and the delight of a good meal and a couple glasses of wine to follow it up.

Grappa pulled out a fat joint, stuck it in his mouth and got ready to light it.

"Who wants to join me?"

"Sorry," I told him. "I'm in charge, and nobody's getting high on my watch."

He made a show of being too shocked to speak as he put the joint back into a metal case and stashed it back in his pocket, still shaking his head.

"Don't feel bad," I told him. "I wouldn't let anybody get drunk either. It's dangerous back here, and I'm responsible. So no getting wasted."

He bounced up from the nest of sleeping bags he'd been reclined on and headed over to check on his snow cave.

Several hours earlier, right when we first got there, he dug a big trench, wrapped his gear in trash bags and covered them over with snow a couple feet deep, firmed it down, and let nature build his snow cave. The natural settling of the snow filtered in around the gear to form a solid pack of snow, and after a couple hours he felt ready to tunnel in, pull his gear out, and there was his snow cave.

"Bud," he said to Mike, "I cannot believe you guys are sleeping in a tent instead of a snow cave."

He had his gear pulled out and had a cave about six feet long, three feet wide, and two feet high hollowed out to sleep in.

Snow caves are warm, much warmer than sleeping outside, and if it had been a cold night we probably would have made one ourselves. But by morning, Grappa would find his ceiling had sagged down to a hands-width above his face. The sagging of the snow would be caused by his body warmth and his breath. To me, that's too claustrophobic. Especially when Mike and I had a lovely warm tent, cold-proof mats, and a platform to keep us off the snow. And we can zip our sleeping bags together.

It was over. We knew what happened, and why it happened. Yet I couldn't help feeling that as long as Jason Riordan was out touting the "clean" energy of natural gas, it would never be completely over.

The cold, the snow, the stars, this life we had all chosen—for one night it was enough. I stared up into the star clouds of the Milky Way and wished Anna, Alexis, and Jennifer safe passage on their journeys. And if they weren't going anywhere, I wished them peace. And even though he didn't deserve it after killing those three women, I sent some positive energy out into the universe for Darnell as well. I sent it out for all four of them. Though I don't pray to any god, I thought good thoughts and hoped it would help them, wherever they traveled. I imagined I saw their spirits zipping across the star-riddled sky.